# DELIGHTFUL DECEPTION

"You know, since we're pretending to be married, we might try acting a little bit more like newlyweds ourselves," Arthur said. And he reached out to take Chelsea about the waist.

Speechless, she looked down to where he held her. In reality, his touch was light, but she swore she felt his fingers burning through the material of her shirtwaist—indeed, through the very layers of her skin—electrifying what lay beneath.

When she looked back up, an impish glint kindled in his eyes; eyes that were the breathtaking blue of a Scottish loch on a midsummer day.

"What's the matter, Miss Delafield?" he inquired suggestively. "Thinking of causing me grievous bodily injury?"

Actually, Chelsea was thinking no such thing. She was wondering instead what perverse part of her yearned to press still closer. She wondered why she suddenly felt so compelled to feed a sensual curiosity she had never even known existed within her.

Books by Donna Grove

*Broken Vows*
*A Touch of Camelot*
*Return to Camelot*

Published by HarperPaperbacks

Harper Monogram

# Return to Camelot

DONNA GROVE

HarperPaperbacks
*A Division of* HarperCollins*Publishers*

This is a work of fiction. The characters, incidents, and dialogues are products of the author's imagination and are not to be construed as real. Any resemblance to actual events or persons, living or dead, is entirely coincidental.

HarperPaperbacks *A Division of* HarperCollins*Publishers*
10 East 53rd Street, New York, N.Y. 10022



Cover illustration by Vittorio

First printing: September 1995

Printed in the United States of America

HarperPaperbacks, HarperMonogram, and colophon are trademarks of HarperCollins*Publishers*

❖ 10 9 8 7 6 5 4 3 2 1

To my critique partners, past and present. Thanks Joann, Heidi, and Ginny. And with much appreciation to the Reading Area Pennwriters, a bunch of critics with heart.

## ACKNOWLEDGMENTS

When I get one of my bright ideas for a new book, I'm often too caught up in the first blush of inspiration to consider the amount of research it will take to tell the story as it should be told. In this case, I bit off more than a mouthful.

Any errors are my own, but the stuff I got right can in part be attributed to Mr. David Bromwich, of the Somerset County Council Library Service; Ms. Janet Graham, of the Glastonbury Library; and John Loveridge, the Honorable Secretary of the Glastonbury Antiquarian Society, all of whom were generous enough to share some of their expertise concerning the history of Glastonbury Abbey and the town of Glastonbury.

My thanks also to the volunteer researchers at the Philadelphia Maritime Museum and Carol Ann Harris of the Temple University Library in Philadelphia.

Finally, thanks to Ann Wozniak, old college buddy and current resident of the United Kingdom, for offering firsthand impressions of life in the British Isles and snapping some great pictures of Arthur's Seat.

## ACKNOWLEDGMENTS

[illegible]

[illegible]

[illegible]

[illegible]

# Return to Camelot

# Prologue

*The young king was not more* than three and twenty when his mighty sword was lost in battle. He was most despondent, for it had served him well.

"My sword has broken," said Arthur.

"It doesn't matter," said Merlin. "The time has come for you to take another. Come with me."

And so, together they rode into the enchanted forest until they came to a clearing in which was cradled a magical lake. All was still. Not a breeze stirred the trees or the glasslike surface of the deep blue water.

Merlin pointed. "Look."

And there, in the middle of the lake, Arthur witnessed a wondrous sight: a woman's arm as it rose to break the water's surface. In her grasp was a sword that gleamed more excellent than any he had seen before.

"It is called Excalibur," Merlin said. "Until now, no knight has been able to claim it."

As Merlin spoke, a woman appeared from out of the mist upon the lake's shore. Of pale complexion, with bright eyes and hair as black as a midsummer night, she was clad in the green of the forest.

Overcome with her otherworldly beauty, Arthur dismounted his horse and knelt before her. "My lady," he said, "you are no mortal."

"Why have you come, gentle king?"

"I have lost my sword in battle, and Merlin has told me of Excalibur. Now, I have seen it with my own eyes, and I want it for my own. To whom does it belong?"

"I am its guardian," she said. "But I will make a gift of it to you upon one condition. You must return a gift to me when the time comes that I ask it of you."

"I will," promised Arthur.

"Then it is done."

And with that, she was gone. Along the shore near where she had stood was a boat.

"Go," said Merlin.

Arthur climbed into the boat, but before he could reach for the oars, it moved of its own accord across the still waters of the lake. It did not stop until it had reached the hand that held the sword.

"The Lady of the Lake has bequeathed Excalibur to me," he said, then clasped its haft. To his astonishment, it felt not as cold as steel, but as warm as living flesh.

The hand relinquished the sword and vanished back into the deep. From that moment on, Excalibur was his.

*The story of how King Arthur obtained Excalibur, as told by Emmaline Pierce to her young son, Arthur Pierce, 1875.*

# 1

**Philadelphia, Pennsylvania, June 1892**

*Her throat was dry* and her palms were wet. Chelsea Delafield's heart thumped against her ribs as she paced the length of the elegant sitting room that adjoined the cavernous assembly hall of the Philadelphia Historical Society.

Clutching a sheaf of dog-eared pages to her stomach, she continued to silently rehearse the opening lines of her presentation. It was always like this when she was called upon to address a group, whether it be five or five score; this wasn't the first time she had been forced to wonder what sort of teacher she would make when, at the end of this week, she accepted her degree from Temple College and set sail for home.

Home.

*Don't think about it*, she berated herself, stopping to adjust her spectacles and refocus her attention on the first lines of her research paper. Its title, *King Arthur and His*

*Role in the Saxon Invasion of Britain: Myth or History?*, written in her own flourishing hand, was, like the rest of her senior paper, indelibly committed to memory. She'd worked bloody hard on this final project, and her dedication had been recognized and rewarded. Professor Hawthorne had declared it worthy of public presentation to his colleagues at the historical society. It was a great honor.

So why did she feel as if she were about to be tossed to the lions?

At this thought, Chelsea raised anxious violet eyes to the forbidding mahogany door that separated her from the rapidly filling assembly hall. From beyond, she could discern the low buzz and hum of a growing crowd. *Bloody hell,* she thought sickly, *I do believe I'm going to lose my dinner.*

A connecting door to a rear corridor opened behind her. There followed a clatter, a yelp, and an earsplitting crash. Chelsea winced. She was expecting only two people. The first was her fellow speaker, Arthur Pierce, another night school student who should have been here more than ten minutes ago, blast him. The second was her, well, beau, for lack of a better term, a mathematics honor student, Miles Middleton.

She didn't need to turn around to know which of them had just stumbled his way into the room, but she did anyway, and her expression fell at the sorry sight that greeted her. Dressed in an ill-fitting black serge suit, Miles's gawky, six-foot frame sprawled atop a mounted map of Arthurian England and a folding wooden easel.

Chelsea set her papers on a lamp table and hurried to his side. "Miles, do stop this nonsense and get up. Can't you see I'm nervous enough as it is?"

"Sorry, Chelsea. I was doing fine until that blasted easel caught in the door jamb."

"Is anything broken?" She dropped to her knees and struggled to tug her map out from under him, no small task, as it measured an impressive four feet tall. Chelsea had slaved over it for weeks.

"No, I don't think so. Except maybe for my—"

"Seems to be undamaged," Chelsea murmured, scrutinizing the map for dents or smudges.

"—spectacles."

Chelsea raised her head as this last comment sank in. "Your spectacles?" She stared at Miles, at the straight center part in his sleek, acorn brown hair, and felt a stab of guilt. "Oh, dear, how inconsiderate of me. Are you all right, Miles?"

He nodded as his long, reedlike fingers searched the floor blindly. "Yes, except for my . . ."

She plucked up his displaced eyeglasses. "Your spectacles."

Miles settled them on his nose. "Oh, much better."

It was true that Chelsea had grown fond of Miles over the past four years. Despite his imposing size, there was an eager, puppy-dog quality about him that was hard to turn away. Ever since their first meeting in a freshman evening course, they had spent many weekends studying together in the library. They'd also passed many hours in the parlor of Chelsea's rooming house, playing dominoes or backgammon.

Now, Miles surveyed the small sitting room as if searching for something. Or someone. "Where's Pierce?" he asked. "Isn't he supposed to be here by now?"

Arthur Pierce. Even at the mere utterance of that cursed name, Chelsea pursed her lips, annoyed. "He's late."

"Late?"

"Late." Chelsea snatched up Miles's stovepipe hat, which had been ejected from his head upon landing. "Here."

Miles took his hat as he struggled to his feet. "But what are you going to do if he doesn't show up?"

Frowning, Chelsea stood and brushed off her dark wool worsted skirt. Her presentation was timed to last exactly thirty-two minutes. If Pierce didn't show up to deliver his companion lecture on William the Conqueror, Chelsea would be left facing an expectant group of historians with another twenty-eight minutes to fill. The very thought of it made her positively ill.

"I don't want to think about it," she replied.

"Well, I daresay you'd better think about it. He's an irresponsible cad, and I wouldn't put it past him to—"

"I don't want to discuss it," Chelsea said irritably. "I'm a nervous wreck as it is."

"Oh." Miles cleared his throat, chastised. "Sorry."

Feeling another stab of guilt, Chelsea apologized. "Oh, I'm sorry, too, Miles. I shouldn't be taking out my frustrations on you. I should be taking them out on Mr. Pierce, but, as you can see, he's not here to receive them."

"Quite all right. I understand completely."

"Thank you, Miles. I do appreciate you offering to fetch my easel and map."

He smiled. "By the way, have I mentioned that you look particularly ravishing this evening?"

Ravishing? Chelsea cocked her head to one side. Poor Miles. He actually meant it, that was the thing. Most young men were intimidated by the company of an intelligent young woman, but not Miles. Quite the contrary. Why, it seemed almost as if the mere thought of Chelsea's brain positively inflamed him.

"No, you haven't," she said, uncomfortable with this turn in conversation. "Thank you."

"Chelsea, I . . ." He trailed off, fingering the brim of his stovepipe nervously. He tossed it down onto a wing chair and began again. "Chelsea, there's something I've been meaning to say ever since—"

Chelsea moved to intercept. "First, let's get this taken care of, shall we?" She bent to retrieve her map.

"Oh, of course." Miles moved at the same time.

Their fingers touched.

Chelsea tried to draw back, but she was too late. Miles caught her hand, grasping her fingers as they both straightened.

"Chelsea, I know you're planning to return to London after graduation, but there's something I want you to think about before . . ."

She found it difficult to concentrate on his words. Instead, she found her thoughts turning to what had precipitated her most recent problem with him. Her birthday.

Although she certainly didn't subscribe to the antiquated notion that, at twenty-two, she was so bad off as to be withered on the vine, she did harbor the sneaking suspicion that it was past time she be properly kissed by a member of the opposite gender. Due to a noticeable lack of candidates, however, she had come to realize that the member in question was bound to be Miles.

Once her decision was made, Chelsea had begun to drop some subtle, then not-so-subtle hints during their times together. Miles, however, had been somewhat slow at taking up the baton. A full week had passed before Chelsea decided that she had no choice but to confront the matter directly.

One balmy, blossom-scented evening, after leaving metaphysics class together, she had thrown all caution to the wind, grabbing her incompetent suitor by the lapels and dragging his face down to hers.

"Don't you want to kiss me, Miles?" she had inquired seriously as they blinked at each other through twin pairs of steel-rimmed spectacles.

They were probably a good match, actually, she being myopic, he being hyperopic. Romance and passion be damned. She was getting too old to be pining away over all that type of nonsense.

". . . and so it has become clear to me that we share a certain intellectual compatibility that is more rare . . ."

As Miles droned on, Chelsea was assailed by a vivid recollection of their lips coming together with all the sensuality and finesse of two battleships colliding at high sea. They had remained thusly positioned for approximately five seconds before drawing apart again. Miles had pinkened a bit about the ears and appeared quite winded by the experience. Chelsea, by contrast, had felt absolutely nothing.

Now, she dearly regretted her decision to conduct her

kissing experiment with poor Miles. Egad, he had been acting like a lovesick nincompoop ever since.

". . . and as I've now been offered a teaching position with the Episcopal Academy next fall—"

A rapping upon the open sitting room door startled them both. Miles swore under his breath, "Oh, diddlysquat."

Expecting her rescuer to be Professor Hawthorne, Chelsea withdrew her hand from Miles's grasp to peer around his shoulder. The portly, well-dressed gentleman who stood in the doorway, however, was not Professor Hawthorne. In fact, he bore no resemblance whatsoever to the diminutive history professor.

With a red-tipped nose, a thick, white beard, and a full head of snowy hair, this gentleman bore more of a resemblance to every small child's notion of that jolliest of old men himself, Saint Nicholas.

"May we help you?" Chelsea asked, noting that in place of a sackful of presents, he carried a leather Gladstone valise. When the man spoke, she was surprised to be greeted with a refined British accent. "I say, sorry to interrupt, but I'm looking for a chap by the name of Arthur Pierce. I was told he was lecturing here this evening."

"He is, but he's late, and . . ." Chelsea's reply tapered off as she noticed an alabaster cat executing a languid figure eight in and around the man's ankles.

"Pierce is always late," Miles said, whipping about impatiently. "That is, when he even bothers to show up."

"Is that so?" the man asked. "Would you have any idea where I might find him? It's quite urgent that I speak to him as soon as possible."

Chelsea tore her gaze from the cat. "Well, you might try his rooming house on Pine Street."

"Oh, yes. I have the address."

"And if he's not there," Miles put in testily, "try an establishment called DeLancey's on Arch Street."

"Jolly good. Thank you, sir." The man looked down as the cat began to mewl at his feet. "What's that, Crystal?"

The cat had stopped meandering and now stood at attention, its white head cocked to one side, its tail pointing toward the ceiling. It meowed again.

"Oh, yes, yes. Quite true, quite true," the man said, as if responding to some form of intelligent verbal communication.

When he looked up, he tipped his black derby and smiled as if nothing were out of the ordinary. "Cheerio, then." Without waiting for a reply, he gestured to the cat with his walking cane. "Come along, Crystal. No time to waste."

And, with that, both the man and his feline were gone.

Miles and Chelsea stood motionless for a long moment before turning to each other. "Did you hear that?" Miles asked. "I believe he was talking to that cat."

"I *believe*," Chelsea said pointedly, "he thought that the cat was talking to *him*."

"Odd."

Chelsea frowned as she pondered the deserted corridor where the gentleman had just vanished. "Yes. Very odd, indeed."

MME. COLETTE'S BRITISH BLONDES!!!
A BEVY OF BUXOM BEAUTIES!!
FEATURING
LILY THE FLYING FAIRY
THE PICADILLY DANCERS
A GRAND FINALE MARCH BY TWENTY LADIES
AROUND THE CIRCLE

So heralded the massive playbill erected outside DeLancey's House of Burlesque on Arch Street.

Arthur Pierce knew it by heart, of course. He had set it up himself this morning, and now, as he and his old Phi Kappa Sigma fraternity brother Bernard Endicott reposed comfortably in the best seats in the house, third row center, he had to admit the playbill hadn't lied.

"*C'est magnifique*," Arthur commented, tilting his head back to squint appreciatively at Lily the Flying Fairy. Clad in a strapless gymnast's costume, a collection of flimsy scarves, and splendidly snug-fitting tights, she arced gracefully through space fifteen feet above their heads on a flying trapeze.

"*C'est merveilleux*," Endicott agreed, as she began her pendulum swing back toward the orchestra pit. "Want a smoke?" He pulled a silver cigar case from his coat pocket and offered it to Arthur.

"No, thank you, Endicott." Arthur settled back in his seat and returned his attention to the rollicking stage where a plump comedian and nineteen Picadilly dancers were busy jiggling and cooching their way through a sheik and harem number.

"What a job you've managed to finagle yourself, Pierce." Endicott chuckled. "British Blondes indeed."

"Unfortunately, it doesn't pay much," Arthur said, "but I suppose there are certain benefits."

"Like free admission?"

"Yes, but you know what they say: If you've seen one leg show, you've seen them all." Arthur propped his feet and then crossed them over the back of the seat in front of him.

The gaslight chandeliers inside the theater were dimmed for the show, but the flickering border lights that spilled out onto the orchestra pit and the first few rows of seats served well enough for Arthur to contemplate the worn leather tips of his shoes. He'd shined and polished and babied them for months, but their life was growing short. Thin spots were wearing through in the soles, and the heels were nearly gone.

Despite the pageantry of frothy costumes and shapely legs on stage, Arthur found himself weighing the approximate cost of having his shoes resoled against how much he would have to shell out to buy a new pair at Wanamaker's. "I'll have to find something else after graduation," he mused aloud.

"What are you talking about?"

"Another job." Arthur cast a side glance at his friend,

who had probably never had to have a pair of shoes resoled in his life. "This one barely pays enough to live on, and my college fund is long gone, you know."

"Oh," Endicott said pensively. Although they'd been the best of friends since their freshman days at the University of Pennsylvania, they rarely discussed finances. "But what about that professorial apprenticeship you were offered at Temple?"

"That won't be available until the fall term, and I haven't decided yet if I want it."

Arthur spoke the truth. After two years of private prep school, three years at Penn, and a year of night school at Temple, he'd had his fill of academic life for a while. He was itching to see the world.

"Perhaps you could get a job from my father," Endicott said.

"Shipbuilding, you mean?"

"Bookkeeping. You always were a whiz at mathematics."

Arthur tried to picture himself stuck behind a desk, running totals on endless columns of numbers. Debits and credits, ad infinitum. He couldn't imagine a worse fate. "Thanks, Endicott, but I'll find something."

"Well, I have no doubt of that. In fact, I'll be disappointed if you're not occupying the White House two decades from now. In the meantime, though, you'll have to eat. I'm going to work for Father after graduation. Why not join me?"

Arthur laughed. "I doubt we'd get much done. Your father would soon have to fire me to get rid of my bad influence."

Endicott took a silver flask from his coat pocket, uncapped it, and offered it to Arthur. "Ah, Pierce, it just hasn't been the same at Penn without you."

Arthur accepted the flask. "Well, the past is in the past."

"But we had some good times. Remember when you picked the lock on Professor Ludwig's classroom so we could whitewash his blackboards?"

"Never got caught on that one, did we?"

"No, and I doubt we would have been caught sneaking out of the Quadrangle after curfew either if it hadn't been for that blackguard, Hughes, ratting on us."

Arthur took a swallow of expensive gin, grimaced at its exquisite potency, then passed the flask back to Endicott. "Hughes was just jealous."

"Oh, no doubt of that." Endicott took a swig and tucked the flask away. "His girl was absolutely wild for you as I recall."

"Ah, yes, Elizabeth." Arthur grinned at the memory of lush blonde curls, flirty baby blue eyes, and an hourglass figure that could bring any red-blooded male to his knees. "She was well worth a few demerits, as I recall."

"That girl was worth expulsion, as I recall."

"Yes," Arthur agreed. "But, in the end, it was that damn incident with the goat that finally did me in."

"The Provost had no sense of humor. Otherwise he would have seen it was just an innocent prank," Endicott said, the nostalgic gaiety fading from his voice. "No sense of humor at all."

But a fine sense of business, Arthur thought, knowing his friend still suffered pangs of guilt over the goat episode. They'd pulled the prank together on a whim, and they'd been called on the carpet together for it, too. Endicott couldn't help that his grandfather served on the board of trustees of the university and that his family had been generous benefactors since the days when Ben Franklin had walked the streets.

In the end, Endicott had stayed, and Arthur had gotten the boot. Two semesters had passed, during which time Arthur had gotten a job as a janitor and stagehand at DeLancey's. He had soon learned of the free evening tuition for working men offered by the fledgling Temple College on Park Avenue. Upon application and examination, he had been accepted into the senior class at fall term.

Now, with Endicott running a year behind on academic

credits, they were graduating in the same year—albeit from different institutions—Arthur with his unshakable A average, Endicott barely squeaking by with his gentleman's C.

In the overhead spotlight, Lily was divesting herself of scarves, unknotting one from her waist and tossing it out into the darkened audience.

Arthur nudged his friend's elbow. "What time is it?"

Endicott pulled out a watch and held it up to the light. "Looks like ten to seven."

"Aw, hell, I've got to go."

"Why?"

"I've got a lecture to give at the historical society. My history professor talked me into it."

"When does it start?"

"Seven."

"Seven? You'll never make it."

"Another student is supposed to speak until seven-thirty."

Endicott eyed him dubiously. "Did you bring your notes?"

"What notes?"

"B—but, well, you're certainly not intending to go dressed like that, are you?" Endicott sounded incredulous.

"Dressed like what?"

"No waistcoat. No tie."

Arthur looked down at his rumpled shirt. "Oh. I suppose I should stop by my room first."

"I suppose you should, although I doubt you'll have time. That professor of yours will probably have your head."

Arthur looked up at the stage ruefully. He was forced to face the depressing fact that he was going to miss the show's grand finale—twenty Buxom British Blondes, no less—in favor of lecturing to a room full of grizzled old fossils. He lowered his feet to the floor and reached for his coat. "Professor Hawthorne is the least of my worries. He may have my head, but no doubt it'll be Delafield who'll be happy to swing the axe."

"Delafield? Who's Delafield?"

"My lecture partner." As Arthur struggled into his suit

coat, he imagined Chelsea Delafield's stiff-necked posture and disdainful expression. "Queen of the Arctic," he added dryly.

"What?" Endicott brightened, then leered. "You mean, your lecture partner is a *woman*?"

Arthur absorbed his friend's lascivious ribbing stoically. Having been educated at an all-boy's prep school before entering Penn, Endicott was fascinated by notions of unsegregated classrooms sprinkled with nubile young beauties.

"A woman?" Arthur repeated absently. "Well, technically, I suppose she is, but, I assure you, Endicott, she's certainly nothing to get your drawers in a knot over." He glanced around for his hat. "Now, where the devil . . . ?"

Endicott chortled. "Maybe so, Pierce, but it's not my drawers we're talking about, is it?"

Arthur spotted his cap on the floor, where it must have fallen during the show. "Oh, darn, look at that." He snatched it up and slapped it against his knee, freeing a cloud of dust before setting it at a careless angle on his head.

"Take heart, Pierce," Endicott gloated cheerily as Arthur edged past him toward the theater aisle. "At least you've got me to fill you in on how the finale turns out."

As a pink and silver dusk descended to blanket the City of Brotherly Love, Maximillian Hamilton paced before the raised stoop of a two-story red brick rooming house on Pine Street. He pulled a gold timepiece from his pocket and flipped it open. Seven o'clock. "Blast," he muttered, snapping it shut.

In the gathering shadows of the evening, this quiet, working-class neighborhood appeared almost deserted. Max knew that most of the residents were probably already in their homes consuming their evening meals, but that knowledge lent him little comfort out here on the empty street.

Sensing her master's uneasy mood, Crystal turned away from her stealthy investigation of the stoop next door. She settled down by Max's foot and cocked her head to peer up at him through glowing amber eyes.

"Yes, Crystal, I quite agree. The sooner we complete our task, the better."

At the sound of footsteps, Max looked up to observe the only other living soul now visible on the block. The brass-buttoned policeman had been strolling in this direction for quite some time, twirling his billy club and stopping occasionally to check the glowing gas lamps that lined the street.

"Good evening, sir," he said, pausing before Max. His gaze dropped to the leather valise that sat unattended by the stoop. "Can I help you with anything?"

Max tipped his derby. "No, thank you, officer. I'm waiting for an acquaintance who seems to be a few minutes late."

"Hmmmmm. Well, at least you've got a nice evening for it."

"That is indeed true."

The peeler touched his cap. "Well, have a good night."

"Thank you, officer. I plan to."

Max watched until the other man disappeared around the corner. While he had never been partial to law enforcement personnel, he nevertheless lamented this particular officer's passing. After all, there was something to be said for feeling secure in one's person, and Max was feeling anything but secure in his person at the moment. He was acutely aware that the invaluable contents of his valise had put him at risk ever since leaving London almost a week ago.

Crystal mewled, breaking into her master's unsettling thoughts. "I know. I feel it too." Max stooped to scratch behind her ears. "It seems unlikely that we could have been followed, but the feeling is there. We're being watched." Max straightened to study the impassive row of red brick buildings across the street. "But from where? And by whom?"

Crystal let out a soft hiss. Max looked down to see her ears perk. Rising slowly from her haunches, the cat tensed and poised. Her back arched. Her tail stiffened in warning.

Max turned toward the street corner around which the peeler had just disappeared, the same street corner with which his erstwhile companion seemed so suddenly concerned.

"What is it, Crystal?" he whispered, one hand dropping to the inconspicuous bulge of a revolver at the side pocket of his tweed cutaway coat. The sound of approaching footfalls on the pavement reached his ears, and it was with a palpable sense of relief that he spotted its source.

Dressed in a rumpled coat and casual brown trousers, a jaunty youth in his early twenties rounded the corner. With his hands in his pockets and whistling a catchy tune, this bloke hardly seemed the type to be called upon to deliver a lecture to a group of socialites. Max, however, who had traveled the world over and then some, knew that Americans were nothing if not delightfully unconventional.

Other than his informal attire, this fine-looking young man fit the description Max had been given of Arthur Pierce. The somewhat tousled, russet-colored hair beneath that flat cap clinched it. Max allowed his hand to fall away from his coat pocket and to move instead to retrieve his valise. "Arthur Pierce?"

The young man halted just short of the stoop. Max found himself faced with a pair of discerning blue eyes. "Yes?"

"My name is Max Hamilton. Might I have a word with you?"

"Well, I don't really have much time right now."

"It's a matter of great importance."

Max saw the young man's gaze flick to his valise. "Look, I'm sorry, mister, but if you're selling something, you're wasting your time. I'm flat busted." He started up the steps.

Max managed to absorb this slight with amused tolerance. The lad, he reminded himself, was oh-so-very young. "Mr. Pierce," he said, injecting a note of polite authority that could not be ignored, "I've come all the way from London to speak with you."

# 2

*Arthur Pierce stopped* and appraised Max with a spark of interest. "London?"

"There's a matter of probating a will that concerns you and your sister, Guinevere."

"Gwin is in Chicago."

"Yes, I understand she lives there with her husband and three children."

"Four children. She popped out another one just two weeks ago. A boy."

"Oh, capital. Then congratulations are in order."

"Who did you say you were?"

"Max Hamilton, solicitor. A friend of your Uncle Sidney's."

"Uncle Sidney? Sidney Pierce?"

"The one and only."

"Well, I'll be damned." Arthur hadn't thought of his Uncle Sidney in years. If he remembered correctly—and, to be truthful, Arthur rarely remembered incorrectly—instead of facing a possible three-year stay at San Quentin, Sidney had chosen to slip away from the San Francisco authorities and flee to a mysterious destination in South America. That was more than twelve years ago. Neither Arthur nor his sister had heard from him since.

"How the hell *is* good old Uncle Sidney?" Arthur asked, recovering from his surprise.

"Dead."

"Dead?"

"Quite."

"How?"

"Heart condition, I'm afraid."

"Oh. Sorry to hear it." Arthur stood motionless for a moment before remembering that he was due to speak in less than half an hour. "Look, I've got to be somewhere, but you're welcome to come inside if you don't mind my changing clothes while we talk."

"Not at all. Might Crystal accompany us?"

"Crystal?"

In answer, the older man inclined his head downward. For the first time, Arthur noticed the cat. White with enigmatic amber eyes, it stared up at him, awaiting a reply.

"Uh, sure." Arthur opened the front door. "Come on in, Crystal."

The cat scooted inside as Max followed Arthur into a shadowed entrance foyer. A gaslight burned at the top of a narrow wooden staircase, illuminating the area sufficiently for Max to note three cast iron mailboxes along the wall inside the door.

Crystal streaked ahead as Arthur started up the creaking stairs. "We never heard from Uncle Sidney after he left San Francisco, but he left a savings account for my sister. I have him to thank for paying most of my way through school."

"He could be most generous," Max concurred, ascending behind him.

"Not to mention, the slickest con man I ever met." Arthur flashed Max a sly half-smile as he reached the first-floor landing. "And that even includes my father, who was no slouch himself."

"So I've heard. You come from quite a long and distinguished line of gifted artists."

"Well, I never knew my grandfather." Arthur proceeded down a short hall to stop before a door marked by a tarnished brass C. Crystal sat waiting directly below it.

"Your mother was quite something, I hear."

"Ah, yes, Mother." Arthur dipped one hand into his trouser pocket to extract a key. "I never knew her when she was in her prime. She died when I was seven."

"According to Sidney, she was quite enthralled with the legends of King Arthur and his Round Table."

"That's how I got my name." Arthur drove his key into the lock and turned it, pushing the door open. "Wait here till I turn up the light."

Max complied as the young man plunged ahead into Stygian darkness. Rustlings of movement came from within, and then there was light. And confusion.

"Good heavens," Max muttered as he stepped inside. His gaze roved over a scholarly muddle of books and papers atop a flat desk before moving on to take in an indecipherable jumble of photographs, football pennants, and variety show posters tacked onto plaster walls. Of the few furnishings in the tiny room, most boasted at least one discarded shirt, sock, or other item awaiting laundry day.

Young Arthur seemed not to notice anything amiss as he yanked open a stubborn closet door. "Only a dollar twenty a week and all the comforts of home."

As Max closed the hallway door, he observed a collection of derbies, caps, dangling bow ties, and boxing gloves hanging from wooden pegs behind it. "A veritable steal," he replied.

Arthur pulled a black waistcoat and matching dinner jacket from the closet. Kicking the door shut, he tossed them onto an iron cot before unbuttoning his shirt. "So, how is it that you knew where to find me, Mr. Hamilton? As I said, we never heard from Sidney after he left San Francisco."

"Once your uncle was settled, he made it his business to

know where you and your sister were at all times. He was always concerned for your welfare."

Arthur moved to a battered dresser. "Really? He could have written."

"That was not his style."

"No, I suppose not." Arthur gestured vaguely behind him. "Have a seat."

Max crossed the room to a lumpy divan littered with discarded garments and student-oriented paraphernalia. Setting his valise down, Max moved most of it aside and made himself comfortable. Crystal was busy investigating the premises, sniffing here and there to get a feel for the place and its current resident.

"So, Mr. Hamilton, what can I do for you?"

Max looked up to see Arthur buttoning his shirt, waiting. Planting his cane down in front of him, Max rested both hands atop its silver wolf's head. "It is not what you can do for me, Mr. Pierce, so much as what I can do for you."

"And what might that be?"

"I don't know whether you were aware of it, but for years your uncle pursued an avid interest in collecting medieval artifacts and weaponry."

As Arthur shrugged into his waistcoat, he didn't divert his measuring gaze from Hamilton's broad, expensively tailored figure. The man knew a lot about his family, more than Arthur had ever bothered to impart to even his closest school chums. In that respect, he certainly appeared to be on the level, but Arthur knew better than most people that appearances could be deceiving.

"I seem to remember seeing his collection in San Francisco," Arthur said cautiously.

This was a blatant understatement. Even now, years later, the very thought of that fabulous collection sent a bolt of excitement through him. As a child, Arthur had strolled the countless rooms and halls of his Uncle Sidney's opulent mansion on Nob Hill in San Francisco. Mounted high upon many of those richly paneled walls had been a dazzling array of medieval fighting weapons: spiked maces, gleaming swords, sleek lances, jeweled daggers. It was, however, the many suits of field armor, those silent, imposing hall sentries, that Arthur remembered best of all. At the time, he'd been most impressed with the grandeur and romance they inevitably conjured, the vivid imagery of a long lost age of chivalrous gallantry, a time of knights, castles, dragons, noble quests and *magic*. Now, he was more impressed with the fact that his Uncle Sidney's weapons collection had been worth an obscene amount of money.

"Then you are aware of his passion on the subject," Hamilton said.

Arthur pulled a tie from his dresser. "His collection was pretty extensive. It must have been difficult for him to leave it behind when he was forced to relocate."

"Fortunately, with the use of certain intermediaries, he was able to repurchase a few of his favorite items later on."

"One of those intermediaries wouldn't happen to be you, would it?"

"Yes, actually. One of my specialties is procuring certain rare items for avid collectors like your uncle."

Arthur eyed him askance as he reached for his suit coat. "Avid, *rich* collectors, you mean."

"Well, the poor have little use for such amusements, do they?"

Arthur thought about the impending holes in his shoes and replied dryly, "I suppose you're right."

Moving back to his dresser, he turned down his collar, doffed his hat, and ran a quick comb through his hair, thus completing his transformation from burlesque theater stagehand to summa cum laude honor student. "Look, Mr. Hamilton, I'd like to talk more, but I'm already late for a lecture."

"Oh, I do apologize for barging in without prior notice, but I'm afraid it couldn't be avoided."

To Arthur, the older man appeared utterly unruffled. As of yet, he had made no move to rise from his seat. He was a cool one, to be sure. Right now, Arthur wished he had more time to play this out, but, then again, perhaps pressing this guy for time would force his hand.

Arthur started for the door. "Well, perhaps after the lecture, we can—"

"Your uncle has left quite a sizable estate."

That stopped Arthur in his tracks. He turned to peer back at Hamilton. "How sizable an estate?"

"Impossible to estimate at this point. A townhouse in London, a banana plantation in Honduras, his collections, of course, and a few other lucrative investments."

"A banana plantation?"

"Yes, they're quite the thing down there."

"I find that a little hard to believe."

"Oh, no, it's true," Hamilton assured him earnestly. "Bananas are their main export."

"No," Arthur clarified, straining to remain patient now that the can had finally been opened. "What I mean is, I was always under the impression that Sidney was forced to leave most of his money behind in his hurry to leave San Francisco."

"Well, most men probably would have, but your uncle was a chap who thought ahead. Only a fraction of his holdings were in San Francisco." Max paused and sighed regretfully. "He did, however, confide in me that he missed his old house."

"I'll bet," Arthur agreed wryly. "That place was a frigging castle."

Neither of them looked away as the lengthy silence stretched out between them. Stalemate, Arthur thought. And he couldn't very well walk out on a stalemate, could he? He was going to miss that damned lecture, after all, and Delafield was undoubtedly going to go for his vitals.

As for Max, he was delighted to realize that the boy had been deftly feeling him out all along. Despite Arthur's apparent nonchalance and inattention to order, Max recognized a keen intellect and an enviable restless energy. After conversing with him for only a few minutes, Max was reassured that Sidney hadn't been wrong about his nephew's potential. What he lacked, Max now decided, was direction.

It was Arthur who broke the impasse. "Exactly why are you here, Mr. Hamilton?"

"Your uncle has left the bulk of his estate to the British Museum, however, he did include two special bequests, one for your sister and one for you."

"And they are?"

"Once the estate has been liquidated and debts cleared, your sister will receive the sum of one thousand pounds."

"Does she know about it yet?"

"No. I haven't had the opportunity to contact her. I intend to do so as soon as possible, of course."

"You said two bequests, one for Gwin and—"

"Yes," Max assured him. "There is also a bequest to you in the amount of one thousand pounds."

The wary expression on Arthur Pierce's face was replaced by a bright, surprisingly disarming smile. "A thousand pounds. I don't know how much that comes to in dollars, Mr. Hamilton, but I bet it'll buy a hell of a lot of shoes."

"Well, I'm afraid there is one stipulation."

Arthur's smile faded. "What stipulation?"

"Your uncle was involved in a search for certain relics and antiquities that, if discovered, would be priceless."

"What kind of relics?"

"At the time of his death, he was specifically involved in the search for Excalibur."

"King Arthur's sword?"

"You're familiar with it, then?"

"Naturally I'm familiar with it. It's part of the legend. Make-believe. Fairy tales."

"Perhaps not. A month prior to his death, Sidney procured a document that seems to indicate the sword does exist."

Arthur didn't bother to disguise the disbelief that edged his voice. "What document?"

Setting his cane to one side, Max retrieved his valise. Unstrapping it, he withdrew a flat, rectangular object swathed in layers of green flannel. He placed it on the divan and unwrapped it to reveal a framed document, which he offered to Arthur.

Beneath the glare of transparent glass, a page of yellowed parchment presented twenty lines of elegantly scrolled Latin. Ancient. Or carefully contrived to appear that way, Arthur mused.

"What's it supposed to be?"

"One page taken from a set of volumes recently discovered in the remains of a razed manor house near Edinburgh, Scotland. Those volumes included a twelfth-century calendar of Glastonbury Abbey as well as other items of historical interest."

Whether Arthur liked to admit it or not, his curiosity was piqued. "Monks?" he asked.

"Benedictine monks, to be exact."

"Where are the rest of these volumes?"

Max offered a crafty smile. "Most have made their way to the British Museum for further study."

"And this," Arthur held up the framed page. "Wait. Don't tell me. This just happened to fall out on the way to the museum and Uncle Sidney just happened to be there to pick it up."

"Something like that."

"Uh huh. What's so special about this particular page?"

"It's part of a preface executed in the sixteenth century. No name or ex libris inscription appears on the first folio, but it may be safe to assume that the author was a Benedictine monk entrusted to smuggle relics from Glastonbury Abbey before its dissolution and impoundment by King Henry VIII."

"Oh, yes. Let's see." Arthur squinted at the ceiling, recollecting his British history. "It was good old Henry who dissolved the Catholic monasteries. He raided their libraries, took what he wanted, and had the rest destroyed."

"Then you understand why the monks would have been

most anxious to have their holy relics removed to safer quarters. If you'll take a look at it, you'll see that clear reference is made to a sword named Caliburn."

Intrigued, Arthur crossed to his desk and sat down to the task of transcribing sixteenth-century letters beneath the unforgiving scrutiny of nineteenth-century gaslight. His Latin was rusty, to say the least, and the Latin composed by this monk—or forger, he reminded himself grimly—was less than textbook correct. Nevertheless, it took him only a few minutes to scratch out a working translation:

> It is fortuitous that we learned of the approach of Cromwell's men in time to hide the books and relics most valued by the Abbey. Among those, the chasuble of St. Dunstan, the holy thorn of the Redeemer, and the royal sword Caliburn. Certain of those were hidden with friends in Glastonbury. The rest we brought with us.
>
> They will be protected by friends of the Benedictines until it is safe for the monasteries to return to England. It is fitting that Caliburn now rests by the seat of the King until he shall rule again.

Arthur stared at the fantastical words he'd just scrawled on the back of an old calculus test: *Gladius Caliburn*. It was not simply a name but an image. An image all the more powerful and seductive because it was a child's image, his own, interlaced with the sweet whispered tones of a spellbinding storyteller he had once called Mother. "*It was magic, Arthur.*"

Sleek, argent steel rising to break the pristine blue surface of a lake. *A gift*. A woman's hand, white and delicate and perfect. *A gift offered to him by* . . . Dripping wet and shimmering, sun's rays dancing off steel forged on the magical Isle of Avalon. "*It was magic, Arthur. That sword was magic unto itself, a gift offered to him by Merlin the Enchanter and the Lady of the Lake.*"

Arthur closed his eyes, trying to dispel the tenacious

remnants of old dreams. When he opened his eyes again, the words were still there, but the images were gone, wisps of smoke stolen back to the deep recesses of childhood memory.

Hamilton broke into his thoughts. "The clue to Excalibur's whereabouts is in the last line. It's interesting to note that the author apparently subscribed to the legend that King Arthur never really died but that he would rise again to reclaim his throne. One can assume that this belief played an important role in his decision regarding where to hide it."

Arthur was familiar with some of those old legends. Many of them contended that King Arthur and his attendants were passing the centuries asleep in an enchanted cave, awaiting the day when they would be summoned to rise again. Was Excalibur to play a role in his resurrection?

Arthur frowned at the ridiculous direction of his thoughts and tossed his pencil aside. He barely remembered his Uncle Sidney, but what little he did remember, he recalled with a certain amount of mixed affection and reverence. Among other things, Sidney Pierce had been a master of the big con. In the end, though, it appeared that he had been reduced to the unseemly role of a gullible mark. This idea not only saddened Arthur, it made him angry. "It's a hoax," he said.

The older man seemed unfazed. "Oh, I seriously doubt it. Before arranging for the purchase of this parchment, I investigated the matter thoroughly and uncovered nothing to indicate fabrication. Whilst I am not an expert on medieval transcripts, I can assure you that the find in Scotland was genuine. The volumes that made it to London have been authenticated by scholarly experts."

Arthur folded his arms, determined to remain intractable despite the current of excitement that raced through his veins. "So, did Uncle Sidney ever find his imaginary sword?"

"No. He was already too weak to pursue his quest by the time he received this last clue. However, he wasn't ready to surrender. That was when he thought of you."

"Me?"

"Sidney knew you were finishing your education, that you were no longer the little boy he remembered but a grown man, an adult capable of pursuing this quest to its conclusion."

"And what made him think I'd want to?"

"The lucrative prospect of five thousand pounds."

"What?"

"Your uncle added a codicil to his will. Five thousand pounds will be held in trust for at least six months, during which time you may claim it by producing Caliburn."

"He must have lost his mind."

"If you are not able to produce the sword, you may still claim your bequest of one thousand pounds by producing adequate proof that you have, to the best of your ability, followed the quest to its logical end."

"Assuming the sword doesn't exist except in my deceased uncle's fantasies, how am I to prove I've followed this thing to its logical end? Especially when that logical end is nothing."

Max closed and fastened his valise. "That I must leave to you, young Arthur."

"Thanks."

Max ignored Arthur's dour sarcasm. "Nothing to thank me for. I'm simply carrying out my duties as executor."

"What are you getting out of all this, Mr. Hamilton?"

Max stood. Crystal promptly turned from her perusals and strolled across the room to join him. "With the exception of a nominal fee for managing the estate, nothing," Max replied. "As I said, your uncle was more than just a valued client. I considered him a friend."

"How very touching."

Max slanted a look at his four-legged companion. "Cynical for one so young, isn't he, Crystal? Remind you of anyone?"

The cat produced something between a growl and a purr, then turned its head to study Arthur with typical feline disaffection.

"Think what you will of me, Arthur, but if you believe any of what I've said tonight, believe this. Be careful who you trust, beware where you step, and watch your back."

Arthur stood. "What are you talking about?"

Snatching up his cane, Max moved for the door. "Men have been searching for Excalibur for hundreds of years. That parchment is as close as anyone's ever come to it. There are certain parties who might be willing to do almost anything to get their hands on it. Do you understand?"

"No."

"Well, you will." Max nudged Crystal with his cane. "It's time we got on our way. If you should need to reach me, my London office is on Little James in Bedford Row."

Suddenly unwilling to let the man go, Arthur crossed the distance between them to block the door before he could pass. "Wait. I don't understand why this was so important to Sidney, why he would pass it on." Arthur hesitated, then reached for what he really wanted to know. "I mean, why me?"

"Your uncle remembered you as an eleven-year-old boy, a very precocious, high-spirited little boy. He once told me that you carried a slingshot named Excalibur."

Arthur stood rooted to the floor, astonished to hear that Sidney had remembered something as insignificant as the two-bit slingshot he'd carried in his back pocket as a child. Arthur had loved that slingshot.

"Is it so surprising, then, that he would choose to offer this gift to you?"

At Hamilton's unsettling choice of words, a window opened in Arthur's mind. *A gift offered to him by* . . . He swallowed hard and deliberately closed that window.

Max adopted a contemplative expression. "As for your other question, I've known many collectors over the years, and I've often wondered myself. What drives them to pursue? What causes them to offer staggering sums of money for that one rare artifact that catches their fancy?"

Arthur had to clear his throat to find his voice. "And?"

"For some it's simply an investment. For most, though, it's a passion; a passion for art, a passion for beauty, a passion for the rare and the truly one-of-a-kind. Your uncle appreciated both aspects, but that wasn't all of it. He pursued what most people would consider the impossible for the same reason he lived most of his life."

"Which was?"

Max flashed a smile. "Why, for the sheer challenge of it, of course."

For once in his life, Arthur couldn't think of a thing to say.

Max tipped his derby. "Good luck to you, Arthur Pierce."

A few moments later, after Max Hamilton and his cat were gone, Arthur closed the door to his room and leaned back against it. The older man's words burned in his mind.

*For the sheer challenge of it.*

# 3

*The following morning,* Lady Spring shook out her skirts and appeared in fine fettle, but Arthur wasn't thinking of the spectacular weather as he pulled open the door of the Parthenonic Ridgway Library at the corner of Broad Street. As it swung closed behind him, the rattling of carriage wheels and the clip-clopping of hooves were stifled to a cottony silence. He was greeted by the scents of wood polish and old books.

The place was nearly deserted. With commencement looming at most schools, final exams and thesis papers were a thing of the past. Most normal students wouldn't be caught dead in a library at a time like this. Arthur, however, was not looking for a normal student.

As he crossed the gleaming marble floor of the entrance foyer, he spotted her at once, a slight, dark-haired figure bent over an open book at one of many empty tables. Nibbling on the remains of a peppermint stick, Chelsea Delafield appeared thoroughly engrossed in her subject. Arthur descended three broad steps to the sunken reading room and approached.

Sliding a leather book satchel from his shoulder, he took a chair across from where she basked in an aromatic aura of peppermint. Today, as always, she was impeccably well groomed—a white leg-o'-mutton sleeved blouse, bow tie, blue skirt, and sleek ebony hair swept up into a fashionable pompadour knot. Arthur concentrated on that neat little knot and waited for her to look up.

She didn't look up.

There was no sound except for the distant ticking of a grandfather clock and the occasional rustle of skirts as an elderly librarian moved from stack to stack in the bookshelves well off to their left.

Drumming his fingers on the tabletop, Arthur contemplated how best to approach the situation. He knew, of course, that Delafield was angry with him. This in itself was nothing new. They'd spent the past academic year grating on each other's nerves so often that each was now capable of annoying the other by virtue of mere proximity. This time, though, she had good reason to be miffed. Normally, he wouldn't have troubled himself beyond offering an apology for not showing up last night, but this time he needed something from her, and so he was forced to consider what it might take to thaw the Arctic Circle.

He cleared his throat, hoping to break the ice. Or at least graze a chip off the edge of it. "My, but you're looking delightful this morning, Miss Delafield."

She pulled the peppermint stick from her mouth. "Go away, Mr. Pierce."

"I stopped by your rooming house before work this morning. Your landlady told me you resigned your job at the bank and that you'd probably be here all afternoon."

"Busybody." She picked up a pencil with her free hand and scribbled something in an open notebook.

Arthur rested an elbow on the back of his chair. "In case you haven't heard, Miss Delafield, the academic year is expired. You've earned your degree, my dear. Take a break."

Her pencil stopped moving. She adjusted her spectacles

and turned to peer at the wall clock. Behind the annoying glare of those thick lenses, Chelsea Delafield had striking eyes, eyes almost the color of amethyst quartz. There was no getting away from them, really, not once they fixed on something, and Arthur certainly felt them fix on him when she turned back around.

"You're eighteen hours, thirty-seven minutes late."

Arthur tried tipping her the crooked grin that had melted countless disgruntled girlish hearts in the past. "Yes, and I'm truly sorry about that, Miss Delafield."

There was no sign of melting. She just stared at him with those eyes, unblinking and expressionless as a stuffed bird.

Arthur's grin faded as he shifted positions—and tactics—bringing his hands around to clasp them humbly on the table before him. This wasn't a girl, he reminded himself. This was a walking bookmark. Better to approach in a more rational manner.

He began again in a sincere tone of voice. "Well, actually, that's why I've come. I wanted to apologize and tell you that there's a very good reason why I didn't make it last night."

"Too bad I don't care to hear it." She returned to note-taking. "Shoo."

"Shoe?"

"Leave." She nipped the end from her candy and munched daintily.

"But I have something to show you, and I'm sure you'll find it interesting."

"Highly unlikely."

"Aw, now, come on, Miss Delafield, relax a little."

"You don't take hints very well, do you, Mr. Pierce?"

"Look, I know we've had our differences in the past, but—"

"Differences?" Her dark head popped up indignantly. "I assume you're referring to Julia."

Arthur appraised her with growing annoyance. She was never going to let him forget that one. Although Julia Tierney and Chelsea Delafield shared a room, Arthur couldn't imagine two women more diametrically opposed in personality.

"So, we're once again back to Julia," he said flatly.

"Poor girl. Cried her eyes out for weeks over you. She soaked through at least a dozen perfectly fine handkerchiefs."

"I never said anything about marriage."

Chelsea resumed taking notes. "No, I don't suppose that you did."

"It wasn't my fault if she assumed—"

"Lace-edged handkerchiefs they were. Very expensive. And quite useless once she was through with them." Chelsea popped the last nibble of candy into her mouth.

"I'm sorry to hear it. If I had the money, I'd reimburse her, but I doubt it would be necessary. I hear she's engaged to be married."

"You hear correctly."

"A Harvard man. Porcellian club."

"Correct again."

"Comes from a good family. Shipping."

"Quite."

"Well, then, Julia's done very well for herself, hasn't she?" Arthur pointed out. "After all, isn't that every common girl's dream? To marry 'up' in society?"

"Regardless of whether she's marrying up or down socially speaking, I agree that she's done well. Her prospects for happiness have improved immeasurably since you broke off with her."

Arthur had to bite back a zinging retort. Ah, well, Delafield was right, wasn't she? So be it. He leveled his gaze at the top of her obstinate head and began again. "As I was saying, I'm sure you'll be interested in what I have to show you." He snatched up his satchel. "I was approached last evening by a very unusual gentleman."

Chelsea raised her head to peer over the rims of her spectacles. "Well-dressed? Abundant white hair? Converses with quadrupeds?"

Arthur was genuinely surprised. "How did you know?"

Those violet eyes chilled, dropping the temperature around them at least twenty degrees. "He stopped by the historical society looking for you. Of course, you weren't there."

"Oh. Well, he found me later, and this is what he gave me." Arthur pulled out the manuscript page and set it down on top of her open book.

It took a moment for realization to sink in. She set down her pencil and examined the document. "Oooooh," she breathed like a woman on the verge of ecstacy. "Where did you get this?"

"I told you. The gentleman you met last night. Turns out he's handling my uncle's estate. This is part of that estate."

Arthur couldn't tell if she heard him or not. She ran an index finger very slowly, almost reverently, over the smooth glass. For the first time, Arthur noticed what slender, delicate wrists and exquisitely tapered fingers she had. Undeniably feminine. Somehow, the notion of elegant femininity didn't fit his image of the curmudgeonly Delafield at all.

"Latin," she said, breaking into his thoughts.

"Yes. Mr. Hamilton estimated its composition to have taken place sometime during the sixteenth century."

"Possible. Yes, yes, quite possible. There seems to be some mention of Cromwell. The earl of Essex, I assume—King Henry's chief henchman in dismantling the monasteries all over England."

"I brought along a translation if you'd like to look at it."

"I am quite capable of translating it for myself."

"Of course you are. I just thought . . ."

But she was already in the heat of scratching out words in her notebook. Arthur could read her flourishing handwriting from where he sat. *It is fortuitous that we learned of . . .*

Stubborn, he thought. She could have saved herself the trouble by just accepting his notes. He drummed his fingers in restless annoyance as he waited.

She spoke through her teeth. "Will you stop that, please?"

Arthur stopped and gritted his own teeth. Chelsea Delafield was a monumental pain in the neck. But a necessary pain in the neck, he reminded himself.

After Hamilton had left last night, Arthur had lain awake for hours, pondering his next logical move. It had been then that he'd thought of Delafield. If anyone could spot a forged manuscript, she could. It wasn't only her specialty, it was her passion. She walked, talked, ate, and breathed European history. Why, if she hadn't come to stay with her widowed aunt in America, Arthur had no doubt she would have excelled at any of the women's colleges on the Continent or her native England. As it was, however, she had chosen to come to America, and Arthur knew that if he could persuade her to cooperate with him, he could save himself days of picking through obscure reference books.

Chelsea looked up, her eyes narrowed. "This isn't one of your infantile practical jokes, is it, Mr. Pierce?"

"No joke, Miss Delafield. This was delivered to me last night, and I need your opinion. Do you think it's genuine?"

She assessed him distrustfully before being drawn back to the parchment. "Well, I can't be sure, but . . ." Once again, she ran an index finger over the surface, and, once again, Arthur was struck by the flawless elegance. A familiar image surfaced in his mind. *A woman's hand rising from the water, white and perfect. The Lady of the Lake.*

"Have you shown this to Professor Hawthorne?"

Arthur jerked his eyes away from her hand. "No, I haven't."

She still looked suspicious. "Why not?"

"If it's genuine, I don't think I'm ready to share it with the world."

Suspicion melted away to cautious interest. "Why?"

"Well, if it's genuine, then that means . . ."

"Yes?"

Arthur felt the threat of a blush coming on for the first time since he was twelve and contemplating his first kiss. She was going to think he was crazy, as crazy as the batty old gent who had delivered this thing. "Well, you saw the last line," he pointed out cautiously. "It could be construed as a clue to the final resting place of King Arthur's sword."

Delicate ebony eyebrows rose. "Excalibur?"

"Yes." Arthur felt three inches high beneath her headmistress-like scrutiny.

"You don't believe all that twaddle, do you?"

Arthur opened his mouth to deny it, then changed his mind. "Well . . ."

"The King Arthur of Camelot legend never existed."

"But I thought—"

She held up a hand. "I said the King Arthur of Camelot *legend* never existed. Now, as for an authentic historical figure upon which extraordinary legends might have been built, that's a horse of a different color, isn't it?"

"You hold that he did exist, then?"

"Possibly."

"When?"

"Well, as you know, Britain was part of the Roman Empire until 410 A.D. That was when the Romans withdrew, leaving the Britons to defend themselves. One of their most pressing concerns was the encroachment of settlers from across the North Sea."

"You're talking about the beginning of the Saxon invasion."

"Precisely. As the Saxons grew in number, they also grew bolder and more violent. By the middle of the fifth century, the Britons were on the verge of being conquered. It was then that a mysterious figure suddenly appeared, a figure referred to as Artorius. Whether he was King of the Britons or merely a war leader of exceptional genius, most historians agree that it was through his military success that the Saxons were beaten back and contained for several decades to follow."

"Well, then," Arthur proposed, "King Arthur did exist. That's basically what you're saying."

"Yes, but you're missing the point." She adopted the didactic tone of a university professor speaking down to a grammar school dunce. "This excerpt has nothing to do with history. It refers to an artifact that was concocted out of pure fantasy. Excalibur is nothing but a supernatural symbol created much later by . . ."

Arthur observed as she presented her scholarly refutation. If it hadn't been for her distracted gaze, which kept dropping to linger a bit too long on the ancient text before her, he might have believed her.

". . . so, you see, much like the Grail and Merlin the Sorcerer, Excalibur is merely a colorful figment of a medieval troubadour's overactive imagination," she concluded.

Arthur opened his mouth to question her, but she didn't give him the chance.

"Why, none of it can be construed as fact. Certainly not. I mean, how could it be?" Her voice tapered off to uncertain silence as her gaze dropped once again to the parchment. This time, it stuck there, and she frowned to herself.

"Uh huh. That's what I thought, too," Arthur filled in after a few seconds.

"Sorcery and magic swords. What rubbish," she muttered.

"Absolutely," Arthur agreed, beginning to sense that he just about had her. He moved to retrieve the parchment. "Well, thanks for all your help, Miss Delafield. I won't bother you again. I'll just take this back, and be on my—"

Her hand shot out like a whip, gripping his wrist with astonishing strength for so slight a young woman. "Not just *yet*, Mr. Pierce."

Arthur looked up in time to see a certain glint flare to life in her eyes. It was a glint he'd seen before, one he had been taught since childhood to recognize.

He had spent the first five years of his life living in the back of a rambling covered wagon, crisscrossing the Midwest as his parents peddled everything from magic pills and hair tonic to lightning rods and Bibles. Why, even now, Arthur was convinced that his father could have pitched repentance to the devil and walked away with a sale.

*"You know that glint when you see it, Arthur, my boy. They're caught. You have them in the palm of your hand. At that point, you may even try to talk them out of it, but they won't listen. Soon they'll be begging you for it."*

That was the glint he saw in Chelsea Delafield's shining violet eyes; the look his father had been referring to, the look that said, *I want it*. It was the look of a mark that was hooked.

Arthur offered a slow smile. "That's all right, Miss Delafield. I don't want to take up any more of your time."

"Nonsense. I've got plenty of time."

"Oh?" Arthur dropped his gaze to where she still latched on like a lobster.

She released him abruptly. "Well, um, what I mean is, regardless of whether King Arthur and his magic sword ever existed, this does exist. We have yet to establish its authenticity."

Arthur didn't miss her *we*, but he refrained from playing with her any longer. She was more than ready to give him what he wanted. "All right. How do we do that?"

Chelsea seemed to relax a bit. "Well, I have a few books back at my room which might help in determining the exact time period this was executed. If it's a forgery, some clue of it may surface through stylistic errors."

"That sounds like a good place to start. Why don't we go now?"

"We?" She looked at him as if he had just proposed ritualistic double suicide.

"Yes, we. This does happen to be my parchment, you know."

"Well, yes, of course it is, but it will undoubtedly take me several hours to go over it in detail. Perhaps you can come round for it tomorrow."

Arthur pretended to chew this over for a bit, then said, "Can I trust you, Miss Delafield?"

"Trust me? What do you think? That I'll abscond with your precious parchment?"

"No, I mean, can I trust you to keep your mouth shut?"

Chelsea looked insulted. "Well, of course. If that's what you want."

"That's what I want. You're not to say a word to anyone about this. Not even . . ." He paused for added effect. "Miles."

Arthur was amused to see two splashes of rose pink bloom high on her cheekbones. While it was common knowledge that she and Miles Middleton were something of an item, Arthur had a hard time picturing them actually doing anything beyond sitting side by side like a couple of bookends. Certainly nothing to blush about. As a matter of fact, if they ever planned to get married, Arthur hoped that, for Chelsea's sake, Miles's father would take him aside and offer him an instruction manual.

"I assure you," she said, her voice icy, although her cheeks still glowed bright. "Miles would have no interest in sixteenth-century scribblings."

"Good." Arthur was unable to suppress a grin of triumph. In the spirit of good sportsmanship, however, he offered her his hand across the table.

Chelsea looked startled. "What's that?"

"We've struck a deal, Miss Delafield. I believe that calls for a cessation of hostilities."

She pondered this for a long moment, then, hesitantly, reached out to accept his offered hand. Arthur was surprised to discover that her skin felt as silky warm and exquisitely feminine as it looked.

"So, what do you say?" he asked, his sparkling blue gaze rising to lock with her guarded, dusky violets. "Truce?"

"Truce," she said, offering him just the whisper of a cunning smile as they shook on it.

Chelsea managed to stay in her seat until Arthur Pierce left the library. But just barely.

After the door swung closed behind him, she forced herself to count to ten. Then she set about packing up her things—the parchment, her notebook, the volume on Egyptology—stuffing them all into her leather satchel and buckling it with trembling fingers. Excited?

Oh my, yes.

She was more excited than she had been about anything

in quite a while. It seemed as if commencement and the daunting idea of returning home to a dull teaching position in London had been glooming her outlook on life for months. But now she had a mystery to solve, a history mystery, no less, a mystery that, if genuine, could not be solved without returning to England. This prospect suddenly made going home seem not nearly as suffocating as before.

Grabbing up her straw skimmer hat, Chelsea set it at a cockeyed angle on her head and flew to the door only to be stopped cold by the shrill chirp-chirping of the librarian. Remembering that she had failed to check out the book on Egyptology, Chelsea slunk back to the checkout desk, blushing hot red and mortified at being called to heel like some lowbrow book thief.

As the old librarian proceeded to write out her cards with excruciating slowness, Chelsea waited, feeling as if she were about to jump out of her skin. The woman obviously hadn't a clue that she was holding up the solution to one of the greatest mysteries of all time.

The very moment Arthur Pierce had revealed the Glastonbury document, Chelsea had felt it was real, as real as the feel of cold, ancient stone beneath her fingers when, at the age of ten, her father had taken her to see Stonehenge for the first time.

With the chill wind whipping at her pink hair ribbons, a newly bespectacled Chelsea had touched one of the bluestone megaliths and had instantaneously sensed the centuries. Five? Ten? No, twenty-one, her father had told her with a strange hint of pride.

Two *thousand* one hundred *years*? But her tingling fingertips could have told her this was so. Chelsea had closed her eyes, knowing then that it was even older. She could feel the lingering presence of countless, very real human souls who had worshipped there even before the ancient Druids.

Legend had it that Merlin himself had transported the seven-ton stones from Ireland. Legends were make-believe, she knew, even at ten, but, at that moment, with her eyes closed and her child's boundless imagination, she believed it. Oh, yes, yes. With all her heart. For how else, if not by magic, could such a wondrous monument have been constructed more than two thousand years ago? How else?

Even now, in the scientifically enlightened year of eighteen hundred and ninety-two, there was no easy answer to that ageless question.

"Overnight only, miss."

Chelsea was snatched from her reverie by the flat monotone of the gray-haired librarian. Grabbing the Egyptology book with a mumbled thank you, Chelsea gave free rein to her itching feet and scooted for the door.

Emerging onto the street and scurrying around the corner of the building where her trusty bicycle was parked, Chelsea stuffed the bulky volume into her satchel. She wondered why she'd even bothered to check it out. She was going to be much too busy investigating the Glastonbury parchment to finish her reading on Egyptian archeology.

Walking her bicycle to the curb, Chelsea slung her satchel over one shoulder, hiked up her skirt, and mounted. With one quick look back for oncoming traffic, she put foot to the pedal and set wobbling rubber wheels spinning merrily down Broad Street.

She knew that if she could successfully prove that the parchment was genuine—as every keen instinct she owned insisted—she would play a significant role in uncovering one of the greatest archeological finds in history.

There was, of course, one problem.

Arthur Pierce.

She could only accomplish so much here in America, and so she was going to have to figure some way to persuade him to let her take the parchment with her to England. She didn't think it would be too difficult. If she was careful to word it right, he might even appreciate the offer. He was, after all, much more interested in chasing lightskirts and high times than in solving scholarly puzzles.

Yes, Arthur Pierce, with his bedeviling grin and off-the-cuff charm, was a potential problem, but Chelsea had dealt with him successfully in the past. She would do so again.

She was confident of it.

# 4

*In his dream, he hit the water hard.* It was skin-ripping cold, and he sank like a stone to the bottom of the lake. All was dark and quiet except for two male voices squabbling in his head.

"'Ey, what did ya go and bash 'im for?"

"Never mind that, ya bleedin' idiot! Check 'is bag!"

Arthur had pause to consider it odd that, as a Midwestern-born American, dream voices of his own invention should come sounding like villainous characters from a Charles Dickens novel. He had little time to dwell on this illogicality, however. He was going to drown if he didn't soon pay attention to his own predicament.

Forcing his eyes open against the cold, he detected traces of light filtering through the murky, fluctuating world above. He pushed off the muddy floor of the lake and swam toward it.

The voices still wrangled. "'Ell's bells and buckets of blood! It's not there! Where did 'e stash the damn thing, 'ey?"

"Well, why don't we wake 'im up an' ask 'im?"

There was a smack, then sarcastic mimicking. "Wake 'im up! You wake 'im up if yer so bleedin' smart!"

Arthur broke the surface in a dazzling burst of light. There was air, clean and sweet, and he gulped it in thankfully. He shook his head, spraying cool droplets, as he squinted against the brilliance of a lovely summer afternoon.

The lake was a deep teal blue, glittering silver and white in the sun, and surrounded by a lush green forest. It wasn't cold at all now that he'd reached the surface. It was perfect. *Avalon.*

Arthur pushed through the water, then floated on his back to observe white puffy clouds. When he came around again to face the center of the lake, what he saw there defied credibility. It was a woman. The most beautiful woman he had ever seen in his life.

Even though she was too far away for him to make out the fine details of her features, the sight of her still took his breath away. Hair of sleek, wet, glistening jet. White, creamy skin. Naked, utterly exquisite shoulders.

Arthur closed his eyes, then opened them again to refocus. She was still there. Soft, lovely, and inviting. She fanned the water with her arms, holding her position with effortless grace.

His heartbeat quickened as she pointed to him, then motioned. It was a beckoning motion, a seductive, come-to-me motion, and Arthur was reminded of the Sirens, those mythical sea nymphs who lured unsuspecting mariners to their deaths with sweet songs. This nymph made no sound, but Arthur was as helpless to resist as any poor, besotted Greek sailor of ages past.

He swam toward her. He wanted to talk to her, to touch her, to find out who she was and where she had come from, but when he neared, she turned her beguiling face away and dove back into the deep water. He caught the teasing flash of a naked hip, a slim flank, and a foot that kicked up a splash before she vanished.

Frustrated, he swore under his breath as he treaded water and scanned the lake's calm surface. Not a ripple remained behind to testify to her presence. Did she expect him to follow her? He would have, but he somehow knew that no mere mortal could hope to follow where she had gone.

He began to wonder if he had imagined her. Good God, who was she? Only a dream?

"Only a dream," Arthur said.

"That's right. Only a dream," came another voice. "Wake up, Pierce."

At least it was a familiar voice. This accent sounded more like Proper Philadelphia.

Arthur's peaceful dream lake drifted away. "Beautiful," he murmured.

Someone tugged on his arm. "Nothing beautiful about you or this room if you ask me. Wake up, Pierce."

Arthur opened his eyes to discover that he was no longer afloat in his sun-warmed dream lake. He was sprawled face-down on dry land. In fact, judging by the putrid lime green shade of the fuzzy wool fibers that now greeted his worm's eye view, he was lying on the threadbare carpet of his own dollar twenty a week room on Pine Street. He had a pounding headache and a dust ball tickled his nose. A far cry from Avalon, he thought dimly, then sneezed, sending the dust ball skittering across the floor.

It was Bernard Endicott who bent over him. "Pierce, roll over and look at me. Can you hear me?"

Arthur groaned and did as he was told. The dull, pulsating pain in his head flared, then settled down once he was flat on his back.

"Good grief, I was ready to go for a doctor. Are you all right?"

With his clean-shaven good looks, his ever-crisp collar and cuffs, and his tailored suits, Bernard Endicott had always cut a dashing figure, but at the moment, he was, as far as Arthur was concerned, a radical and extremely disappointing departure from the lady of the lake.

Arthur cleared his froggy throat. "What happened?"

"That's what I was about to ask you. I arrived just a few minutes ago to see if you wanted to go out for some fun, and I found you like this."

Arthur started to sit up, then stopped as a sharp pain tore

through the base of his skull. Its source seemed to emanate from somewhere between his occipital bone and mastoid process if he recalled his freshman anatomy correctly. He grimaced and tried again. "Give me a hand up."

Endicott grasped his wrist and pulled. Once upright, Arthur held his throbbing head in both hands. "Christ, I feel like I died and went straight to hell."

"Looks like you took a nasty bump. You'll be in for a bugger of a headache."

"Thanks, Dr. Endicott. Just tell me, is it bleeding?"

"A little. Here, take my handkerchief."

Arthur accepted the handkerchief and pressed it to his aching wound.

"Don't you remember anything?" Endicott asked.

"Not much."

"Say, you haven't gone and gotten yourself mixed up with people you shouldn't have, have you?"

Arthur raised his head very slowly so as not to antagonize the sleeping dragon at the base of his skull. "What are you talking about?"

"Well, I know you're low on funds, and—"

Arthur waved his friend's concern away. "No, of course not."

"Well, then, how do you explain this?"

"I think I was robbed." As soon as the words were out, Arthur began to remember.

"Robbed?" Endicott echoed. "Robbed of what, for God's sake?"

Arthur concentrated, trying to bring it all back. "After I left the library, I stopped for a sandwich and coffee. It was close to five by the time I got back here. I remember I had my key, but the door was ajar. At first I thought my landlord . . ." Arthur trailed off as the last few seconds of his conscious recollection finally took shape.

He surveyed his small room bleakly. The quilts and linens of his cot had been torn off. The mattress itself had been slashed and gutted. His dresser drawers had been yanked out, and his clothes were strewn on the floor. Likewise, his desk had been nearly disassembled, its contents tossed about like so much worthless confetti.

"I must have interrupted them," Arthur finished. "I think one of them came at me from behind the door."

"Hmmm, strange, isn't it?" Endicott stood and began to pick his way around the room. "You'd think if they wanted to rob someone, they'd pick a fellow with something worth taking."

Endicott's observation brought to mind Max Hamilton's warning from the previous night. "*Men have been searching for Excalibur for hundreds of years. That parchment is as close as anyone's ever come to it. There are certain parties who might be willing to do almost anything to get their hands on it. Do you understand*?"

Arthur hadn't understood then, or hadn't cared enough to try, but he was beginning to understand now. Regardless of whether the parchment was genuine or a fake, someone out there apparently believed it was real, and that someone was willing to commit robbery and assault to get it.

"I know what they were after," Arthur said.

"Oh?" Endicott turned to him with interest. "What?"

As Arthur struggled to his feet, he suddenly remembered Delafield, who had the Glastonbury parchment in her possession at this very moment. His heart plummeted at the awful thought that the men who had attacked him might have left here only to go after her.

"Oh, my God, what if they know about Chelsea?"

"Who?" Endicott asked.

Arthur raised a hand, trying to calm himself enough to think past the pounding in his head. "Wait a minute. Let me sort this out logically."

"Make sense, will you, Pierce?"

Arthur wasn't concerned with making sense. He was too busy trying to remember if anybody had followed him into the Ridgway Library this afternoon.

"Who's Chelsea?" Endicott persisted after a few moments.

"There's no way they could know about her," Arthur said, reasoning aloud. "Even if they were following me earlier, they didn't go into the library. I would have noticed them because the place was almost empty."

"I think that knock on the head did some real damage, Pierce. You're still not making any sense."

"No, it makes perfect sense," Arthur insisted, beginning to feel confident that Chelsea was indeed safe from harm. "I didn't go into the library with her, and I didn't leave with her. There's no way they could have seen her. The parchment is probably safer with Chelsea than with me."

"Sorry. I still don't understand. Is all this good or bad?"

"It's good. I bet they came back here when I stopped on my way home for a bite to eat. They figured they'd have plenty of time to locate the parchment and be long gone, but they couldn't find it because it wasn't here."

"The parchment? What parchment?"

"And when I returned home, they figured I must have had it with me all along." Arthur glanced about the floor for his leather satchel. He spotted it by the door, open and empty. "They searched but they didn't find it because, by then, I'd already given it to Chelsea."

"What is this 'it' you're blathering about? A parchment, you say? A piece of paper?"

"You wouldn't believe me if I told you."

"Sounds like trouble to me. Perhaps you should report this to the police."

"They wouldn't believe me, either. No, this is something I have to handle on my own, but you can do me a favor."

"What's that?"

"Do you think I could stay with you for the next few days?"

Endicott shrugged. "Certainly, if that's what you want. Do you think they'll be back?"

"I don't know, but I'd rather not take the chance."

Stuffing Endicott's handkerchief into his pocket, Arthur moved to his closet to find his suitcase lying open on the floor by his feet. "After I get some things packed, I'd appreciate it if you'd come with me to DeLancey's. If I'm being followed, maybe we can work together to lose them in the theater crowd. I can't risk being followed to Chelsea Delafield's rooming house."

"Wait a minute," Endicott interjected. "Delafield. I've heard that name before, haven't I? Isn't that the ice queen you mentioned last night?"

"Yeah, that's her all right." Setting his suitcase out on the floor next to him, Arthur stooped before a distressing conglomeration of clothing and scattered papers.

"But I thought you didn't like her," Endicott said.

"Like has nothing to do with it," Arthur replied. "As Shakespeare might have put it, sword-hunting acquaints a man with strange bedfellows."

Endicott sounded confused. "Did you say *sword-hunting*?"

"I'll explain on the way," Arthur assured him. "Oh, and there's one more thing you could do for me."

"Name it."

"I may need to borrow some money. I have a feeling I'm going to need it."

"For what?"

Arthur pulled a shirt from the pile and folded it into the suitcase. "For a trip I plan to take very soon."

The clock on the mantle in the parlor read six forty-five. Chelsea forced her gaze away from its impassive face to Miles, who sat motionless across from her at the open game table.

He was preoccupied this evening, and Chelsea was beginning to get the dreadful feeling that he was going to try to propose to her again before the night was through.

For the moment, however, she assumed that she was safe as he studied the triangular points on the backgammon board. He had been thusly occupied for more than four minutes, during which time Chelsea had found her thoughts being drawn back to the Glastonbury parchment. At this very moment, it lay next to an open book on her bed. She could literally feel its arcane pull on her nerves even from where she sat, and she was eager to get back to it.

She tapped two fingers on the tabletop, then, upon remembering that this was one of Arthur Pierce's most aggravating mannerisms, she promptly curbed herself and spoke. "Miles, for God's sake, *move*."

"Well, I seem to have encountered a rare mathematical problem. You see, the probabilities of getting hit are essentially the same for both of the strategies I'm considering."

"Then it doesn't matter what you do."

"Yes, but, how to choose? How . . . to . . . choose?"

Chelsea eyed the center part atop his head and wondered what the mathematical probability was of getting caught if she popped him with one of the fireplace implements that seemed to wink so invitingly at her from across the room.

Just then, a flash of something at an open window behind Miles diverted her attention. A bird? Curious, Chelsea leaned to the left to gain a better view. Dusk was descending, but she easily recognized Arthur Pierce standing outside her window.

A very annoying bird indeed.

He wore the insufferable grin Chelsea's enamored roommate Julia had once described as irresistible. Irresistible or not, at the sight of him, Chelsea felt an unwelcome surge of warmth rise to her cheeks. Egad, how long had he been standing there watching her like some unconscionable voyeur?

Upon noting that he'd captured her attention, he began gesturing. Still disconcerted at finding him lurking at her window, however, Chelsea completely missed his meaning. She frowned and shook her head.

Obviously exasperated with her thickheadedness, Arthur pointed at her and jerked a thumb toward the back of the house. Then he forked two fingers and walked them along the window sill.

Chelsea straightened in her seat. It was obvious that he wished to meet with her in the backyard, but why? And why in heaven's name hadn't he just come to the door like a civilized human being?

The most logical answer to this second question came to her instantaneously. Julia, of course. He had no desire to run into his jilted paramour, and Chelsea couldn't blame him. These days, Julia was likely to shoot him down like a pheasant.

Chelsea addressed Miles. "Will you excuse me for a moment?"

He mumbled, not looking up from the gameboard. "Hmmm? Oh, yes, of course."

He was still mumbling to himself as she swept the parlor doors closed behind her. Picking up her skirt, Chelsea hurried back a narrow corridor and through a deserted kitchen. It now occurred to her that Arthur might have come to demand the return of his parchment. What would she do then?

Pushing open the back door, Chelsea stepped outside to meet a warm spring breeze. The moon was rising. Perfumed scents of fresh-cut grass, blooming lilacs, sweet alyssum, and honeysuckle put Chelsea in mind of her mother's slavishly tended garden back home.

Descending three steps to a brick walk, she squinted as she scanned the darkening yard for Arthur. She called out his name in an impatient whisper.

"Here."

Startled, Chelsea spun around to see him leaning up against a nearby rose trellis, his arms folded casually across his chest. She scurried toward him. "What's the meaning of all this sneaking about? Couldn't you see that I was busy?"

Smirking as if at some private joke, he straightened to meet her halfway. "Ah, yes. Sorry to interrupt you and Middleton in the heat of passion, Miss Delafield."

Chelsea was grateful for the shadows of twilight that served to camouflage both the renewed heat which rose to her cheeks as well as the disconcerting deep blue of Arthur

Pierce's gaze. This wasn't the first time she was driven to curse his confounding ability to make her blush like a ripe peach seemingly at will. It was most unsettling.

"I thought you were supposed to be working on the parchment," he said, after she deigned not to reply.

"I was, but I forgot Miles was coming round this evening. I couldn't very well tell him to leave, could I? If you'll recall, you swore me to absolute secrecy."

"I recall."

"So, what is this all about? I have to get back to Miles before he becomes suspicious."

"There's been a new development."

"A development?" Chelsea's heart began to pound. He was going to demand return of the parchment. She was sure of it.

"When I got back to my room this afternoon, it had been ransacked. Before I knew what was happening, I was attacked from behind. When I came to, it was obvious that someone had been searching for something."

"Oh, dear heavens!" Chelsea forgot her own anxiety in light of this startling new revelation. "How exciting!"

"Exciting?"

"Yes!"

"That wasn't exactly the first adjective that came to mind upon waking in a pool of my own blood, but—"

"Don't you realize what this means?"

"It means someone out there thinks that parchment is worth braining me for."

"Precisely! And I couldn't agree with them more."

"Pardon me? Bloodthirsty little wench, aren't you?"

Chelsea ignored the question. "What I mean is, from what I've found so far, there's nothing to indicate it's a forgery. Stylistically, it corresponds perfectly with what one might expect to find in a sixteenth-century manuscript."

Only the hint of a smile played up the corners of Arthur's mouth as he listened, but the light of triumph in his eyes was unmistakable. "It's real."

Chelsea looked up into his glittering gaze and imagined that she saw therein a reflection of her own most cherished dreams and desires. For the briefest of moments, they shared a perfect understanding. "Yes," she whispered.

A slow moment passed before Chelsea remembered that his next move could be to reclaim his parchment. She turned from him and added, "Of course, I can't be absolutely certain until . . ."

"Until what?"

Chelsea sucked in a hopeful breath. "Until it can be authenticated by an expert." She waited, breath still bated, for his reply.

"Like who?"

Chelsea turned back to him cautiously. "There's a friend of my father's in London, a retired Oxford professor."

"Good," Arthur said before she could continue.

Chelsea was unable to credit her own ears. She opened her mouth, but no words issued therefrom. *Good?* Would he really allow her to leave the country with his parchment so easily?

"When do we leave?" he asked.

Chelsea felt as if he had snatched a rug out from under her feet. "Wha-wha we?" she repeated stupidly.

"How much is a second-class ticket to England going for these days, anyway?"

Chelsea's mouth had gone too dry to speak.

"What's the matter, Miss Delafield? The scuttlebutt is that you plan to return to England. I assumed it was going to be soon."

"Friday," she croaked.

"Day after tomorrow," Arthur said. "Not much time to make arrangements, but I can probably manage it."

Chelsea shook her head to gather her scattered wits. "I'm sorry, but I'm afraid you won't be able to secure a steamer passage, at least not this week. I happen to know that we took the last cabin to Southampton on a last-minute cancellation."

It was Arthur's turn to repeat the most popular pronoun of the day. "We? Who's 'we'?" Then, he adopted a baiting tone. "You and Miles? Do I hear wedding bells?"

Chelsea felt the first glimmerings of another blush brewing and fought valiantly to control it. "Certainly not! If you must know, my traveling companion is a woman named Mrs. Putnam. Papa hired—" Chelsea cut off too late, cursing her own tongue and wondering what it was about Arthur that so unsettled her nerves and muddled her thoughts.

His eyes took on the knowing, privately amused glint that she so detested. "What about your father? Go on."

She folded her arms and raised her gaze to fix on the glowing face of the moon. It too seemed to be smirking at her. "Nothing."

"What's the matter, Miss Delafield? Embarrassed?"

"Oh, really, Mr. Pierce. Don't be juvenile."

"Mrs. Putnam is your chaperone, isn't she?"

Chelsea set her teeth together. "She's my traveling companion."

"Uh huh. You've managed to live on your own for four years now, but Daddy thinks you need protection from all those lascivious young men who prowl steamships at night."

Chelsea turned away and worried her lower lip in annoyance. Whether Arthur was extraordinarily perceptive or just stabbing in the dark, Chelsea didn't know, but he had nevertheless just hit upon a particularly sensitive issue. Her sense of independence.

She had spent her first three years in America staying with her widowed Aunt Geraldine, but after her aunt had been called to return to her missionary work in Africa the previous summer, Chelsea had begged her parents to allow her to come back to Philadelphia to finish her last year at Temple. To this end, she had found herself a room, secured a modest-paying typewriting job during the day, and was now looking forward to graduating with honors tomorrow evening. What she was not looking forward to was the day after tomorrow when she would set sail for home.

Although Chelsea loved her parents and missed the company of her older sisters, she knew this would mark the end of her adventure in self-sufficiency. The fact that her father had seen fit to hire a chaperone to watch over her only added insult to injury. For weeks now, she had felt the walls of her family's unbearably conventional expectations closing in, and Mrs. Putnam's imperious presence aboard ship would be just one more reminder that her days of freedom were numbered.

Chelsea turned back to Arthur, determined to ignore his childish taunts no matter how close they cut to the bone. "I have a proposal."

"Do you?" He still sounded amused, blast him.

"If you leave the parchment in my care until you gain passage to England, I would be willing to ask Professor Doyle to take a look at it in the meantime."

Chelsea had difficulty reading Arthur's expression as he appeared to consider her offer. Just about the time she was ready to allow herself a sprig of hope, he shook his head. "Sorry, but where that parchment goes, I go, and I have no intention of waiting around for a week or more if I can help it."

"But I told you—"

"Why don't you do us both a favor and get rid of Mrs. Putnam?"

"What?"

"If you get rid of her, our transportation problem will be solved," Arthur said matter-of-factly. "By the way, her passage has been paid for, hasn't it?"

"Yes. My father saw to that when he engaged her."

"Good. Then I can take her place."

Chelsea didn't follow his reasoning. "But we've only booked one cabin."

"Oh, I don't mind bunking with you, Miss Delafield. Just so long as you promise to keep your hands to yourself, of course."

"Oh, honestly! The whole idea is preposterous!"

"Why? Are you afraid I'll make advances?"

"No!"

"Are you afraid *you'll* make advances?"

"Oh! You . . . you . . ." Before she could think of a properly scathing retort, she heard Miles call from inside the house. By the sound of it, he was already passing through the kitchen and heading in this direction.

Chelsea's natural inclination was to answer, but just as she turned back to the house, it occurred to her that she had good reason to hold her tongue. While Arthur could easily duck out of sight, she would be left standing in the open like a dolt, unable to explain what she was doing out here by herself in the dark.

Before she knew what was happening, Arthur made her decision for her. Catching her up about the waist from behind, he pulled her back around the east corner of the house.

When he pressed back up against the brick, Chelsea was plunged right along with him into a web of creeping honeysuckle vines. Their sweet fragrance rose to overwhelm her, but it wasn't the woodbine that set Chelsea's senses to spinning. For the first time in her life, she was stunned to find herself snugly braced, inch for shocking inch, against the length of a fully developed male physique.

The fact that it was Arthur Pierce who held her with such intimate familiarity and that she should have been outraged by his audacity failed to even register. What did register was the surprising realization that the unfamiliar physical sensations that were washing over her were not at all unpleasant. In fact, they were most interesting.

The back door squeaked open and Miles called out. "Chelsea? Are you out here? Chelsea?"

She was almost afraid to move. Because of Arthur's superior height, his forearm had inadvertently slipped up to hug her about the rib cage rather than the waist. Now, with every shallow breath she took, Chelsea clearly felt his thumb grazing the underside of her left breast.

"Oh, dear. Oooh, dear heavens," she whispered, more to herself than to Arthur, but it was Arthur who replied.

"Shhhhh!"

His head was bent, and Chelsea felt a whisper of warm breath flutter over her ear. In fact, he felt warm all over, very warm. And firm, so very *interestingly* firm.

Miles was calling out into the backyard. "Chelsea? Are you out here?"

A woman intervened. Chelsea recognized this new voice as her landlady, Mrs. Hess. Miles had apparently roused her from the sewing room, where she spent most of her evenings. "Is there a problem, Mr. Middleton?"

"I can't seem to find Miss Delafield. We were in the middle of a game when she excused herself. Have you seen her?"

"No, but perhaps she's just gone to use the necessary."

Miles sounded doubtful. "Perhaps, but she's been gone for quite some time. I thought maybe she came out for a breath of fresh air."

"Well, it's obvious she's not here. I can check her room if you'd like."

"Oh, I hate to put you to the trouble."

Their voices receded as the back door shut behind them.

Arthur spoke against Chelsea's ear. "They're gone."

Chelsea felt his hold on her loosen, then his arm slipped down so that his fingertips brushed lightly over her abdomen before he released her.

"Ahhhhhh," she whispered, wondering at the buoyant little flip her stomach did in answer to this casual contact. It reminded her of the delightful sensation she had once experienced while riding a carousel at Smith's Island Resort.

"Miss Delafield? Are you all right?"

She felt strong fingers grip her shoulders before he turned her to face him. "Chelsea?"

She couldn't seem to take her eyes off of him. In the deepening darkness, she could make out the strong, square cut of his jaw and the undeniably appealing lines of a sensual mouth.

Oh dear, but he *was* exceptionally handsome. Chelsea had seen as much before this, of course, but she had always considered herself immune to it. Now, though, his hair shined soft and thick in the waxing moonlight, autumn russet shot through with streaks of gold, and Chelsea suddenly wondered how it would feel to touch.

He bent his head close to hers, his eyes searching her face. Chelsea imagined that she felt his warm breath on her cheek. Oh dear, was he going to . . . ?

"What is it?" he asked. "Are you sick in your stomach or something?"

"Wha—what?"

"You look sort of funny."

What was the matter with her? Arthur was good looking, yes, but Chelsea had always been intelligent enough to see through that. She had recognized him for what he was from the very first day she had laid eyes on him in astronomy class. He was an unabashed flirt, an unmitigated cad who went through paramours like so many old socks. And he had soon proven her correct when he had taken up with Julia and just as quickly left off, hadn't he?

Apparently convinced that she intended to keep her evening meal where it belonged, he released her and stepped away from the house. "Look, we don't have much time, but I have an idea."

Chelsea was still too bewildered to concentrate on what he was saying. "I'm sorry?"

"Do you have Mrs. Putnam's address?"

"Um, yes. She's a governess for a family named Morgan on Rittenhouse Square."

"Good. I think I can arrange for Mrs. Putnam to receive a telegram from your father disengaging her from her duties as chaperone."

"But how?"

"I have a friend who works for Western Union."

"You mean, a falsified telegram? Isn't that illegal?"

"Probably." Arthur appeared unconcerned with fine points of the law as he brushed a honeysuckle leaf from his coat sleeve. "It'll probably cost me two free tickets to DeLancey's, too, but if it works, it'll save me a week's worth of time. I can pay you back for the passage once my uncle's will is settled."

DeLancey's. At the mention of his disreputable place of employment, Chelsea couldn't help wrinkling her nose scornfully. She had a good idea of what went on at DeLancey's House of Burlesque—dancing tarts in tights—and it only served to reinforce the stark reality that Arthur Pierce was nothing more than what she had always thought him to be.

"Julia told me you have an aunt living here in Philadelphia. Is that right?"

"What?" Chelsea asked absently, then shook her head as his question sank in. "Um, yes. I mean, no, not anymore. She's in Africa."

"Africa?"

"Missionary work," Chelsea clarified impatiently, aggravated more with herself than with him. "Why do you ask?"

"Does Mrs. Putnam know that?"

"No, I don't believe so. Papa initially engaged her through mutual acquaintances. What's that got to do with this?"

"Mrs. Putnam will receive a telegram tomorrow afternoon stating that she's being excused from her duties as chaperone. Your Aunt, uh, what's her name?"

"Aunt Geraldine."

"Your Aunt Geraldine will be accompanying you back to England. What do you think?"

Chelsea set aside her irritation as she mulled this over. The idea of allowing Arthur to share her stateroom aboard ship was highly improper. Scandalous, really, but, dash it all, did she have any other choice? He had made it abundantly clear that he wasn't about to allow an ocean to get between him and his blasted parchment.

She assessed him skeptically. "Do you really think you can pull it off?"

A white smile flashed in the dark. "No problem at all, Miss Delafield. Just leave it to me."

# 5

*The docks along Delaware Avenue* bustled with riverfront activity. Carpetbag in hand, Chelsea tapped her foot impatiently as she waited beneath a lamp post by the Christian Street piers. The rattling of wagons and the calls of street vendors mingled with the wail of steam whistles, the clatter of winches, and the multilingual chatter of immigrants, stevedores, and sailors to create a cacophony that numbed the ears.

To a young woman faced with the prospect of traveling alone, this spectacle of confusion might have been intimidating, but Chelsea had already crossed the Atlantic six times since first coming to stay with her Aunt Geraldine to pursue an American education. She was anything but intimidated; in fact, her heart pumped strong and fast with the barely suppressed excitement she always felt before embarking on a new adventure. This excitement was dampened only by the sobering realization that this might be her last ocean voyage for quite some time. Maybe forever.

From behind came a tap on her shoulder. She turned to be confronted with a pair of wicked blue eyes and a devilish grin. Dressed in a double-breasted lounge jacket and crisp tan trousers, Arthur Pierce appeared exceptionally dashing this afternoon. A brown derby sat at a cocked angle on his head, lending him a bohemian air. "Lovely day for a boat ride, Miss Delafield."

Chelsea bristled, annoyed with herself for even noticing his appearance. Her loss of good sense two evenings ago was still appallingly fresh in her memory. "Mr. Pierce, you seem to be forever lurking up behind me."

"Well, a fellow has to have a hobby."

"What took you so long? I was ready to board without you."

"Oh, you wouldn't do that to me, would you, Miss Delafield? Not after all we've meant to each other over the past year?"

"Do stop your theatrics. We haven't the time for it. They've already cleared the decks of visitors, and we're due to set sail in less than fifteen minutes."

"Hey, I'm lucky I made it at all. I had to stop by DeLancey's to pick up my pay. Ever since I told him I was leaving, getting money out of that guy has been like squeezing blood from a turnip."

Unconcerned with Arthur's monetary tribulations, Chelsea glanced over her shoulder before dipping into her reticule to produce a boarding pass. "Here. Take this before Miles sees you."

"Ah, yes, Miles." Arthur accepted his steamship ticket. "I should have known he wouldn't miss this chance to see you off. Where is good old numberhead, anyway?"

"Seeing to my baggage." She was determined to ignore his infantile witticisms. Good God, but it was going to be a tediously long voyage.

Arthur let out a low whistle as he scanned his boarding pass. "Hey, first class. Remind me to thank your father personally. He really knows how to travel in style."

"If my father had any idea we were taking advantage of his generosity in this manner, he would no doubt experience an apoplexy."

"Don't worry, Miss Delafield. When I get my inheritance, I'll pay back every cent." He frowned at the ticket. "This is made out for Althea Putnam."

"Well, it was purchased in her name. What did you expect?"

"Oh, well. A minor inconvenience." Arthur slid the ticket into his coat pocket. "By the way, I didn't get to talk to you last night at commencement. How did Mrs. Putnam take the news?"

"I assume you're referring to the telegram you sent her."

"You assume correctly."

"Well, she was quite put out, but I assured her that Aunt Geraldine's decision to accompany me was totally unexpected. I explained that a dear old friend of hers has taken ill, and she's most anxious to see him once more before he pops off."

Arthur appeared amused by this imaginative embellishment. "It's for certain that he's on his deathbed, then?"

"Yes." Chelsea straightened her beribboned straw boater hat with dignity. "You're not the only one who can spin a good yarn."

"Well, I'm damned impressed, Miss Delafield. Well done."

"Thank you."

"So, are you ready to go?"

"Not quite. Miles hasn't returned from—" Before she could finish, Chelsea caught sight of Miles Middleton's gray top hat amidst the milling crowd of tearful well-wishers.

"Oh dear," she said. "Here he comes. Maybe you should make yourself scarce."

"Too late. Looks like he's already seen me."

Even as Arthur spoke, Chelsea saw Miles's eyebrows draw together into a fierce scowl. She closed her eyes and raised one hand to pinch at the bridge of her nose where she had good reason to believe a headache would soon be forming.

Those two had never hit it off, not since Arthur had enrolled at Temple and then proceeded to unseat Miles as head of their class. Chelsea knew how hard Miles had worked to earn his outstanding grades, and she could understand why it had nettled him to watch Arthur outscore him on every examination without so much as cracking open a book.

"Pierce! What are *you* doing here?"

Chelsea opened her eyes to see Miles towering over Arthur, his nostrils flaring, then thinning, flaring, then thinning.

"Why, Middleton, what a small world," Arthur said brightly. "You wouldn't be coming along, too, would you?"

"What? Coming along? What are you talking about?"

Chelsea laid a calming hand on Miles's arm. She knew that they were as good as off to the races if she didn't nip this confrontation in the bud. Nothing delighted Arthur more than to goad Miles to the point of turning scarlet with rage.

"It seems he's been invited to visit Cambridge," she said, uttering the first explanation that flashed to mind.

Miles gaped at her in disbelief. "Cambridge? *Cambridge*? He's been invited to visit *Cambridge*?"

"Yes."

"Well, I simply can't believe it!"

Sensing that Arthur was about to open his big mouth, Chelsea shot him a censorious look. "Will you excuse us for a moment?"

For once, he tactfully acquiesced. "Certainly, Miss Delafield. I'll wait for you on the pier." But he couldn't resist tipping his derby at Miles. "*C'est la vie,* Middleton."

Miles tracked him with murderous eyes until he was out of earshot, then whipped around to face Chelsea. "I can't believe it! Who invited *him* to visit Cambridge? Nobody invited *me* to Cambridge. He hasn't snagged himself a fellowship, has he?"

"There, there, Miles," Chelsea soothed. "I'm sure nothing will come of it once they meet him."

"Well, that's a good point," Miles muttered grudgingly before changing the subject. "Hasn't Mrs. Putnam shown up yet?"

Chelsea hesitated only briefly before reeling off yet another stretcher. “She’s already boarded. Didn’t you see her?”

“No. Already boarded, you say?”

“You must have just missed her.” Chelsea marveled at what a jolly good fabricator of tall tales she had become since linking up with Arthur.

Behind them, the steamship whistle bellowed.

“Oh, dear, I’ve got to go,” Chelsea said.

Miles began shifting his weight from one foot to the other and back again, a sign that he was growing agitated. It was also an indication that he was about to try to propose again, and Chelsea’s heart dove straight to her feet.

“Chelsea, my dear, I’ve been trying to—that is, I’ve tried to find a way to ask you this for weeks now, and all I’ve done is botch it up terribly.”

Chelsea wished that a passerby would ask for the time, that the steamer’s whistle would burst forth again to drown out his words, even that Arthur would interrupt them with one of his inane comments.

“And now it’s almost too late,” Miles was saying, “and so, perhaps the best way to ask is to just ask. Chelsea, will you—”

“Will I write to you? That’s what you wanted to ask, isn’t it?”

He looked stunned. “Write to me?”

“The answer is yes.” Chelsea rushed on before he could recover. “As soon as I arrive home and every week thereafter. Please promise you’ll do the same.”

“But I . . .” His shoulders slumped. “Yes, I promise.”

On impulse, Chelsea rose up on her toes to hug him. She knew that she had hurt him, but it was better this way. Better that he hadn’t asked and she hadn’t had to answer. She did love Miles, but she loved him like a brother, not a husband, and that wouldn’t have been fair to either of them in the long run.

“You’ve been a dear friend, Miles, and I shall miss you awfully,” she said, fighting an urge to free the tears that burned at the corners of her eyes.

She felt his large hands settle tentatively about her waist. "I shall miss you, too, Chelsea."

She held tight for another second, taking in a deep breath to compose herself before pulling away and stepping back. "This isn't good-bye, this is merely farewell. I shall certainly visit America again, and if you ever get to London . . ."

"Yes," Miles said forlornly. "Of course."

"Farewell, then."

"Farewell, Chel—"

The rest was drowned out by another thundering blast from the steamship. Chelsea turned and walked away. Her feet felt as if they were encased in lead as they crossed over brick pavement to wooden planking. It was all she could do to keep her head high and her watering eyes fixed on the looming black hull of the passenger steamer docked along the pier.

Arthur, who was waiting by a post with one foot resting atop his battered suitcase, straightened and moved to join her. "Say, are you all right, Chelsea?"

She didn't look at him. Couldn't. Not without bursting into a ridiculous torrent of tears. "I'm fine," she managed to clip off, determined to keep her numb feet moving toward the steamship *Salacia*'s gangway where six other Johnny-Newcome passengers had formed a line to board.

Chelsea was acutely aware of Arthur's touch, a light, reassuring pressure near the base of her spine, as they mounted the gangplank to take their places in line, and she was oddly grateful for it.

She wondered if she had just made a terrible mistake. Perhaps love was love. Perhaps one was lucky to find any type of caring at all in this world. Many successful marriages had been built on much less. Why was she so determined to hold out for something more?

She was suddenly helpless to keep her lower lip from quivering. Confound it! She would not cry. Not in front of Arthur.

"Here."

A white handkerchief dangled in front of her face. She stared at it, speechless.

"Take it, for chrissake."

She set down her carpetbag and took it.

"One gets used to leaving places," Arthur said. "But I doubt one ever gets used to leaving people."

Chelsea blew her nose and peeked up at him sideways. She was relieved to see that his attention remained tactfully trained on the uniformed purser ahead of them. "How do you know so much about it?"

"My family moved around a lot when I was a kid."

"Oh." Still clutching his handkerchief in one white-gloved hand, she retrieved her carpetbag and concentrated on the steel-hulled ship that would carry them across the Atlantic.

Long and sleek, stretching over five hundred feet from stem to stern, the *Salacia* was three decks high and equipped with two thick steam-breathing funnels and three sets of auxiliary sails. Set high and forward of the funnels was an immaculate officer's bridge, and, from the foremasthead, the Union Flag of Great Britain fluttered proudly against a clear, blue sky.

Arthur spoke in a low voice next to her ear. "Here, I've got something for you."

Wresting her attention from her native flag, Chelsea saw he proffered a small, round gleaming circle in the palm of his hand.

"A ring?" she asked, questioning the obvious.

"A wedding ring."

"A what?"

Arthur laid a finger to his lips. "Quiet down, will you? Since we're sharing a cabin, it'll keep up certain appearances if we seem to be married."

"I see your point." She took the band, removed her glove, and slipped it onto her third finger to examine it. "Gold?"

"Close enough."

"Where on earth did you get it?"

"A pawnshop. Look, from now on, just keep your mouth shut and go along with whatever I say."

Chelsea didn't appreciate being dictated to in such a high-handed manner, but, as the line in front of them began to move, she saw no benefit in offering any further argument.

Soon they stood before the brass-button uniformed ship's purser, a broad-shouldered man with graying sideburns, a subtle Scots accent, and an air of indisputable nautical authority.

"Tickets?"

"Ah, yes," Arthur said pleasantly, rearranging the thick leather strap of his satchel, then setting down his suitcase. He produced the requested document from his coat pocket. "Darling?" He held a hand out to Chelsea. "Your ticket, darling?"

Darling? Chelsea curled her lip at this endearment but accommodated by withdrawing her ticket from her reticule and slapping it into his waiting palm.

Arthur offered them to the purser. "Beautiful day for a cruise, isn't it?"

"Aye, that it is." The purser paused as he scrutinized Arthur's ticket. "There seems to be some mistake."

"Oh, I assume you're referring to the name," Arthur said. "Obviously a clerical error. It should read *Arthur* Putnam, not *Althea* Putnam."

"Oh." The man examined Chelsea's boarding pass. "And this is Miss Delafield?"

Before Chelsea could reply, Arthur cut in. "She's Mrs. Putnam now."

Chelsea was surprised when he wrapped an arm about her shoulders and heaved her smack up against him. She was struck again by male strength and firmness, but, with her shoulders hunched up to her ears, she was thankfully too uncomfortable to go all weak-kneed over it.

"We were joined in holy matrimony just yesterday morning," Arthur was saying. "This is to be our honeymoon trip." He squeezed her again, causing her carpetbag to thump against her leg. "Isn't that right, tootsie?"

Tootsie? Really, he was going much too far. It was all Chelsea could do to hold her tongue.

"As you can see, she's still so overwhelmed with happiness, she's speechless." Arthur released her so abruptly, Chelsea almost stumbled back down the steep gangplank.

The purser motioned for a steward. "Stateroom fifteen. That's on A-deck, first cabin."

"You bet! First class all the way." Arthur swept up his suitcase. "Uh, say, my good man." He stopped and winked at the purser. "There wouldn't happen to be a wedding suite equipped with a big brass bed available, would there?"

Oh! That was the last straw!

Chelsea lifted her skirt and sent the toe of her button-up shoe slamming into Arthur's shin. Her lower digits throbbed upon contacting solid bone, but her physical discomfort was greatly mitigated by the sound of his strangled bleat and the sight of him nearly crumpling to the gangway.

"Problem, sir?" The purser bent over him with concern.

Chelsea answered. "Bad knee. It goes out on him at the most inopportune moments."

"That's a shame. Will you need help boarding, Mr. Putnam?"

"No . . . I can manage just fine on my . . . own."

"Do hurry along, *tootsie*." Chelsea accepted the assistance of a steward to step up onto deck. "We don't want to keep first class waiting."

Beneath the lamp post where Chelsea Delafield had earlier fretted over a tardy Arthur Pierce, Horace "the Spider" Doolittle, Thames riverfront thief and Whitechapel ruffian of the lowest order, stalked back and forth on the long, spindly legs that had earned him his nickname among the street urchins that swarmed London's notorious East End.

Behind him, two blasts from a steam whistle drew his vexed attention to the transatlantic ship that now prepared to depart from its berth. He stopped his pacing long enough to shake a bony fist in the air and let out a string of invectives that might have turned the air purple if he were the least bit intelligible to the people who swept by. As it was, his thick cockney accent made no meaningful impression on the ears of middle-class Philadelphians and immigrants just arriving from eastern Europe.

"'Orace! 'Ey, 'Ooorace! I got 'em, I did! I got 'em!"

At the sound of his brother's call, Horace turned to see Bert alighting from the opposite curb of Delaware Avenue, waving something over his head. His next words were drowned out by the clatter of an ice wagon as it passed between them.

"'Urry up, ya bleedin' fool," Horace muttered as his brother scuttled across the street.

Although no one would have guessed it to look at them, they were fraternal twins. If Horace's six-foot cadaverous frame and unsightly dark countenance had earned him the nickname of Spider, his rotund little twin more resembled a hairy species of garden beetle.

"See 'ere, 'Orace, I got 'em, I did!" Bert's round face was suffused red from exertion. "Two tickets to Mother England! Right 'ere they are!"

"'Old yer bleedin' noise and give 'em 'ere!" Horace grabbed the tickets and smacked his brother on the ear with one quick, well-practiced motion. "Blimey! What took ya so long?"

Bert managed to catch his dusty bowler before it flew off his head. "Well, I 'ad to find the blinkin' ticket office, then I 'ad to queue up."

"We've almost missed the boat, ya bleedin' fool!" Horace turned and stalked up the pier, long arms swinging. "Come on and step lively. We ain't got no time to waste."

Bert hurried to catch up, wheezing and gasping as he gamefully skipped two steps for every one of his brother's protracted strides. "Say, 'Orace, who do you think the bird is with the Pierce cove, 'ey? Do you think maybe she's got the blinkin' parchment? Maybe that's why we couldn't find it on 'im. Maybe 'is doxy's 'ad it all along!"

"'Old yer bleedin' noise, you idiot! 'E wouldn't give it to no bird. 'E's got it on 'im somewhere, and we're going to find it this time."

"Well, I 'ope so, 'Orace, 'cause Mr. Blake ain't goin' to be 'appy at all if we come back empty-'anded. I think we'd be better off staying 'ere in the States if that 'appens. Till 'e cools off some, ya know?"

Horace knew. Mr. Blake's employees had a disturbing propensity for turning up as bloated corpses in the Thames. While the man paid uncommonly well, he was explicit in his instructions and demanding that they be followed to the letter. In this case, no killing and a minimum of bashing, which, quite frankly, for Horace, took all the fun out it. It also made their job much more difficult. How were they supposed to get their hands on the bloody parchment, anyway? Say "pretty please" for it?

He offered up no more than a disgruntled growl in reply to his brother's merited concerns as they approached the steamship. The purser had just checked the last passengers aboard.

"'Old it there a minute, me covey! Two more to go," Horace called in his most pleasant voice. "Almost missed the bloomin' boat!" Horace held out his tickets and offered the purser a black-toothed grin.

The purser didn't smile back. In fact, he frowned as he took in Horace's scruffy boots and weedy coat. He did, however, accept the tickets.

Bert came wheezing from behind just as the purser's frown deepened. "I'm sorry, sir, but these are for the *Indiana*."

"Wot's that?" Horace's grin froze into a grimace.

"These tickets are for the American Line. They dock in Liverpool."

"Oh! Well, that's all right, ain't it, Bert?" He winked and poked his brother with an elbow. "Our mum lives in Liverpool, ain't that right, Bert?"

Bert nodded. "Thas right! Thas right!"

The purser gave the tickets back to Horace. "You don't

understand. Your ship doesn't depart until next week. Check the date on your tickets."

Horace tried to pick out a date amongst a jumble of letters and numbers. He had never been much of a literature student. "Wot? Where?"

The purser tapped the upper left hand corner. "There."

"Oh, no, no, that won't do. That won't do at all!"

"It'll have to do, sir. This ship is full."

"Oh, no, no," Horace protested again, straining to remain calm as his mind threw itself into gear and began to grind squeaking wheels. "You see, uh, er, it's me mum, sir! She's taken awful bad sick, and she ain't got much more time left."

Horace felt Bert's pudgy fingers press through the sleeve of his coat. "Wot?" he gasped in shock. "Mum's blinkin' sick, ya say? Why didn't you *tell* me, 'Orace?"

Horace's tenuous poise snapped. He smacked his half-witted brother on the ear. This time, Bert's derby went spinning into the air like a pie plate. "I *did* tell ya, ya bleedin' idiot!"

"Curse yer eyes, 'Orace! Ya went and knocked off me 'at!" Bert scrambled back down the gangplank to rescue it from the dock below.

The purser's voice lost all semblance of politeness. "Please step down from the gangway, sir. This ship is ready to cast off."

At the infuriating thought of Blake's parchment slipping through their fingers yet again, Horace grabbed the purser's spiffy lapels. "'Old it a minute, me covey! I'm sure we can work somethin' out if ya know what I mean! A few extra bobs for yer pocket? What'll it take, 'ey?"

"Sir, if you do not release me and clear the gangway immediately, I'll have you forcibly escorted!"

"What'll it take? What'll it take, 'ey?"

The purser was already signaling. Out of the corner of his eye, Horace saw perhaps half a dozen uniformed seamen hurrying across the deck.

Knowing when he was outmatched, Horace backed off,

raising both hands. "'Ey, no 'arm done! I just lost me 'ead there for a minute! No 'ard feelin's, 'ey?"

When he had retreated to the dock, he watched in helpless, broiling frustration as the gangway was hauled up, cutting off their last access to the steamship *Salacia* and the precious parchment it carried.

"'Ey, 'Orace! They're leavin' without us!" Bert wailed. "They can't do that! We've got tickets, we do!"

Normally, Bert would have suffered dearly for his infuriating stupidity, but Horace was already too horrified to react. A disturbing mental picture had formed as he watched the great ship cast off its moorings, that of their ill-matched twin bodies floating and bobbing amongst the flotsam of the river Thames. Bert's earlier suggestion concerning an extended stay in the States suddenly didn't strike him as such a bad idea after all.

# 6

*"You're a real hellhound,* Chelsea Delafield."

Arthur dropped onto the lower bunk and lifted his trouser leg to examine his shin for any signs of bruising. They had lingered topside long enough to observe as their ship was led from its berth by the mighty little tugs.

Now, in their midships first class cabin, the great sea vessel's motion was barely detectable. The gentle vibration of its propeller, noticeable in the walls and the carpeted floor beneath their feet, was the only indication that they were no longer docked at Pier 46 in Philadelphia.

Delafield was ignoring him as she bustled about the cabin. Dressed in a cocoa brown skirt, white blouse, and matching jacket, she epitomized the seasoned traveler as she moved from closet to dresser to writing table, whisking open drawers and doors to take note of various stashes of blankets, stationery, candles, and towels. "Yes, yes," she would clip off at one stop, only to shake her head and express at the next, "No, no, that won't do at all."

Arthur was hard pressed to understand what she found wanting with their accommodations. He had never traveled by boat, but he'd traveled plenty by train. Although their cabin was small, it was private, a luxury not found in land conveyances unless one had the considerable wherewithal to engage his own Pullman car.

"I was just trying to inject a little humor into our situation," Arthur said, raising his voice so she couldn't ignore him so easily. His shin still smarted, damn her pointy English shoes.

"I suggest you curb your wayward sense of humor, Mr. Pierce. You have met your Waterloo." She slipped the latch to their private lavatory, another luxury unheard of in land travel, and popped her head inside for an inspection. "Oh, dear. No soap."

"Well, that tears it for me," Arthur said. "Let's get off this floating ragbag and demand our money back."

"Don't be ridiculous." She closed the lavatory door and opened one of three steamer trunks that took up most of their floor space. "We'll simply inform the steward."

Curb his sense of humor, she'd said. Arthur thought he'd be lucky if it wasn't bled from him, drop by painful drop, by the time they docked in Southampton. God, but this was going to be a tediously long voyage.

He watched as Chelsea began to unpack her trunk. Her movements were quick and sure as she pulled out, not clothing as he expected, but bottles, little brown medicine bottles and ointment tins. One after the other. *Slap, slap, slap*. They soon lined up like a row of miniature pharmacopeia soldiers on the chest of drawers that was bolted securely to their cabin wall.

Arthur strolled over to survey the odd collection. Arnica, ammonia, ginger, French pills, quinine pellets, smelling salts. He wondered wryly if she had remembered to pack splints for fractured shin bones.

Chelsea pulled out two woolen shawls, a winter coat, a pair of thick gloves, and a knitted scarf.

"Planning to stop off at the North Pole?" Arthur asked, no longer able to contain himself.

"The North Pole?" Chelsea looked up as she draped her garments over the back of a chair.

"It's seventy degrees outside."

"You've never traveled the North Atlantic before, have you, Mr. Pierce?"

"No, I haven't."

She smiled then. Just the whisper of a smile, a typical Mona Lisa-like Delafield smile, and it occurred to Arthur that he might never have had occasion to actually see her teeth. "Hmmmm, well, you'll find out."

Her smug tone gnawed at him. It was the same kind of tone married men often adopted when addressing grooms-to-be. Before he could ask what she meant, there was a knock at their door.

"Are you expecting someone?" Chelsea asked.

"No." Arthur had to step around a trunk to get to the door. "It's probably just the steward come to tell us you're weighing down the boat with all your baggage."

Her pert nose wrinkled at this, but he managed to scoot past her before she had time to cause him serious bodily injury. When he opened the door, he found not a steward, but a beaming, nattily dressed young couple in their early twenties.

The man, of solid build but an inch or two shorter than Arthur, offered a manicured hand. "Say, my good man, I hope we're not interrupting. My name is Fred Sherman."

"Not at all," Arthur said as they shook hands. A private school boy, he guessed. Yale. Class of '90. Member in good standing of the Germantown Cricket Club.

"And this is my wife, Bernice."

Bernice, a plump blonde with dimples, smiled up at him from beneath a massive ribboned hat. "Delighted to make your acquaintance." She disentwined her arm from her husband's long enough to offer him a white-gloved hand in greeting.

Old family. Rittenhouse Square, Arthur decided. Bryn Mawr Ladies College. Class of '92.

"The steward mentioned that we weren't the only newlyweds on board, and we just couldn't wait to introduce ourselves," she gushed. "I hope you two don't mind."

"Not at all," Arthur said again, noticing that Chelsea had made her way over to stand next to him. "My name is Arthur Pier—uh, Putnam, and this is my, um, wife, Chelsea."

"How do you do," Chelsea said. Arthur noticed that while she didn't frown, she didn't actually smile, either. Typical Delafield.

Fred chuckled and nudged his wife. "Listen to that, dovey, he still can't quite get used to that word, *wife*." Offering Arthur a wink, he added, "You're not the only one, my good man. We've only been married a little over a week ourselves."

"You're English, aren't you?" Bernice asked, obviously picking up on Chelsea's accent.

"Yes," Chelsea said.

"How delightful! Are you going home to visit family?"

"Yes."

"So, this isn't your first transatlantic trip. Perhaps you can give us landlubbers some traveling pointers. Say, how long have you two been married?"

Chelsea looked at Arthur. Arthur looked at Chelsea. "Since yesterday," he said.

"Isn't that wonderful, Freddy?" Bernice melted up against her husband so that, except for the color of their clothes, it was hard to tell where one of them ended and the other began. "They're even newer newlyweds than we are! What fun!"

Fun. Arthur caught a slithering look from Chelsea. She had already distanced herself, not physically but emotionally, donning her British reserve like an invisible cloak of dignity.

Fred and Bernice didn't seem to notice. Fred was clapping him on the shoulder in a comradely fashion and Arthur was forced to pay close attention to follow the gist of his conversation.

Chelsea folded her hands primly and observed without joining in. *Americans*. Overall, they were a pleasant lot, but they did tend to get a bit sloppy about it. Even after four years, all of their ebullient chatter, back-slapping, and handshaking was still a bit much for her to fathom.

"Fred's family is in textiles," Bernice said.

Chelsea realized the other woman was speaking to her. "Oh? Isn't that interesting."

"What's your husband in?"

Chelsea should not have been taken off guard by this inquiry. The American preoccupation with occupations was another oddity she'd never learned to understand. She looked to Arthur only to find that he and Fred were immersed in a conversation about boxing or fencing or some such barbaric male pastime.

She knew nothing of Arthur's background. In fact, now that she thought about it, she couldn't recall seeing even one member of his family at commencement the previous night.

Left to fend for herself, Chelsea looked back at Bernice and answered truthfully. "I haven't the foggiest."

Bernice's forehead wrinkled in puzzlement. Luckily, Fred chose that moment to nudge his young bride. "Say, dovey, why don't we go take a spin around the promenade deck?"

"Oh, let's do, dear!" Bernice turned dancing bright eyes upon Chelsea again. "Would you two care to join us?"

Chelsea looked at Arthur, who, for once, seemed to read her thoughts and agree. "We would, but I'm afraid we're right in the middle of unpacking."

"Oh, that's all right," Freddy assured him. "Perhaps we'll see you two again at dinner."

"We'll look forward to it," Arthur said.

"Till then." Freddy turned to leave. "Come along, dovey."

As soon as Arthur closed the door to their stateroom, Chelsea resumed unpacking her trunks. "Ridiculous," she muttered.

"What? The Shermans?"

Chelsea was surprised to realize Arthur had followed her and now stood directly behind her. She had to force herself not to look around. "Oh, really," she said, wondering why his nearness seemed so disturbing. "They were draped all over each other like a couple of wet towels."

"They're young, rich, and in love, Miss Delafield. Typical world-traveling Yankees. What can you expect?"

"A little decorum, a little discretion in public." Chelsea hung her coat in the cubicle that would serve as their closet.

"They're newlyweds. They can't get enough of each other."

"Oh? And how would you know?"

"I've heard that's how it is. At least until the bloom wears off her rose."

This typically male comment was so nettling that Chelsea couldn't resist turning around. "What about his rose?"

"Doesn't apply. It's his wealth and family name she's concerned with."

"But doesn't that fly in the face of all that democratic heritage you Americans are always spouting off about? What happened to 'all men are created equal'?"

"Well, when it comes to money, Miss Delafield, some men are created more equal than others." His lips crooked into a playful grin that caused her stomach to flutter apprehensively.

She was right to be apprehensive, but she realized this too late to avoid being caught when he reached out to take her about the waist. Instinctively, her hands flew up to his chest to fend him off. They stopped just short, however, of actually pushing him away.

"You know, we might try acting a little bit more like newlyweds ourselves," he said.

Speechless, Chelsea looked down to where he held her. In reality, his touch was light, but she swore she felt his fingers burning through the material of her shirtwaist—indeed, through the very layers of her skin—electrifying what lay beneath.

When she looked back up, an impish glint kindled in his eyes; eyes that were the breathtaking blue of a Scottish loch on a midsummer day. "What's the matter, Miss Delafield?" he inquired suggestively. "Thinking of causing me grievous bodily injury?"

Actually, Chelsea was thinking no such thing. She was wondering instead what perverse part of her yearned to press still closer. Until thigh met thigh, until breasts met chest, until lips met lips. She wondered why she suddenly felt so compelled to feed a sensual curiosity she had never even known existed within her until so recently.

She would think back later and know that the only thing that saved her was that maddening glint in his eyes. As always, he was merely teasing her, testing to see what she would do, and there was nothing Chelsea hated more than to be teased.

"Oh, really!" She found her voice and her indignation in the same instant. She turned her back, effectively removing his hands from her waist in one movement.

*I don't like him*, she reminded herself. She had never liked him. Yet, she wondered why Miles's touch had never had the same effect on her and tried not to contemplate the fact that if it had, she wouldn't have been nearly so quick to deflect his proposals of marriage.

"You know, you might take a lesson from Bernice Sherman, Miss Delafield. At the very least, you're going to have to stop stiffening up like a fence post when I touch you. We're supposed to be happily married."

Chelsea didn't reply as she yanked a day dress from her steamer trunk. How was she supposed to stop stiffening up when his touch seemed to have the same unsettling effect as a static electric charge? Somehow, she was going to have to rein in her illogical emotions. In these close quarters, she feared it was going to be a treacherously long week.

It was only by lucky chance that they arrived in the dining saloon too late to be seated near the Shermans. Bernice waved as they passed, and Freddy called out a jovial good evening.

The passengers seated with them at the purser's table, the owner of a Philadelphia newspaper, his snobbish wife, a pleasant elderly couple, and two mutton-whiskered English stockbrokers, were markedly uninterested in each other's business. Except for introductions and a smattering of small talk, Arthur and Chelsea consumed their meals in peace.

Later, Arthur suggested they tour the public rooms. Chelsea had never sailed on this particular vessel, but she knew that most passenger steamers were set up in a similar manner. The thoroughly modern *Salacia*, although a shining example of the very latest in *tourisme de luxe*, was no exception.

Located forward was the library, a writing room, and a drawing room for the ladies. Progressing aft, a staircase led back to the dining saloon and embarkation hall. Behind that, the grand saloon and the gentleman's smoking room. Chelsea noted that the decor was more lavish than those she had seen before. Rich paneling of maple and walnut, Rubenesque oil paintings, wall tapestries, and thick carpeting greeted their every stop.

As for Arthur, he was most impressed with the gentleman's gym on the boat deck. After emerging, he informed her that not only was it equipped with foils, dumbbells, and a punching bag, it actually featured a mechanical horse, too.

A mechanical horse?

Chelsea tried to picture such a horrific contraption, to no avail. She was much more interested in the wide reading selection offered in the library and made a mental note to browse its shelves at another time.

After a brief stroll about the promenade deck, they returned to their cabin. As it was not yet time to retire, Chelsea brought out the one interest they had in common. The parchment.

As she pulled it from her carpetbag, she felt its ancient vibrations thrumming through her fingertips, and a familiar thread of anticipation wove through her.

"All right," Arthur said as he paced the short length of their cabin. "Putting aside the question of its authenticity, let's think about what the monk meant when he said he hid the sword by the king's seat."

With well-practiced effort, Chelsea reined in her native enthusiasm, made herself comfortable at the writing table, and recited aloud. "'It is fitting that Caliburn now rests by the seat of the King until he shall rule again.' I think he was speaking of King Arthur, not his present king. The reference to regaining his crown makes that clear."

"I agree," Arthur said.

"So, where and what is King Arthur's seat?" Chelsea set the parchment down in front of her. She was careful not to touch it any longer than necessary. "Do you think he meant an actual throne?"

"If he did, then we're in trouble."

"Perhaps he meant a place from which King Arthur might have ruled, the seat of his government."

"You're talking about Camelot."

Arthur was still pacing restlessly, and Chelsea wondered how he was ever going to withstand being cooped up on a steamer for seven days. "Yes," she answered.

"But no one knows where Camelot was located, do they?"

"Not for certain, but there are some theories."

Arthur stopped pacing. "What theories?"

"There are historians who believe Camelot might have been located in south Somerset. The town of Glastonbury is nearby."

Arthur raised a finger. "Now, that's interesting. If this monk believed Somerset to be the lost site of Camelot, he might have considered it the perfect place to stash the sword. Remember, he believed that the king would rise again. Where better for Arthur to go search for his sword than near his old stamping grounds?"

"Interesting theory," Chelsea allowed. "However, I can't seem to get past the fact that it would have been much safer if the monk had taken the sword with him to Scotland. It was likely he would have found friends sympathetic to his Catholic cause."

"But then, how to explain the monk's reference to the king's seat?" Arthur asked. "Are there any places in Scotland rumored to be possible sites of Camelot?"

"Perhaps. Almost every inch of Britain lays claim to some aspect of Arthurian lore, but most historians tend to agree Arthur was probably based in southern England."

Arthur shook his head and smiled. "Ironic."

"What is ironic?"

"Wouldn't it be something if our monk decided to hide Excalibur right beneath the very noses of King Henry's monastery-dismantling henchmen?"

"Yes," Chelsea admitted. "It would."

"It reminds me of a little pearl of wisdom my father passed down once. If you want to hide something well, stash it in the most obvious place. Right under their noses."

"Perhaps, but I'm not sure that it would always work."

"Nothing works all of the time, Miss Delafield. That's why you should always vary your strategy. Keep them guessing."

"Another nugget of wisdom from your father?"

"No. A guy I once knew named Fuzzy Garrison."

"Fuzzy," Chelsea said with a dry little smile. "How charming. An astute philosopher, no doubt."

"Among other things."

Chelsea rose to her feet. "Well, it seems our monk promises to keep us both guessing. If his intention was to be mysterious, he was certainly successful."

"Whatever the case, I think our search has to start in Glastonbury. That's where our Benedictine friend started from. That's where we need to begin."

Chelsea warmed at his words. *Our search*, he'd said. Whether he realized it or not, he was including her in his plans. Until now, she hadn't been sure where she stood in that respect.

"It's late," she said. "I suggest we turn in."

"I heartily agree."

As Chelsea collected her nightdress, dressing gown, and slippers, she reflected on how smoothly the evening had passed. Not once since dinner had they exchanged sniping words. Even if she hated to admit it, the effect was quite pleasant.

At this thought, she cast a cautious glance in Arthur's direction to see that he was busy extracting his suitcase from beneath the lower berth. She rcmembered Bernice Sherman's question from earlier this afternoon and was suddenly curious.

Pulling her hairbrush from the top drawer, she asked, "You mentioned your father. Is he still alive?"

"No. He died a long time ago."

Chelsea sneaked another glance to see that he seemed occupied with gathering up his own night gear. She wrestled with herself only briefly before posing the question that burned on her mind. "So, what was it you said he did for a living?"

There was a pause. She heard Arthur stop what he was doing and turn around. "I didn't say."

Biting her tongue, Chelsea looked at him. She couldn't tell if he was offended or not, but he wasn't answering her, so she could only assume that she had committed an unpardonable social gaff. Leave it to her to succumb just once to American nosiness only to run up against the only American loath to impart every scintillating detail of his personal history.

"I'm sorry," she said, then lied through her teeth. "I thought you did."

He gave her a slow, cunning smile before turning back to rummage in his suitcase. "My father was a thief."

Chelsea blinked at his impassive back. Was he pulling her leg? Repaying her for being so forward? With Arthur, one could never quite tell. "You're joking."

"Nope. He was a thief, a swindler, a flimflam man, a grifter, a con artist. So was my mother, for that matter. What do you call them in England?"

"I don't—that is, I . . . I'm not quite sure."

"So was my Uncle Sidney. He was the one who left me the parchment in his will." Arthur faced her, gesturing with his toothbrush. "Now, he was a real master. One time, they almost elected him mayor of San Francisco. I'll have to tell you that story someday. It's incredible. What does your father do?"

"He edits encyclopedias."

"Sounds fascinating."

"Yes." Chelsea was too flabbergasted to think of anything else to say.

Arthur pointed at the door to their lavatory. "You want to go first or shall I?"

"I'll go now, if you don't mind."

"Not at all."

Chelsea walked to the lavatory on wooden legs, flipped the latch, slipped inside, pulled the light chain, and locked the door. A mirror fronted the medicine chest over the washbasin. Chelsea stared at her reflection to see that her cheeks were parched white. Setting her bundle down on the sink, she reached up to pinch them back to life. "Never," she scolded herself. "Never again."

When Chelsea emerged in her nightdress and dressing gown, hairbrush in hand, she was confronted by the scandalous sight of Arthur Pierce in flagrante delicto—that was, in the act of donning his nightwear.

"Oh, my God!" She turned away too late to keep from catching her first view of an unclothed adult male chest.

Even with her back turned and her eyes squeezed shut, Chelsea could envision every distressing detail. Instead of a calf-length nightshirt like her father had always worn, Arthur wore pajamas. And only the bottom half, at that. She was immediately put in mind of a conversation she'd once overheard on Derby Day at Epsom. *"Strapping healthy specimen, that one. A thoroughbred stallion born to stud."*

"Oh, God!" she gasped again. Her heart pounded and her stomach seemed to be executing a breathtaking series of swoops and curls that she knew from firsthand experience had nothing at all to do with seasickness.

"What's the matter, Miss Delafield?"

"You're naked!"

"Not quite. My best part's covered."

"For God's sake, Mr. Pierce!"

"All right, all right. You can turn back now."

Chelsea spun around, vastly relieved to note that he was finishing off the top button of his pajama shirt. Not an inch of firm, muscled, hairy male flesh in sight.

"Why couldn't you wait until your turn in the lavatory?" she demanded.

"You were taking too long."

"If we are going to learn to get along together in such close quarters, I think it behooves us to set down some rules!"

A corner of his mouth quirked up. "Rules? Whose rules?"

"My rules! If you can't wait your turn, then, from now on, you shall go first, and I shall go second! That way, there will be no more gallivanting about in the . . . in the . . ." Chelsea waved her hairbrush as she stumbled, fumbled, then recovered. "Improperly attired!"

"Heaven forbid that."

She could tell he was enjoying the situation, and, although this realization rankled her to no end, she drew in a tremulous breath to calm herself. "As for sleeping arrangements, I think it only fair that you take the top and I'll take the bottom."

"Fine, tootsie." Arthur sent her a rakish wink as he brushed by her to the washroom. "Maybe later in the week I'll let you be on top."

When he was gone, Chelsea marched over to the dresser to put away her clothing. It was only as she slammed the drawer closed that the meaning of his words sank in, and a hot blush swept over her from head to toe. Her knowledge of sexual matters was limited to anatomy textbooks and what she had gleaned over the years from her married sisters and other girls' giggling innuendos, but she wasn't altogether ignorant.

Julia Tierney had been a particularly enlightening roommate. "Gentleman on top, lady on the bottom," Julia had joked one night before retiring. "They say, though, that it can be done the other way around. But I can't imagine how. Can you?" No, Chelsea had not been able to imagine how. Quite frankly, she had already gotten hopelessly stuck while trying to imagine the first.

She scurried over to her berth, raising cold hands to press down hard on her burning cheeks. It was the only way she could think of to douse them before he emerged from the lavatory. He was too bloody observant to miss her flush, and he would no doubt pounce upon any sign of embarrassment to amuse himself. Damn him.

Damn him to hell!

With that scorching epithet ringing in her mind, Chelsea tried to calm her overactive heart and bobbing stomach as she kicked off her slippers, ripped off her dressing gown, and climbed into her lower berth. *Lady on the bottom.*

"Stop it," she commanded from between clenched teeth. She snatched off her spectacles and stowed them in a small bag for personal items that hung inside her berth.

"Stop what?" Chelsea heard the door latch snick closed behind him.

"Nothing." She pulled her blanket up to her ears and rolled over so her back was to him. Her cheeks were heating up again.

"A bit cranky, aren't we?"

"Go to sleep, Mr. Pierce."

"Gladly, Miss Delafield." There was a pause, then, "Ready or not, out goes the lamp."

A click. Darkness.

Chelsea felt him step up onto the frame of her bunk. Then, just as quickly, he pushed off and was gone. Wooden beams creaked overhead as he settled in. *Gentleman on top.*

"Stop it," she said again.

"Stop what?"

"Oh, shut up! None of your business!"

"All right, but, just tell me one thing. Is this some sort of bizarre ritual you go through every night before falling asleep?"

Chelsea closed her eyes only to be confronted once again by a smirking, virtually naked Arthur Pierce. Lean muscle, chiseled chest. Broad shoulders. *Strapping. Healthy. Thoroughbred.*

*Stud.*

With a groan of misery, Chelsea burrowed her head deep into her pillow and willed herself to sleep.

# 7

**London**

*With his portmanteau in hand,* Emory Blake, son of a long-deceased earl's bastard and a bastard himself in every sense of the word, stepped down from a hansom cab into a pea-souper fog that all but blotted out the gaslit windows of his Park Lane townhouse.

Broad-shouldered of stance and with a generous crop of silver hair, Blake's distinguished figure did brash justice to his tailored Savile Row suit. The diamond-studded tie-pin that secured his cravat was from Garrard & Co., Crown Jewelers and Goldsmiths. Nevertheless, the tip he flipped the cabman was paltry. Two silver bobs.

He was not in a generous mood.

Unmindful of the scowling driver behind him, he cut briskly through the evening mist, causing it to wisp and curl in his wake as he passed through a wrought iron gate and took the flagstones with long, impatient strides.

Within seconds of setting foot inside the foyer, he was

besieged by a middle-aged housekeeper and two bustling maids. As the women hurried to relieve him of his silk top hat, his walking cane, and his coat, Blake handed his portmanteau to the butler who silently materialized by his side.

Expressionless and unflustered as always, Geoffrey Dark observed his employer through the saurian, unblinking eyes of a lizard. "How was your trip, sir?"

"A disappointment, Geoffrey, an abysmal disappointment."

"I'm sorry, sir." Geoffrey gave the leather suitcase to one of the housemaids, and, with a slight inclination of his bald head, indicated it should be taken up to Mr. Blake's dressing room posthaste. The women soon scattered and vanished, melting back into the woodwork until called upon again to perform their duties. They had long ago learned not to tarry needlessly in the master's presence.

Geoffrey Dark had no fear of tarrying in Blake's presence. In truth, by now, it was expected of him to do just that. The diminutive butler had outlasted two wives and the first Swiss timepiece Blake had purchased on Regent Street.

"I take it the South African situation has not improved," Geoffrey said tonelessly.

"Damned Boers." Blake didn't bother to elaborate as he moved to a side table to flick through calling cards and dinner party invitations. He didn't need to explain his discontent. Geoffrey had often accompanied him to his Kimberley diamond mine and understood the unstable governmental situation that threatened his holdings there.

"Will you be taking a late dinner in the dining room, sir?"

"No, Geoffrey. I will, however, take claret in my study."

"Very good, sir."

Blake soon finished glancing through the pile of unopened letters delivered by penny post. No doubt, many of them were groveling requests for extensions on repayment of personal loans. Nothing that couldn't wait until tomorrow for his attention; all except the transatlantic telegram from the States. News of the parchment, he thought, a swell of excitement bubbling in his chest. It was a feeling that had become more rare and precious as he had grown older. It was the old excitement of the chase.

Taking the telegram, Blake followed Geoffrey into the study. To say that it was expensively furnished and lavishly decorated was a ludicrous understatement. Blake was a collector; a collector of elegant furnishings, of fine wines, of classical art, of rare artifacts, and of priceless antiquities.

The paintings on his wall were not reproductions, they were originals. The volumes that lined his bookshelves were not off-the-rack but first editions. He collected everything and anything that he set his mind to.

As his personal fortune had burgeoned, his tastes had grown more exotic and eclectic. The furnishings were authentic Chippendale. The rich carpet had been imported from China. Priceless jade figurines and Ming pottery dotted the veined marble mantle over the fireplace. Upon a corner table, next to a potted rhododendron, rested a limestone statuette of an Egyptian cat goddess, a souvenir from an excavated tomb.

Settling onto a cushioned sofa, Blake unfolded the transatlantic telegram he had been waiting for. A frown cut his brow just as Geoffrey approached with his claret.

"Something wrong, sir?"

Blake crumpled the telegram. "This is intolerable!"

"Sir?"

"They've botched it again!"

"I assume you're referring to the Doolittle brothers, sir."

"Those dunderheads!"

"I see that you are referring to the Doolittles, sir."

With a scowl and an oath, Blake stood and flung the telegram into the licking flames of the fireplace. "Blast Sidney Pierce and his confounded luck. It follows him even to his grave."

"I take it the Doolittles were unable to liberate the parchment from Mr. Hamilton."

"Correct. And now the parchment seems to have passed to Pierce's heir, an American lad barely out of knee pants."

"That would be Arthur Pierce."

Blake glared at his imperturbable butler. "Obviously you've already looked into it."

"As you requested before you left for the Kimberley mine," Geoffrey reminded him. "Pierce's will names three beneficiaries. The British Museum, an American niece, and her brother, Arthur Pierce. Although there's no direct mention of the parchment, there is a provision for a trust to be set up for the nephew. According to our sources at the Bank of England, Max Hamilton set up an account just before he left for the States."

Blake scowled again. "Hamilton. Damn, but he's been as much a pebble in my shoe as Pierce ever was. Sneaky old scoundrel. Remember that shady business in Cairo a few years back?"

"Vividly, sir."

Blake turned to stare into the licking flames of the hearth. "It must have something to do with the parchment."

"What, sir?"

"The trust for the nephew."

"Oh, undoubtedly, sir."

The sound of light, pattering footsteps interrupted their exchange. A tousled blonde head poked around the corner to peer at them through wide azure eyes. "Father! You're home!"

Blake turned, his dour expression at once softening to one of paternal pride as his six-year-old son, Duncan, bounded into the room. Clad in his nightshirt and stockings and toting a wooden sword, his pale brows drew down to a threatening glower as he struck a warrior's pose. "Lay down your arms! You are surrounded!"

This child, borne by his forgettable second wife, a theater actress he'd married on a whim after the death of his first spouse, was Emory Blake's most prized objet d'art of all. That after twelve years of marriage to a titled but barren widow, he had coupled with a lowbrow nymphet to sire such a perfect specimen of boyhood never failed to amaze him.

That face, cherubic in both innocence and beauty, almost brought tears to eyes that had not so much as misted over upon hearing that the boy's mother had perished in childbirth.

He crossed the room to kneel by his son's side. "Ah, I see you have become quite formidable with your sword, my little knight. Perhaps you're ready for something more substantial."

Duncan's face lit with childish delight. "Really, Father? Might I have a new one? A real one?"

Blake chuckled. "Yes, I think so."

"Might I have one from your collection at our 'shire house? The one with the ruby in the scabbard? I like that one best! It's such a fine sword!"

"It is a fine sword, but you deserve one even finer."

"I don't think there is one finer than that one, Father!"

"Oh, but there is, Duncan. There's one finer than any other on earth."

"But which sword is that?"

Emory raised an eyebrow. "Which sword do you think?"

Duncan's eyes grew wide. "You can't mean Excalibur?"

"Can't I?"

Duncan bounced excitedly on stockinged heels. "Oh, Father! They say it's magic!"

"Yes, it is. Very powerful magic. And someday soon that magic shall be yours."

"When? When?"

Emory patted Duncan's head and stood. "Soon, my little knight, soon."

"Oh, Master Duncan! There you are. You gave me a frightful bad start, you did."

Duncan's new nursemaid appeared in the open archway. A sumptuous, titian-haired lass of perhaps eighteen years, she appeared shocked at discovering the master of the house.

"Oh, blimey, sir! You're home!" Hastily covering for her verbal slip, she curtsied and dropped her eyes. "I'm sorry, sir. I only turned me back for a minute and he was gone."

Blake took in the ripe, buxom figure that strained beneath the bodice of the nursemaid's dark uniform. "Don't worry, my dear. He must have seen my cab through his chamber window."

"Yes, sir, I believe so, sir. Might we be excused now? It's past time for his bed."

"I think that might be best."

"Oh, Father, no! Must I?"

"Yes, Duncan. We'll talk in the morning. Now, off with you."

With a heavy sigh, the boy turned away, dragging his toy sword behind him. "Good night, Father."

"Good night, Duncan. Sleep well." Blake took pleasant note of the nursemaid's swishing derriere as she led Duncan from the room. After their footsteps receded, he turned to Geoffrey. "Does she have a name?"

"Lucille Merriweather, sir."

"Lucille." Blake nodded his approval. "A fine choice, Geoffrey. I assume she also has some affinity for children?"

"That too, sir."

"Very good." Blake turned his mind to more pressing matters. "The telegram indicated that Arthur Pierce is now on his way to Southampton by steamship."

"Did they mention the name of the liner, sir?"

"The *Salacia*."

"He should pose no real problem for us once he lands, sir."

"You're right, Geoffrey, but I think that you should handle this personally. I want it accomplished with the utmost discretion. I cannot afford any more incompetence."

"Certainly, sir." Geoffrey began to glide from the room.

"And Geoffrey?"

"Yes, sir?"

"When this is all over, remind me to do something about the Doolittle brothers. This matter was to be short and simple. They've disappointed me one too many times."

"Yes, sir. Very good, sir."

* * *

Arthur awoke to the gentle sensation of floating. Squinting in the dim light, he had to think for a moment to recall where he was. A boat. A very big boat. And sometime during the night, they must have left the Delaware River behind. The subtle rocking motion he now detected came from the pitching North Atlantic.

Enough daylight filtered through a porthole to assure him that it was indeed morning, but its gray, gloomy cast hinted that the weather had taken a turn for the worse.

When he sat up, he barely missed grazing his head on the ceiling of the cabin. Top bunk, he reminded himself. He was here by Delafield's unilateral decree. And judging by the soft snores that drifted up from the lower berth, her royal highness was still asleep. He took the short ladder down to the floor, then crossed to the porthole to peer outside.

Fog.

He drew back, undeniably disappointed. The child in him yearned to throw on some trousers and dash topside for a better view; the adult in him, however, would settle for waiting until after breakfast.

Wondering whether he should wake Delafield, he turned to observe her sleeping figure in the lower bunk. A devilish smile curved his lips. Last night she had emerged from the lavatory swaddled from neck to toe in a flannel dressing gown. Now, he knew she would be furious to know that, as she lay on her side, one leg happened to be poking out from beneath the blankets, scandalously exposing her from knee to toes.

Knee, calf, ankle, Arthur thought wickedly, his gaze traveling down the exposed limb. Then his smile began to fade as his eyes moved back up at a more leisurely pace. Actually, it was a very nice knee. An exceptionally nice leg. Perhaps even nicer than Julia Tierney's, and definitely nicer than any of the varied and shapely feminine limbs he'd had occasion to study while working at DeLancey's House of Burlesque.

*I'll be damned, but Delafield has magnificent legs.*The thought floated unbidden into his mind. It hovered for just a moment too long before it popped and evaporated.

Arthur shook himself back to his senses, crossed to the lavatory, pulled the lamp chain, and slammed the door. He plugged the sink basin, turned the cold tap, and stared at the mirror.

Delafield with legs. A startling thought in itself, but not nearly so mind-boggling as the one that followed. If Delafield had legs, she obviously came equipped with every other female part of intrinsic male interest. Breasts, hips, thighs . . .

*Stop*!

With a muttered oath, Arthur slammed off the tap just before the basin would have overflowed.

Delafield was Delafield, no more, no less. She was the human equivalent of an iceberg. An iceberg had no legs, no breasts, no hips, no thighs. And certainly no . . .

Arthur splashed his face with cold water. What the hell was the matter with him?

Perhaps he was coming down with something. He frowned at the mirror. By golly, now that he thought about it, he did feel a little headache. He tested his forehead. No sign of fever, but that didn't mean anything. He'd planned to try out the gym this afternoon, but perhaps the best thing to do was to take it easy.

Yes. Take it easy, he thought, reaching for his shaving kit. And stop thinking about Delafield's legs.

A most wise prescription.

The purpose of the overhead skylight in the dining saloon was to emit natural illumination and give passengers a sense of the great outdoors; all of this while they were actually trapped in a gigantic floating box of steel. These illusions were poorly executed as far as Arthur was concerned. The daylight that filtered through the glass was nothing but a gloomy, gray wash, and, as for a sense of the great outdoors, Arthur felt as if he was cooped up in a dry aquarium.

He stared miserably at his poached eggs on toast. It seemed that ever since he had taken notice of Delafield's leg, his entire morning had gone downhill. His headache had grown worse, and now he was beginning to lose his appetite.

"Something wrong?" Chelsea asked as she finished the last of her scrambled eggs and asparagus.

In his present state of malaise, Arthur couldn't help noticing that, in addition to her main course, she had put away two biscuits slathered in marmalade, a bowl of pineapple and mandarin slices, and a side dish of fried potatoes. Quite a hefty appetite for someone with such dainty ankles.

He pushed his plate away. "I think I need some air."

"But aren't you going to finish your breakfast?"

Arthur didn't look at her as he rose from the table. If he looked at her, he'd think about her legs, and he didn't want to think about her legs right now. He didn't want to think about them ever.

"Why?" he asked. "Do you want to finish what's left?"

"Well, if you aren't going to eat that biscuit, there's no use letting it go to waste."

Now, he did look at her and cursed himself for noticing that she peered up at him through dark-lashed, violet eyes. What had he likened their color to in the past? Amethyst quartz. Very unusual. And very attractive, too. Even from behind misleading glass lenses.

"Well?" she asked expectantly. Innocently. As if she weren't perfectly well aware that she had been hiding magnificent legs beneath those conservative wool worsted skirts for the past year.

"You can have it," he said curtly.

"If you're going out on the weather deck, you'd better be sure to wear your . . ." Her last words were lost as Arthur crossed the spacious dining saloon. He needed air. Fresh air. And he needed it now.

He wasted no time finding his way topside. The first thing that struck him was the cold. If he'd wanted air, he'd come to the right place. The calming sea breeze he had expected felt more like the punishing slap of a sharp northern wind, and its effect, even through his suit coat, was surprisingly chilling.

As it was still the breakfast hour, few passengers strolled the deck. Arthur couldn't resist moving straight to the iron railing to take in his first impression of the great North Atlantic from aboard ship.

It was big.

He could make out not even the merest hint of land in the vast fog-wisped distance. Nothing but water; water that varied from a dank, grayish green where white foam lapped up against the steamship's hull to a deep, rich blue on the far-off horizons.

It was a sight so awe-inspiring that it diverted his attention from his nagging headache for a few moments. Too soon, though, he felt the pounding return with a renewed vengeance. He rested his elbows on the rail and bent his aching neck in an effort to ease the pain, but it didn't help. To make matters worse, he thought his stomach was angling to join the party.

"Deck blanket, sir?"

Arthur looked up to see a uniformed deck steward with a bundle of gray blankets beneath one arm. "No, thank you."

As the steward continued on his way, a brisk wind whipped across the deck, lifting Arthur's hair and biting through the meager protection of his spring suit coat. It was getting damn cold out here.

Finding an empty deck chair, he sat and rested his head against its back. He closed his eyes, feeling worse. The rocking motion of the ship seemed more pronounced, and his stomach wasn't taking this new development well at all.

Determined to stick it out, he folded his arms and gritted his teeth. He remembered Delafield's cryptic words from the previous afternoon. "*You've never sailed the North Atlantic before, have you, Mr. Pierce*?" She might have had the common decency to mention then that, with the wind, the temperature above deck sometimes fell as low as fifty degrees below zero, but no. She had chosen instead to give him that smug little Delafield smile. Oh, she was an iceberg, all right. An iceberg with legs.

Damn.

He hadn't meant to think that. Why did his mind keep circling back to her legs? Was God punishing him for something?

He might have actually dozed off for a few blissful, painfree minutes. When he began to come around again, it was to the sound of his name on *her* tongue. He knew then that God was definitely punishing him for something.

"Arthur? Is that you? Of course it's you. Are you mad? You'll freeze to death out here like this."

He cracked one eye open. Swaddled in her toasty winter coat and knitted scarf, she perched on the edge of the neighboring steamer chair, looking as at home and comfortable as a wool-wrapped penguin.

"Pneumonia," he said hoarsely. "It'll be on your head."

"Don't be absurd. Come down below. You look positively awful."

"Flattery will get you nowhere." He tried to offer a weak smile, but failed even at that. While he had dozed, his stomach had not been idle.

She frowned and leaned closer. "Egad, you do look frightful. Are you feeling all right?"

The sea air was as brisk and snapping as ever. Arthur's fingers were frozen stiff, but he was breaking into a cold sweat. "I think I'm coming down with something."

"You're seasick."

"Seasick?" Indignant, he sat up too fast. The pain in his head bloomed savage and bright, spinning the deck into a blinding menagerie of colors before fading back to a dull throb. "That's ridiculous! I don't get seasick."

"How do you know? You've never been at sea."

"I've been on plenty of boats before." He had to swallow down a sudden urge to retch.

"When?"

Arthur's stomach rose, then fell, rose, then fell, keeping perfect time with the rocking ship. He gritted his teeth. "I've taken the ferry countless times."

"Oh, yes. I remember Julia telling me you took her to Smith's Island Resort. Fifteen minutes each way."

Even through a swirling haze of misery, Arthur detected a certain condescension in her tone that he didn't care for at all. "And to New Jersey! I took her to Camden! Did she mention that?"

"I don't recall."

Arthur closed his eyes, fighting as his stomach prepared to rise in full revolt. "And I never once got seasick, goddamnit! I hope she mentioned *that*!"

"I think you'd better come back to the cabin. You can take the lower bunk, and I'll ring the steward for a chamber pot."

"No!" he yelled. "No chamber pot!"

"What would you suggest, then?"

"Ahhhhhh! Friggin' hell!"

Arthur had no further suggestions. He was too busy running for the rail.

# 8

*The lunch hour came and went.* Dinner passed. The sun set. Through it all, Arthur huddled in his bunk, silently and not so silently cursing the *Salacia* and everything wet, salty, and nautical.

Between fitful bouts of sleep and misery, Chelsea was in and out of their cabin, inquiring if he needed anything. His answer was always the same. No. What he needed was to be left alone to expire in peace. Now, though, as he opened his eyes to the glare of incandescent electric light, he realized it must be later than he thought. He heard something, the crackle of a page being turned, and knew he was not alone.

His head still ached, but his stomach had settled. It was certainly about time. He had consumed nothing but a few swallows of tap water since breakfast.

He turned over to see Delafield seated at the writing table, nibbling on a peppermint stick and reading a book. Once again bundled in her dressing gown and slippers, she appeared ready for bed. Except for her hair. She had braided it the night before, but tonight it hung loose and damp, brushed out to a blue-black shine to run as smooth as water down to the middle of her back.

Something like a memory flashed in his mind. *A raven-haired beauty swimming naked in a lake.* The image vanished as quickly as it came, but it left behind a lingering sense of sensuality that was unexpectedly arousing.

Chelsea looked up from her book. "Oh, you're awake. How are you feeling?"

It was Delafield, just Delafield, he reminded himself, trying to play down the fact that his body, ill and drained as it was, seemed to be reacting in quite a healthy manner to the naked-woman-in-the-lake image his delirious mind had created.

He grumbled and turned away, hoping this would cure his lower extremity problem. "All ye who enter here, abandon hope."

"I see we're still feeling a bit sorry for ourselves."

"Maybe we could trade places for a few hours. Then we'd find out who's feeling sorry for whom, wouldn't we?"

"Hmmm. Still touchy, too, I see."

He didn't have the physical or mental strength to retort. He heard her rise from the writing table and move to the lavatory. Good. Maybe she'd braid her hair.

A moment later, she emerged, smelling like a heaven-sent combination of flowers and peppermint. She perched on the edge of his berth. "Here."

Arthur turned over to see that she hadn't done a thing to her hair. It was still parted in the middle, with wispy soft tendrils hanging loose over each shoulder. She offered a small glass of fizzing clear liquid and a plate of crackers.

"What's that?" he asked.

"Cold champagne and rye crackers. I brought them from the dining saloon. Try some."

He looked up into dark-lashed violet eyes only to find himself thinking about her legs again. "I can't."

"You must. You haven't eaten anything since breakfast."

He meant to look back down at the plate, but, instead, his

gaze followed the fluid line of sable tendrils to stop dead on her chest. The breasts she hid there might be small by some men's preferences, but Arthur was suddenly certain they must be utterly perfect. Delightful and delectable. Just like her legs. Hidden treasures that no one would ever suspect.

"No, I shouldn't," he said, not altogether sure he spoke only of the crackers and champagne.

"Arthur, just try them. I promise they'll be better than you think."

"I can't!"

"You're acting like a child."

That did it. Her tone. That voice. Delafield.

All erotic imagery fled. Sanity returned. He looked straight into the electric glare of those schoolmarmish spectacles. "I am not acting like a child. I am acting sick. I can't eat, I can't sleep, and I feel like hell."

"Well, you're not the only person to ever get seasick. It happens to a lot of people their first time out."

"Oh, well, that makes me feel better. Why didn't you tell me that when I was hugging the rail?"

"It's unavoidable," she continued as if he hadn't spoken. "A combination of the immutable laws of wave-motion physics and human physiology. Why, it's a wonder our land-dwelling bodies don't rebel much worse than they do. Just think of it. An ocean wave slides beneath the ship's keel, causing the great vessel to bob and pitch, fore and aft, fore and aft, fore and aft."

Arthur started to grow queasy as she demonstrated this movement with the champagne glass.

"Then, before you know it, another comes in from the side, causing the ship to roll to and fro, to and fro, to and fro."

He stilled the waving champagne glass. "Delafield, please."

"Oh, sorry. What I mean is, with all that constant motion stirring up one's insides for days, it's a wonder we humans ever managed to cross the great oceans in the first place."

"Uh huh. And did this ever happen to you?"

"What?"

"Did you ever get seasick?"

"Yes, but only once. I seem to be blessed with a hearty constitution. Here." She offered him a cracker from the plate.

Arthur took it and examined it. "'To be, or not to be, that is the question: Whether 'tis nobler in the mind to suffer the slings and arrows of outrageous fortune, or to take arms against a sea of troubles and by opposing . . .'" He sighed miserably and took a bite. "'End them.'"

"Oh dear. First Milton, now Shakespeare. And *Hamlet*, at that. You are feeling low, aren't you?"

"Low isn't the word."

"Be sure to wash it down with some champagne."

"A sure cure?" he inquired doubtfully, taking the glass.

"Well, there are other methods."

"Such as?"

"The cook told me to give you water and vinegar. The steward suggested mustard pickles, and one of the gentleman at dinner insisted you should drink at least a pint of seawater before turning in for the night."

"I think I prefer crackers and cold champagne."

"I thought you would."

"Well, bottoms up." He took a sip, then waited to see if this modest repast would threaten to make a return appearance. His stomach, however, remained calm. After a few moments, he gave her a grudging smile. "Thanks, Miss Delafield."

If he wasn't mistaken, she almost smiled back.

Chelsea hesitated outside the door to their stateroom. Having just come from breakfast, she was laden with a library book under one arm, a cribbage board beneath the other, and a covered platter for Arthur. With no hands to spare, she kicked the door with her heel and waited.

She heard him call out from within. "Who's there?"

"Me."

"Me whooooo?"

Chelsea grimaced. His health had obviously improved since yesterday. That infernal sense of humor was back.

A second later, he appeared in the open portal, wiping remnants of shaving soap from his chin with a towel. "What have you got there, Miss Chelsea?"

"Your breakfast."

He stepped aside, allowing her entrance. His hair was wet, combed back from his forehead, and he smelled of spice and soap. Chelsea tried not to notice that his shirt was unbuttoned, revealing a heart-stopping glimpse of bare chest.

"I thought you might like to have a go at some toast and coffee." She first set the platter down on the writing table, then the book and the cribbage board, being careful to keep her eyes averted. She hoped he was buttoning his shirt.

"That was really nice of you."

"Oh, it was nothing." She turned to see that he hadn't buttoned his shirt, so she looked at the ceiling instead. "I gather you're feeling better."

"I still have a headache, but my stomach has settled down."

"It's raining, but the sea is much calmer today," she said.

"Expecting the sky to fall?"

"Hmmmm?"

"What are you looking at?"

"The ceiling."

"Have we sprung a leak?"

"No. It's your shirt."

"Oh, sorry. Sometimes I forget there's a woman in the room."

"Quite all right." When she sensed that he was decent, she found his eyes fixed on her and his lips crooked into a smile that fired her cheekbones scarlet.

"And then again," he added rakishly, "sometimes I find it impossible to forget there's a woman in the room."

Chelsea swallowed hard. Had she just imagined that look in his eye, that blatantly flirtatious tone?

Before she knew what was happening, he took her right hand. A tingling warmth seemed to emanate and spread from where his fingers touched her flesh. "Thank you for thinking of me, Miss Chelsea."

He kissed her hand, then released her. Then, as if nothing were out of the ordinary, he sat down to his Spartan breakfast. Chelsea's heart thumped. Her arm hung stiff in midair. She marveled that his lips had felt so . . . so . . .

"Mmmmmmm." He lifted the lid of the platter. "Toast and strawberry jam. My favorite."

Chelsea stared at his back, at his hair, thick and soft, brushing over his collar, at the broad male shoulders moving beneath the crisp blue-striped linen of his shirt.

"Even the coffee is still hot. This is wonderful."

Chelsea detected nothing in his manner to indicate that she had *not* just imagined the suggestive nature of his previous words and actions. He was playing with her again, damn him. Feeling foolish, she snatched her hand back to her side. "It was really nothing."

Scurrying to the dresser, she snatched the book she'd begun the night before, then perched stiffly on the lower bunk to stare at meaningless lines of print as Arthur finished his breakfast. Something about history. Something about Egypt.

"Another book?"

Chelsea's head popped up too quickly. "What?"

"I see you borrowed another book." Arthur nodded toward the volume that sat next to his breakfast platter.

"I thought you might like something to read during your convalescence."

"Convalescence?" He sounded as if his male pride had been stung. "You make it sound like I'm on my last legs."

Quite involuntarily, Chelsea glanced at his legs. Even through his trousers, they appeared quite solid and strong. She wondered what his legs might look like out of his trousers.

"*Le Morte d'Arthur*," he said, examining the flyleaf. "I never much cared for the title of Malory's work, but the stories are wonderful. Do you remember how Arthur gained Excalibur?"

Chelsea struggled to quash thoughts of Arthur Pierce sans trousers. "Merlin took him to meet the Lady of the Lake."

"Yeah, that's the one," Arthur said, paging through the book. "In one version, it was said that the lake itself was just an illusion for the benefit of mortal eyes, that beneath the illusion, the lady and her fairy sisters lived in an ivory castle."

"Oh, yes, I remember." Chelsea was relieved to find something innocent to concentrate on. "The imagery is quite rich and beautiful. The forest, the lake, a jeweled sword offered from the water."

"I agree." Arthur stopped paging through the book. His arresting blue gaze grew speculative as it settled on her. "Quite beautiful."

Chelsea was suddenly certain that he could read her mind, that he knew exactly what lewd and licentious thoughts had occupied her for the past few minutes. She retreated to her book again. She had read the same paragraph three times, still unable to make one jot or tittle of sense out of it when he spoke.

"And what's this?" He had set the book aside and was examining the cribbage board.

"It's a cribbage set."

Arthur lifted the pegged lid to look inside. "I've never played the game."

"You've never played cribbage?"

"No." Arthur removed a set of playing cards from their box. "Are you willing to teach a beginner?"

Chelsea glanced at the port window, its glass streaked and running rivulets of rain. She wasn't sure what had possessed her to borrow the cribbage set from the ladies lounge except that she had no urge to wander the public rooms today.

Yesterday, in an effort to leave Arthur alone in his misery, she had run into Bernice Sherman time and again in the library, in the ladies lounge, and in the dining saloon. Bernice Sherman and her steady stream of questions regarding Chelsea's relationship with Arthur. How had they met? How long an engagement had they had? Were they planning on living in England or America? Did they want children?

Children? Egad.

Chelsea had soon wearied of spinning tales to feed Bernice's never ending curiosity. Soon, she might even begin to start believing her own flapdoodle. How else to explain her recent distraction with Arthur as a man, as a possible lover, rather than the constant nuisance she had always considered him to be in the past?

When she looked back at him, he seemed to be observing her with his usual amusement. Once again, she had the disturbing sense that he could read her mind. "Certainly I'll teach you if that's what you want."

"Good." He cleared the writing table of his breakfast tray, setting it outside their cabin for the steward, then he grabbed an extra chair from one corner of the room. "Have a seat."

Chelsea sat. She noticed that he was rolling up his sleeves as if preparing to pluck a chicken

"Before we start, Miss Delafield, I have to warn you, I'm pretty good at card games. Hope you're not a sore loser."

"If I were you, Mr. Pierce, I wouldn't be so quick to count my chickens."

He chuckled as he shuffled the cards with brisk efficiency.

"You do that quite well," Chelsea commented.

"You ain't seen nothin' yet."

Setting the deck on the table, he squared it neatly, then drew the top card, a seven of clubs. With a sly wink, he replaced it facedown on top, then, in a trice, cut the deck three times and squared it. When he drew from the top again, he showed the seven of clubs.

Snatching up the deck once more, he shuffled, then cut by

executing a smooth, one-handed shift. As a child, Chelsea had seen a magician do this, and she had been amazed. Today, she was no less amazed by the manual dexterity necessary to complete this maneuver without a hint of hesitation.

"How many?" he asked.

"Six," she said, still somewhat awed. "Where did you learn to do that?"

"My sister." He flipped them each six cards.

"I didn't know you had a sister," she said, then was quick to add, "I mean, I didn't see her at commencement."

"She lives in Chicago now."

"Is she a thief, too?" This question tumbled out too late for Chelsea to censor herself. Arthur, however, laughed, clearly unoffended by the blunt nature of her inquiry.

"Well, she was a bit of a cardsharp, but she gave it all up for love."

"For love?"

"She married a policeman, a Pinkerton detective. Maybe you've noticed their office on Third Street?"

"Oh, yes," Chelsea said, brightening. She remembered their sign. The picture of an eye and the slogan, We Never Sleep. She had passed it everyday on her way to her typewriting job.

"My brother-in-law worked out of that office for a few years, but they moved back to Chicago just before I started my first year at Penn."

"Is that all the family you have?"

"Yes, unless you count their children. As of last month, I now have two nieces and two nephews."

"I have three nieces and three nephews," Chelsea offered.

"A prolific older sister?" Arthur asked with a grin.

"Actually, I have two prolific older sisters, but I can't say that either of them ever fleeced unsuspecting victims at cards."

At this, Arthur laughed again, a clear, honest, uplifting sound that brightened their dreary cabin. Chelsea was surprised to feel herself beginning to relax in his presence.

"Enough chitchat, Auntie Chelsea," he said, slapping the remainder of the deck down next to the cribbage board. "Let's play cards."

The lunch hour came and went. Dinner passed. The sun set. Through it all, they ordered light meals from their cabin as Chelsea introduced every two-handed card game she could think of in an attempt to stump Arthur. First, cribbage, at which, after an initial practice round, he went on to outscore her at every game. Then, beggar my neighbor, at which he ended up with all the cards on his very first try.

Over lunch, Chelsea had proposed a game of all-fours. "High-low-jack!" he had exclaimed, apparently recognizing it by a different name after she'd explained the rules. He had then proceeded to knock the spots off of her.

Ecarte. Vingt-et-un. Euchre. Now, commerce.

Chelsea was rapidly discovering that this game was much too close to the American game of poker for her to have a prayer at winning even one hand, and so, upon seeing her poor draw, she threw in her cards with a petulant scowl. "Enough!"

Arthur seemed surprised. "What's the matter? Are you giving up?"

"Oh, honestly, Arthur, I don't know how you do it."

"Do what?" he asked innocently.

"Win at everything."

He started gathering up the cards. "Well, I'm not cheating if that's what you're getting at."

That was exactly what she was getting at. She had watched him like an eagle each time he'd dealt but couldn't figure out how he was pulling it off. Now, she folded her arms and eyed him doubtfully from across the table. "Oh, really?"

"Yes. If I wanted to cheat, I could, but I don't need to. It's as simple as that."

"How modest of you to say so."

"Modesty has nothing to do with it. The secret to winning at cards is either to keep track of what's been played or to calculate the odds of obtaining certain combinations."

"And that's what you do," Chelsea said sarcastically.

"That's what I do."

"Simple," she said, tapping her foot in annoyance.

"Simple."

She didn't reply, but her foot kept tapping of its own accord, an outlet for her growing vexation. He lifted a quizzical eyebrow. "You still think I was cheating, don't you?"

"Did I say any such thing?"

"No, but you were thinking it."

"You couldn't possibly have any idea what I was thinking."

"Of course I do, Chelsea. I can read you like a book."

She remembered the unsettling premonition she'd had earlier, that he *could* read her mind and every wicked thought that crossed it. "Poppycock," she muttered, not nearly so sure as she sounded.

"I can prove it."

"Then, do so," she challenged, all spit and bravado.

He held out the playing deck. "Pick a card, take a look at it, and remember it."

"Don't be silly. Parlor tricks prove nothing."

"Come on, I'll close my eyes so there's no way I can see what you pick." He did as promised and even turned his head.

"Oh, this is a childish waste of time."

"Are you afraid that I can read your mind?"

"Of course not."

"Perhaps you're afraid of what evil thoughts I'll find lurking there."

Chelsea's spine straightened. "Rubbish."

"Then pick a card."

"Fine, I will." Chelsea was now game for the challenge. He was always so bloody sure of himself, wasn't he?

She kept a sharp eye on him to make sure he didn't peek as she inched one card from the center of the deck, lifted its corner, and glanced at it before nudging it back into place. Queen of hearts. She folded her arms again triumphantly. "Done."

Arthur turned back to her, squaring the deck with his right hand and setting it facedown on the writing table between them. He tapped it with his forefinger a few times, then winked and smiled. "You can't rush these things. It'll take a few minutes for the right card to rise to thc top."

Chelsea wrinkled her nose. "What do you take me for, an imbecile?"

He feigned surprise. "You don't believe in magic?"

"Sleight of hand, perhaps, nothing more."

"Miss Chelsea, how are you ever going to help me find a magic sword if you don't believe in magic?"

She was determined not to allow him to distract her with verbal patter. "Just finish your little trick."

"Okay." He leaned forward to look deep into her eyes. "It's time to find out what you're thinking." After a long moment of deep study, he frowned. "You know, this is very strange. Are you sure you're thinking of the card?"

"Yes, of course." But she had grown uncomfortable beneath such intense scrutiny. Those eyes were really much too blue.

"Hmmm, that's not what I'm getting."

"Could you please just get on with it?"

"No, I mean it," he insisted, his expression serious. "This doesn't make sense. It's almost as if . . ." His lips curved in a slow, playful smile. "Why, Chelsea Delafield, I'm shocked."

She shifted in her seat. "I beg your pardon?"

His smile widened into a grin that flipped Chelsea's stomach right over. She became acutely aware of how close he was, and all thoughts of the queen of hearts fled. She thought instead of how he had almost caught her looking at his legs earlier and felt a hot, guilty blush creep up the back of her neck.

"Chelsea, Chelsea, Chelsea, you lusty wench. I never would have suspected."

"Oh, do stop all this nonsense, and guess a blasted card!"

"You know what I see on your mind? Miles Middleton in nothing but his union suit."

"Oh!" Chelsea shot up so fast, she almost knocked the chair back off its legs. Arthur jumped up at the same instant, catching her wrist before she could pummel him. She tried to wrest away. "You are abominable!"

"Methinks the lady doth protest too much."

"Don't be absurd! I was thinking no such thing!"

"On the contrary. I must have come real close to hitting the mark or you wouldn't be so angry about it, would you?"

Real close was right. But it wasn't Miles Middleton she'd been envisioning in his under flannels, it was . . .

Infuriated, Chelsea tried again to twist free. "I regret ever allowing you to accompany me on this trip!" she shouted. "I don't like you at all, Arthur Pierce! I've never liked you!"

At her heated declaration, his eyes narrowed and his grip tightened. "I know you've never liked me, but the question is, why? Why exactly is it that you've never liked me?"

Flustered, she fell back on the first reply that came to mind. "It was Julia!"

"Julia didn't have anything to do with it," he shot back, calling her bluff. "You took a disliking to me the minute I walked into your precious classroom, and I didn't even know Julia then. What is it about me that bothers you so much, Chelsea? Let's get at the truth once and for all."

"All right!" She ceased her struggles and lowered her voice, ready to lay her cards out on the table. He'd asked for it, hadn't he? "It's that childish sense of humor of yours."

"My sense of humor?" His brows rose in honest disbelief. "You don't like it?"

"I hate it!"

He leaned in close. "Okay. So, my natural charm eludes you. I'll give you that. Is there more?"

"Oh, there's more. Much, much more," she assured him.

Now that he'd set the kettle to the flame, there would be no stopping her. "To start with, you're too bloody smart for your own good!"

There. She'd said it.

They stared at each other, eye to eye, toe to toe, for a long time before he released her and stepped back. "You're jealous of my brain? That's it?"

Frustrated, Chelsea clenched her fists. No, that wasn't it. She had never been the sort to waste time and energy on useless emotions like petty jealousy. No, that wasn't it at all.

"You take it for granted," she said, putting tumbling thoughts into words. "Some of us had to work hard for our grades. You're gifted, Arthur Pierce, and you don't even seem capable of appreciating it."

He folded his arms. His expression was neutral, but Chelsea sensed that she might have finally succeeded in stirring up some honest-to-goodness anger beneath that smooth, carefree veneer. "Well, I appreciate the backhanded compliment, Miss Delafield, but just what would you have me do to correct this shortcoming?"

Chelsea cut the air with one hand. "Oh, I don't bloody know! Go out in the world and do something! Make something of yourself!"

He nodded slowly, seeming to assess her. "Fine, but turnabout is fair play. You know what bothers me most about you?"

She lifted her chin bravely. Let him take his best shot. "What?"

"Your teeth."

Had she heard correctly? Why, she had always considered her teeth to be one of her best features. Not only were they straight and white, she actually had them all, every last one of them. Not just every Harriet or Jane on the street could say that. "My teeth?" she echoed indignantly.

"That's right. Your teeth. I've never seen them."

"What are you talking about?"

"You don't smile, Miss Delafield, and when you speak, your lips barely move."

Chelsea was insulted. Her lips? Barely moved? What sort of twaddle was all this? "That's utter nonsense! Of course my lips move!"

"Ah ha!" Arthur pointed. "See there? You just did it! Your lips barely moved! I couldn't see your teeth."

"Preposterous," she denied heatedly, yet at the very same instant sensing that he was right. Her lips *had* barely moved. She frowned to herself. Why, she had never thought about it before. Had her elocution teachers ever mentioned such a thing?

"Take a look in the mirror sometime, Chelsea. You'd be damned pretty if you smiled once in a while." He brushed by her roughly and, headed for the closet, covering the length of their stateroom in three angry strides.

She was stunned. It was as if he'd knocked the wind out of her. Pretty? No, *damned* pretty, he'd said. Damned pretty.

Arthur snagged one of his coats from the closet and whirled on her, pointing. "And you know what else? You snore!"

Pretty. Damned pretty. The words swirled around in her head. She watched dumbly as he shrugged on his coat and stormed to the door. "Where are you going?" she asked.

"I'm going for a walk on deck."

"But it's raining."

"I don't care!" he bellowed.

The stateroom door slammed behind him. Unable to move, Chelsea stared at it for a long time before remembering the deck of cards that still rested undisturbed on the table. She reached down and cautiously turned over the top card.

It was the queen of hearts.

# 9

*It wasn't exactly raining.* It was drizzling. A silky gray fog shrouded the *Salacia*, casting ghostly halos about the outside deck lamps and blotting out most of the star-studded night sky. Moisture dripped steady, fat drops from the riggings overhead as the steamship crawled along at well below its optimal pace of seventeen knots.

Arthur had taken two brisk walks around the open promenade. With his shoulders hunched, his hands shoved deep into his coat pockets, and blowing out angry little puffs of air, he encountered no one but two deck stewards as they gathered up the few steamer chairs still out. He had caught a few looks from them, too, as he'd stalked past on his solitary trek. Knowing looks. Have a row with the wife? looks. You poor old dog, you looks.

Well, the hell with that.

Now, he leaned over the cold iron railing, shivering in his flimsy suit coat, staring down into a void of fog and swirling black seawater.

"*You're too bloody smart for your own good.*"

"Ha!" he scoffed to no one in particular. "Too smart!"

Those words, Chelsea's words, inevitably brought to mind another woman's words, those of his sister, Gwin, who had not only raised him since the age of eleven but had unselfishly spent the money his Uncle Sidney had given them on Arthur's private schooling. "*You're special, Arthur. Someday you'll do us proud.*"

Special. Gifted.

Well, perhaps they were both right, but he hadn't asked for such a special gift. He had put off the wanderlust in his soul long enough to complete his formal education, a dream that had always been more his sister's than his own, and now he was free to do as he pleased. If he wanted to take his abilities for granted, he'd damn well take them for granted. It was his brain, not Chelsea's.

Chelsea.

Damn it. She had gotten to him tonight. And he, apparently, had the same effect on her. He had never seen her lose her composure before. Over the past year, he'd annoyed her, teased her, prodded her, and nudged her, never failing to elicit a gratifying flush or quelling glare for his efforts, but she had never lost that cool British poise. Not until tonight. He had finally nudged her right over the edge, and he couldn't say that he was sorry. Quite the contrary. There was a part of him that had set out from the very beginning to do just that.

"She's no iceberg," Arthur muttered aloud, raising his head to stare out into the clammy mist.

"I'm afraid that the blissful sea of matrimony has its share of those."

Arthur was so preoccupied, he had not heard Fred Sherman approaching from behind. He turned to see the other young man wrapped in an expensive overcoat and observing him from beneath the brim of a soggy brown bowler.

"Its share of what?" Arthur asked.

"Icebergs. Death defying obstacles." Fred moved to lean against the rail. "Snags, if you will."

"Snags?"

Fred gave him a wise married-man-to-married-man look. "Oh, come now. You're not going to tell me you and the wife didn't have a bit of a spat, are you?"

"What makes you think that?"

Fred pulled a silver case from his coat pocket and extracted a cheroot. "Well, for one thing, you're standing out in the rain talking to yourself."

Arthur scowled at this bit of irrefutable logic, and Fred chuckled as he struck a match, then cupped his hand to light his smoke. "I also couldn't help overhearing your stateroom door slam a few minutes ago. Anything I can do to help?"

Arthur turned up his coat collar against the cold and plunged his freezing hands back into his pockets. He thought of Chelsea, of her warm winter coats, of her goddamned beautiful legs, and scowled again. "No, we're fine. I'll handle it."

"Handle it? Oh, my good man, that's the last thing you want to do."

"What do you mean by that?"

Fred pointed authoritatively with his cigar. "Let her think she's handling you. The first thing you must do is apologize. In fact, the more obsequious, nose-to-the-ground dirt-eating you do the better. See if you can't find some fresh flowers or candy, too. They really go in for that."

Despite the fact that his marriage to Chelsea was nothing more than a convenient charade, Arthur felt a swell of righteous indignation. She had started it. She'd accused him of cheating. "Apologize? I didn't do anything wrong."

"Doesn't matter."

"But what if she's the one in the wrong?"

"Doesn't matter," Fred said again as he turned to contemplate the hazy North Atlantic.

"What makes you such an expert? You've only been married a week."

"True, my good man, but I've learned a lifetime's worth

of hard lessons in that week. Bernice and I had one devil of a spat on our wedding night. She locked herself in the bathing room and wouldn't come out. She wouldn't even speak to me for two days much less . . . well, you know."

Arthur knew. Poor Fred had been left high and dry on his wedding night. *You poor old dog, you,* he thought, then turned back to the darkened seascape where another ship's running lights appeared in the far-off distance.

"So, what did you two fight about?" he asked.

"Well, I found out—" Fred cut off, then cleared his throat self-consciously. "I found out Bernice wasn't what she seemed."

The other ship's running lights winked out then appeared again as it passed through a distant pocket of woolly fog, headed west. Perhaps a sister passenger steamer bound for New York City.

Arthur gave Fred a curious side look. It was obvious the man wanted to get something off his chest. "Wasn't what she seemed?"

"No." Fred glanced over his shoulder to make sure they were still alone, then leaned closer. "It turned out she wears one of those gadgets. You know, those what-do-you-call-thems."

Arthur looked at him blankly.

Seeing that his companion wasn't following, Fred cupped his hands in front of his chest in the time-honored male sign for bounteous female breasts.

Arthur caught on fast. "Bust improvers?"

"Shhhh!" Fred threw another furtive glance over his shoulder before continuing in a low voice. "She'd kill me if she knew I was telling you this, but, well, I just can't keep it to myself any longer. It was such a blasted disappointment, you know. A fellow has certain expectations and, poof, just like that, they're discarded and lying on the floor like a couple of upended turtles."

"What a blow."

"Yes, well, I just couldn't stop staring at them. At those

*things,* I mean. For a moment, I completely forgot that Bernice was even there. Shock can do that to a fellow, you know."

"Naturally," Arthur agreed.

Fred turned back to the ocean, puffing thoughtfully on his cheroot. Its tip bloomed bright orange then faded to dull red in the dark. "Well, before I knew it, Bernice had dissolved into tears and gone running down the hall to shut herself up in the bathing room."

"How did you get her to come out?"

"I didn't. Not that night, and that's my point."

"I don't understand."

"I failed to apologize. You see, I thought I was in the right. I mean, I love Bernice with or without her—" Fred stopped, shook his head, then took another stab at it. "What I mean is, I had a right to know ahead of time is all. I just wasn't properly prepared."

"A valid point," Arthur agreed. "You were right."

Fred didn't reply. Instead, he frowned up at the hazy night sky. A young Socrates pondering the incongruities of holy matrimony.

Arthur pressed him. "You *were* right, right?"

"Right."

"So?"

"So, that's it."

"What's it?" Arthur was losing patience.

Fred let out a doleful sigh as he flipped his cigar out to sea. He turned to Arthur and rested a mentor's hand on one shoulder. "Look, you've got to apologize whether you're right or not. In fact, you've got to apologize especially when you're right. The sooner the better, and don't forget the flowers. As I said, they really go in for that."

"That's ridiculous."

Fred grinned and clapped him on the back. "Absolutely. Now you've got it."

"That doesn't make any sense at all," Arthur insisted.

Fred's philosophical mood had vanished. Getting the bust

improvers off his chest had apparently worked wonders. "Well, you're married now, my good man. Nothing is going to make much sense anymore."

Arthur didn't reply. He'd apologize to Chelsea Delafield, all right. When it rained peanuts and not a minute before.

Fred turned up his coat collar and shivered against the bone-chilling damp as he changed the subject. "We heard you were a bit under the weather yesterday."

"A little." Arthur wondered what Chelsea had been telling everyone while he was so humiliatingly indisposed.

"A touch of seasickness, eh? I had a bit of it myself. Today's much better, though. The sea has calmed down."

"Yes."

"Well, I must be off." Fred moved to leave. "Bernice is waiting up for me." He stopped then as if struck by a sudden thought. "Say, perhaps you and the wife would like to join us for dinner tomorrow night. I hear there's going to be a fancy dress dance in the grand saloon afterwards."

Arthur was about to decline, then thought better of it. Spending too much time alone with Chelsea had caused him nothing but problems so far. Perhaps if they spent more time in the company of others, it would serve as a much-needed distraction. For the both of them. "All right," he agreed. "That sounds like a good idea."

"Wonderful. Bernice will be thrilled. It's the dancing, you know. The women really go in for that."

"Sure they do," Arthur agreed amiably. He wondered what Chelsea would do when she learned that he had committed her to spending an entire evening with Bernice Sherman. Did it really matter? He thought perhaps it would serve her right.

"I don't understand." Arthur leaned up against the lavatory door, his arms folded stiffly across his chest. It seemed to him that he'd been expressing this sentiment quite a bit lately.

Wearing a yellow shirtwaist and a prim gray skirt,

Chelsea sat at the writing table where she had been studying the Glastonbury parchment and a Latin dictionary for the past ten minutes, ever since they had returned from breakfast in icy silence. Now, she looked up to meet Arthur's stony gaze, her expression aloof. "I will not go. Which part presents you with difficulty?"

Arthur had expected her to be displeased. He had even expected her to argue, but he hadn't expected her to flat out refuse to dine with the Shermans this evening. How was it going to look to Fred when Arthur told him Chelsea couldn't make it? Fred would know immediately they were still spatting and he would know Arthur hadn't apologized. Why, it would look like Arthur couldn't handle his own wife.

Wife?

Hell, this was getting downright ridiculous.

"How can you say you're not going?" he demanded.

"In any number of spoken languages. English, French, German. Perhaps you'd even prefer to see it written out in Latin."

"Ha. Very funny."

"Oh, my," Chelsea admonished in a tsk-tsk tone. "You don't much care for a sense of humor once it's put on the other foot, do you?"

Arthur glared at her. She, it seemed, had managed to regain her composure since the night before. He, however, was ready to strangle her, to wrap his fingers around that slender pale throat and . . .

"You should have checked with me before you accepted Fred Sherman's invitation," she continued. "What kind of marriage is this supposed to be?"

"It's a regular kind of marriage. The kind where the wife does what her husband tells her to do."

"Then I want a divorce."

"Well, you can't have one." He pushed off from the door and moved to tower over her in what he hoped was an intimidating manner. "At least not until we dock in Southampton, and by then you'll have to run pretty fast to beat me to the nearest magistrate."

Her eyes narrowed dangerously. "I'm sorry I ever married you."

"Well, the feeling is mutual. That doesn't mean we can't suffer through one dinner with Fred and Bernice Sherman."

"You may suffer what you please, but I won't be in company."

"Why?" he shot back.

Her composure finally cracked. "Because, Arthur Pierce, you pretentious popinjay, you want me to!"

So there it was. The ugly truth. She was blackmailing him. Her price? An apology. A sniveling apology. He was sure of it. She was a woman, wasn't she? It was as plain as the pert little nose on her face. Well, she could wait until the sun rose in the west and set in the east. Sackcloth and ashes did not become him.

"I hope you realize that you're the one acting childish now," Arthur pointed out.

At this, her chin tilted. Rose pink lips thinned into an intractable line. With an indignant little "hmph!" she returned her attention to the parchment.

Oh, Arthur thought, now she wasn't speaking to him. As if that were supposed to be some kind of punishment.

Snatching up the volume of *Le Morte d'Arthur*, he stalked to the lower berth, pulled off his shoes, then made a grand show of fluffing up a pillow before collapsing onto his back. Cracking open the book, he settled in to read.

For a long time, there was no sound in the cabin but the occasional footfalls of passengers strolling by on the deck overhead, the faint churning of the ship's screw propeller, and the steady scritchy-scratching of Chelsea's pencil.

Arthur read Malory's opening paragraph three times to no understandable end. Aggravation churned his stomach. He didn't usually allow anything to get to him like this, especially a woman. What was the matter with him? *She* was the matter with him.

He slapped the book closed and sat up. "Look, Chelsea, when I told you your lips don't move, I was stating a fact. When I told you that you snore, I was stating a fact."

She lifted her head to glower at him.

"Some people would consider it a favor," he pointed out.

Her nose wrinkled ever so slightly.

Arthur stood. "It's a far cry from insulting my personality and implying that I lack ambition."

Chelsea frowned but still said nothing.

"Well, for your information, I've got plenty of ambition!"

She returned her attention to the parchment.

Arthur began to pace. "Just because I'm in no big hurry doesn't mean I don't have ambition."

He stopped to see if she was paying any attention to him. She wasn't. Or she was pretending not to. He noticed that her pencil was poised but not moving.

He resumed pacing. "How does Professor Pierce strike you, hmmmm?"

He checked again. Not looking. Pencil still not moving. He resumed pacing. "Or, how about Senator Pierce?"

This time, he whipped around just in time to see her head jerk back down to her book. Ah ha!

She knew she'd been caught. She nibbled at her lower lip, then set her pencil down and studied him before speaking. "Why fool with small potatoes? What about President Pierce?"

"I was going to mention that, but I thought perhaps it would sound a bit presumptuous."

What might have been the hint of a reluctant smile tugged at the corners of her mouth. "And modesty, after all, is one of your most endearing qualities."

"Absolutely," he agreed.

It seemed as if they had both taken one halting step toward the middle. Who would take the next? Arthur had the passing thought that Chelsea might be as inept at humbling herself as he was. At this, his stubborn resolve splintered for just a moment, but it was a damning moment.

"I'm sorry," he said.

Her eyes widened. She had been waiting for him to apologize, but she obviously hadn't expected him to. "What?"

"I said, I'm sorry."

"You are?" She appeared innocently surprised, but she was far from innocent. She was going to draw this out, make him grovel.

His next words seemed to stick in his throat like rocks. "I'm sorry I said your lips don't move when you talk."

She looked hesitant, cautious, then sly. "Are you admitting, then, that they do move?"

"Don't push me, Chelsea."

"What about my snoring? It's a wicked lie, isn't it?"

"No, but I'm sorry I mentioned it."

She frowned at this, a clearly unacceptable compromise, but after a moment seemed to relent. "Fine. Then, I forgive you."

Arthur's pride had ingested about all the humble pie it could take at one sitting. "Forgive me?" he repeated, teetering on the edge of taking it all back.

"Yes." She cleared her throat and swallowed hard, indicating that there might be a few rocks sticking in her throat, too. "Perhaps I was a bit harsh," she said, her gaze shifting to fix on some point about twelve inches to his left. "Your sense of humor isn't that dreadful. I don't like it, really, but I don't suppose I actually detest it, either."

"Okay," Arthur said, relaxing a bit. "Then, I guess we're back to where we were before, right?"

"Yes." Her gaze returned to meet his. "I suppose so."

Sleek raven tresses were pinned into a loose pompadour knot atop her head. Steel-rimmed spectacles glinted in the lamplight. She looked the same as she always had. Nothing different. Nothing at all. Except that she was quite pretty. Oh, it wasn't an obvious kind of pretty, not the flashy, eye-catching kind of pretty that took a young man's notice on the street. It was a quiet type of pretty.

With some effort, Arthur shifted his attention to the

notebook she had been writing in earlier. "So, uh, what are you doing there?"

She replied quickly, obviously as eager as he for a change in subject. "I'm doing a bit of playing about with words."

Arthur pulled up a chair to sit next to her. She smelled like spring flowers. One glance at her notebook seemed to indicate that she was translating the parchment from Latin to English all over again, except that in place of a number of words, she had crossed out the original translation and replaced it with an alternate possibility. Most of them, when taken into account with the surrounding context, didn't make sense.

She adopted a scholarly tone. "I wondered if there might be double meanings for some of these words or perhaps archaic connotations we've failed to take into account." With the tip of her pencil, she indicated two of the monk's inscribed words. "For example, right here. *Sella regis*. We both interpreted it to read 'seat of the king,' correct?"

Arthur nodded.

"If you recall, we discussed the possibility that our monk might have been referring to a king's throne, but now I doubt it. Otherwise, I think he would have utilized a more precise noun, one that had royal connotations. *Solium* or *regnum*, for instance."

Arthur was impressed with her reasoning. "Good point."

"However," she continued, "the word he does use, *sella*, could have referred to any common sort of seat or chair. I've found no royal connotations attached to it." Chelsea looked up, awaiting an opinion.

"Do you think it could mean something?" he asked.

She let out a weary sigh. "Oh, I don't know. Probably not."

"Chelsea, you're pretty darn smart yourself. You might just come up with something useful if you keep at it."

At this, she ducked her head and turned back to her work, but not before Arthur saw her cheeks flush a fetching shade of pink. His heart unexpectedly softened. He knew well enough how to make a girl blush. One complimented her hair or her eyes or her appearance in a new dress, certainly not her intelligence. Chelsea's reaction to his passing remark indicated how vulnerable she might be beneath that unflappable exterior, and he suddenly regretted all the teasing he'd subjected her to over the past year.

"Chelsea," he said quietly, "won't you please have dinner with me tonight?" These were humble words, granted, but Arthur now felt no qualms at expressing them.

Her answer was just as subdued as his question. "I can't."

"Please, Chelsea," he urged. "Bernice Sherman isn't that bad. You can stand her company for just one evening, can't you?"

"It's not Bernice," she said, still not looking at him.

"Well, then, what is it?"

"I don't dancc."

"You don't dance?"

"No."

Arthur wasn't sure how to respond. He noticed the back of her slender neck, where a gentle shade of pink now rose to join the blush that no doubt still stained her cheeks. "You mean, you can't dance?" he ventured.

"No, no, no!" She spoke rapidly, impatiently. Either she was embarrassed or she was growing peeved with him again. "I didn't say I *can't* dance. I said I *don't* dance. There's a difference."

"What's the difference?"

"I simply don't dance!"

"You mean, you don't know how. That's what you mean, right?"

"No!" Her pencil skittered across the desk before she shot up from her seat. "I know how to do it, I just don't do it well. I've never done it well, no matter how much I practiced, no matter which partners my instructors matched me with, I just never could get the bloody hang of it!"

Arthur smiled up at her. "Is that all?"

"Isn't that enough? I have no desire to make a fool of myself in front of the entire ship's company!"

"You've just never had the right partner."

She rested a hand on each hip and looked down her nose at him. "And you, I presume, are the right partner."

"Yes." Arthur rose from his seat so he could look down at her. "They don't call me Twinkle Toes Pierce for nothing."

"Twinkle Toes Pierce?"

"Don't go spreading it around."

"Egad," she rejoined dryly, "who on earth would be interested?"

Arthur had to bite back a chuckle. It seemed that Delafield was back to her old scrappy self. Good. He didn't like going all mushy over her, anyway. It was unnatural.

Deliberately donning the smile that he knew no female in her right mind could resist, Arthur offered her his hand. "May I have this dance, Miss Delafield?"

"Oh, I don't think . . ."

Not waiting for her to acquiesce, he took her right hand. "Please, Miss Delafield." He led her out to a small square of open floor space in their cabin. "There are times when one must throw all caution to the wind."

"Oh, this is silly," she protested, but it was a halfhearted protest, mumbled under her breath.

"Put your other hand on my shoulder," he instructed, taking her about the waist.

"I am well aware of the positioning," she said huffily; however, when she rested one palm on his shoulder, it was with a shy hesitancy that belied her bluster.

Violet eyes climbed very slowly from his chest to his chin to his eyes and stopped. Arthur sensed that she held her breath, and suddenly he felt awkward despite his self-proclaimed expertise. Her hand felt so soft, so small and delicate in his own. Her waist was so slim that the length of his palm and fingers spanned over half its length across the small of her back. Despite her exasperating bull-headedness and formidable intellect, Chelsea Delafield seemed, at that moment, very fragile and very in need of male protection.

Arthur brushed these thoughts aside. "If we can get

through a few waltzes, that should be sufficient, don't you think?"

"I suppose so." She blinked up at him through those damned spectacles, all violet-blue orbs and thick black lashes.

"Let's begin," he said gruffly.

As soon as he started to guide her into a basic three-count box step, however, he began to feel a great deal of sympathy for her past dance instructors. She was stiff, and he could feel her pulling back at each turn. It was almost as if she were deliberately fighting him.

"Chelsea, stop trying to lead," he said as they lurched about.

"I'm not."

"Yes, you are. Just follow me."

"I am."

Arthur had to bite his tongue. If he didn't, they were going to end up arguing again. "Relax," he said. "And stop looking at your feet. You're doing fine."

But she wasn't doing fine. She kept stepping on his toes.

After another five minutes of agony, he stopped, his patience wearing thin. "Chelsea, are you lifting your knees?"

"Lifting my knees?"

"You seem to be stomping your feet."

"I beg you pardon?"

"Chelsea, there will be a dance orchestra in the grand saloon tonight, not a toothless fiddler from the Ozarks."

"A what from the where?"

"Step lightly."

"I was."

"Never mind. Let's try again."

And so they tried again. And again. And about the time that Arthur thought she was right about never getting the hang of it, she began to loosen up. Just a little.

"Lightly, step lightly," he reminded her, and soon, despite her protestations and grumblings, she began to do it. She soon stopped pulling back from him, too, finally relinquishing control and trusting him to lead her. He sensed that this last was no small accomplishment. If, as she had said, Arthur was a little too smart for his own good, Chelsea was clearly a little too independent-minded for her own good. They were quite an unlikely pair, but they were dancing. And not half badly, either.

Arthur grinned down at her. "We're doing it."

"By Jove, we are, aren't we?" She wore a smile when she looked up at him, her eyes bright, her cheeks flushed with pleasure rather than embarrassment.

Undeniably attractive, Arthur thought as he assessed the graceful arc of high-set cheekbones and finely sculpted coral pink lips. He had known her for almost a year, yet he had never been able to see her subtle beauty before being forced to spend time with her. Now that he had seen it, though, he doubted he would ever be able to un-see it.

At some point, without him realizing it, they stopped dancing. They stared at each other, with no more than three inches between them, and Arthur had serious pause to consider that teaching her to dance while they were alone and in such close quarters might not have been the brightest idea he'd had all morning.

He let go of her. "See, it was just as I said. All you needed was the right partner."

"Yes." Her eyes dropped to the floor, her hands dropped to smooth the folds of her skirt. "So it seems."

Without another word, Arthur turned away and headed for the lower berth where *Le Morte d'Arthur* lay discarded. It suddenly seemed a very good idea to lose himself in other-worldly fantasies for a while. At least those fantasies were less likely to lead him into trouble.

# 10

*"Peter Piper picked a peck* of pickled peppers."

No, no, that wouldn't do at all. No teeth. Chelsea frowned critically and leaned farther over the washbasin to get a better view of her reflection. She wasn't concerned with her painstakingly arranged curls or her scrubbed and powdered face.

She moistened her lips and tried again, this time pulling air up from the diaphragm as her elocution teacher had taught her.

"Eeny, meeny, miney, moe!"

Better. If he wanted to see teeth, by Jove, he'd see teeth. Allowing herself a smile of satisfaction, Chelsea checked the small satin bows in her hair and smoothed out the snug bodice of her evening dress.

Since she had crossed the Atlantic on numerous occasions, she knew that the general rule for first-class gatherings was to dress to the nines, so, on sudden inspiration, she had sent for one of her trunks to be brought up from the baggage hold. The steward had not even blinked when she asked if her gown could be pressed by this evening. He had taken the wrinkled garment with him a little after two, and it had magically reappeared, crisp and perfect, on a hook outside her stateroom door by four o'clock.

Chelsea had reserved a turn for a scented bath in one of the ladies bathrooms before returning to slip into her freshly pressed dress. It was a lavender taffeta with cap sleeves and crystal beading about the neckline, the one that her sister, Cornelia, had once told her brought out the color of her eyes. At this thought, Chelsea's smile faded. Ugly, glaring lenses.

She had been cursed with them since the age of ten. Cursed and blessed. Before then, she had suffered increasingly painful headaches, but they were nothing compared to the paralyzing fear that she was going blind. If the terror of living the rest of her life without precious light weren't bad enough, she suspected what people did with blind children. They sent them away to horrid institutions or locked them away in the cockloft.

It was only because of an attentive teacher that the problem had been brought to her parents' attention. Could Chelsea's difficulties in reading be due to poor eyesight? The woman had noticed her stalwart little pupil's painful squint, and, despite Chelsea's vehement denials, she thought perhaps an eye examination might be in order.

Astigmatic myopia.

Chelsea still remembered the day her papa had taken her to be fitted with her first pair of spectacles, how the world had suddenly come into sharp and vivid focus, how on the way home, she had stared at the bricks in the sidewalk and the leaves on the trees, marveling that she had long since forgotten they were not just flat blurs of dull red and green. She had pointed at a passing hansom cab, at the driver's bushy moustache and his riding crop, at the horse's reins, which were clearly distinguishable against the animal's chestnut coat. She had even stopped to recite from a shop sign across the street. "*I can read it, Papa*! *C-U-R-I-O*! *Curio Shoppe*!"

She still had the music box her father had bought for her from that little shop, a music box with a pair of clockwork dancers, for the spectacular sum of twelve shillings and sixpence. In celebration, he'd said, for it was a fine and most noteworthy day altogether, was it not?

Oh, yes, it most certainly was.

As Chelsea studied her bespectacled reflection in the looking glass now, she knew it was petty of her to disparage those steel-rimmed lenses. They had given her the world back. How could she begrudge the small price they exacted in exchange? Beauty. A shallow type of beauty, too. Still, just once . . .

"Chelsea!" A sharp rap at the door.

Startled, she knocked a perfume bottle off the side of the basin to clatter into the washbowl.

"Chelsea, it's six o'clock. They'll be seating for dinner in a few minutes."

Oh dear, it was Arthur. It seemed as if he'd tapped on the door only moments ago to tell her he was going to play a round of billiards with Fred Sherman. How long had she been daydreaming?

Chelsea laid a hand over her pounding heart and willed herself to calm. It didn't work. The white-gloved fingers that hastily replaced the upended perfume bottle trembled with dread.

"Chelsea! Are you in there?"

"I'm coming!" She threw one last, desperate glance at the mirror. Pretty, he'd said, *damned* pretty. She was vaguely aware of his good-natured ribbing from the other side of the door.

"Fred was right. He told me you'd still be primping, but I said, 'Oh, no, not Chelsea. She's much too practical to be frittering away all this time in front of the mirror.'"

Quickly, on pure, illogical impulse and before she could change her mind, Chelsea snatched off her spectacles, folded them, then pulled open the medicine chest door to slip them in lengthwise between two bottles of God-knew-what. She could no longer read the labels.

Slamming the cabinet closed, she stood stiff, motionless, blinking at the fuzzy, unfamiliar world that surrounded her.

The medicine chest was a brown and silver blob on the wall, her hands . . . She looked down. White, knob-ended clubs. Oh, dear, beauty didn't come cheap, did it?

She reached up for the lamp chain and pulled it. She had never liked the dark, but at least it was neutral, with or without her spectacles.

"Chelsea, am I going to have to break down the door?"

She smacked her knuckles on wood before locating the latch and releasing it. Light once again flooded her field of vision. Light and Arthur. Or, at least, she thought it was Arthur.

"It's about time. For a minute—" He cocked his head to one side. At least, she thought it was his head. "Are you all right?"

"Absolutely. Shall we go?" Chelsea had to resist an urge to thrust her hands out before her as she stepped into the stateroom. Oh dear, it had been years since she had tried to negotiate without her spectacles.

"I'm sorry. It didn't occur to me that you might not be feeling well. I just thought—" He stopped again. "Chelsea, what's wrong with you?"

"Nothing." She hazarded a few more steps, these more cautious, toe-sliding movements. The last thing she wanted was to trip over something on her way to where she believed the stateroom door was located. She had not noticed before that the blasted thing was stained the same color as the cabin's paneled walls. Now she could barely make out its rectangular outline in the distance.

"Chelsea, where are your eyeglasses?"

She stopped, her eyes beginning to water from trying too hard to focus. "I seem to have misplaced them."

"How could you do that?"

"I don't know. Could we go? I don't want to be late."

"Wait." She felt warm, strong fingers wrap around her forearm, stopping her before she could get off to a good start again. "Do you have an extra pair I could get for you?"

"My extra pair is packed in one of my trunks down in the hold. It's not worth the trouble. I'll be fine."

He let go of her, but he still sounded bothersomely concerned. "We should look for the ones you lost. They can't be far. Did you have them when you went into the lavatory?"

Chelsea's fingers curled into fists at her sides. She heard the lamp chain click in the lavatory, then the soft clink and rustle of bottles, hairbrushes, and powder boxes being sifted through. "Hmmm, I don't see them. Wait a minute." Medicine cabinet hinges squeaked. "What in the world are they doing in here?"

Feeling infuriatingly helpless, Chelsea could do nothing but look down at the floor where the carpet's elegant floral pattern now appeared as indistinguishable red and grayish black splotches. Bloody hell, what had possessed her to do such a silly thing? She felt like a complete fool!

Arthur was beside her again. "Here." Lifting her right hand, he placed the folded spectacles in her palm. "You left them in the cabinet."

Chelsea allowed her fingers to close over the fragile constructions. Old friends. Despised appendages. "I must have put them there when I washed up." She was unable to bring herself to look at him. "I do so hate it when they get splashed with soap."

"Oh." The soft tone of voice hinted that he didn't believe her for a second.

Chelsea couldn't remember when she had ever been so embarrassed. "Terribly difficult to get the streaks off."

"Of course."

When she settled the spectacles onto the bridge of her nose, she couldn't help but feel some measure of relief as the tips of her opera shoes and the floral print of the carpet slipped back into reassuring focus. When she looked up at Arthur, however, her heart skipped a beat and her breath deserted her.

Dressed in black tie and tail coat, he cut the most princely figure she had ever seen in her life. It was difficult to believe she was going to dine and dance on such a dashing young man's arm.

He broke the awkward silence. "So, what do you think?" He patted his waistcoat proudly. "Lucky I decided to bring along my best suit, isn't it? I wasn't going to, but then I thought, what the heck, I might get invited to dinner with the Queen."

"Yes." Chelsea could not manage much more than a whisper.

"You did something different with your hair."

She felt her cheeks warm and dropped her gaze again. "One of the women in the ladies lounge suggested I might try her curling rod."

"I like it."

"Thank you." She wanted nothing more than to disappear. She felt worse than foolish.

"You look very pretty tonight, Chelsea." She felt his finger slip beneath her chin, then, with no choice but to look up, she was suddenly lost in the clear lake blue of his eyes. She could see therein no smirking amusement, no sign of insincerity, just a gentle understanding that melted her weak and fluttering heart.

*Pretty*. He'd said that, hadn't he? First the other night without thinking. Now, he had said it again. Could it possibly be that he meant it?

"Thank you," she said, too numb to say anything more. Luckily, she didn't have to.

He smiled. "Shall we go, Mrs. Putnam?" He offered her his arm. "We don't want to keep first class waiting."

It was past midnight when they bade goodnight to the Shermans and returned to their stateroom. As Arthur closed the door behind them, he watched Chelsea breeze to the dresser, remove her gloves, and begin to pluck the tiny satin bows from her coiffure. She was humming.

What a night it had been. They had dined and danced and conversed and laughed together. Yes, laughed. Chelsea had laughed. Not once, but twice. The first time at one of Fred

Sherman's awful jokes and then again as she and Arthur had attempted to stumble their way through a lively polka.

"I thought it went rather well tonight," she said, unwittingly echoing Arthur's thoughts.

"Yes." He sat on the lower bunk and loosened his tie as she pulled pins from her hair, one by one by one, setting black silk waves tumbling down her back.

"They collected quite a tidy sum for the Seamen's Orphanage," she added.

"Hmmm."

"Well, at any rate, it's all over now." She turned to face him, and he noticed, not for the first time tonight, that her eyes seemed all the more luminous and mesmerizing against the lavender of her gown.

"Yes," he said, belatedly realizing that she had been waiting for him to answer.

The silence that followed was so long and profound, Arthur could make out snatches of conversation from the next cabin. Something about lost shoes.

"Is there something wrong?" she asked.

"Wrong?"

"You're looking at me strangely."

"Am I?"

"Yes."

"I'm just tired."

"Oh."

The tension between them was now palpable. Normally, Arthur would have tried to defuse it with a light comment, but now he could think of nothing to say as she stood before him, nervously twisting the gold wedding band around and around her finger. She had lovely hands. Feminine. Graceful. When had he first noticed them? That day at the Ridgway Library? Was that when all of this had started?

"Well, it's past time to turn in," she said. "Would you like to go first?"

"First?"

"In the lavatory."

"No. You go ahead."

She gathered her nightdress from the bureau and her dressing gown from the closet, obviously relieved at something to occupy her attention as Arthur continued to brood from his place on the lower bunk.

They had taken so well to their roles as the happily married Putnams, they now seemed to be having trouble reverting back to plain old Arthur and Chelsea. For some reason, it was hard to remember where their former battle lines had been drawn. It should have been simple. After all, they had drawn those lines from the first moment they met. He was cocky and conceited. She was stuffy and puritanical. It was in the natural order of things that they should drive each other to the brink of murder. There was no reason they should be getting along any better now. But they were. That is, they had. Well, just for a little while, anyway. Arthur had enjoyed himself tonight.

"I won't be but a moment," she said crisply, not sparing him a glance as she crossed to the lavatory. She almost sounded like the old Chelsea.

Nice try, Arthur thought as the door shut behind her. But she wasn't the old Chelsea, and he wasn't the old Arthur. Something was terribly wrong.

He rose to his feet, shedding his suit coat and yanking off his tie. Crossing the stateroom to the closet, he busied himself by hanging up his coat. He couldn't help wondering what she was thinking. Surely, she couldn't be thinking what he was thinking. He was thinking about sex. She couldn't be thinking about sex. The Chelsea Delafields of this world didn't think about such things. They thought about art and literature, history and philosophy. Certainly not sex. Yet, he had seen The Look.

Tonight, as they had danced in the grand saloon, Chelsea had gazed up at him, and there it was, in the dark, swirling violet of her eyes. As plain and compelling as he had ever seen it. The Yes Look.

Arthur removed his waistcoat and flung it down on a chair

before moving to their berth. Kicking off his shoes, he climbed to the top bunk, where he had again taken up residence after his brief bout with seasickness. Without bothering to even take down the cover, he collapsed facedown onto the mattress. It was the act of a man exhausted and defeated, and that was exactly how he felt. If God was merciful, He would put Arthur to sleep right now. He would order a dream chock-full of buxom blondes to ease the carnal frustration that surged through his veins and tensed every muscle in his body.

But God was not in a merciful mood.

Turning onto his back, Arthur groaned and threw one arm over his eyes to shut out the light. Oh, something was terribly wrong. Chelsea was all wrong. Arthur's new and confusing attraction toward her was all wrong. This was not how things were supposed to be between them, and nobody knew that better than Arthur.

Over the years, he'd developed a certain talent that had grown to be much envied by his prep school chums. He could size up romantic prospects after spending as little as five minutes in an unsuspecting young lady's company. Will she or won't she? There were Yes-Girls and No-Girls, and then there were those most challenging of young ladies, the Maybe-Girls.

He took pride in this unique ability that had served him so well. That was why he was so troubled tonight. Chelsea's signals were all wrong. In fact, they had started to go wrong soon after they had boarded ship. While she was the most emphatic example of a No-Girl he had ever stumbled across—indeed, perhaps the only girl he had ever met who seemed totally immune to him—she was now sending out unmistakable "yes" signals. But why now? Hell, before this, he'd never been able to wheedle so much as one page of borrowed class notes from her. Frankly, Arthur didn't know what to make of it. Add to all of this his own illogical emotions, and he was in a hopeless state of sexual quandary.

Arthur closed his eyes and succumbed to the weariness caused by thinking too hard in too many circles for too long.

Perhaps the seasickness hadn't only stirred up his stomach; perhaps it had addled his brain. Yes. The more he thought about it, the more this rang true. It made perfect sense. Why, Delafield was no more likely to be throwing out "yes" signals than he was to be contemplating joining the priesthood.

*It's the seasickness*, he thought as he descended into a restless doze. Yes signals, no signals, maybe, maybe, maybe.

# 11

*She was thinking that she felt* like Cinderella. Clad in her corset and petticoat, her hair loose and spilling about her shoulders, Chelsea stood in the lavatory with her eyes closed and a smile curving her lips as she savored the last few remnants of the most wonderful night of her life. If Arthur had asked her tonight if she believed in magic, she would have been forced to reconsider her original answer.

"Ah, magic," she whispered as a flood of intoxicating memories washed over her. Parquet floors and swirling silks. Candlelight and mirrors, music and champagne.

For the first time ever, as she had danced in Arthur's arms, she had imagined herself as weightless as a sunbeam and as graceful as a prima ballerina. When he held her, one hand so capably anchored at her waist, the other so easily and perfectly clasped with her own, she had become lost in the rhapsody of the music.

Step, step, close, step, step, close. Around and around they had swept from one end of the grand saloon to the other. Why, so light were her steps and so sure was his lead, Chelsea could not have sworn for a fact that her feet ever touched the floor. She had imagined that he held her just a little closer than he had this morning, their bodies just a whisper apart, and that she saw deep in his eyes a certain light, a certain spark she had never seen there before. She even dared to imagine what it would be like if he kissed her. Spark, light, magic.

But now it was past midnight. Cinderella's coach had turned back into a pumpkin and her footmen back into mice.

Chelsea's eyes flickered open to behold a disheveled stranger in the mirror. She had been foolish to think that Arthur had enjoyed their evening together. His easy smiles and smooth conversation were for Fred and Bernice's benefit. The warmth she had seen in his eyes was nothing but her overactive imagination at work. That was obvious now. His cold silence upon returning to their stateroom attested well enough to that.

Chelsea struggled to put Arthur from her mind as she finished getting ready for bed. Gathering up her gown and undergarments, she prepared to face Arthur's disconcerting blue gaze once again, but when she emerged, he was gone.

"Arthur?"

His shoes lay on the floor, his waistcoat hung off a chair by the dresser, but where was . . . ? And then she heard it. A snort, a mumble, and a deep, rumbling sigh. Following its source to the top berth, she saw the unlikely object of her amorous fantasies lying on his back, fully clothed, with one arm thrown across his face.

"Arthur?"

No answer. Just a soft, snoring in breath followed by a soft, whistling out breath.

Chelsea laid her clothing out across the back of a chair, then approached, rising up on tiptoes to examine the situation. Snore in, whistle out. Snore in, whistle out. By all appearances, her gallant prince was asleep. Frankly, she was pleased with all the racket he was making. She couldn't wait to inform him that she wasn't the only one with an audible nasal impediment.

"Arthur." She tugged on his sleeve. "Don't you want to get ready for bed?"

"No, no, yes, yes, maybe, maybe, maybe," he mumbled, then resumed his whistling and snoring.

Chelsea sank back down onto slippered heels. Oh, dear. What was she to make of that? She couldn't very well undress him herself, could she? Her eyes took on a speculative glint as they roved down the appealing masculine length of him. Strapping healthy specimen.

No, no, of course not. Shocking to even entertain the thought.

Turning quickly, Chelsea set about hanging up her gown and stowing the rest of her clothing before grabbing an extra blanket from the closet. Gripping the berth's post, she stepped up onto the lower berth only to be caught up short upon seeing that the arm which had been thrown over his face earlier now rested more naturally across his middle. In profile, his handsome features appeared relaxed and unburdened.

Chelsea felt a tug of guilt at stealing this chance to observe him while he was unaware, but she couldn't help it. At this moment, it was not difficult at all to imagine that he resembled the young hero king he was named for, and all her efforts to remain rational fled. Her heart swelled, taking her very breath away. Oh dear, what had she done? Not fallen in love?

The very possibility froze her blood. Down that path lay nothing but tragic disappointment. The inevitable hopes that would follow, that Arthur would ever look upon her with anything more than polite interest, were ludicrous. She had none of the qualities he obviously sought in a woman, and she had no clue of how to go about attracting his attention. She was not pretty or adept at coy flirtation. Dash it all, she had never even been kissed. Not really. She couldn't even count Miles in that respect. That had been all wrong. Timed wrong. Executed wrong. A hopeless failure. No spark. No light. No magic.

*It's not love,* she thought, moving hastily to cover him and step down from the bunk. Infatuation, perhaps. A temporary manifestation. She had felt it once before. A neighbor's gardener. She had been thirteen at the time. That had soon passed, hadn't it? So too would this. Wouldn't it?

Yes, a calm rational voice soothed in her mind. As soon as she got off this ship. Chelsea doused the light and climbed into the lower berth, stowing her spectacles, and burrowing beneath the blankets. They had been cooped up too blasted long on this ship. It was an explanation that made good sense, the kind of sense Chelsea was used to, the kind she could latch onto and keep hold of.

"And there is no such thing as magic," she added for good measure before closing her eyes and surrendering to the welcoming open arms of sleep.

Oh no, not this dream again, Arthur thought as he fought through a tangle of underbrush only to be smacked in the forehead by a low-hanging tree branch. He slapped it away with a muttered oath and continued to pick his way through a thicket of scrub.

His waking mind had no memory of this quest, but his dreaming mind knew that he had been negotiating the unmarked trails of this ancient, dark-shadowed forest for the past three nights. Around and around in circles, it seemed, always searching but never finding, and no company but a lordly voice that spoke to him only in his mind; an omniscient counselor he had soon recognized as none other than the eccentric Max Hamilton.

"Where art my buxom blondes?" Arthur complained, yanking a corner of his cloak free from the greedy clutches of a thorn bush. "Doth not a man deserve some earthly diversion from time to time, even if it can be had only in his dreams?"

*Try not to think of buxom maidens,* the Hamilton voice replied. *Concentrate instead on thy quest. It is—*

"My quest," Arthur interrupted, "is to find some respite in the arms of a willing lass. Thou hast no understanding of what I hath been through of late."

*Thy recent difficulties will not be relieved by indulging in a lusty tumble, young Arthur.*

"Oh? And to whom doth this dream belong? As I recall, thou wert not even invited."

*Cease thy tiresome whining.*

"Whining?" Indignant, Arthur stopped. "I understand not why I must continue to fight my way in circles night after night."

*Thou wilt understand soon enough.*

"There!" Arthur jabbed an angry finger at the air. "Thou art doing it again! Thou answereth questions with platitudes, and I am tired of it! I want to know why I am here."

*Thou art here because thou fell asleep.*

Arthur gestured angrily at the tunic, hose, and leather buskins he wore in lieu of trousers, shirt, and shoes. "And why am I garbed thusly? And why do I speaketh in the manner of a medieval troubadour?"

*Mayhaps thou hast been reading too much knightly adventure.*

Arthur could think of no good answer to refute this. Instead, he glared up at heavens barely visible through thick layers of ageless boughs. For a long time, there was no sound but the whispering of windsong and the fluttering of dark leaves overhead.

His anger receded. He had two choices. Either he could wait here until he awoke many hours hence, or he could get on with things. "Which way?" he asked flatly.

*Continue to keep the sun at thy back.*

"East, east, always east," Arthur grumbled, but, as he took up the inhospitable trail this time, it was with a renewed sense of determination.

He climbed over decaying logs the size of war horses and slashed his way through low-lying scrub. The rotting stench of old detritus and sodden earth filled his nostrils. It seemed like a very long time until the voice spoke again. *Thou art drawing nigh.*

"To the sword?" he asked hopefully.

*Nay. Thou hath a long journey yet ahead. One step at a time. To make haste is to stumble, and patience is a virtue.*

Arthur's optimism withered. "Much thanks, Oh Proverbial One." Soon, though, he began to sense a change. The all-encompassing gloom that had dogged him since first entering the woods was lifting. The shrubby undergrowth was thinning. The air itself seemed lighter, less drugged with fungus and eternal rot.

*Look ahead. Behold a break in the trees.*

Yellow, mote-swirled beams of sunlight lanced through the branches overhead. Puddles of light splashed the ground at his feet. Beyond the murky trees, he could now make out something else, something bright and alive with color and life. A glade?

Arthur stepped up his pace. When he reached the outskirts of the forest, he stopped, his eyes full to brimming, his brain numbed by the stunning medley of color that greeted him.

Not an open glade, but a vast lake. Tall reeds and sundry other marsh grasses grew along its gently lapping shores. Water lilies floated upon its shimmering blue surface. The air was sun-warmed, perfumed with the fragrance of spring blossoms, yet there was something out of place. In his present state of euphoria, it took him a moment to put his finger on it.

The air was still. No sound or movement at all. No birdsong, no breezes, not even the lazy drone of summer insects. He was confronted with a solitude so total and complete, he had never known the likes of it before. Except once.

"I remember this place," Arthur said, his voice a whisper in the pristine silence. "I dreamed of it before. Where are we?"

*Some call it Avalon.*

Arthur heard a splash and looked to behold a woman bathing just off the near shore of the lake. A thin barrier of water rushes separated them, but not enough to keep him from observing the glistening drops of water that dappled her naked shoulders, or her hair, sleek and wet and black as jet, streaming down her back in fluid lines to disappear into the water.

"God, she's beautiful," Arthur whispered as she vanished beneath the lake's surface, then smoothly re-emerged, shaking the water from her eyes and smoothing her hair back with both hands. "Is she the Lady of the Lake?"

*Nay, not the Lady of Legend, but thou hast sought her out for good reason. Trust thy instincts.*

Instincts, Arthur thought as she turned and began making her way back to shore. Ah yes, he was feeling plenty of those. At the sight of uptilted, rose-peaked breasts, it seemed as if every drop of blood in his body rushed to flood his nether regions with warming concupiscence.

*Young Arthur?*

He knew he should retreat from this wondrous place, give the lady her privacy, but, by now, his buskin-clad feet had grown stubbornly intractable. They had joined ranks with his eyes, which refused to look away as, with each step she took, yet another glorious inch of ivory skin came revealed. A smooth navel, the gentle flare of feminine hips, the dark thatch at the apex of her thighs, slim flanks.

*Arthur?*

She was a work of natural art. All sleek lines and coltish legs. Her lissome figure was revealed to him in stark relief when she reached the shore. For one brief moment, she tilted her face up to the sun, eyes closed as she absorbed its life-giving heat.

*Arthur!*

"Whaaat?" His reply came out a strangled rasp. The last thing he wanted was for her to discover him standing here, gaping and drooling like a besotted schoolboy, but Hamilton, it seemed, was damnably intent upon interrupting.

*In sooth, mayhaps thou shouldst set aside certain of thy instincts for the moment,* Hamilton advised. *Thinketh with thy brain, not thy britches.*

*Wert thou not ever young?* Arthur thought back furiously.

Ponderous silence, then a rumbling sigh of acquiescence. *Yea, thy point is well taken. The damsel is comely, but thou must try to remember why thee sought her out from the beginning. She will lead thee to thy sword.*

"The sword?" Arthur's attention shifted for the briefest instant to sweep the vast expanse of the lake and its farthest shores, but he discerned nothing aside from the occasional silver-white flash of waterlights in the sun.

*She will lead thee to thy sword.*

"But who is she?" Arthur asked. His lady was now in the act of donning a long, white silken tunic. Sheer and light as gossamer, it did precious little to mask the lake-wet curves of her figure. In fact, Arthur thought as she turned to face him and he observed the clearly delineated peaks of her breasts, it clung most deliciously in all the right places.

"Who is she?" he murmured again, mesmerized by the graceful movements of her hands, hands that now struck him as strangely familiar, as she tied a flowing sash at her waist.

*Why dost thou ask? Thou dost already know her.*

And even as his guide spoke, Arthur's gaze lifted to her face. Their eyes locked, and he knew, with a jolt, that it was true.

# 12

*Silly dreams. It was just Arthur's* bad luck that he remembered the last one so vividly. As if things hadn't been bad enough before, now, whenever he set eyes on Chelsea, he no longer saw the disagreeable bluestocking who had made his academic life so difficult. What he saw was a lovely brunette swimming naked in an enchanted lake, rivulets of water running off skin of ivory cream, firm, young breasts, slim, flaring hips, legs that made him want to bite a bullet.

Wrong, wrong, wrong, his rational mind insisted time and again, adding its own confusing two cents to the mix, upon which time Arthur would have to excuse himself from her presence in order to regain some perspective. It would be easier, he decided, if he didn't have to spend so much time with her.

For the remainder of their week at sea, Arthur spent most of his time in separate areas of the ship from Chelsea. Yes, he, Arthur Pierce, who had always preferred thinking about sex to just about any other subject on earth, found himself engaging in brisk walks and energy-depleting bouts with weights and mechanical horses in an effort to cleanse himself of unchaste thoughts. More than once, as he fell exhausted into his berth after an ice-cold shower bath, he wondered if he wasn't going just a little bit crazy.

It was overcast and drizzling the day they docked in the thriving port of Southampton. After passing through a deck full of stewards, all with their palms out for parting tips, Arthur discovered that his funds were running dangerously low. During the voyage, he had won a few gentlemanly wagers at billiards to supplement his meager resources, but what with all the lavish tipping and the contribution he had made to the Seaman's Orphanage, he was left with what he had borrowed from Bernard Endicott before leaving the States. Fifty dollars.

With his satchel strapped over one shoulder and carrying his worn suitcase, he took his place next to Chelsea in line to disembark. He silently lambasted his deceased uncle for not thinking to leave him a few extra shillings to aid in pursuing his outlandish quest.

Even as these curses passed through his mind, however, he knew that the likelihood it had been an oversight was slim. As his late father would have been quick to remind him, a Pierce was expected to make his own way in this wicked and wonderful world.

His gloomy thoughts grew gloomier as the drizzle that sprinkled his derby turned to a steady, pattering rain.

*Fooo-fump!*

Arthur barely jerked aside in time to avoid being impaled as Chelsea snapped open a voluminous black umbrella.

"Did you forget to bring yours?" she asked in that dignified unruffled tone that usually made him want to strangle her.

"I don't have one." He pulled down on the brim of his hat and squared his shoulders to face the soggy onslaught with masculine fortitude. It had always been a point of pride with him. No one but the idle rich, fat businessmen, and frail women carried umbrellas.

"Perhaps you should invest in one." She peered up at him reprovingly from beneath the brim of an unembellished royal blue hat. The arresting violet shade of her eyes mixed darker blue than usual today, a reflection of the somber shirtwaist dress she had chosen for disembarking.

"Perhaps." Arthur glanced over the rail to see that a crowd awaited on the dock below. Relatives, friends, and servants prepared to meet arriving passengers. A veritable sea of tweed and dark wool serge. It wasn't long before, one by one, a line of black mushrooms bloomed in response to the quickening rain. They couldn't all be fat businessmen.

"Would you care to share mine?" Chelsea pressed, breaking into his thoughts.

"No, I'm fine." The light pattering rain was now a full-fledged downpour. The water that dripped from the brim of his hat was fast developing into a steady trickle. He was getting soaked.

"You're being ridiculous," she pronounced, offering him the umbrella. She wore her schoolmistress look, and there was no point in arguing with that.

Arthur ducked beneath the portable canvas roof and took charge of the contraption, holding it aloft as they proceeded to press a little closer together to take shelter. With passengers lined up in front and others pressing from behind, they found themselves standing intimately close, body-touching close, and Arthur's thoughts immediately took flying leaps of fancy. *Rivulets of water running off skin of ivory cream . . .* Dear God, stop, he thought miserably.

The staccato tempo of needling raindrops seemed to fill his ears to bursting until she spoke. "Perhaps we should review a few rules before you meet my father."

"What rules?" He tried not to notice the traces of perfume that rose to tickle his nose. That alluring garden scent.

"Social etiquette."

"Etiquette? Uh, golly gee whillikins, Miss Delafield, you afraid this Yankee bumpkin will embarrass you in front of the family?"

"Please just try to behave yourself," she said, ignoring his sarcasm as they moved a few mincing steps toward the gangway.

"Sure I'll behave myself. No scratching or spitting, right?"

"Oh, dear Lord." Chelsea bent her head and pinched the bridge of her nose.

"You mean there's more?" He was gratified to see he was annoying her. Served her right after insinuating that he was an uncultured heathen.

She sucked in a breath and trained her eyes on the dark overcoat of the gentleman ahead of them. "Upon first introduction, you should avoid becoming overfamiliar too soon. Handshaking, for example. Not necessary at all."

"Wait a minute. Maybe I should write all this down. No handshaking. What's the word on foot kissing?"

"When entering a carriage with a lady," she continued with bulldog determination, "a gentleman always takes the seat facing the back."

"Okay, clear enough. But where do I sit?"

"As we walk to the station, be sure to take the outside of the pavement so that I may take the wall."

"And how many times shall I fling my coat across mud puddles for you, Miss Delafield?"

There was a pause before she condescended to gift him with a grudging side look. "I think once should be sufficient to create a favorable impression."

"I'll try to keep that in mind."

Chelsea offered nothing more as the line of passengers made its way down the ramp to the dock.

In addition to disembarking passengers and their families, scores of able-bodied seamen in dark slickers crisscrossed the wharves. Others moved with confident dignity and wore the crisp uniform suits of seasoned officers. Among most, Chelsea recognized the varied accents of home. Liverpool Irish, Welsh, Scots, West London, the East End.

Her life was over, she thought bleakly. From this day forward, she would have obligations to meet. She would have to see about finding herself a suitable situation as soon as possible. Whether it be teaching at a public school or securing employment as a private governess, her parents would be most eager to see her safely settled in either way. Next, she knew, would be marriage. If it wasn't already too late.

Something inside of her wilted.

"I say! Chelsea Anne, my dear, you look positively splendid!"

From out of the swimming crowd of colliding umbrellas and dark wool ulsters appeared a black bowler hat, gleaming round spectacles, and a drooping, gray-speckled moustache. Chelsea found herself looking up into her father's beaming countenance.

"Papa," she said, the word coming out more a strangled croak than the exclamation of happiness she had planned. Because of their umbrellas and her hand luggage, it was difficult to embrace. He clasped her forearm instead. "How was your trip, my dear? Everything satisfactory?"

"Satisfactory. Oh, oh yes," she replied, trying to shake free from the fog that had settled over her brain.

"But where is Mrs. Putnam, and . . . and who is this?"

Before Chelsea could answer, Arthur introduced himself. "The name is Arthur Pierce, sir. It's a pleasure to meet you."

All hint of human color departed her father's normally ruddy complexion. "How do you, uh, er, do."

Egad, Chelsea thought, he believed she'd brought home a Yank husband. No doubt memories of his sister, Geraldine, were flashing through his befuddled mind. Dear Geraldine, his ever unconventional younger sibling, who had left the sisterhood to elope with a globe-trotting American journalist. Chelsea hastened to explain. "He's a classmate of mine from Philadelphia, Papa."

Arthur picked up smoothly. "Miss Delafield and I have shared classes for more than a year, so you can imagine how surprised we were to discover after boarding that we had booked on the same crossing. It's such a small world, isn't it?"

"Er, yes," her father mumbled, then turned to Chelsea, "but what of Mrs. Putnam?"

Chelsea struggled to appear innocent beneath such intense parental scrutiny. "She's already disembarked. Didn't you see her?"

"Already disembarked?" Her father scanned the crowded docks. Fortunately for Chelsea, among the affluent mass of scurrying umbrellas, it was impossible to tell one personage from another.

"Oh well, no matter," she interposed quickly. "Her niece has probably already met her, and they've gone to board their train. We can't blame them for wanting to get out of the rain."

"Her niece, you say?"

"Charming woman, Mrs. Putnam," Arthur put in. "Delightful sense of humor."

Chelsea's father stared at him quizzically. "Sense of humor? Mrs. Putnam?"

Chelsea hastened to deflect her father's attention. "Arth— I mean, Mr. Put—, um, Mr. Pierce has come into possession of what may be a historically significant parchment, Papa. In fact, he's been invited to Oxford to have it analyzed, but since he doesn't have to travel to the university until the day after tomorrow, I thought perhaps he might consult with Professor Doyle in London. I trust he's well?"

"Doyle? Oh, er, yes. A touch of the gout. Nothing serious." Chelsea's father addressed Arthur. "Been a fellow at Oxford for more than forty years now. Specializes in restoring old manuscripts."

"Mr. Pierce has always had a keen interest in medieval history," Chelsea threw in, feeling a tug of guilt at greeting her father with a peck of fibs that put her few adolescent indiscretions to shame. "Isn't that right, Mr. Pierce?"

"Oh, yes," Arthur agreed. "Your daughter and I have had some stimulating discussions on the subject."

"I have no doubt," Mr. Delafield answered, casting Chelsea a fond paternal look.

"I thought perhaps Mr. Pierce could stay with us while in London," Chelsea said, disguising the silent hope that caused her heartbeat to quicken. "Cornelia's room is still empty, isn't it?"

"Oh, no, that's quite all right," Arthur cut in. "I planned to stay in a hotel."

Mr. Delafield frowned. "Tush, tush, we can't have that. Chelsea Anne is quite right. My eldest daughter's room has been left unused for years. We planned to have it turned into a sitting room for Mrs. Delafield, but she so detests sitting, you know, it hardly seemed worth the effort."

Arthur shot Chelsea a questioning look. "Uh, well, if you're sure it's not any trouble."

"No trouble at all," Chelsea said.

Her father extracted a silver watch from his fob and took quick note of its face. "Well, then, there's nothing more to be said about it. The next train up to London is scheduled to depart in twenty minutes. What do you say I dash over to check your baggage? Won't take but a moment."

"Sounds splendid," Chelsea agreed. "We'll wait for you over by the train shed."

"Very good. Cheerio, then."

Chelsea held her breath until her father melted into the crowd.

"Smooth work," Arthur said next to her ear.

Chelsea jumped. Her nerves were on edge. She calmed herself before peering up at her partner-in-crime. They had discussed his Oxford cover story before disembarking this morning, but she had chosen not to mention that she fully intended he take lodging with her family in the meantime. "I hope you don't object to being a houseguest," she said, gauging his reaction.

"Not at all." Those deep blue eyes sparkled to warm her insides. "But I already owe your father about seventy dollars in passage. It seems that I'm forever finding myself in your debt, Miss Delafield."

"I rather like it that way." She turned her face away, trying to keep her voice unaffected, although she was anything but. In fact, she was greatly relieved that he would be staying with them, even if only for a short time. It would put off parting ways with him, an idea that seemed to hold less and less appeal for her with each passing day.

For some inexplicable reason, the reality of separating

from Arthur and the prospect of facing her own dreary future had become intertwined. While she wasn't quite sure of the connection, she had already convinced herself that it certainly wasn't because of her temporary infatuation with him. No, no, of course not. It was not Arthur Pierce she was infatuated with at all. It was the parchment, and soon after their consultation with Professor Doyle, Arthur would have no other reason to stay in London. He would take his parchment and go off to pursue his quest, leaving her behind to . . .

No, she thought firmly as she started in the direction of the train station. It wasn't over yet. Not just yet. She would think of something, or her name wasn't Chelsea Anne Delafield.

"What was that name again?" The young steward spoke with a Liverpool accent, his blue company cap perched askew after loading bags and trunks into an expressman's coach that awaited on the dock.

"Pierce," Geoffrey Dark repeated. "Arthur Pierce. My employer has sent me to meet him. He was to be traveling on the *Salacia*."

"Pierce?" The steward removed his cap and scratched his head, seemingly oblivious to the rain that pelted his hair and streaked down his forehead. "I don't recall any Pierce. Perhaps there's been a mistake."

"There is no mistake."

"Oh." The steward ran a forearm across his brow and replaced his cap. "Could he have been traveling in steerage?"

"I'm quite sure I have no idea." Switching his umbrella from one hand to the other, Geoffrey dipped into his coat pocket and produced a shining gold sovereign. Were they in a dark alley, he could have just as easily produced a razor-edged flick-knife along with no trace of compunction at using it. He knew from experience that between the sovereign and the flick-knife, the latter was the more effective means of stirring immediate recollection, but there was a time and place for everything, and discretion, after all, was the watchword of the day.

"It is urgent that I locate him," Geoffrey said. "It would be most unpleasant if I were to miss the poor chap and he ended up boarding the wrong train, you see."

The steward's eyes rounded upon spotting the coin that winked enticingly from between Geoffrey's forefinger and middle finger. "Oh, er, uh, well, let me think a minute. You're sure he was on board the *Salacia*?"

"Most certain."

"Well, let me see . . ."

Geoffrey knew the seaman was testing his limited brain capacity to its pitiful limit, and therefore he had no choice but to wait as that incompetent organ went through its paces. There was nothing he could do in the meantime except perhaps further lament the fact that they were not in a dark alley after all.

The steward finally shook his head, his brow wrinkled in worriment. He was honestly concerned, of course, that he might not be able to collect his bribe. "I'm sorry, sir, I just don't recall an Arthur Pierce. There was a Nicholas Pearson in second cabin and an Arthur Putnam in first—"

"Young, good looking, reddish hair?" Geoffrey interrupted.

The steward's expression brightened. "Yes, that's Mr. Putnam, but . . ." His brow furrowed again.

"Yes?"

"He was traveling with his wife. You didn't mention that your bloke had a missus."

"Wife?" Geoffrey repeated sharply. That fool, Horace Doolittle, had made mention of a dark-haired woman in the telegram he had sent Blake. Wife? Perhaps. Perhaps not. Geoffrey was beginning to suspect that young Arthur Pierce could be as clever and duplicitous as his deceased uncle if the occasion called for it. The young lady could have been a diversion or simply a means of getting on board the *Salacia* without having to travel under his real name. Very clever indeed.

The steward prattled on with the enthusiasm only a queen's gold sovereign could inspire. "It was the first leg of their wedding trip. A pretty young thing, a bit stuffy, but—"

"Have they debarked?"

"Yes, just a few minutes ago. They went—there, look!" The steward pointed toward the train station. "See the bloke sharing his umbrella with the missus? That's him!"

Geoffrey caught a glimpse of the fellow's profile, a square jaw and a flash of red-gold hair, then he and the woman turned away, two of many indiscriminate figures beneath wide umbrellas moving to seek shelter beneath the cavernous, soot-covered train sheds. Geoffrey's quarry had been spotted, and not with a second to spare.

With a curt inclination of his head, he sent an unspoken command to his swarthy companion, a behemoth package of pure muscle named Beck, who hovered a few feet away on the dock. Beck's head turned to pick out the pair Geoffrey had indicated. Looking back, he nodded and lumbered across the docks in their direction.

Geoffrey returned his attention to the steward. "Very good."

The seaman grinned, all teeth and bright, sated eyes beneath his crooked company cap as he accepted the sovereign Geoffrey dropped into his waiting palm. "Quite a bit of luck, there, 'ey?"

"Yes," Geoffrey agreed. "Quite a bit of luck indeed."

Except for the British and Continental accents that surrounded him in the train's coach, Arthur might have mistaken the lush countryside of Hampshire for the rolling green farmlands and pastures outside Philadelphia. It was only as they passed through the suburbs and approached the outskirts of London that he sat up to take notice.

He had lived in and visited a number of American cities. Philadelphia, New York, Chicago, Kansas City, San Francisco. While they all shared certain inalienable urban characteristics, each had a distinct and separate personality, a certain ambiance that was uniquely its own. London was to prove no different, except perhaps even more so.

As her dark spires and domes emerged on the overcast horizon, Arthur immediately sensed her character, a majestic imperturbability that could only arise from wisdom borne of a millennium's worth of hard-learned lessons. Drenched in history and shrouded in yellowish mist, she was all black and every variation of gray. She should have been ugly, but she wasn't; she was London, pure and unmistakable.

Arthur grinned as he snapped open Chelsea's umbrella and stepped into a torrential downpour outside Waterloo Station. By then, he was thoroughly undaunted by the weather. He had always dreamed of seeing the far-off places he'd only read about, and, by George, here he was! London!

Later, when Chelsea's father hailed a growler carriage to take them home, he made it a point to catch Chelsea's eye as he dropped into a seat facing the back. He thought she looked incredibly appealing this afternoon, her ivory complexion flawless against the shadowed interior of the carriage, her navy blue hat pinned atop her head just so, her gloved hands folded over her carpetbag. Why, she was so adorably stiff and British in her father's stodgy presence Arthur had to fight a sudden urge to grab her and kiss her right then and there.

It was a good thing that Mr. Delafield chose that moment to address Arthur. "How long did you say you were staying in London, Mr. Pierce?"

"Only a day or two," Arthur replied. "After I'm done at Oxford, though, I'd like to come back, perhaps do some sightseeing before returning to the States."

"Ah, yes, splendid idea. There's a little bit of something for everyone in London, you know."

Now that was a prime example of British understatement. As their carriage started across the teeming Westminster Bridge, Arthur saw on the opposite riverbank what he knew from photographs were the Houses of Parliament. After they passed over the Thames, they joined a stream of coaches, cabs, and omnibuses traveling north on Parliament Street. Big Ben, the most famous clock tower in the world, soon loomed far behind them.

Continuing north, they found themselves embroiled in the swarming traffic of Trafalgar Square. Arthur caught a glimpse of Nelson's Column as their coach driver took a street headed northwest, soon whisking them away from the busy confusion of the pumping heart of London.

As they passed Leicester Square and continued through Soho, the neighborhoods began to take on a less spectacular character. It was then that Arthur realized Chelsea had spoken only a few cursory words since Parliament Square. Now, as she stared out her window, she didn't seem at all impressed by the breathtaking sights they had just witnessed.

Well, of course not, Arthur had to remind himself. This was home to her, same as those rundown flats in Kansas City and that ramshackle medicine wagon on the prairie had been home to him as a child. Yet Arthur now began to sense that her passivity might be due to something more than a simple case of overfamiliarity.

"Your mother received a letter from your Aunt Geraldine just yesterday," Mr. Delafield said.

"Aunt Geraldine?" This seemed to pique Chelsea's interest. "How is she?"

"Quite well. She's apparently gone in for Buddhism or some such nonsense."

"Oh, Papa," Chelsea admonished, "stop joking or Mr. Pierce will get the wrong idea entirely."

Undaunted, Mr. Delafield looked to Arthur. "Did you happen to meet my daughter's infamous Aunt Geraldine during your sojourn at Temple College, Mr. Pierce?"

"No, I'm afraid I only transferred to Temple for my senior year. She'd already left for Africa, as I understand."

"My sister was a nun for eight years. That was before she met up with that American poet of hers."

"Uncle Hugh was a journalist, Papa, a travel writer."

Mr. Delafield waved this minor distinction away. "They met while she was school teaching in India. I remember our dear mother, God rest her soul, had to be roused with smelling salts when she heard Geraldine had up and run off with the fellow."

"Oh, Papa, Grandmother had to be roused half a dozen times a day." Chelsea turned to Arthur to explain. "It got to be such a regular sort of thing, we all had to keep a fresh supply of salts in our pockets."

Mr. Delafield continued. "Next thing we knew she was alighting all over the globe. Africa, Egypt, Nepal, Zanzibar. We couldn't keep up with her. No sooner would we post a letter than it would come back straightaway unopened. Good heavens, until we would receive her next missive, she could have been devoured by some wild carnivore for all we knew."

"Oh, that's just plain silly," Chelsea put in. "Aunt Geraldine would never have allowed herself to be devoured by a wild carnivore. I always looked forward to her letters. It was such a delightful surprise to learn where they would come from next."

Mr. Delafield chuckled. "Oh, yes. Her missives were anticipated with the same sort of suspense that used to accompany a new installment of Dickens."

"Well, she did settle down for a short while, Papa."

"But she was a widow by then, and instead of coming home, she chose to stay in Philadelphia with Hugh's family."

"Nothing wrong with that," Chelsea said.

Arthur took this opportunity to interject a diplomatic observation. "From what I understand, she was a great supporter of Reverend Conway in founding Temple College. It's an admirable idea and gaining more support each year, a rare opportunity for working men to pursue a free education even if they have a family to support."

"Oh, she's done good work, no doubt of that," Mr. Delafield conceded. "We only wish she could have gone about it a bit more conventionally. Always stirring up the old pot."

"Sometimes the old pot needs stirring up," Chelsea grumbled, turning back to the window. "Otherwise it just sits there and coagulates."

Mr. Delafield smiled at Arthur. "Chelsea Anne always adored her aunt, so you can imagine how she reacted when she received Geraldine's letter inviting her to come to America to finish her education."

Chelsea looked back at her father, her tone subdued. "It was a unique opportunity."

"Yes, and now it's all done with." Mr. Delafield patted Chelsea's gloved hand. "Your mother and I are happy to have you home again and safe, my dear."

Chelsea's tremulous smile was late in coming and not too convincing. "And I'm happy to be home again, too, Papa."

Happy? Even in the muted light, Arthur saw that "happy" did not describe the truth he saw in Chelsea's eyes as she turned away to resume her pensive study of the brick pavements that passed outside the carriage window. No, Chelsea was not in the least bit happy to be home.

# 13

*Mrs. Delafield was an attractive,* dimpled woman with lively eyes and hair the color of star-dusted night. She was younger than her husband or perhaps it was just that Arthur thought she behaved much younger than the stiff and proper gentleman she had married. While Mr. Delafield clearly perceived himself to be king of his castle, his bustling little wife commenced to run verbal circles around him soon after they deposited Chelsea's trunks and baggage inside the front door of their brick townhouse on Montague Street.

"Perhaps you'd care for a spot of tea, Mr. Delafield?" she inquired, taking his coat.

He swept off his derby, revealing a bald pate fringed about the ears and nape with gray. "No, thank you, Mrs. Delafield."

"But it's already half past the hour. You never miss your tea, Mr. Delafield."

He tugged at his waistcoat and smoothed his moustache. "Yes, but I don't seem to be in a tea sort of mood today."

"As you say, Mr. Delafield. Do come along, Chelsea Anne, we have got so much to talk about."

As Chelsea and Mrs. Delafield bustled down a corridor, her husband led Arthur into a heavily draped parlor cluttered with ponderous furniture, chintz tidies, potted plants, flowered throw rugs, and a hodgepodge of generally useless bric-a-brac.

Mr. Delafield added some wood to the fire and stoked glowing embers to life as Arthur strolled over to a small cottage piano to examine a collection of oval-framed family photographic portraits. Except for the fact that each of the children grew several inches from one year to the next, they were almost identical: one top-hatted, rather dazed patriarch surrounded by his serene wife and a trio of ebony-locked female offspring.

Mr. Delafield soon appeared by Arthur's side, polishing his spectacles with a handkerchief. "Mrs. Delafield has always been a great one for family photographs."

"I can see why, Mr. Delafield. You have three very lovely daughters."

"Oh, thank you. Our eldest, Cornelia, is living in Leicester now with her husband and three boys. Married into wool, you know. Lucky thing, that. Crochets like the wind. Constance, on the other hand, married a paperhanger. I must say, though, the chap does quite well at his trade."

With a serving tray in hand, Mrs. Delafield blew into the room like a fresh spring breeze. Chelsea came close on her heels, pulling the doors closed behind them.

"Who does quite well at his trade?" Mrs. Delafield inquired as Chelsea produced an immaculate white linen tablecloth and draped it over a coffee table.

"I was just speaking of Constance's husband," Mr. Delafield said, settling his spectacles back onto his nose.

"Oh, yes. A paperhanger. They live in Hampstead. Quite delightful if you like leaves." As Mrs. Delafield set her serving tray on the table, Arthur noted a gleaming silver teapot, a sugar bowl, a creamer, silverware, bone china cups and saucers, and a serving plate with thin sandwiches and biscuits.

Chelsea chose a chair by the fireplace. “Oh, Papa, surely you’re not dragging Mr. Pierce through all those old family photographs.”

“Not dragging at all,” Mr. Delafield said, pointing to a frame on the far end of the piano. “This one was taken in ’79, I believe.”

As Arthur bent to get a better look, he couldn’t suppress a grin. Except for the short white muslin dress, the enormous bow attached to the back of her head, and the childish patent leather shoes, little Chelsea didn’t appear much different than she did today. Somber and bespectacled, she stood next to one of her adolescent sisters looking as if she were cogitating upon a particularly knotty mathematical problem.

Mrs. Delafield trilled from across the room. “Did you say one lump or two, Mr. Delafield?”

Apparently forgetting that he had requested neither, her husband huffed. “One, Mrs. Delafield, one. When in thirty years of marriage has it ever been two?”

“One, then, just as you say, Mr. Delafield.”

Chelsea’s father clasped his hands behind his back and returned his attention to Arthur. “Now, what was I saying?”

“You were saying that the portrait was taken in ’79.” Behind them, amidst the delicate tinkling of silverware and china, Arthur swore he heard two distinct wet plops before Mrs. Delafield approached. “Your tea, Mr. Delafield. Would you care for a biscuit?”

He accepted the fragile teacup and saucer. “No, thank you.”

His wife glanced at the portrait Arthur had been examining. “Oh, no, Mr. Delafield, that one was taken in ’78, don’t you recall?”

“What? ’78, you say? Are you certain, Mrs. Delafield?”

“Oh, yes, quite certain. That was the year we misplaced Chelsea Anne at the British Museum.”

“Oh yes, quite right.” Mr. Delafield arched a bushy eyebrow at Arthur. “We were ready to notify the metropolitan police.”

"Misplaced her at the British Museum?" Arthur threw Chelsea a questioning look.

In response, she shot to her feet. "I hardly think Mr. Pierce is interested—"

"She gave us quite a fright that time," Mrs. Delafield said with a titter. "Tea, Mr. Pierce?"

"Yes, thank you."

Mrs. Delafield beamed as she puttered back over to her tea service and proceeded to pour a splash of milk into a cup. "It was a lovely day in May, as I recall. We had just finished touring the—"

Chelsea piped up in a shrill tone. "Mother, really! I don't think—"

"—King's Library and the ancient Egypt collection and had moved onto the Assyrian galleries, or was it the Greek antiquities, Mr. Delafield?"

"I believe it was the Roman antiquities," he replied, settling onto a medallion back sofa by the hearth and sipping from his cup.

"Oh, yes, quite right. One lump or two, Mr. Pierce?"

"One, thank you." Arthur threw Chelsea a teasing wink. She promptly sent him a nonverbal dagger in response.

He looked back just in time to see Mrs. Delafield drop a sugar cube into his cup. "As I recall, Cornelia and Constance had gotten into some sort of ridiculous argument over the Theban tomb paintings," she said. "It was just as we got it all straightened out that we realized Chelsea Anne had vanished completely."

"Mother! This is hardly the sort of—"

"None of us could quite remember if we had last seen her in the ancient Egypt collection or the Assyrian galleries, so we retraced our steps throughout the entire museum." Mrs. Delafield gave Arthur his tea. "She was nowhere to be found, not even in the old manuscript saloon. By then, we were frantic, envisioning our defenseless daughter kidnapped by ruthless ne'er-do-wells, you know. The curator and museum guards were in a frightful state, too."

"Oh, Gawwd," Chelsea groaned from somewhere behind them.

"Just a moment, dear. I'm not finished. Where was I, Mr. Pierce?"

"The curator was frantic," Arthur supplied.

"Oh, yes. Well, we did find her, or rather one of the guards found her, fallen asleep beneath a table in the ancient Egypt collection. She wanted to be alone with the stone, you see."

"The stone?" Arthur asked, testing his tea. Sweet and smooth as ambrosia going down. Darjeeling, he guessed.

"The Rosetta Stone," Mrs. Delafield clarified. "It seemed that viewing it in the display case wasn't sufficient. She had to be alone with it to be sure it was genuine."

"Genuine?" Arthur peered over his cup at Chelsea. Her arms were folded rigidly across her chest, her cheeks flamed like two firebugs.

"Yes," Mrs. Delafield said, "she claimed that she couldn't tell how old it really was unless she could talk to it alone or some such thing."

"That wasn't it at all, Mother. I didn't say I wanted to talk to it, I said I wanted to touch it."

Mrs. Delafield blinked at her daughter. "Oh, yes, you're quite right, my dear." She turned back to Arthur. "She wanted to touch it, that was the thing."

"And did she get to?" Arthur asked.

"Why, I don't quite recall." Mrs. Delafield looked to Chelsea again, inquiring. "Did you ever get to touch it, dear?"

"No," Chelsea replied from between clenched teeth. "The display case was locked."

"No," Mrs. Delafield translated, turning back to Arthur and flashing a smile that could have melted butter. "The display case was locked. Amusing little story, though, isn't it?"

*Amusing*. Tea time was a nightmare. Dinner was worse. As her mother commenced to dredge up every humiliating detail of her childhood, from her catechism to the dormouse she had kept as a pet, Chelsea had slunk down lower and lower in her dining room chair. Arthur had been no help whatsoever. He had encouraged her mother every step of the way. Each time his bedeviling gaze had turned back to Chelsea, she had wished for nothing more than to disappear in a pop and curl of smoke.

Now, it was all she could do to try to put the evening's tribulations from her mind as she peeked out the casement window of her bedroom. Except for the hazy glow of a street lamp, the neighborhood below was darkening and quiet, bathed in swirls of gray city fog. Her father was already out of sight, on his way to deliver her telegram at the post office. Her mother was in the kitchen, overseeing their new maid as she cleaned up after dinner. Chelsea had excused herself on the pretense of unpacking, and Arthur, she knew, had gone to his room to freshen up before returning downstairs to commence an obligatory chess match with her father. It was now or never.

Dropping the curtain, Chelsea scooted from her room and hurried down the carpeted hallway to Arthur's door. Rapping twice, she heard a muffled response from within to enter. She slipped inside and closed the door behind her. The room was as dimly lit as the corridor, one gas lamp set low.

Arthur's back was to her as he rummaged through his open suitcase on the four-poster bed. He glanced over his shoulder. "Is your father waiting for me?"

"No. He's gone out, but he'll be back momentarily. I just wanted to be sure your accommodations are satisfactory, and . . ."

Chelsea knew she was blathering. Thanks to her overtalkative mother, her stomach was in knots and she had a headache. She was strung tighter than an Irish harp.

"And?" He turned back to rifling the contents of his suitcase. Socks, trousers, and shirts were piling up on the bed.

"And to let you know I dashed off a quick telegram to Professor Doyle," she finished. "I told him we would drop round at eleven in the morning if that's acceptable."

"Eleven o'clock sounds fine."

"Good."

Unsure of what to say next, Chelsea cast a quick glance about the room. The shuttered casement window, the colorful quilted spread on the bed, the armoire, the writing table where Cornelia had bent over her studies for so many years. This room was not much different from her own. All very familiar. Like the rest of this house, it was home. She should have felt comfortable here, but she didn't. Arthur's presence caused her great discomfort indeed.

"I'm sorry about Mother," Chelsea blurted. "She has a tendency to monopolize the conversation. Perhaps I should have warned you."

Arthur gave a soft laugh, then turned, clutching something in one hand. "Nonsense. I like your mother, Chelsea. And your father, too, for that matter."

"Well, I'm sure all those old stories were—"

"Charming," he finished. "I enjoyed hearing about your childhood. It sounds like it was very nice and normal." He paused, then added with a gentle smile, "Different from my own."

Chelsea wondered for the first time what his childhood had been like. He would have been a precocious little boy. And mischievous? Oh, yes, she thought, recalling the traces of boyish roguery that characterized the tilt of his lips whenever he teased her. No doubt Arthur had been quite a little gremlin in his time.

"You managed to get into a lot of trouble, didn't you?" Arthur asked lightly, scattering her pensive mood.

Chelsea wrinkled her nose. "Not as much as it seems when one hears it all dredged up at once."

"We've all got skeletons in our closets, Chelsea. My sister could fill you in on a few childhood stories of mine that would curl your hair."

"I have no doubt that she could."

"I think you would like my sister if you met her. She's a lot like your mother. Refreshingly candid. Not afraid to speak her mind."

"I'm sure I would like her very much," Chelsea said, "but somehow I doubt that I'll ever have the chance to find out."

At her words, something in his eyes seemed to cloud over. "No, I suppose not."

There was an infinite stretch of uncomfortable silence. Chelsea knew that propriety dictated she leave right this moment, yet her feet seemed in no hurry to comply. With great effort, she dragged her attention away from his face to see that he held a familiar flannel-wrapped parcel.

"The parchment," she said.

"What?" Arthur looked down as if he'd forgotten. "Oh, yes. I was thinking about our visit to Professor Doyle before you knocked." Freeing it from its protective wrapping, he took it to Cornelia's writing desk and laid the frame face-down upon its surface. From a pocket in his trousers, he extracted a jackknife and flipped it open.

Chelsea darted to his side. "What are you doing?"

"I'm removing the parchment." Applying the tip of his knife to the inner edges of the frame, he began to pry the backing loose.

"But it's very fragile." She spoke in a stringently controlled voice even as her breath jammed in her throat. "It should be kept under glass."

"There are three people who have read these words and understand their significance," he explained calmly. "You, me, and Max Hamilton. I don't see any reason to add to that list, do you?"

His question remained unacknowledged as he turned the frame over and slid the brittle paper out from beneath its protective glass. It was all Chelsea could do to keep from batting his hands away. Still, her nagging premonition of disaster was nothing compared to the inner alarms that screamed murder when he laid the fragile parchment on top of the glass and poised the cutting edge of his blade directly over it.

"Noooo!" Her hand shot out to lock upon his wrist. Her panicked eyes riveted with his, and time came to a screeching halt.

She tried to speak, to draw in another breath, but fresh air seemed in short supply. What was even more odd was that her concern for the parchment, so urgent only seconds before, suddenly fled.

Arthur had held her gloved hand the night they'd danced aboard ship, but Chelsea had never actually touched him like this, flesh to flesh. She was acutely aware of the feel of him, the unexpected thickness of his wrist, the wisps of fair hair beneath her fingertips, the texture of his skin, so warm yet so different from her own. She felt it all, that and more.

For a fleeting second, those tactile sensations mixed with nameless impressions of Arthur then and now; Arthur as a boy and as a man. They swirled and collided and bounced off one another as they raced back and forth along nerve endings from her fingers to her brain.

Just as quickly, the stunning rush of images and sensations faded. The past merged back into the present; the present back into the physical. So male, she thought, her senses still reeling from the unexpected onslaught. So young and vital. Such strength.

"Chelsea?"

"What . . . what are you doing?" she managed, finally remembering what all of this was supposed to be about.

"Exactly what it looks like."

"But why?"

"Don't you trust me?"

"What?" Chelsea was still too shaken by the intensity of her own reaction to pay much attention to what he was saying.

He moved closer then, his free hand rising to caress her chin. "Don't you trust me, Miss Delafield?"

Oh God, he was going to kiss her.

The flickering lamp gave off not nearly enough light to interpret his strange expression. His eyes. She needed to see into his eyes because that was where his playful spirit danced, but no playful spirit lighted their depths now. Was he serious or was he baiting her yet again? She didn't think she could stand it if he was.

"I . . . don't understand the . . . question," she whispered.

"I don't understand the attraction," he whispered back.

How often had she wondered what his kiss would be like?

It was heaven-sent, she thought, purely heaven-sent. Light and gentle and wickedly tantalizing all at once. His warm and compelling lips brushed over hers, once, twice, just touching.

Chelsea closed her eyes and imagined that she felt his heartbeat through the touch of his fingertips as they feathered very slowly down the line of her jaw to her neck to rest on her shoulder. She lost herself in a whirling carousel of light. Spark. Magic.

Then it was over.

He pulled back.

Chelsea's eyelids flickered open as if awakening from a disorienting dream. For a second that was how she felt; as if she had forgotten where she was, lost all track of what she was doing.

He watched her. Not moving, not speaking, not anything. Chelsea could read nothing in his uncharacteristically shuttered gaze. Nothing. Her pounding heart death plunged to her stomach. Not at all a comforting feeling.

"I'm sorry," he said. His hand slipped from her shoulder, down her arm to her elbow, then, after lingering for a second longer than necessary, fell away to his side.

Suddenly realizing that she still clamped his wrist tight enough to shut off life-giving circulation, Chelsea released him and stepped back. "Sor—sorry?"

"I asked you if you trusted me, then I took advantage of you. I don't know why I did that."

"I—I don't feel taken ad—advantage of." Chelsea swallowed hard before turning away. She had to get hold of her emotions. She was trembling and stuttering like an idiot. "I can take ca—care of myself," she said.

"Oh, I know you can. I didn't mean—I mean, it was just a kiss. Miles probably kissed you lots of times, right?"

Just a kiss. Chelsea squeezed her eyes shut and bent her

head. She could not stop trembling, confound it. "Oh, ye-yes. Of course. Con—constantly."

"Constantly?"

"Quite, um, often, I mean."

He sounded doubtful. "In between backgammon games?"

Chelsea drew in a breath and let it out in slow increments before replying. "Well, it was rather difficult to do so during a game, of course."

"Maybe, but I can't help thinking that if I were him, I would have found a way."

He spoke the obvious truth. Unlike poor Miles, no woman of Arthur's would remain unkissed for long. It was no wonder that Julia had returned from their clandestine, late-night meetings so starry-eyed and flushed. Chelsea had suspected then that much more than just kissing had gone on between the two of them and now she was sure of it.

Of course it was just a kiss. To him.

"Perhaps it would be best if we just forget it happened," he said after an interminable moment. His words were tentative, testing. Swellheaded male that he was, Chelsea thought he most likely expected her to dissolve into a quivering mass of sniffles and hiccoughs.

"Yes," she managed through clenched teeth. Her stomach felt as if it were chock-full of plum pits, but sniffles, she decided, were most definitely out of the question.

"Good," he said with an unmistakable note of relief.

Chelsea gathered her wits, then raised her head and forced herself to face him. "You were about to destroy the parchment."

"I was about to *cut* the parchment," he said, correcting her.

"It amounts to the same thing. Why?"

"As I said, only three people have read it and understand its possible significance. I have no desire to widen the circle."

"But you can't be concerned about Professor Doyle?"

"I understand that he'll need to see the document in order to authenticate it, but he doesn't need to have knowledge of the entire text. The most valuable clue to Excalibur's whereabouts is in those last lines. I propose to remove them before Professor Doyle sees the parchment."

"But he's entirely trustworthy," Chelsea protested, "I would stake my life on it!"

"I don't doubt it," Arthur said as if calming a pouting child, "but there are people who would do just about anything to get their hands on this thing. Why drag the good professor into it?"

Chelsea opened her mouth to argue, then stopped. Although she didn't agree with keeping Professor Doyle in the dark, she could understand his reasons for wanting to keep their quest a secret for now. If news were to get out that Excalibur might exist, it would set off an explosion of Fleet Street publicity. Arthur and his parchment would not only become the objects of public curiosity, they would become perfect targets for other would-be treasure-seekers.

"All right," she said, still not liking the idea but not able to think up another workable solution. "Do it if you must."

"It's for the best." He seemed to search her face for agreement that wasn't there before giving up and turning back to his dreadful task.

If Chelsea needed any more proof that their kiss had meant nothing to him, she had it now. Her knees had just barely ceased knocking together, yet his hand was as steady as that of a well-trained surgeon. Making a neat lateral cut straight across the paper, he sliced the bottom half off with one clean stroke.

Chelsea expected to feel as if she had been wounded herself, but the parchment had withstood the assault better than anticipated. Since the cutting edge of Arthur's knife was in good condition, only one brittle corner had broken off the top of the severed half. The monk's pen strokes were not marred.

She raised her eyes to meet Arthur's waiting gaze. He had just coldbloodedly destroyed the integrity of a historically significant document, and she, contrary to her earlier anxiety, could now feel nothing more about it. She wondered instead how many pairs of female lips he had sampled in the past. Ten? Twenty? She frowned. Thirty?

Arthur raised a cautious eyebrow. "Do you have a place we can keep this?"

More than thirty, Chelsea thought. She didn't know how she knew, she just knew. It was as good as written all over that maddeningly sensual mouth.

"Chelsea?"

"What?"

"Is there somewhere to keep this bottom half until tomorrow?"

Furious with herself for being such a ninny, Chelsea yanked open the top drawer of Cornelia's desk to pull out a King James Bible. Just a kiss. One of dozens! Hundreds!

Flipping it open to Ecclesiastes, she thrust the book toward him sharply. "If it can't be under glass, the next best thing would be to keep it pressed between pages."

Chelsea knew that he was perceptive enough to realize she was annoyed. He was also enough of a dense-headed male to assume it was the mere destruction of the parchment that nettled her. Just a kiss indeed.

Picking up the severed bottom of the parchment between two fingers, he laid it flat atop chapter eight, then looked back up at her again, waiting. Well? his eyes seemed to ask, Forgive me?

You profligate cad, Chelsea thought.

In answer, Arthur's expert mouth tipped into a crooked grin. Chelsea knew that grin. He was apparently unable to resist badgering her even though it had to be plain from her expression that it could prove suicidal.

"Are you sure you wouldn't like to touch it or be alone with it for a few minutes before we put it away?"

The Rosetta Stone. Blast her mother's incessant chatter. Just as it had been with the Stone all those years ago, Chelsea had felt an immediate and undeniable attraction to the Glastonbury parchment. Even through its glass frame, she had felt the parchment's age, its authenticity, its urgency; all of that despite her rational reservations concerning the possibility of Excalibur's actual existence.

Now, unbound from its protective barrier, part of the parchment lay only inches from her tingling fingertips, exercising an almost irresistible pull upon her senses, but she could not surrender to it. Not in front of Arthur; not in front of anyone.

She slapped the Bible closed, cutting off the parchment's seductive vibrations. Stuffing it back into its drawer, she slammed that closed, too. "I must go. Father will be back soon."

Arthur's bantering tone softened, turned almost apologetic. "Ah, come on, Chelsea. Don't be angry. I was just trying to get you to smile. It's not the end of the world."

Despite herself, Chelsea's anger began to ebb. He was speaking of the parchment, of course. It wasn't his fault that he was all wrong for her, that she had lost all sound judgment and become infatuated with him. He had no way of knowing that one simple kiss would practically unravel her stockings, that getting off the blasted boat hadn't done one thing to cure her of him.

Straightening her skirt, Chelsea moved briskly for the door. "I must go."

"Chelsea, wait."

But she didn't wait, didn't dare even look around as she passed through the open portal into the hall. "I'll see you in the morning."

# 14

*Located above an apothecary shop* near the British Museum, Professor Frederick Doyle's quarters were perfectly suited to a confirmed bibliophile: a cozy fireplace, an overstuffed sofa, cushy armchairs, fat ottomans, jostling-full bookshelves, and an expansive desk cluttered with scholarly journals.

"Professor Doyle, I'd like you to meet Mr. Arthur Pierce, the colleague from Temple College I mentioned in my telegram," Chelsea said.

Swathed in a brown serge waistcoat and shirtsleeves, the septuagenarian's egg-shaped figure perched upon two bird-like legs. His feet were encased in worn leather slippers.

"Oh, yes, Mr. Pierce." Although he stood a head shorter than Arthur, the older man managed to peer down through his spectacles. "Graduated from Geraldine Delafield's Temple College in the States, did you? What was it you went in for?"

"Mathematics," Arthur replied, opting for the first of many possibilities that came to mind.

"Teaching?"

"I hope to, sir. I've been offered a professorial apprenticeship for the fall term."

"You have?" Chelsea sounded dumbfounded.

Despite a stab of annoyance, Arthur resisted an urge to gift her with a smug I-told-you-so look. Make something of himself indeed. It wasn't as if he were completely devoid of potential. By her astonished tone, one would think she'd expected him to remain a theater stagehand for the rest of his life.

Doyle nodded his bald head in approval. "Very good. I'm sure you'll find teaching a most rewarding profession."

"I'm sure I will."

"And Miss Chelsea." Making use of a malacca walking cane, the professor shuffled toward his desk. "Your father tells me you will be applying for your teaching certification very soon."

Chelsea wore a pine green skirt, a matching jacket, and a small hat trimmed in light green silk, cool colors that matched the aloof manner she had adopted toward Arthur since the previous evening. At the professor's comment, however, her cheeks visibly colored. "Oh, um, of course. Very soon."

"Do have a seat, the both of you." The professor gestured as he snail-stepped around the corner of his desk.

Chelsea crossed the room to help. "Oh, dear, your gout is acting up again, isn't it?"

Arthur's gaze immediately dropped to follow the alluring movement of her hips from behind. He wondered if she had any idea what a boon that little swish-swish was for his lately repressed sexual drive.

"Frightful, my dear." The professor waved her off as he sank into a swivel chair. "The doctor ordered me down to Bath two weeks past. Didn't do a thing to help. All I received was a new batch of wrinkles from rotting about in the springs."

"Sorry to hear it." Chelsea turned to Arthur, hands on hips. "Mr. Pierce, are you going to just stand there all day?"

Arthur jerked his gaze back up where it belonged, chastising himself for taking notice of her feminine accoutrements. There had been a time when he had firmly believed Chelsea Delafield had no feminine accoutrements. Ah, for the good old days.

Chelsea gestured for him to join them, then chose a chair facing the desk. "We don't want to keep you from your work, professor. Perhaps we should get down to business."

"So, what is it you need?" the professor asked as Arthur took a chair next to Chelsea. "Your telegram was most cryptic."

"A necessary precaution. Mr. Pierce has come into possession of a document that may have great historical significance."

Arthur unbuckled his satchel and produced the framed top half of the parchment. "I received it through a testamentary bequest."

"Only part of one page?" the professor asked suspiciously.

"Do you need more in order to authenticate it?"

"No, but I might inquire as to what has become of the missing portion."

"I have it in a safe place."

"This wouldn't be connected with a set of religious volumes that recently turned up at the British Museum, would it?"

"That I wouldn't know."

"Hmmmm, I see." Doyle cast a doubtful look at Chelsea.

"He's telling the truth, professor, but because of certain circumstances, we've agreed that it would be best to keep this whole affair quiet for the moment. I've not even informed my father of the particulars, and it's imperative that we can rely on your discretion in the matter."

"Hmmmmm. Very well." Doyle removed the parchment from its frame. He ran the pad of one gnarled forefinger over the brittle surface of the paper, then tested a few ink strokes with his thumbnail before holding the sheet up to the sunlight that filtered through lacy summer curtains behind him.

"Hmmm, yes," he muttered before returning it to his desk. "Miss Chelsea, would you be so kind as to fetch me the fourth volume on the shelf to your left? The one on the Benedictines."

She was up before he finished his request, quickly retrieving the requested reference book. Despite her collected demeanor, Arthur could sense barely suppressed excitement. She was more anxious over this thing than Arthur was, and she didn't even have five thousand pounds riding on the outcome of Doyle's pronouncement.

Withdrawing a magnifying glass from a drawer, the professor emeritus bent to examine the document for a few more moments before setting it aside and ending the suspense. "It is my considered opinion that this was composed by a moderately well-educated Benedictine monk in the autumn of 1539."

"Oh!" Chelsea lost all semblance of composure as she shot forward in her seat. "1539? How can you be sure?"

Doyle gave her a mildly reproving look. "As you know, Glastonbury Abbey was dissolved in the autumn of 1539."

"Oh, yes. Yes, of course." Blushing, Chelsea adjusted her hat and tried without great success to relax back into her chair.

Doyle turned his attention to Arthur. "The last abbot of Glastonbury, Richard Whiting, has gone down in history for attempting to resist the dissolution of his abbey. He was later accused of stealing from his own church, charges most historians assume were fabricated in order to silence him."

"What happened?" Arthur asked.

"He was hung and quartered on a hill known as the Tor near Glastonbury. His head was fixed upon the abbey's gate as a warning to anyone else who might have contemplated taking a stand against the king."

Arthur had to resist an urge to adjust his collar. "Jeez, what a way to go."

"Yes, quite untidy."

Chelsea spoke up. "But this parchment indicates the

charges may have been justified. Perhaps the abbot himself ordered that certain relics be smuggled to safety before they could be destroyed or impounded for the royal treasury."

The professor raised a finger. "Precisely. If what this monk wrote is true, it will make a most interesting historical footnote."

Arthur's heart sank. "Wait a minute. What do you mean, 'if' what this monk wrote is true? You said the parchment is authentic."

"Oh, I have no doubt that the parchment is authentic. It's the authenticity of the relics we must question."

Arthur knew that the disappointment he felt was irrational. He had taken up Sidney's fanciful quest fully expecting it to be a hoax. All he had to do was follow the trail of clues to their logical end in order to collect his one thousand pounds, sword or no sword.

He glanced over at Chelsea to see that she sat straight as a pin. Her tension was palpable, and he suddenly felt like a lout for neglecting to mention that his own reasons for setting out on this quest were primarily financial.

"Please explain, professor," she said anxiously.

"Well, as you may know, the larger monasteries earned a good portion of their income from the donations of travelers who came from all over Britain to make pilgrimages that would cure them of their ills and cleanse them of their sins."

"Like in Chaucer's *Canterbury Tales*," Arthur said.

"Precisely. Due to the shrine of St. Thomas Becket, Christ Church in Canterbury was a premier attraction. They made out quite well, so you can see why the monasteries were in competition to attract visitors. Their economic well-being depended upon the collection and exhibition of holy relics."

"What was Glastonbury's claim to fame?" Arthur asked.

"The tomb of King Arthur and Queen Guinevere, of course."

Arthur was surprised. Before becoming involved with Sidney's crazy quest, he had always assumed King Arthur and his Round Table were the stuff of fairy tales. Even now, to think that the man had walked upon the earth was hard to fathom. "I never realized—I mean, did they really find King Arthur's body?"

"So they claimed. The remains, along with a leaden cross identifying the body, were unearthed in the monks' graveyard in 1191, however many historians believe the find was staged in order to enhance the prestige of the abbey."

"Well, I can understand if the bones are quantitatively unidentifiable," Arthur said, now unwilling to let all this go with a shrug, "but isn't there some way to determine if the cross they found is authentic sixth century?"

"The tomb itself disappeared after the Dissolution, and, as for the cross, it mysteriously vanished sometime in the last century. As it stands now, we may speculate all we wish, but, without the remains or the cross, we can never know the truth."

Maybe not, Arthur thought. But what if the remains were real, and what if the monks had found more than just a leaden cross buried with the dead king?

"At any rate, the relics listed here by your monk are quite extraordinary," the professor continued. "I'm speaking specifically of the alleged sword of King Arthur, of course."

"Excalibur," Chelsea murmured.

The professor flipped through his reference book until he found what he was looking for. "Here it is. A fourteenth-century list of the relics at Glastonbury Abbey. It's general in nature, but see for yourself." Turning the book around, he pushed it back across the desk.

Both Arthur and Chelsea scanned the page. Arthur looked up first. "Sorry, I still don't understand."

"Even if you read onto the next page, you will find no mention of a sword named Caliburn."

"So?"

"Not only is it not mentioned here, to my knowledge, it's never been mentioned anywhere. It's highly unlikely that such a spectacular find would go unrecorded. Imagine the swarms of eager pilgrims it would have attracted."

The man had a valid point; nevertheless, Arthur had to struggle to remain objective. No doubt about it. Logical or not, he wanted the sword to be real. When had that happened? "All right," he said, piecing all of this together. "Correct me if I'm wrong, professor, but a lot of church records were lost after the Dissolution, weren't they?"

"Yes," Chelsea joined in eagerly. "In fact, most monastic books and records were deliberately destroyed because they were considered offensive to the Church of England."

"True," the professor allowed. "What you need is an expert on Glastonbury Abbey. For that, you should contact a friend of mine who lives in Glastonbury. Not only is he an avid historian, he's spent a lifetime studying the Arthurian folklore that abounds in Somerset. If such a sword was ever reputed to have existed, Jeremy Hunnicutt will know about it."

"He sounds like exactly the man I need to talk to," Arthur said, willing himself to remain calm. He wondered if Chelsea's harebrained historical enthusiasm was contagious or if somewhere along the way he'd simply gone soft in the head.

The professor produced a sheet of notepaper and dipped a pen into ink. "If you like, I'll write a letter of introduction."

"That's very kind of you, sir. I appreciate your going to the trouble."

"No trouble at all. I'm sure Jeremy will be most eager to have a firsthand look at your parchment."

As the professor composed his message, Arthur replaced the parchment in his satchel and looked at Chelsea. "Maybe I'll be able to catch a train this afternoon, what do you think?"

"Well, I . . . I don't know," she stammered softly. "Perhaps you can telephone from the post office to find out."

The bewildered expression on her face made Arthur want to snatch his words back. For the second time this morning, he felt like an insensitive lout. She had helped him come all this way, and now she thought he couldn't wait to leave her behind.

He *did* intend to leave her behind, but not for any reason she would believe. Kissing her had been one of the stupidest things he'd done yet. Such an innocent kiss should not have stirred him, but it had, and despite his misgivings, he knew that if he were left alone with her, he would do it all over again.

The professor sealed the letter of introduction and gave it to Arthur. Grasping his cane, he pushed up from his seat. "Good luck, Mr. Pierce. I hope you find what you're looking for."

"I hope so, too. Thank you, sir."

As they exchanged farewells and Arthur opened the door to let Chelsea pass into the hallway, he didn't miss the grim set of her mouth. Later, as they emerged on the busy street, he had to remind himself that it was for the best that they get on with their own lives. As for the fact that she was clearly unhappy to be home and pursuing a career she didn't want, well, that was simply none of his concern. She was capable of handling her own troubles. After all, with a letter of introduction in hand and a clear-cut destination, Arthur now had his own fish to fry.

He was going to Glastonbury.

Arthur Pierce was going to take his parchment and walk out of her life and there wasn't a blasted thing she could think of to do about it.

Brandishing her mother's gardening shears, Chelsea clipped the stem of a budding tea rose and added it to a growing collection in the basket she carried looped over one arm. Normally, she didn't care much for gardening, but today she found the privacy afforded behind the rose arbor gratifying. She needed the quiet, the peace, the soothing fragrances of wisteria and roses. She also needed something to keep her idle fingers busy and her itching feet planted in one place. At this very moment, Arthur was in Cornelia's room packing his belongings to catch a four-fifteen train out of Paddington Station.

She snipped off the head of a dying blossom and watched it hurtle to the ground. The sight reminded her of Arthur's offhand comment regarding the bloom soon wearing off a woman's rose. Soon was right. He had kissed her just last night, and already it was clear that he couldn't get away from her quickly enough.

Men, she thought, snipping off another dying bloom. She hated them. All of them. Well, perhaps she could allow one exception for her father and one exception for Professor Doyle, who was too old and crippled to wreak havoc with a woman's emotions and then expect to dart off to Paddington Station.

Hate them, hate them, hate them, she thought savagely, beheading one blossoming pink rose after another. What was the point of waiting for the poor things to wither and die? Their days were numbered. Better to get it all over with quickly and painlessly. As for Chelsea, she would remain a spinster for life and rejoice in the fact.

She held the shears aloft and stared at the bright blooms scattered at her feet. Only then did it dawn upon her that she had just sheared one whole section of her mother's prize rose arbor quite bald. Oh, blast.

"Chelsea?"

Despite her hatred of the male gender, and this male in particular, her heart froze then began to flutter at the sound of his voice calling from the house.

"Chelsea? Are you out here?"

Stop it, she commanded her frantic heart, but it paid no heed as she stooped to toss roseheads pell-mell into her basket. "I'm here!" she called out, jumping back to her feet. She tried her best to appear composed by the time he rounded the corner of the rose trellis. Her gaze immediately riveted upon his suitcase.

"I just wanted to say good-bye."

He had changed into a fresh suit and tie; his derby was set back at an angle on his head. The afternoon light played up the gold that streaked through the autumn russet of his hair.

One leather satchel and one battered suitcase, and he was apparently prepared to leave her without a trace of regret.

She tried to sound casual. "You needn't be in such a rush. Mother would be happy to have you stay for dinner, and you would be able to get a fresh start for Glastonbury in the morning."

"I know," he said, the gentle understanding in his eyes reflecting back the fruitlessness of her facade, "but there's no real reason to wait . . . is there?"

Chelsea tried to distract herself by transferring her flower basket from one arm to the other. "No, I suppose not."

"I want to thank you for everything."

"It was nothing."

His slow smile was self-deprecating, a rare expression for him, and it nearly did her in. "No, really, Chelsea, you've been more help than I deserve, and I want you to know that I appreciate it. As soon as this sword thing is done and my uncle's will is straightened out, I'll be back to reimburse you for my ocean passage. Count on it."

"Is that all you'll be back for, Mr. Pierce?" she asked, her voice trembling on his name. Did he hear it? She couldn't tell.

He took a step toward her. "No, of course not. I wouldn't dream of going home without filling you in on all the details. After all, you're the one who pointed me in the right direction."

"Oh, I hardly think that." He would have found his own way to Glastonbury and they both knew it.

"Well, anyway, I couldn't have found a more charming cabinmate." His eyes kindled with old devilment.

Instead of being cheered, as he obviously intended, Chelsea had to fight a threat of tears. She was determined not to make a fool of herself, however, so she set down her flower basket and reached into the pocket of her skirt. "I have something for you."

She pulled out the wedding band he'd given to her in Philadelphia. A sunbeam caught and flashed gold in the palm of her hand as she offered it to him.

The playfulness in his eyes flickered out as he stared at it. "Why don't you just keep it?"

"It's yours."

He took it and shoved it into his coat pocket. "I can't imagine what I'll do with it. It's not like I'm planning on getting married anytime soon."

"Well, you never know."

He didn't answer. Instead, he studied her face, and Chelsea suddenly felt as transparent as window glass.

"Chelsea," he began, taking a deep breath.

"You should go. You'll miss your train."

After a moment of awkward silence, he nodded, then turned and started to walk away.

Chelsea squeezed her hands into fists as he took a few more steps, then slowed, then stopped, then swung around to face her. "Oh hell, why don't you just come with me?"

"What?"

"Come with me."

Chelsea's heart thumped. All it would take was one word from her. *Yes.* Her feet almost moved. Almost. Her heels rose off the ground for one indecisive second. *Yes!* a voice urged in her mind.

But she couldn't.

"I can't," she said numbly.

"Why not?"

Dropping his suitcase to the ground, Arthur suddenly had her by the shoulders, his fingers burning through the material of her blouse, his mesmerizing blue eyes threatening to make mincemeat of her newfound resolve. "Why not?" he repeated.

Why not? Oh, there were lots of why not's. The very idea of traveling alone with him was preposterous. They'd pulled it off aboard ship, but that had been more of a daring lark than an honest-to-goodness adventure. They couldn't hope to get away with it again, not here at home where Chelsea's parents would also suffer if she sullied her reputation. Four years ago, she'd promised them that she would pursue her teaching certification after returning from America. They didn't deserve to have the family name dragged through the mud for the sake of a fluttering heart and an ancient sword that might not even exist.

She didn't need to put her answer into words. He knew. They both knew. It was time to grow up. For Chelsea, anyway.

He blew out a sigh and let go of her. "Yeah, you're right. Stupid idea. Forget I even mentioned it."

"Stupid idea," she said, "but I won't forget."

His lips curved in a wistful smile. "Neither will I." Then he kissed her. It was just a mere touching of the lips, but it sent Chelsea's world spinning.

Drawing back, he muttered something unintelligible before gathering her up in his arms and kissing her again.

This was not supposed to be a gentle or innocent kiss; this was intended to be an entirely different kind of kiss. Chelsea knew what he wanted. The instant her lips parted, his tongue joined with hers, touching and probing, then retreating only to begin its scintillating dance all over again. Once, twice, a touch, a stroke, another, then another.

Her stomach did a pirouette. Her bones disintegrated to the marrow. Chelsea sagged against him, no longer able to tell up from down, down from up, but what did it matter? Nothing mattered except that he was leaving and she seemed to have no rational choice but to let him go.

When Arthur was finally able to command himself to pull away, his breathing came too quick and shallow, his blood pumped much too warm. When her eyelids fluttered open, he looked down into bottomless pools of aching violet and felt a knot of regret tighten in his gut. Why was it so difficult to leave her behind?

He released her abruptly and stepped back. "A memorable farewell."

"Most memorable," she said softly.

Turning away, Arthur retrieved the suitcase that only moments ago had taken little effort to carry. Oddly enough, as he strode past Mrs. Delafield's rose arbor and around the corner of Chelsea's childhood home toward Montague Street, it felt as if he were dragging along nothing less weighty than the *Salacia*'s starboard anchor. He was going to miss Chelsea Delafield.

It was the last thought he had before boarding the four-fifteen express out of Paddington Station.

# 15

*"Mr. Dark to see you, sir."*

Emory Blake looked up from his desk to see that his valet, Thackery, awaited a reply. Nondescript in appearance and disdainful in expression, Thackery's butlering skills were exemplary. In any other household, he would have advanced to the station of head manservant long ago. In Blake's household, however, it took a bit more than traditional butlering to rise to the esteemed rank of Man Friday.

"Show him in, Thackery."

"Yes, sir."

Thackery's immaculate shoes made no sound as he strode across the floral carpet and vanished through the open double doors. Moments later, Geoffrey Dark was sweeping those doors closed to gain privacy from unseen ears.

"You have it?" Blake closed an account book and pushed it to one side. He rubbed his hands together, then began cracking his knuckles, an exercise designed to distract him from the burgeoning swell of anticipation that might overwhelm him at any moment. That swell was both exquisite and painful, almost sexual in its intensity, an approaching climax that, in this case, was almost ten years in building. That was how long Blake had been searching for the sword.

"Not precisely, sir."

Not precisely? Blake stopped cracking his knuckles. Geoffrey remained still as a lizard. One blink. Two. That was all. Geoffrey's reptilian stare seemed even deader than usual. Blake suspected Geoffrey was experiencing a certain level of job frustration.

"I'm afraid there is a problem, sir."

"Oh?" Very carefully, Blake interlaced his long, restless fingers on the desk in front of him. Patience, he reminded himself. He shouldn't jump to conclusions. Still, it was not like Geoffrey to be so indirect.

"Circumstances have not been working to our advantage," Geoffrey said.

Blake's clasped fingers tightened. Frustration knotted in his chest. "You've lost him?"

"No, sir. We located him after he disembarked in Southampton. We followed him here to London."

"He's here, then."

"Mr. Beck is with him at Paddington Station. He's purchased a ticket to Glastonbury. They should be on their way now."

"Glastonbury?" Blake flexed his fingers. A minor setback, he told himself, only one in what seemed an ever lengthening chain ever since they had run into competition with that wily old sharper, Sidney Pierce.

But Pierce was finally in his grave, and Blake was more determined than ever to have the sword. Sooner or later. One way or another. "Well, of course. That makes perfect sense," he said to Geoffrey in a tightly controlled voice. "According to our sources, the parchment originated at Glastonbury Abbey."

"Yes, sir."

"Why haven't you been able to lay hands on it?"

"It's your concern for discretion, sir. Mr. Pierce has kept himself in public to such an extent that it's been impossible to get him alone. Also, he failed to check into a hotel last night, opting instead to stay with a family named Delafield in Bloomsbury. Slipping into a hotel room is one thing. Slipping into an occupied private residence is quite another thing entirely."

Blake grimaced and cursed what he believed to be phenomenal Pierce family luck. It couldn't possibly be intentional, could it? Determined not to succumb to his vexation, Blake focused on the brilliant greens and blues of a Chinese landscape painting across the room.

Patience. Ten years of patience. He could wait a few more days if it meant getting the blasted thing done without drawing undue attention to the sword's existence. "Yes, I see your point," he said. "You were correct not to take a chance. No matter how close we may be to success, employing reasonable discretion is preferable to risking police involvement."

"Yes, sir."

Blake met Geoffrey's bland stare. "But an opportunity will present itself, and you will be there to take advantage of it."

"Yes, sir. I left Mr. Beck with instructions to follow Mr. Pierce, but he is to wait until I arrive to take any action."

"Good. Then you should be on your way."

Geoffrey, however, made no move to leave. "There is one more detail I should mention."

"Yes?"

"Arthur Pierce and his lady friend, Miss Delafield, paid a visit to one retired Professor Frederick Doyle. From what I've been able to learn, he's a well-known expert on incunabula."

"Old books and manuscripts," Blake mused aloud. "No doubt they requested that the good professor take a look at the parchment. I wonder why?"

Geoffrey didn't answer.

"Well, it's of no matter," Blake said. "This could be just the break we need, especially if Mr. Pierce manages to slip through our fingers yet again."

"Yes, sir."

Blake pushed back from his desk and stood. "I want you to proceed to Glastonbury as planned. If we cannot lay our hands on the document soon, I may have to arrange for two emissaries to pay a call on Miss Delafield and Professor Doyle. A verbal summary of the parchment's contents may be all we need to determine the sword's whereabouts."

"Yes, sir."

As Geoffrey prepared to leave, Blake turned to the window behind his desk and observed grimly as a four-wheeled brougham passed on the street. "Three days, Geoffrey."

"Sir?"

"Master Duncan and I will be spending this weekend in the country. For Professor Doyle's sake as well as Miss Delafield's, I do hope Mr. Pierce can be persuaded to turn over the parchment, otherwise we may need to reconsider our tactics. I'm growing frightfully impatient."

If Blake was not mistaken, he detected a note of approval in Geoffrey's parting reply. "Yes, sir. Very good, sir."

As the sun began to dip into the west, the ever present blanket of fog that hung over London thickened. A light drizzle began to fall. On Montague Street, middle-aged couples bound for the Strand emerged from their townhouses to hail hansom cabs from the host of conveyances that clip-clopped along the street.

Safely tucked inside her childhood home, Chelsea felt about as festive and useful as a bug in a jar. She sat with her shoulders hunched, pushing a green pea around in circles on her dinner plate and half-listening as her mother tried to convince her father to allow a telephone in the house.

"Constance assures me that it's a wonderful convenience," she was saying.

"Convenience? Pah!" he snorted. "Ring-ring all day long. It's bad enough that I must listen to it at the office. Pointless chatter. A waste of time. If it's not worth writing down, it's not worth communicating."

"Then we might as well all fall silent right this moment, Mr. Delafield."

"Oh, that's not what I'm speaking about at all. Can a man not expect to have some peace and quiet in his own home?"

"Absolutely not. A man should never expect to have peace and quiet in his own home. You should know that better than anyone."

He gave a grudging chuckle. "Insolent woman. Difficult to recall why I was so eager to marry you in the first place."

"Precisely because of my insolence. I recall it vividly, Mr. Delafield. You positively adored my insolence."

There was a significant pause. "Indeed?"

"Indeed yes."

It took a second or two for Chelsea to realize that the room had fallen altogether too quiet. No scraping of silverware or tinkling of glass, only the steady tick-tick-tick of a cuckoo clock on the wall behind her. When she looked up, she saw that her parents had taken to gazing into one another's eyes from across the table. Why, it was as if they had completely forgotten their daughter's presence.

Her father raised an eyebrow at her mother. "Infallible memory you have, Mrs. Delafield."

Her mother arched an elegant brow right back at him. "That, too. You were enamored of my . . . infallible memory."

"Hmmmmm, yes."

Horrified, Chelsea jerked her eyes back down to her plate. This was almost as embarrassing as the time she'd gotten up during the night only to discover her father, clad in nothing but his nightshirt, tiptoeing from her mother's chamber. He had tried to pretend that he'd gotten lost on his way to the water closet, but, even at eleven, Chelsea had been skeptical of that.

It seemed forever until her father cleared his throat gruffly and resumed his meal. "I say, what were we speaking of, Mrs. Delafield?"

"I don't recall, Mr. Delafield. More peas, Chelsea Anne?"

"No, thank you." Giving up on her nonexistent appetite and eager to leave her parents to their mid-life frolicking,

Chelsea dabbed at her mouth with her napkin. "I don't seem to be hungry this evening. Would you mind terribly if I went to my room?"

Her mother's teacup stopped midway to her lips. "Are you feeling ill, my dear?"

"Oh, no." Chelsea stood. "I'm simply tired. The ocean voyage took a bit more out of me than I thought."

Her father pointed his fork at Chelsea's mother. "It's because of those newfangled steam vessels."

Mrs. Delafield sent him a mildly reproachful look before returning her attention to Chelsea. "Are you sure you wouldn't care to accompany us to the theater, my dear? Perhaps that would help buoy your spirits."

"Another night. Do go on and enjoy yourselves. There's a book I've been meaning to finish for weeks."

"A book? Well, I should have known." Her mother sipped daintily from her cup. "Be sure not to stay up too late reading, or you'll feel even more frightful tomorrow."

"Yes, Mother." Chelsea was already on her way out of the room, passing into a darkened hallway and bound for the privacy of her own bedchamber. She had lied about the book, of course. No book could absorb her attention tonight.

Once inside her room, Chelsea didn't bother to light a lamp to ward off the shadows that would soon encroach like stealthy fingers across the carpet. By ten o'clock, the soft glow of the streetlamps below her window would be sufficient to illuminate all that she needed to see; a child's room where she no longer belonged, a way of life that bored her to tears.

"Oh, blast," she muttered, determined to stop feeling so sorry for herself. Crossing the room, she pushed aside the window curtain to look down upon the rain-glistened street. Pairs of black umbrellas floated by beneath her window. Across the bustling thoroughfare, she saw couples walking their dogs and couples out for a night on the town.

"No," she said aloud, not bothering to wonder why she had lately taken to conversing with herself. "I will not think of him. I won't."

But it did no good. The more she tried to convince herself that her decision to stay behind was the right one, the more uncertain she became.

*"Come with me."*

*"I can't."*

*"Why not?"*

Lots of why not's, she had thought at the time, but, for the life of her, now, Chelsea could not think of one.

One, she thought, just one more adventure. At this, her yearning heart beat a little faster. Her heavy spirits began to lift. But then she caught herself and gripped the window sash tightly.

It was a childish thought, a selfish thought, an irrational, irresponsible reaction to the feelings of uncertainty she was experiencing concerning her own future. It was time to put childish notions of romance and adventure aside and begin behaving like a rational adult.

Wasn't it?

Yes. That was exactly what she had done this afternoon when she had sent Arthur to pursue his quest alone. She had behaved like a rational adult. It *was* the right decision.

Wasn't it?

Just below her window, Chelsea caught sight of her parents as a hansom cab drew up to the curb. After helping her mother inside, Chelsea's father followed suit. The door closed behind them, and the black cab moved off down the street. By then, Chelsea was staring out her window, seeing nothing, her thoughts drifting inexorably back.

*"Come with me."*

*"I can't."*

*"Why not?"*

Chelsea's fingers tightened on the window sash. Her voice was not much more than a tremulous, unconvincing whisper in the fading light. "Foolish to even think . . ."

To think what? That Arthur might actually need her help?

Turning from the window, Chelsea tried to separate her turbulent emotions from the facts of the situation. Why so foolish? Professor Doyle's authentication of the parchment was no more than a scholarly validation of what she had known from the start. The parchment was real, the sword was real, and, whether he realized it or not, Arthur would need her help to find it.

And that wasn't all there was to consider. What if the same men who had ransacked Arthur's room in Philadelphia had somehow picked up his trail here in London and were following him to Glastonbury at this moment? What if Arthur really did need help? What if he was in danger?

Moving quickly, much too quickly to pause long enough to consider sensible options such as dispatching a telegram or notifying local authorities, Chelsea strode to her armoire and flung open the doors. Within moments, her carpetbag was tossed open onto her bed and she was rifling through the drawers of her dressing table.

To hell with behaving rationally. She was going to Glastonbury.

# 16

*Time to kill and funds to replenish.* That was what had brought Arthur to a pub called the Red Rooster. The men that made up the small crowd gathered around him were not exactly the crème de la crème of Glastonbury society. The crème de la crème would not be taken in by an old three-card-monte game; at least, he didn't think so. Still, at the moment—as he crouched behind an overturned crate in a back street behind the Red Rooster—Arthur felt closer to his roots than he had since his transient childhood; perhaps a sign that the many generations of grifter's blood that flowed through his university-educated veins had not gone to complete waste after all.

"The lady, gentleman."

Splaying three playing cards in his right hand, Arthur tapped the queen of diamonds. He held it up to show the circle of pipe-smoking, ale-swilling farm laborers and tradesmen above him, then passed it under the nose of his latest mark, a hefty, foul-tempered blacksmith, who squatted directly across from him.

With a theatrical flourish, Arthur spread all three cards

facedown in a row on the crate, then made a series of sliding passes, rearranging them as quickly as he could. He had no choice but to play it straight since he had no confederate to distract the group from what his hands were doing. Tonight, he was relying on the odds, his own nimble fingers, and Lady Luck.

When he was done, Arthur turned an open palm over the row of cards. A scatter of coins—a shilling, a sixpence, two threepence, and a collection of coppers—winked in the witch's glow of an old lantern that was their main source of light. All laughter and ribald comments had now cut to a hushed silence.

Arthur met the bleary-eyed stare of the hulking smithy called Osgood—"Oz" to his many and sundry pub pals. Oz was well into his cups. His eyes were pink-veined road maps.

"Where's the pretty lady, Oz?"

Slapping his half-drained beer mug down on the crate, the blacksmith chose the card to Arthur's left. "That 'un."

Arthur frowned with apparent concern. "Are you sure, chum?"

In response, Oz opened his mouth and emitted a belch that would have grounded a herd of stampeding buffalo. It was all Arthur could do to remain upright and clear-thinking as Oz grinned, displaying a gap where his right incisor had once dwelt. "Aye, chum."

Arthur flipped over the indicated card.

Two of clubs.

There was a group gasp.

Oz's steel jaw clamped. His chunky features mottled red. Throwing his head back, he howled like a wounded wolf and struck out to send his mug flying. It exploded against the white stone wall of the Red Rooster to spray foaming ale and shards of glass over the both of them. "Ye cheated, ye bloody bastard!"

Arthur ignored the fact that he now had beer in his hair, not to mention a sliver of glass or two, as he pocketed most of the money. He laid out one threepence, flipped another to a chap named Knox—the only one who'd had enough sense to bet on Arthur to win—and looked up to meet Oz's homicidal glare.

"No, chum. It just proves my point. The hand is quicker than the eye."

Clenching his fists, Oz rose to his feet. He was a man of impressive measurements, in both height and the substantial girth of his belly. "Ye're cheatin'."

"Aw, come, Oz. We all be watchin' him. He's lost some turns too, ain't he? You had one pint too many, that's what."

This was Knox, the villager Arthur had pegged early in the evening to be his unknowing shill. Upon first entering the Red Rooster, Arthur had befriended Knox by allowing him to win half a dozen pints at darts. Knox had also won back his own sixpence at the cards. As far as Knox was concerned, he and Arthur were practically brothers by now.

"Thas right, Oz. Ye're too drunk to hit the ground with your own arse!" This candid observation came from a pudgy wagoner named Jackson.

Oz shifted his enraged attention long enough to curl a lip at his chortling companions. After a long, broiling moment, however, he backed off. Since no one else had stepped forward to agree with him, he apparently reasoned that it wasn't worth acquiring a reputation as a welsher over a lousy sixpence.

Muttering curses, Oz retreated into the shadows to mope among the spent casks that were stacked by the rear entrance to the pub. Arthur figured he was safe. For the moment. He turned away from the man with only a few misgivings.

"Any more takers, gentlemen?" Arthur scanned the small group, noting that most of them had already laid out more than a few coppers, and lost them, too. His eye quickly fell, however, upon a new face that lurked in the shadows near the back. No, not new, he corrected upon closer examination. He remembered that the man had been nursing an ale inside the pub earlier. In fact, while that grizzled countenance might be forgettable, the rest of him was not. Towering, muscular, and bald as an egg beneath his flat black cap, he made Oz look like an elf.

Arthur scooped up the cards. "How about you, chum? Care to try your luck? A thruppence is all you need."

The small group parted as Arthur's new mark stepped forward. When his face came fully revealed in the glowing circle of light, it was clear that he was not as inebriated as the others.

"A bob," the man said.

Reaching into his pocket, Arthur laid out another threepence and sixpence of his own as the bull-necked newcomer crouched opposite him, fishing one large hand into his pocket to extract a coin. "Show me yer lady, guv'ner."

Arthur made a few idle passes with the cards. This guy was extravagant compared to the others. "What do they call you, chum?"

"Beck."

"Mr. Beck?"

"Just Beck."

"Good enough, Beck." Arthur splayed his trio of cards and flashed the lady of diamonds for the benefit of his audience. "Let's get this show on the road, shall we, gentleman?"

It was close to midnight by the time Chelsea made it to Glastonbury. She might not have arrived at all if not for a young sheep farmer who was determined to return from his wife's family gathering in time to put in a full day's worth of haymaking after the next sunrise. The wife, a sullen-mannered woman about Chelsea's own age, said little throughout the bumpy wagon ride from the nearby town of Wells; in fact, she said nothing at all.

If Chelsea had known beforehand that she would be plunking herself down in the middle of a newlywed spat, she might have resigned herself to staying the night in Wells, after all.

Then again, perhaps not.

According to the guard at the train station, Chelsea could have caught a connection to Glastonbury the following afternoon, but that would have been much too long to wait. Her premonitions of doom had grown more compelling as the evening express from London had steamed across the invisible boundary of Somerset. By the time she stepped off in Wells, she was frantic with the certainty that Arthur was in danger.

Perhaps it had been the panic in her voice that had caught the attention of the young farmer as he'd passed; that or the fact that he wasn't looking forward to traveling alone with his furious bride. Whatever the case, he had offered her a ride to Glastonbury for the price of a shilling, and Chelsea had pounced upon the opportunity. It was a good omen, she had thought at the time. Arthur needed her help, and the gods would lead her to him.

Now, she wasn't so sure.

With her carpetbag and furled umbrella hanging from nerveless fingers and her hat drooping from the night mist, Chelsea stood on a glistening wet pavement, watching as the farmer's open wagon rattled off down the unlighted, empty street.

Crickets chirped night songs in outlying meadows and a three-quarter moon cast a silvery glow over the sleeping village. The damp air smelled of wet fields and white fog.

The farmer had given her directions to High Street, in which she could locate a reputable inn. It had sounded simple as he'd explained it, but she had assumed that there would be street lamps to light her way or people from which to inquire help.

As Chelsea trekked past a series of dwellings, a hay and corn merchant's, a tailor's shop, and a smithy, all dark and dead as tombs, her heels clipped against the pavement. The sound echoed dully in the still night air, reminding her all the more that she was quite alone, more alone than she'd ever felt in her life.

Soon, she approached a quiet intersection at the top of an incline, and it was just as she turned to look for a street sign that she caught her first glimpse of the imposing, five-hundred-foot blackened silhouette of Glastonbury Tor. It was the hill where the last abbot of Glastonbury had been executed. To Chelsea, it looked like a defiant human fist raised against the glazed, starry heavens.

As she turned away and continued across the street, she wondered if her monk had witnessed his abbot's tragic execution that day more than three hundred and fifty years past, and quite without realizing it, her pace began to slow. By the time she came to a dead halt and turned again to stare at the talismanic silhouette of the Tor, it felt to her as if an unseen hand had reached out to cup her by the jaw and hold her transfixed.

*No. The monk was long gone when his abbot met death. He was already safe in Scotland where he learned of it much later.*

Chelsea suddenly knew that she was not alone at all. Beneath her feet, beneath the cracked pavement where she somehow knew a young boy of seven had skinned his knee just this morning, time seemed to stretch taut then double back to loop and interlace—once, twice, again and again—to converge like a cosmological slipknot.

Oh, yes, her monk had walked these streets, as had many people before and after him. Men, women, children, all with their own peculiarities and preoccupations, too many to count, too many to make any sense of, but they were all there, all of them, now, right beneath her tingling feet.

*He needs you.*

The thought came like a soft whispered reminder in her ear, but it was enough to snatch Chelsea from her reverie.

Arthur was here in Glastonbury.

She tore her gaze from the midnight shadow of the Tor and shook off the fogging anesthetic in her brain. How long had she been distracted? Ten seconds? Thirty? A minute? She looked down at her feet. Her soles were tingling. It was a familiar sensation that resembled gentle needlepricks; not painful, not terribly pleasant, either, but impossible to ignore.

Lifting her feet slowly, she stepped down off the curb to stand in the street. As she knew it would, the tingling ceased.

She had experienced similar episodes in the past, but never to this extent. If she didn't stay on her guard, a spell might come over her in public in broad daylight, and what then? Off to an institution where they cinched their guests to the bedposts, that's what.

"Step on something, miss?"

Startled, Chelsea spun around to discover a diminutive gentleman leaning up against the front of a bootmaker's shop. He hadn't been there before. How long had he been watching her?

Minutes, she thought as their eyes met. He must have had time to emerge from around the corner or from up the street behind her.

The man struck a match, cupped a hand over the tip of his cigar, then tossed the match away, all without taking his eyes from her. "Lost your way, miss?"

Wearing city clothes and carrying a furled umbrella, he spoke like a Londoner and appeared perfectly harmless, even if drastically out of place. Chelsea would have welcomed his company if it weren't for the way he moved, slow and languorous, like a lazy snake in the sun. She sensed, however, that he could move very quickly if he wanted to, and she took a hesitant step backward. "I'm sorry, sir. I didn't see you there."

Out of the corner of her eye, she caught a flash of movement across the street and was relieved to see that yet another man had emerged from an alley next to a glowing pub. Wearing a seedy coat and ill-fitting trousers, he sported a head of straw yellow hair and a cowlick problem severe enough to be noticeable even from where Chelsea stood. Upon espying her, he offered a besotted grin and a wave. "Ahoy there, missy!"

Ahoy? Sailor or not, the scarecrow man swayed like a ship's mast in a squall. He was drunk as a piper, but at least he belonged here, and Chelsea sensed none of the subtle menace emanating from him that she sensed from the better-dressed man.

"A vagrant."

Chelsea looked back at the source of her apprehension. Although he still leaned up against the bootmaker's shop in a deceptively casual posture, his eyes were sharp as beaks. "A friend of mine," she said, swallowing hard.

"Indeed?"

"Ahooooy there, missssy!"

"Ex—excuse me." Chelsea tripped over her words in a rush to get away. "But, as you can see, my friend is calling, and I must be going."

Chelsea didn't look back as she dashed across the street to where the drunken scarecrow awaited. By all appearances, he was delighted to meet her.

" 'Ey there, missy, missy! Tha' bloke your husband?"

The man reeked of alcohol and other ingredients Chelsea didn't care to dwell upon long enough to identify. She was close enough now to hear muffled laughter and string music coming from the shuttered windows of the alehouse. The knowledge that there were conscious, if not entirely sober, humans within shouting distance made her feel a little bit more secure.

"No, he isn't," she replied, trying to straighten her hat and regain some semblance of dignity. "Would you be so kind as to point me to the Crown Hotel?"

"The Crown?" Scarecrow scratched his head, inadvertently loosing a windfall of flaking dandruff. "That be in the next street, missy. Ye're goin' the wrong way."

He mumbled something else, but Chelsea wasn't paying attention. Male laughter reached her ears again, only this time it was much closer and not coming from inside the pub at all. A rich, masculine voice carried clearly on the still night air, a voice she recognized.

"Go on, pick another card, chum! Any card at all. It only costs a thruppence to play."

*Arthur.*

Forgetting her distaste for the foul-smelling drunkard, Chelsea snagged a filthy sleeve. "Is that an American named Arthur Pierce?"

"How's this? An American named Price, ye say?"

"No, no, no!" Chelsea gritted her teeth and forced herself to speak slowly. "Tell me, are they playing cards back there?"

"Oh, no, missy. We just be havin' a bit o' fun, thas all. No harm in that, is there?"

Tired of wasting time, Chelsea dropped his sleeve and tried to pass him into the alley. "Excuse me, but I must get through."

"Wait here, missy." Scarecrow shot out a cadaverous arm to bar her progress. "That ain't no place for a lady."

Chelsea was growing impatient. She'd come eighty miles by train, six miles in a bumpy dray, nearly been accosted by a masher, and now her delicate sensibilities were being protected by a spindly, malodorous vagrant with unkempt hair.

She jabbed a finger at his gaunt chest. "Listen, you, that Yank happens to be my husband. I've come a very long way to find him, so I would appreciate if you would let me through."

"But the bloke said he ain't married. He be a peddler, thas what he said."

"Well, that may be what he said, but I must speak with him immed—" Chelsea cut off as another rumble of laughter rolled out from the narrow alleyway. Straining to see around Scarecrow's shoulder, she made out a glow of light coming from round the back of the alehouse. Frustrated, she muttered to herself. "I risk my neck and my good reputation to rescue him, and he's running about town doing card tricks."

"What tricks?"

"I'm sorry?" Chelsea looked back at her antagonist with annoyance.

"What tricks?" Something in the besotted man's expression had sobered considerably.

"Card tricks, of course. That's what he's doing back there, isn't it? Card tricks?"

Scarecrow stared at her, apparently uncomprehending, and so Chelsea pressed on in exasperation. "See here, I can prove to you that he's my husband. He's about this tall, reddish-gold hair, and he's good with playing cards. He does all sorts of fancy shuffles and mind-reading tricks."

Scarecrow's eyes narrowed. "He be a sharp."

Now it was Chelsea's turn to be baffled. "No, he's not a Sharp, he's a Pierce."

"He stole a thruppence from me, he did."

Suddenly, bony fingers were tightening around Chelsea's elbow. "Come along, missy. I think yer husband has a bit o' explainin' to do."

Arthur thought for a moment that he was dreaming, but, of course, that was just plain wishful thinking.

"Unhand me this minute or I shall call for the police!"

*Chelsea.*

But he'd left Chelsea in London.

Hadn't he?

When the villager called Puck rounded the rear corner of the Red Rooster, he was attempting to dodge a series of smacks from her umbrella without letting go of her arm. They were greeted by a stream of overlapping, excited babble from the group.

"Look ye there now!"

"Who's that?"

"A woman!"

"A *woman*?"

"*Whose* woman?"

"He be a sharp!" Puck was calling out between umbrella blows. "He be a sharp!"

"I demand that you cease manhandling me this instant!"

It was Knox who pushed through the little crowd to take charge. "Say, Puck, how's this? Let the lass go before she brings the whole bloomin' town down on us. Who is she?"

Puck released Chelsea, who promptly desisted from her struggles and proceeded to smooth her skirt and check the status of her hat.

Even though the others hadn't caught on yet, Arthur hadn't missed the significance of Puck's words. Leaving the cards lying facedown on the crate, he rose to his feet.

"By what I can make out, she's his missus," Puck was saying, pointing a finger at Arthur, "and she told me he be a sharp!"

"I never said any such thing," Chelsea protested. "I know nothing about this Sharp person you keep referring to."

But no one was listening. All eyes were now trained on Arthur. The inebriated group formed a semi-circle before him, cutting off access to the lane from which Puck had just emerged. Even Knox seemed to be assessing him through distrustful eyes.

"Look, I don't know what she told you, but you must have misunderstood." Arthur turned his hands up. "I'm just a peddler."

None of them replied. Not an optimistic sign, so Arthur considered his options. Access to the alley ahead was cut off, but the alley that ran parallel to the street in front of the pub was clear. There wasn't a man here Arthur couldn't easily outrun, but there was, unfortunately, one small problem.

Chelsea.

Now, she stood quiet and dignified, her little hat straight, her skirt and jacket crisp, one gloved hand primly clutching her carpetbag and umbrella. She should have come wearing a banner that read, Ball and Chain.

What the hell was she doing here?

Arthur glanced at the man called Beck, who still hadn't moved or said a word. He'd won a round of cards and lost another, coming out even thus far. That might have explained the absence of anger in his expression, but it did little to explain his lack of attention to what was going on around him. His attention seemed fixed instead on the satchel Arthur had brought with him from his hotel, the satchel that held the parchment. At the moment, it leaned up against the crate by Arthur's left foot.

Arthur didn't have much time to puzzle over Beck's odd preoccupation. A low voice growled behind him. "I told ye he was a-cheatin'."

Oz. Damn. Arthur had almost forgotten him.

Puck was babbling and waving his arms. "He's good with the playing cards, she says. Does tricks and fancy shuffles, she says. Sounds like he be a cheat to me!"

"Me, too," said the pudgy wagoner named Jackson.

"That's not what I meant at all," Chelsea tried to protest again, but it did no good. The other men were grumbling their assent. The tide had turned. Angry, ale-flushed faces scowled out from beneath tattered hat brims.

Arthur's gaze dropped to his satchel, then went to Beck, who looked up from his crouched position at the same moment. The man smiled. Beck was ready to go for the satchel the moment everyone was sufficiently distracted. Arthur didn't have time to dwell on this new problem because that was when he felt a heavy hand clamp his shoulder from behind.

# 17

*As Arthur turned to face the hulking* monstrosity that loomed over him, Chelsea began to get the feeling that her idea of coming to Glastonbury to rescue him might not have been divinely inspired after all.

The men around her were buzzing with excitement. From what she could determine, they were wagering on how long Arthur would last before the monstrosity succeeded in flattening him into a hapless pudge of dough. The situation was getting out of hand.

She tapped Scarecrow's shoulder. "There's been a dreadful mistake."

Scarecrow was taking a bet that Arthur would go down in less than two blows. "Stand back, missy. This ain't no place for a lady."

"You don't understand. When I referred to Mr. Pierce's skill with cards, I merely meant—"

Scarecrow paid no attention to her. Chelsea turned to the gentleman who had stepped forward earlier to order Scarecrow to unhand her. "Pardon me, sir, but I shall have to go for the police if something isn't done to put a stop to this at once."

The man spared her only a glance, but in that fleeting instant, Chelsea saw that his eyes glowed with ale and anticipation. "Don't you worry, now, mum. He'll still be in one piece when you get him back, just not as pretty is all."

Chelsea rose on tiptoes to see that Arthur had his arms spread and seemed to be taking one step back for every step his opponent advanced. The monstrosity did not appear to be in a negotiating mood.

Knowing that Arthur could be pudding by the time she located a town constable, Chelsea cast about for a more timely solution. Her eyes alit upon a thick-necked man who now rose to his feet by the crate where Arthur had been dealing cards. He was easily as large as the monstrosity and didn't appear to be as tipsy as the rest of the group. At the very least, he wasn't wagering on Arthur's impending incapacitation.

Pushing by Scarecrow, Chelsea tugged on the large man's sleeve. "Pardon me, sir, but there's been a mistake. You see, Mr. Pierce wasn't cheating at all, he was just—"

Chelsea cut off when the man turned his head to glare down at her. There was something in those eyes that chilled her to the marrow. She would get no help from him.

Just then, the little crowd burst forth with a chorus of whoops and hollers. Chelsea whirled around in time to see the monstrosity take a swing at Arthur. Luckily, Arthur managed to elude the blow.

Catcalls and boos erupted at this near-miss, but Arthur wasn't paying attention to the audience. All of his concentration was reserved for his opponent, a specimen that outweighed him by a good fifty pounds worth of hammer-and-tongs muscle. Even if this were a supervised ring and they were wearing gloves, Arthur would be in big trouble. As it was, here in a dark alley with a bloodthirsty crowd to cheer him to victory, Oz's eyes had developed a crazed glow that proclaimed he was in his most cherished element.

With a grunt, the drunken smithy swung again, a real haymaker that whistled through the air over Arthur's head as he ducked beneath it.

Too close. If it weren't for Chelsea, Arthur would have made a run for it by now. To hell with masculine honor; he much preferred to keep his teeth.

Oz swung again. Arthur dodged again, knowing that he couldn't go on like this forever. Sooner or later, he would misread one of Oz's punches and then it would all be over. He had no choice but to bow to the inevitable.

"All right!" Arthur threw up both hands in a warding-off gesture as they danced around each other. "If you want to fight, we'll fight, but let's get the rules straight first."

Oz stopped moving and let his guard drop slightly. "How's this? Wot rules?"

Arthur stopped moving, too, letting his arms fall to his sides and hoping that Oz had enough pride to resist delivering a sucker punch. "Queensbury rules, of course."

Oz sneered. "Wot rules is they?"

"Well, first and foremost . . ." Arthur truly hated to do it; any man would, so natural was it to empathize, but, what the hell, he thought and sent the toe of his boot hurtling into Oz's unprotected groin.

With a gut-wrenching howl, the blacksmith's knees crashed to the pavement. Arthur joined both hands to make a tight-fisted club then swung hard, cold-cocking his adversary with one solid blow to the jaw.

Oz toppled like a felled oak.

The crowd was stunned silent. The slugfest they had been salivating over for the past five minutes had lasted roughly three seconds.

No one moved; no one but Arthur. With Oz out of the equation, he spun around, his eyes first going to Chelsea, then to his satchel, then back up to find Beck.

The other man's eyes met his at the same instant. They lunged. Unfortunately for Beck, Chelsea was in his way. With a frustrated growl, he shoved her aside, sending her stumbling into the wall, but it was too late. Arthur snatched the satchel a split second before Beck's fingers closed over empty air.

The man recovered quickly, nabbing Chelsea instead. She let out a squeak of surprise as he wrapped a massive arm around her waist from behind and swung her around to jerk her back up against him. He cupped her jaw in one meaty hand.

Arthur was poised to run, his heart pumping, his eyes locked with Beck's. Not a word passed between them, but the threat was clear. One neat twist of the wrist, and Chelsea's neck could snap. This guy was no petty thief, and this had nothing to do with cheating at cards.

"Son of a bitch," Arthur muttered, then tossed the satchel so it landed a good five feet off to his left, well out of reach for both of them.

Beck grinned and released Chelsea, shoving her forward.

"Dear heavens!" she exclaimed as Arthur caught her, then spun her around again to link hands.

They were suddenly airborne. Or something close to it.

With Chelsea trailing behind like the fluttering tail of a kite, Arthur led them skimming over cobbles and across a deserted street to shoot down an alley opposite. By then, the others had recovered from their shock. In the distance, Arthur heard infuriated shouts and pounding hobnail boots as their pursuers poured out onto the street from the lane behind the Red Rooster.

Arthur took a sharp right onto another back street, heading toward the northeast end of town. They passed a blur of stone cottages with garden walls, many of which Arthur would have put between him and his pursuers had Chelsea not been in tow.

No doubt about it. He could have moved quicker without her, but they were lucky. Most of the Red Rooster's patrons had been propping up the bar for a few years too many. Suspenders had been stretched to their limits, and the footraces of youth were but vague and distant memories. The sounds of hot pursuit began to fade.

Dashing down a sparsely populated lane and cutting through a small apple orchard, Arthur spotted the back end of a barn ahead. "Come on," he called. "In here!"

Amazingly enough, Chelsea held her own as Arthur led her careening around the corner to the front. He spotted double doors and hoped they weren't padlocked. They weren't. Trusting souls, Arthur thought as he pulled Chelsea inside.

The door slapped shut behind them, plunging them into deeper darkness. Moonlight streamed in an open window over a stall at the far end of the building, but it would be several minutes before Arthur's eyes adjusted enough to make out their surroundings. It was warmer here, the air close with the pungent aromas of old leather, straw, horseflesh, and fresh droppings. They had stumbled upon a livery.

"Chelsea? You all right?" Arthur still had her by the hand. She was gasping and gulping in great lungfuls of air. "Chelsea?"

"Ye-yes!"

"I think we lost them."

Somewhere off to the left, a horse whickered and rustled in its stall, a subtle hint that they were disturbing the equine peace. The knuckles on Arthur's left hand, the ones that had delivered the knockout blow to Oz's jaw, now throbbed with heated vengeance. He hoped he hadn't broken anything.

It took Chelsea a few more seconds to collect her breath enough to speak. "I thought you killed that man."

"Not quite." Arthur let go of her and moved back to the stable door to listen for their pursuers.

"I do hope he'll recover."

Arthur grimaced as he flexed his fingers. "Don't worry about Oz. His wife was probably tired of being pregnant all the time, anyway." Using his good hand, he cracked the door open to peer out onto the peaceful, moonlit country lane. In the distance, he heard a few shouts and decided it might be best to wait a bit before returning to town.

He let the door close and turned back to his other problem. By now, he could make out her petite figure against a shadowy backdrop of hay bales and feed sacks. She still had her umbrella and carpetbag, although it appeared that she had lost her hat. He couldn't see her eyes, of course, but he could feel those violets boring into him, waiting, and so he posed the obvious question. "Chelsea, what are you doing here?"

"I thought you might need help."

It was all Arthur could do to hold back the sarcastic response that strained to escape, but he was glad of the effort when she continued in a small voice. "I had an awful feeling that you were in trouble, and, oh, dear . . ." She trailed off miserably. "That man got the parchment, didn't he?"

"Yes."

She moaned and dropped her head. "It was all my fault."

Arthur sighed, then approached. "He probably would have gotten it sooner or later anyway. That's what he came for. I was just too distracted to realize it until it was too late."

She raised her head. "Do you think he was one of the men who ransacked your room in Philadelphia?"

"I don't know."

"What are you going to do now?"

"I'll go see Jeremy Hunnicutt tomorrow morning as planned."

"You haven't spoken with him yet?"

"No. His wife said he was out and was expected late this evening. I told her I'd be by in the morning."

Chelsea was quiet, then, "Do you want me to leave?"

Her face was upturned, her expression bathed in shadows. A ray of moonlight caught and reflected off the lenses of her spectacles. No, Arthur didn't want her to leave. Despite the fact that she'd nearly gotten him pulverized and might have hastened the loss of the parchment, he was glad to see her. He just wondered if she had done irreparable damage to her reputation by following him here. What would her parents think was going on between them? What, for that matter, was going on between them? Arthur wasn't sure at all.

"Do you want to leave?" he asked.

"No. I want to help you find the sword."

He'd expected no other reply. Still, he shoved his hands into his trouser pockets and turned away in an effort to think clearly. "I don't know. After what happened tonight, you could end up getting hurt, and I don't like that idea at all."

"That man wasn't going to hurt me in front of all those people."

"Maybe not, but—"

"You need me."

Arthur couldn't help an amused smile at her subdued, yet supremely confident tone of voice. "Do I?"

"Absolutely, Mr. Pierce. You may be an exceptionally gifted cardmaster, and you may even pack a pretty good punch when you trick your way into it, but you're certainly nothing to howl about when it comes to British history and geography, are you?"

Arthur still had enough money to put her on a train back to London. For her own good, and perhaps for his own as well, he knew he should do just that. "Your parents will be frantic."

"I left them a note."

"Oh. Well, that's different. I'm sure they won't give your disappearance another thought."

"I'm an adult. I make my own decisions."

He turned back to her. "Even if they're bad ones?"

"Especially if they're bad ones. I may be a woman, but no one is responsible for my actions but myself."

"Ah, so what you're telling me is that your womanly mind is made up."

"What I'm telling you is that I want to help. If you wish me to leave, I will, but I'd hoped—" She stopped, then plunged ahead. "You did ask me to come with you."

"Yes, I did," he admitted, "in a particularly weak moment."

When she didn't offer any more argument, he gave her a tired smile. "Do you want your ring back?"

"Is that a proposal?"

"I don't know. The last time I asked you to run away with me, you refused. Do I dare risk another rejection?"

In answer, she tossed her bag and umbrella to the earthen floor, tugged off her gloves, and offered her left hand. "Since when has Arthur Pierce ever been daunted by the idea of taking a little risk?"

Reaching into his coat pocket, Arthur produced the plain gold band he'd picked up in a pawn shop in Philadelphia. "Your tone, Miss Delafield, has a ring of challenge to it, and, as you know, I've never been able to resist a challenge."

"Then don't even begin to try."

Taking her smaller hand in his, Arthur felt for her third finger, then slipped the circlet down the slender length of it. Her skin felt as soft to him as it had that day in the reading room of the Ridgway Library. How long had he known her before then? Nine months? Why had it taken him so long to notice the rest of her?

A rapt silence had fallen over the stable. Even the horses in their stalls had gone still. Here in the dark, it was all too easy for Arthur to picture Chelsea swimming naked in a magical lake.

"From now on, we stay together," he said, trying with little success to tamp his ardent imagination. "Not a moment out of my sight."

She answered in a soft, breathy voice that heated his blood. "I do believe that it's customary for a groom to kiss his bride."

Arthur lifted her hand to his lips. "Is that so?"

"Not that kind of kiss."

"Oh?" Arthur turned her hand to interlace his fingers with hers, then took up her other hand, gently locking them together in a similar fashion. "What kind of kiss would you prefer?"

"I prefer the kind of kiss you offered this afternoon."

"I somehow doubt that's the type of kiss a groom bestows upon his bride at their wedding."

"But this is a different sort of wedding."

"So it is," he agreed, willingly surrendering to feminine logic as he bent his head and pressed his lips to hers.

*Cool British miss melts like butter on a hot skillet*, he thought, sliding his tongue between her sweet, parted lips. Unschooled in erotic kissing as recently as this afternoon, Chelsea made up for her lack of experience with eager, unguarded innocence.

They kissed not once, but again and again, leisurely and unhurried, as they moved in a slow mating dance, back one step, two, then another and another until the wall of the stable came up against her back.

Arthur released her hands, allowing his own to close about her waist. Her palms pressed flat to explore his chest before skimming up to clasp behind his neck. They merged closer still, their bodies meeting inch for inch, chest to breasts, hips and thighs, layers of clothing luckily impeding what might evolve too naturally otherwise. Head-clearing air seemed in short supply. So was Arthur's dwindling sense of self-control.

When his state of physical arousal could no longer be ignored, Arthur forced himself to break away, raising his head to concentrate on her face in the dusky shadows. Her eyes were closed, her lips were parted, her breath came soft and shallow. He was waiting for her to pull back, to be shocked by the feel of him against her.

Her eyes fluttered open, but she didn't move. "Oh, dear," she whispered, "is that you?"

"It's difficult for a man to control when he's . . . interested."

"Interested?"

"Very."

"I must confess, I find you quite interesting, also." Then, with no further delay, she pressed up against him again, her fingers threading in his hair to draw his mouth down to hers.

Frigid? Had he really once assumed Chelsea to be frigid? Lord almighty, she was like a milk-starved kitten, soft and snuggable, lapping up every drop of nourishment he could offer.

And Arthur took for himself, too, drinking in her sensual hunger as his hands caressed over her corsetted ribs, around her back, down to her waist and up again. He imagined how it might feel to burrow into her woman's softness, to have her delicious body moving in perfect synch with his own as they made love by a lake in an enchanted vale called Avalon.

Chelsea made an almost undetectable whimpering sound in her throat, a sexual cue that, with any other girl, Arthur would have taken to mean his way was clear. They were alone, she was willing, and . . . Jeez, no, he thought, snapping back to his senses.

He broke off the kiss. "Chelsea, we've got to stop."

"Ohhhh, but no." Her breath fluttered like warm silk against his mouth. Her arms tightened about his neck, and she moved against him in such a way that, if Arthur hadn't known better, he would have sworn he was being professionally seduced. He knew his noble intentions weren't going to amount to squat if she kept this up.

He took her firmly by the shoulders and set her away from him before releasing her. By now, more than just his sore knuckles throbbed. His blood raced hot. Every muscle felt tight, poised, ready to snap. He could barely think straight, but think straight he must. For both of them, apparently.

She didn't move. "What's wrong?"

"Nothing. It's just time to stop, that's all."

"You're angry."

"No." But even as he denied it, Arthur knew that she'd hit on the truth. He was struggling with an irrational surge of frustration. He didn't want to think straight. Thinking straight was supposed to be the woman's job. It was her role to set the limits; his was to push those limits. He was darned good at it, too. Chelsea, however, seemed hell-bent on getting her part all wrong. She was wreaking havoc with every carefully conceived preconceived notion he possessed, damn it.

"We should get some sleep if we're going to see Jeremy Hunnicutt in the morning," he said.

She didn't reply.

Turning his back, Arthur moved to retrieve her carpetbag and umbrella. "We'll have to share my room at the inn," he said, "but don't worry, you can have the bed. I'll take the floor."

"I wasn't worried," she said.

Crossing to her side, Arthur took her by the elbow. He didn't look at her as he guided her to the door. "Maybe you should be."

Soft-bellied, bearded, balding, and almost comically short-legged, Jeremy Hunnicutt was somewhat younger than Chelsea had expected. A former student of Professor Doyle's, he had returned to his native Glastonbury to marry his childhood sweetheart. Now, as vicar of his church and a father of six, he took great joy in indulging his two most passionate avocations, local history and Arthurian lore, a combination that was not in the least bit mutually exclusive as far as he was concerned.

"Such a pity that you lost the parchment," he said as he led Arthur and Chelsea across the west end of High Street, the bustling center of Glastonbury. He had procured permission from the landowners for them to inspect the abbey ruins that stood behind the present town. "I should have liked to take a look at it myself. Have you informed the authorities?"

"Informed them of what?" Even though Arthur was a head taller and considerably longer-limbed than their amiable guide, he had to keep up a good pace to stay abreast of the energetic little man. "That a clue to the location of King Arthur's sword was stolen? Who would believe it?"

Hunnicutt chuckled as they left the public walkway to cut through a tree-dappled green. "In Glastonbury? Why, just about anyone, Mr. Pierce, just about anyone at all."

Chelsea had done her best to keep up with the two men

even though she hadn't bothered to join in their discussion. Now, however, her heels sank into the rain-soaked earth, slowing her down so that Arthur and Hunnicutt pulled ahead, both of them so preoccupied that they didn't notice she was lagging. Chelsea didn't mind. She was otherwise preoccupied herself.

In her mind, she again played over what had happened between Arthur and her in the stable, trying in vain to determine what she had done to aggravate him. Wasn't it Julia who had told her that men enjoyed kissing, that they enjoyed it so much, in fact, that they schemed to steal as many as they could?

Chelsea had become worried that, in her overexuberance, she might have gotten the tongue thing all wrong. Perhaps she wasn't supposed to join in the festivities, perhaps she was just supposed to stand there with her mouth open, allowing him to have his way with her, yet that didn't seem fair at all.

"Mrs. Pierce! I say! We almost lost you, madam!"

A little ahead, Jeremy Hunnicutt beamed and waved from where he and Arthur waited by a weeping willow. It was a warm, slow-to-brighten morning, the breeze just strong enough to wreak havoc with the chestnut brown wisps of hair the reverend had carefully combed over the top of his balding pate.

Even though the man could not have known what was on her mind, Chelsea felt her cheeks flush hot with embarrassment. They flushed even hotter when she reached them and was forced to take Arthur's outstreatched hand.

"Sorry, my dear," he said. "We got so caught up in our conversation, we didn't realize we'd left you behind."

"Quite all right." Chelsea was exquisitely aware of his touch even through her gloves. She addressed their guide, who was busy taming his misbehaving hair. "I was enjoying the scenery. Such a pleasant morning."

"Indeed it is." Jeremy Hunnicutt smiled and motioned for them to follow. "Come. The ruins are just over here."

Moments later, they emerged from a covering of trees to behold a verdant meadow by the foot of Glastonbury Tor. It struck Chelsea as ironic that a handful of sheep now grazed so benignly amongst the skeletal gray stone ruins of what was once the richest and most powerful abbey in England. Against a backdrop of lifting clouds and splinters of late morning sunlight, the crumbling, fragmented walls and violated stone arches stood silent and reproachful, bleak testaments to man's greed and folly.

Hunnicutt spoke with pride as they approached the roofless remains of St. Mary's Chapel. "In the days before the great marshes of Somerset were drained, before the time when Joseph of Arimathea came here to build the world's first Christian church, Glastonbury Tor was known throughout Europe to be a holy place, an island of enchantment. It was the mystical Isle of Avalon, the resting place of departed souls."

"The Isle of Avalon is where the three queens took King Arthur to die from his battle wounds," Arthur said.

"Yes, and it's here that he was buried with Queen Guinevere."

Arthur's expression was skeptical. "I suppose people would believe anything back then."

The vicar paused in the doorway of the chapel. "In the light of day, we all find it easy to scoff at the quaint beliefs of our scientifically ignorant ancestors, yet, there are times, usually at night, when we approach Glastonbury from a great distance, when we contemplate the dark and silent Tor as it rises from the eerie flatland mist, that we begin to wonder if our ancestors weren't actually on to something. Who is to say?"

Chelsea listened with only half an ear as they strolled through the chapel and admired the detailed reliefs of biblical scenes that still survived on the north door. Soon, they were crossing the green to the less well-preserved abbey church. It was in the church, or rather, what little remained of its once massive structure, that Hunnicutt pointed out the site of the high altar where, in 1278, Arthur and Guinevere's disinterred bones had been placed in a sarcophagus of black marble. Like most of the holy relics of the Abbey, the magnificent tomb disappeared at the Dissolution.

It was then that Arthur broached the subject of Excalibur, asking the vicar's opinion regarding the possibility that the sword might have been uncovered with the remains of King Arthur. When the two of them moved toward a building known as the Abbot's Kitchen, Chelsea lingered behind. She needed to be alone.

Once the men were a safe distance away, she removed her gloves and slipped behind one of the piers of the chancel arch. Closing her eyes, she pressed her fingertips to the cold, gritty stone.

Immediately she sensed a potent concentration of the mystical undercurrents that had been tugging at her ever since she'd arrived in Glastonbury. Layers upon layers of human history were stored here, agonies and ecstacies, glories and desecration, a virtual kaleidoscope of ever shifting impressions, but, unlike the previous night, she could detect no traces of her monk.

Frustrated, she moved on to the site of King Arthur's tomb. Dispensing with ladylike propriety, she dropped to her haunches and pressed both palms flat against the wet grass. *Warm.* Much warmer than the ground even just a few feet away, she decided after shifting about and experimenting. This was a special place, perhaps even a holy place, but if the mysterious Dark Age king had ever really been here, he was here no longer.

Disappointed that her efforts had yielded no practical results, Chelsea gave up and hurried after Arthur and Hunnicutt. They were engrossed in conversation by the Abbot's Kitchen some distance off and didn't appear concerned over her absence. All for the better. Chelsea was aware of how odd her actions might appear and had no desire to explain herself.

". . . however, I find it interesting that of the three relics mentioned in your parchment, one did turn up in the seventeenth century," Hunnicutt was saying as an errant breeze played amusing games with wisps of his hair.

Arthur stood with his arms folded, listening to the vicar. Although he didn't look up when Chelsea rejoined them, he had indeed noticed her absence, not to mention her odd behavior. For one thing, it wasn't like her to be so quiet. "Which relic is that?" he asked.

"The Holy Thorn of the Redeemer. It's never been known exactly how it was saved, but it turned up in the hands of a family here in Somerset and was presented to the Chapel of the Holy Rosary in London in the seventeenth century."

"That lends weight to the monk's claim that he left some relics in the hands of local friends," Arthur said.

"Yes, it does, but we're still left with the question of whether the sword he took with him was authentic."

"I suppose that will have to be determined if and when we ever find it."

"True. Your immediate concern is to determine whether your monk left it here as he apparently did the thorn or whether he took it to Scotland."

Arthur allowed his gaze to shift to Chelsea. "Unfortunately, it's a mystery we may never be able to solve."

"Oh, you shouldn't give up the ghost just yet," Hunnicutt said brightly. "There is that last clue you spoke of."

"The seat of the king," Arthur said, regarding Chelsea with growing speculation. She said nothing; she simply stared back at him, those long-lashed violet eyes luminous and guilty as Judas behind her spectacles. What was she hiding?

"Perhaps we should let ourselves stew on it for a bit," Hunnicutt said. "You never know what might come to mind."

They spent the remainder of the morning touring the Abbot's Kitchen and the crumbling remains of the Almonry and the Abbey Gateway. Later, they stood before a well at the foot of Chalice Hill, the place where legend had it Joseph of Arimathea hid the Cup of the Holy Grail. They took a light midday repast in the parlor of the George Inn.

"Really, our only hope of finding Excalibur is if the monk

left it here, otherwise, it could be almost anywhere in Scotland," Arthur said.

He sat directly across the table from the vicar. Chelsea was seated next to the older man, finishing off the last of her bread and cheese. Even though she'd been acting decidedly un-Chelsea-like all morning, Arthur noted that her appetite hadn't suffered one whit.

"Yes, I see your point." The vicar pushed his plate away and refilled his teacup. "It would be like trying to find the proverbial needle in a haystack."

"Worse," Arthur said. "Now that we've lost the parchment, I have a feeling we've got competition to find that needle."

Chelsea addressed Hunnicutt. "It was the monk's reference to the king's seat of government that led us to believe he hid the sword somewhere in Somerset. Aside from King Arthur's burial here, weren't there legends that suggested Arthur was based in this area?"

"Oh, yes. As you may know, Henry VIII's antiquary, John Leland, was adamantly convinced that Camelot was located in Somerset." Hunnicutt surveyed the cake plate for a suitable confection to top off his snack. "It's less than ten miles from here, actually."

Arthur and Chelsea looked at each other, then back at Hunnicutt, who was still immersed in making a culinary choice. "*What* is less than ten miles from here?" Arthur asked, not sure he'd understood the man.

"Cadbury Castle."

"You mean . . . the *real* Camelot?"

"Why, yes." Jeremy Hunnicutt looked up quite innocently. "Would you like to see it?"

# 18

*They could see it from the road* long before they reached the village of South Cadbury. Cadbury Castle was not a castle at all; it was a flat-topped hill, a rounded square that rose from the surrounding moors like a colossal tortoise shell. Dazzling green in the summer sun, its perimeters were fortified by four ascending concentric circles of earthwork defenses, ancient manmade ramparts and ditches that had, over the last few centuries, become almost entirely hidden by forest growth.

Hunnicutt snapped the reins and raised his voice over the clatter of the phaeton's wheels as they neared their destination. "Since King Arthur was a military leader, it's logical to assume that he would have had a military base from which to operate. We already know from studying relics that have turned up that Cadbury Castle was utilized since the Bronze Age by the Celts. Later it was staked by the conquering Romans. As you can see, the hill itself was a formidable vantage point for purposes of defense."

Arthur was looking forward to reaching their journey's end. With Chelsea seated in the middle, the three of them were packed into Hunnicutt's small four-wheeled rig like peanuts in a shell.

Hunnicutt kept up his monologue as he eased the hack off the road toward a group of beech trees near an empty church. "Historical references from King Arthur's time are silent on the subject of where he was based. The first mention of Camelot didn't even come until the fourteenth century, and it was actually a French poet who coined the term."

"Chrétien de Troyes," Chelsea put in unexpectedly. It was one of the few comments she had offered since they'd left Glastonbury. She leaned forward in her seat, shading her eyes to peer up the wooded slope of Cadbury Castle.

"Very good, Mrs. Pierce," Hunnicutt complimented as he drew their little gig to a halt.

Arthur stepped down from the rig and reached up to hand Chelsea down. Their eyes met only briefly before she looked away, turning her back to him as soon as her feet contacted solid ground. She *was* hiding something.

Taking his horse by the bridle, Hunnicutt spoke as he led it to the nearest beech tree to graze. "It was in 1542 that John Leland proposed Cadbury Castle as the site of Camelot. Aside from its ideal location and the fact that its ramparts were still visible at the time, he may have derived the idea from the local population. There's a rich abundance of Arthurian folklore surrounding this place."

Chelsea wasn't paying attention. Instead, with her umbrella hooked over one arm, she strolled a few yards away. Having lost her traveling hat the night before, she was bare-headed, her raven hair reflecting blue-black in the sun. Due to the active afternoon breezes, tendrils had blown free of her pompadour knot to frame her face and stir gently down her back.

Arthur turned back to the vicar. "So, what old stories have you found to be the most prominent?"

"There are a number of different versions of the sleeping king legend, but the most colorful is that this hill is hollow and that once a year, a pair of golden gates opens along its side. That's when one may catch a glimpse of King Arthur and his knights asleep in their enchanted cavern. The story goes, of course, that he will one day awaken to reclaim his throne."

Arthur couldn't resist a dubious smile. "Any eyewitnesses to this who haven't had a pint too many?"

Hunnicutt chuckled. "Not that I'm aware of. Come. Let us climb to the summit. I'm sure you and Mrs. Pierce will find the view most spectacular."

Leaving the phaeton tethered to a tree, Hunnicutt led Arthur and Chelsea up a winding trail along the northeast slope. Disused for years, it was muddy, overgrown, and rocky, but, luckily for Chelsea, who was burdened with a skirt and at least one petticoat, it wasn't too steep to negotiate with care. Arthur helped her over the rougher spots, taking her hand in his, becoming more uncomfortably aware of her each time they touched.

Throughout the climb, Hunnicutt expounded upon the history of Cadbury Castle, and, even though most of Arthur's thoughts continued to dwell upon Chelsea, upon his disturbing attraction to her as well as her curious behavior today, he made sure he absorbed every word their enthusiastic guide uttered. For once, his ability to concentrate on more than one subject at a time was coming in handy outside the classroom.

Extrapolating from examinations of the crumbling walls and foundations that remained of the ramparts and some of the relics that had turned up, Hunnicutt was convinced that Cadbury Castle had been built up yet a third time after the Roman withdrawal from Britain in 410 A.D. This third reincarnation would have dated during King Arthur's lifetime. Unfortunately, not many experts agreed with him, and the vicar lacked the financial backing to conduct a massive dig to support his theory.

Soon they emerged from the forested footpath into the sun. When they reached the crest of the hill to stand upon the fringe of an eighteen-acre greensward, Arthur couldn't help but be impressed by nature's splendor. This might have once been a place of tall battlements and castle keeps, but it was now a peaceful bucolic paradise.

A spread of field grass, shrubs, and some trees cut sharply to a clear, pale blue sky. Except for the calls of skylarks and cuckoos, and the soft, steady drone of honeybees as they dipped among the buttercups, all was quiet.

Hunnicutt paused to catch his breath. "If we had approached from the south side, you might have seen some of the ramparts through the trees."

"Fascinating," Arthur said, striding through shin-deep grass to gain a better view of the vast green and brown patchwork of fields and peat moors that was south Somerset.

Ten miles away, Glastonbury Tor rose from the flatlands, jutting against the hazy outline of the Mendips. To the west were the Poldens, and in the sweeping distance, the Blackdown Hills. Truly, Arthur thought, this would have been an ideal location for purposes of defense. From this very vantage point, a young monarch might have once surveyed his fledgling kingdom while carpenters and masons worked to erect an impenetrable fortress behind him.

"The mound at the top of the hill is still called Arthur's Palace," Hunnicutt said, approaching from behind. "Up here you will also find Arthur's Well and, if you look off to the northwest, you can see an old track that leads back to Glastonbury. They call it King Arthur's Hunting Causeway."

Chelsea joined them just as a falcon cruised by overhead. "I remember once, when I was very small, we were traveling through the countryside when my father pointed out a boulder the size of two carriages. It was called Arthur's Stone. He then proceeded to relate an outlandish David and Goliath story of how, upon that very spot, King Arthur once battled a ferocious giant. I was quite enthralled. I thought King Arthur must have been quite a large and very imposing fellow."

Arthur and Hunnicutt turned together to stare at her. She offered them a disarming Mona Lisa smile. "Well, what could you expect? I was only five."

Hunnicutt chuckled as she strolled away, carrying her furled black umbrella like a walking stick. "I'm afraid your wife has just put me in my place."

"How so?" Arthur's gaze dropped to follow the soft movement of her hips until she was some distance away.

"Actually, very few geographical locations that claim Arthur's name have any historical connection with him. All throughout England, as well as Wales and Scotland, you'll find boulders known as Arthur's Stone, hills known as Arthur's Seat, battlefields named after the Round Table itself. Why, I believe there's even an Arthur's Oven."

"Arthur's Oven?"

"An unusual rock formation."

Arthur laughed. "Well, don't feel too bad about my wife getting the better of you. She does it to me all the time."

"Indeed. I'm afraid my wife has a way of doing that, too." Casting a look over his shoulder in Chelsea's direction, the vicar abruptly frowned. "Oh, dear, whatever is she doing?"

Following the man's puzzled gaze, Arthur looked back to see Chelsea standing by a cluster of hawthorns, alternately stamping her foot and jabbing at a section of ground with her umbrella.

"Good heavens!" the vicar exclaimed. "I do hope she's not stumbled upon a snake!"

Before Arthur could react, Hunnicutt was off to the rescue, his arms waving, his hair flying askew, his coattails flapping. "I say, madam! Stay calm!"

Arthur didn't react nearly as quickly. Not that he had any particular sympathy for reptiles, but he doubted Chelsea needed any help. If she'd uncovered a snake, the poor creature hadn't a chance, not the way she was stabbing at it.

By the time he reached their side, it was clear that Chelsea had not been battling a snake. She was gouging a hole in the ground with the sharp end of her umbrella.

The reverend was perplexed. "What's that? You've found something, you say?"

Looking as intent as a cat at a rabbit's burrow, Chelsea

dropped to her knees in the deep grass, trying to dig still deeper with her umbrella. "There's something buried here."

Hunnicutt looked to Arthur. "I'm afraid I don't understand."

Arthur didn't either. He hunkered down next to Chelsea, lowering his voice as if addressing an asylum lunatic. "Mrs. Pierce, what exactly are you doing?"

Her head popped up. She glared at him with impatience. "What does it look like I'm doing? I'm digging!"

"Why?"

"Something is buried here."

"*What* is buried here?"

Her gasp of exasperation expressed the opinion that he was being unbelievably obtuse. Her eyes were almost wild with restrained excitement. "Well, we won't know that until we dig it up, will we?"

As she returned to her bizarre mission, Arthur craned his neck to squint up at the vicar. Instead of attempting an explanation, he shrugged and glanced around for something to help her with. Whatever she was up to, the intensity that burned in her eyes was unmistakable. There was something contagious about it.

Locating a flat, sharp-edged stone nearby, Arthur joined her, cutting a wider arc into the earth where she was tunneling. "How do you know something is buried here?"

"I just know," she said evenly. "Dig."

And so they dug.

*Never try to scam a scammer*. It was advice Arthur's older sister had given him whenever she'd caught him trying to pull the wool over her eyes while he was growing up. Wise advice considering they came from a family in which deceit had developed into an art form as well as a livelihood. Arthur was reminded of those words as he followed Chelsea's shapely behind up the staircase of their inn and down a corridor to their room.

Although it was after ten, the sun had set only a short time ago. Arthur turned the key in the lock and pushed the door open for Chelsea. He reached into his coat pocket for a box of matches. In the process, his fingers encountered the metal object they had unearthed on Cadbury Castle.

Their room was plain. A brass bed, a chest of drawers, a washstand, two straight-backed chairs, and a dressing screen. After lighting a paraffin lamp, Arthur watched Chelsea as she turned her back and began to unfasten the buttons on her navy blue jacket.

When it slid from her shoulders, he saw, or imagined that he saw, the faint outline of her corset beneath the thin white cotton of her blouse. He had explored the construction of that feminine undergarment just the previous night. In fact, he knew exactly where the fastenings were and how little effort it would take to tug them loose.

Balling his hands into fists, Arthur shoved them deep into his trouser pockets and forced his attention back to the subject at hand. "Chelsea," he began, "all day you've been—"

"Oh, yes, such an invigorating day," she interrupted, folding her jacket and draping it over the back of a chair. "I'm utterly exhausted."

She avoided his gaze as she found her carpetbag atop the dresser and set about unbuckling it with nervous fingers. "It must be all this splendid country air." After extracting her toothbrush, she finally looked at him, quite innocent by all appearances. "If you'll excuse me, I think I'll go see if the lavatory is available."

"Fine," Arthur said. He'd bided his time all morning and afternoon because of Hunnicutt's presence. After the bizarre incident on Cadbury Castle, he'd held his counsel still longer through their ride back to Glastonbury. It hadn't been easy, but because of other hotel guests, he'd even managed to suffer through Chelsea's innocuous chitchat at dinner. Now, he'd have to wait longer as she exhausted her last avenue of escape, running off to the lavatory, but he'd damn well be waiting when she got back.

Taking a towel and washcloth from the washstand, Chelsea ducked her head as she scurried past him.

*Lies,* Arthur thought as the door closed and her footsteps faded down the corridor. There were all sorts of lies—white lies, bald-faced lies, lies by exaggeration, lies by insinuation, and lies by omission—but they all smelled pretty much the same. Little did Chelsea know that she was dealing with an expert, a lie-detector extraordinaire if early family training had anything to do with it.

Arthur took off his coat and hung it on a peg behind the door before yanking open the buttons of his waistcoat. Yes, he could smell a lie brewing a mile away, and he smelled one now. She was hiding something, something big, something she was afraid to tell him. There hadn't been any secrets between them before this. Why now? Why couldn't she trust him? It was this last question that nagged at him the most.

Arthur took off his shoes, then tossed his waistcoat on the chair before being drawn back to the peg where his coat hung. Reaching into the side pocket, he extracted the mysterious item that so stimulated his curiosity.

An inconsequential scrap of corroded metal. That had been his first impression when they'd pulled it from the mud on Cadbury Castle. Hunnicutt had dispelled that notion in a hurry. Rushing off to wash it in a watering hole, he had used Arthur's jackknife to chip away some of the centuries-old dirt that obscured its intricate ironwork etching. When he was done, it was clear that they had uncovered the broken hilt of a broadsword.

Holding the L-shaped scrap of iron up to the glow of the lamp, Arthur examined the scrolled foliage along the grip and the two-headed serpent engraved on the pommel. Even though the left half of its guard had broken off, the hilt was solid and heavy, well balanced; it fit Arthur's hand well.

*"She will lead thee to thy sword."*

Arthur tossed the hilt down onto the bed and loosened his tie. It had been on their way back to Glastonbury that the prophetic words from his dream had come back to him. The disembodied voice belonged to Max Hamilton, but the other-worldly maiden had Chelsea's face, and damn if she *hadn't* just led Arthur to a sword.

But was it his sword? Could the scrap of metal they had uncovered this afternoon possibly be the legendary sword they were searching for?

Arthur rolled up his sleeves as he crossed to the wash-stand. He removed his collar and poured some clean water into the basin. As he washed up, the ancient handpiece on the bed behind him remained out of sight but not out of mind.

Hunnicutt was eager to compare it to other samples of sixth-century weaponry. If he was correct in his assessment of its late Celtic workmanship, the relic would help prove his theory that Cadbury Castle had been occupied during King Arthur's reign.

*"She will lead thee to thy sword."*

Adjusting the mirror on the washstand, Arthur stared at his reflection in the glass. Could it be mere coincidence that Chelsea had known exactly where to find that fourteen-hundred-year-old hilt? No, he just couldn't believe it. The odds against coincidence had to be even more astronomical than the odds against . . . what? Dreams coming true?

Preposterous.

Neither possibility was logical or credible. Perhaps more important was the fact that something inside of him, something instinctive and surprisingly passionate, refused to believe that the pitiful remains they had discovered this afternoon could be all that was left of the wondrous Excalibur. That something inside of him had nothing to do with mathematical probabilities. In fact, it had nothing to do with logic at all. To be honest, it had more to do with the awe-inspiring image of a splendorous sword thrusting skyward from the deep; it had to do with a mysterious woman's hand clasped about a jeweled hilt; it had to do with the shimmering dance of sunlight on polished steel; it had to do with a little boy's idea of what magic should be.

That was what told Arthur this was not the legendary sword he searched for. If that scrap of metal was all that remained of Excalibur, he would have known it the moment he'd touched it.

Wouldn't he?

Maybe not. Arthur reached for a towel. All right, probably not, but he was beginning to think he knew who would know, and it wasn't Reverend Hunnicutt or Professor Doyle or any other scholarly male expert in history or archeology, it was—

"The lavatory is free if you want to use it," Chelsea said, breezing into the room. After draping her damp towel over the rack on the washstand, she whisked past him to replace her toothbrush into her carpetbag. She sat on the bed and bent to unlace her shoes. "I'd go while there's no queue if I were you."

Something very unusual was going on, and Arthur was determined to get to the bottom of it. He folded his arms and shrewdly regarded his dreamlake-swimming, battlesword-detecting brunette. "So, are you ready to explain?"

"Explain what?" Her voice was muffled as she tugged off one shoe and set to work on the other.

"Explain what's been going on."

"I'm sure I don't know what you're talking about."

"Why don't we start with how you knew where to dig for the hilt of that sword."

She sat up, still managing to avoid his gaze as she reached to undo what was left of her windswept pompadour. Her tone was casual, but her hands trembled as they worked. "I had no idea what was buried there."

"But you knew something was buried there."

She freed waves of jet black silk to spill down her back. "It was just a coincidence. What does it matter? It didn't turn out to be anything important, did it?"

"Oh, I don't know. Reverend Hunnicutt nearly snapped his suspenders."

Chelsea crossed to the washstand and snatched up her hairbrush. "The good reverend is a historian. Historians get agitated over all sorts of queer things."

Arthur was suddenly out of patience. He moved quickly, taking her by the arm just as she raised her brush. He whipped her around to look at him, but her guilty gaze dropped to the floor. "Chelsea, tell me the truth. What happened on Cadbury Castle?"

"Nothing, nothing. I don't know what you're—"

Using his free hand, he cupped her chin, forcing her to look up at him. Her amethyst eyes were wide, almost frightened. If he hadn't felt so urgently compelled to get at the truth, he would have released her with a mumbled apology for behaving so rashly, but the fact remained, he was urgently compelled.

"It wasn't just on Cadbury Castle," he pressed. "You've been acting odd all day. I felt it even when we were touring the ruins of the abbey. What's going on, Chelsea?"

She shook her head, but her apprehensive gaze remained fastened on his, belying the feeble denial. Arthur could sense the agony of her indecision, but he couldn't understand it.

"Trust me," he urged.

After an interminable moment, she tried to speak. "Sometimes . . . when I touch things, I feel . . ."

Arthur looked deep into those beautiful troubled eyes and suddenly knew. *Touching, touching, touching*. He remembered how she had touched the glass face of the parchment in the Ridgway Library. Not once, but twice, caressing it with such reverence. And today at the abbey, so often running her fingers over the stone ruins. More importantly, he remembered the amusing little anecdote her mother had imparted over tea the other day. Not so amusing now as startling and illuminating. The Rosetta Stone. "*Oh, yes. She wanted to touch it, that was the thing.*"

Of course Chelsea had wanted to touch it. How else could she have convinced herself that what she felt was real?

"The Rosetta Stone," he said.

"What?"

"It talked to you."

Her mouth fell open. Her gaze remained locked with his.

Arthur doubted they could have drawn apart at that moment even if they'd tried. Except for the physical act of sex, they could not have been more closely fused.

"The Rosetta Stone talked to you, but you couldn't talk back because it was under glass. You couldn't touch it because you were only a little girl, and it was against the rules."

"No." The denial came out on a little puff of expelled air. Her eyelids fluttered. Her complexion went chalk white.

Chelsea was going to faint.

# 19

*One moment she was staring up* into Arthur's all-too-knowing eyes; the next she was flat on her back, her legs dangling like puppet strings from the side of the bed.

Chelsea blinked as thick oak rafters swam into focus. "Oh, dear," she mumbled.

She felt Arthur's mild touch on her cheek, then the mattress shifted as he leaned over her, wearing an expression of concern. "Chelsea? You okay?"

"What happened?" She raised a trembling hand to adjust her spectacles.

"You fainted."

That got her attention. "Fainted?"

"Yes."

Scowling, she tried to push up onto her elbows. "I do not faint. I have never fainted in my life."

"Well, you fooled me."

"Don't be absurd," she said, finally righting herself. "There must be another explan—"

Black dots mushroomed before her eyes. The room tilted, swirled, then swept her right along with it.

* * *

"Chelsea?"

She forced her eyes open. Oak rafters. "Blast," she muttered.

Arthur's face appeared over her. "Welcome back."

"Don't say it."

"You fainted again."

She sighed and closed her eyes in defeat. "It's been such an exhausting day."

"Sword-detecting really takes it out of you, huh?"

"It would seem so."

"You want some water?"

"Perhaps that might be the thing."

The bed slats creaked and the mattress shifted as he slid off of it. Chelsea didn't move as she listened to the sound of water pouring from pitcher to glass. A moment later, he was back, settled on his side, holding her glass and regarding her calmly. "Maybe you should wait before you try to sit up again."

"I'll be fine."

"Sure you will."

Blast him, Chelsea thought. He was altogether too perceptive, too intuitive, too bloody smart. In less than a fortnight, he had guessed the secret she'd managed to keep hidden from even her immediate family. She wondered dismally if he could also see that she was falling in love with him.

She drew in a deep breath to steady herself. "I'm ready."

He sat up ahead of her, then she felt his hand on her shoulder. "Let's take it a little slower this time, shall we?"

It seemed very natural that his arm should slide so easily around her back for support as she sat up. "Okay, just sit tight for a bit."

Chelsea was still too lightheaded to protest. Instead, she closed her eyes and allowed herself to huddle against him for a moment, to take respite in his warm strength and the unfamiliar security of a firm male arm encircling her shoulders.

"Still awake, Miss Delafield?"

"Hmmm." She didn't want to move.

"Still interested in that water?"

Chelsea forced her eyes open and lifted her head. "Yes, thank you."

He pulled his arm from around her shoulders as he offered the glass to her, but he didn't move away. Chelsea straightened her spine as she drank. The water was cool and refreshing, but did absolutely nothing to relieve the knots that were tightening in her stomach. Nevertheless, it did furnish her with a few seconds to collect her thoughts before Arthur broached the inevitable.

"You want to tell me about it?"

*It.* Chelsea felt warmth seep back into her cheeks. She couldn't bring herself to look at him as she handed back the drained water glass. "What is there to tell?"

"How long have you had it?" he asked, reaching over to place the glass on a night table.

"For as long as I can remember."

"What is it?"

"I don't know."

"Well, what does it feel like?"

She chanced a cautious look in order to read his expression. Curious. Curious and somewhat perplexed, that was all. She saw no shock, no disbelief, and, most thankfully of all, no disgust, and so she made an effort to quell her dread and pluck up her courage.

"It's very much like any other sense, like touch or smell, but it's also very different. As a child I soon came to realize that not everyone had it, so I tried to ignore it, to block it out. That works quite well most of the time, but sometimes it's overwhelming, it's as if . . ." But now, for the first time in her life when she was ready to confide her darkest secret, Chelsea found herself at a total loss for words. How did one describe color to the blind? Sound to one who could not hear?

"As if what?" he urged.

Chelsea tried again, reaching for a concrete reference. "Sometimes it's as if a curtain stirs, then parts, then draws closed again. Sometimes I get no more than a glimpse."

"You see things?"

"No, not *see*, precisely. It's more like voices in the dark, traces of thought, a scent I can't place, warmth without a source. It's like . . ." Chelsea paused again. It was indescribable. Arthur would never know what it felt like, not without feeling it himself, and that was never going to happen. He was normal.

He prodded. "You were feeling it today. At the abbey."

"Yes, it was very strong there, but I've been sensing something very unusual ever since I arrived in Glastonbury."

"There's a lot of history here. Even I can feel that."

"Yes, but that's not what I mean. There's a lot of history everywhere. I couldn't have grown up in London without learning to block out all that constant chatter. This is different."

"Different how?"

"I'm not sure. Whatever it is, it's very deep, very entrenched. This place is a taproot, a center for something I don't understand. There's a great deal of whispering going on. I just can't make out the words."

"Whispering?" he repeated, puzzled.

Chelsea shook her head and mused to herself. "What was it Reverend Hunnicutt said? An isle of enchantment. Perhaps that's not very far from the truth."

"What about this?" From somewhere behind her on the bed, Arthur produced the broken hilt they'd found on Cadbury Castle.

"What do you want to know?" she asked.

"Is it what Reverend Hunnicutt thinks it is?"

"Part of an old sword, you mean?"

"Sixth century?"

"All I can tell you for certain is that the knight who carried it felt an unswerving loyalty to his king, whoever that king might have been."

"The *knight* who owned it," Arthur said, his heart-stopping blue eyes alighting with hope. "Then it's not . . ."

Chelsea realized then what he must have been wondering. If the pitiful relic they'd found today was Excalibur. "No," she replied firmly.

"You're sure?"

"At first I thought perhaps it was, but after we dug it up and I touched it . . ." She didn't finish; she didn't need to.

Arthur eyed the broken hilt and nodded to himself before placing it on the night table next to her drinking glass. "I knew that. I just wanted to make sure. Tomorrow we get back to work looking for the real thing."

"It's not here."

Arthur stared at her. "Not here? What do you mean it's not here?"

Chelsea couldn't have said it any plainer. He just didn't like what he was hearing; neither did she, so she patiently rephrased. "I don't believe our monk left the sword here in Glastonbury."

"Cadbury Castle?" he asked hopefully.

Chelsea shook her head.

"Are you sure?" He sat forward, picking up her hand as he spoke. Chelsea's gaze dropped to where they touched. *Tingling.* "Chelsea, how do you know?"

"I just know," she said, noting how small and pale her own hand appeared compared to his. She remembered how deftly his clever hands dealt with a deck of cards, and the tingling in her fingers began to spread like warm molasses into her veins. This was a very different sort of tingle than she had felt last night on the street.

"What are we going to do?"

Chelsea forced herself to look up. "We must go to Scotland."

"Edinburgh?"

"I daresay that would be most logical. It was where the parchment was first discovered."

"Logical?" he repeated, staring at her as if she'd lapsed into Greek.

"What other choice do we have?"

"Edinburgh is a big town. How will we know where to start?"

"I don't know. Perhaps once we arrive, we'll uncover a clue."

He didn't reply, but a smile lifted the corners of his mouth, and his eyes shined with a shrewd kind of delight. Young Edison might have worn a similar expression upon witnessing his first spark of electricity.

Chelsea was suddenly very uncomfortable to be the subject of that look. "Do you think I'm crazy?" she blurted, daring for the first time to voice the fear that had nagged at her since childhood.

His brows shot up in surprise. "Crazy? Chelsea, I was there when you stabbed your umbrella into the ground and uncovered the remains of a fourteen-hundred-year-old sword. It was probably the strangest thing I've ever seen, but you're definitely not crazy."

"Strange." She pounced on the word like a damning clue to murder. "You think I'm strange?"

He grinned. "Well, yeah, but then again, I always thought you were strange."

Chelsea blinked at him woodenly.

Arthur leaned closer and squeezed her hand. "A joke."

"What?"

"It was supposed to make you smile."

A joke! "Oh, yes, yes, of course," she said, gasping the words out on a rush of bated breath. She bent her head as an intoxicating wave of relief washed over her. A joke. Of course it was a joke. Hadn't his timing always been dreadful? A sense of newfound freedom burst and blossomed inside of her.

Arthur let go of her hand only to place two fingers beneath her chin and lift her face to his. "Perhaps it's time you stop trying to block out these feelings. Perhaps you should start looking at your abilities as a gift and not some sort of curse."

His sleeves were rolled up to the elbows and the top of his shirt hung open. His hair was hopelessly tousled from their day's outings, and the hint of a day-old beard shadowed his jaw. By such accounts, Arthur should not have appeared so devastatingly handsome, but Chelsea thought he most certainly did.

"A gift?" she echoed.

"Yes. A very special, very unique gift." His fingers stroked back along her jaw to trail very slowly and suggestively down the side of her neck. "Others may not understand it, but does that matter?"

A dark light had kindled in his eyes, a light Chelsea now recognized as erotic interest, and the tingling heat that had started in her fingers now spread to every part of her body. It was a tingling that had nothing whatsoever to do with moldy parchments, dead monks, or rusty swords.

Chelsea wasn't sure who moved first, perhaps they moved at the same time. They kissed once, lightly, then again, much longer and much more thoroughly as Chelsea clasped her arms around his neck and sifted her fingers through the soft thickness of his hair. He bent her back then, slowly lowering her onto the bed to half-cover her supine body with his own.

As they kissed, Chelsea became aware of Arthur's hand at her waist, gently caressing up along her ribs and back down again. Little spirals of delight exploded along each nerve-ending his talented fingers encountered, even through the blasted nuisances of cotton and boning, and she yearned to know what his touch would feel like against skin that had never seen the light of day.

When his mouth left hers to press hot little kisses down the sensitive column of her throat, she knew that he was slipping open the buttons of her blouse. She also knew that when their adventure with the sword was done, he would leave her because that's what footloose young men like Arthur did; they made love, trampled hearts, then blithely set off to seek greener pastures, but she didn't care about that now. She wanted him to keep doing what he was doing, she wanted to feel his hands on her breasts, she wanted him to make love to her. It was shocking and indecent, but it was true, and Chelsea had never been one to shy from the truth.

Arthur was not thinking of greener pastures; the pasture he was in right now was plenty lush and green for him. He hadn't slept with a woman for months, not since a French cancan dancer whose name he couldn't remember, and now he was primed to surrender to his baser instincts and lose himself in the mindless pleasure of exploring Chelsea's ripe young body.

*In sooth, mayhaps thou shouldst set aside certain of thy instincts for the moment.*

Arthur tried to ignore the admonishing voice that whispered in his mind. Instead, he nibbled a trail back up Chelsea's sweet, delectable throat. He could smell her hair, that elusive floral scent he always seemed unable to place. One of these days, he might ask her what it was. At the moment, though, he didn't care about much of anything but getting her clothes off.

*Thinketh with thy brain, not thy britches.*

"Go away," Arthur mumbled against her collarbone as he pushed aside her blouse to reveal a lace-trimmed corset of yellow satin. When he pressed his mouth to the soft rise of one breast, Chelsea arched her neck and let out a small sound that kicked up the fever in his blood. His right hand was already set to work, executing one of those skills it knew best, slipping open buttons and hooks and loosening corset fastenings, artfully, quickly, and sight unseen.

*Act in haste, repent at leisure.*

His fingers abruptly fumbled, clumsily entangling in what was suddenly a confusing mass of lacings and hooks. What was going on? What was wrong with him?

Perhaps sensing something amiss, Chelsea's grip on his shoulders tightened. "Oh, Arthur, please," she whispered, her eyes closed, her head moving from side to side as if fighting a bad dream.

This *was* a bad dream, Arthur thought, an awful bad

dream. Thanks to his proverb-spouting conscience, he could feel his erection—the manly tool that only moments ago could have pleasured a whole harem of lake-swimming brunettes—beginning to fade at an alarming rate.

Unsure of himself, he raised his head to look at Chelsea in the warm, flickering glow of lamplight. Her ebony hair, rich and lustrous, spread out behind her head, her coral pink lips were well-kissed, her pale breasts swelled over the top of her corset with each quickened breath. Why, the mere sight of her would be sufficient to arouse any sexually healthy male, and Arthur was nothing if not that.

Just a temporary lull, he assured himself, willing all inner voices silent as he set back to work on her fastenings. He took her seeking lips with his own, kissing her hot and hard enough to rekindle his floundering passions. In response, Chelsea moaned into his mouth, turning so that her belly pressed against the rapidly reviving swell below his belt. Arthur was homeward bound.

*Wedding bells and babies.*

"Ah, hell!" He pulled away from her, rolled onto his back, and threw an arm across his face.

Chelsea was stunned to find herself clutching at empty air. Her eyes opened to stare at rafters for the third bloody time in one evening. What the devil was happening?

She tried to straighten her spectacles and sit up at the same time, but her blouse was hanging open and her corset was loose. It kept slipping down, threatening to bare her breasts, an occurrence which only a few seconds earlier had seemed immensely desirable but which now seemed horrifyingly inappropriate.

"I don't . . . I don't understand." Clutching her corset to her chest, she sat up. She felt as if she'd been led to dare soaring heights only to have her wings clipped and come crashing down to earth.

Arthur was mumbling into his sleeve. "This is all wrong, all wrong, all wrong."

Wrong? Dash it all, what had she done this time? "I don't understand," she said again.

He pulled his arm away from his face to focus on her. "Chelsea, a few minutes more and we wouldn't have stopped at just kissing and touching."

She stared at him incredulously. Well, of course she knew that. What did he think she was, a total and complete idiot?

Apparently taking her silence for naive distress, he sat up and reached for the hand she wasn't using to cover herself. "There's no denying that there's an attraction between us, but to act on it would be irresponsible."

She could do nothing but gape. Irresponsible? Arthur Pierce, who before this probably hadn't kept his trousers buttoned in the company of God-only-knew how many twitty, brainless trollops, was now lecturing *her* on responsibility? The ludicrousness of the situation was beyond words.

"Do you understand now?" he asked in a gentle tone. "I don't want you to get the wrong idea about what's happening here."

"No. I do not understand." Chelsea yanked her hand away and tried to get up off the bed and away from him. Instead, she got tangled up in her skirt and petticoats, all of which were loose and sliding down to twist about her hips and legs. She could already feel the threat of tears behind her eyelids, and this . . . well, this was simply the final straw!

"Oh! Bloody hell!" Gritting her teeth, she pushed both garments down over her hips and bicycled furiously with her legs to kick them off.

Arthur watched in astonishment as Chelsea's skirt and petticoats flew through the air to slap against the opposite wall and slide down to the floor. What the hell was she so fired up about? He was behaving like a gentleman, wasn't he?

"What about Julia?"

Arthur tore his gaze from her skirt heap to find that she had turned her back and appeared to be wrestling with her corset. She was on her knees with her legs tucked beneath her. The curvaceous crescents of her rump were quite obvious and appealing through the flimsy material of her yellow cotton drawers.

"What about Julia?" he asked back, trying not to ogle her scantily clad behind. Now was no time to be regretting his chivalrous decision.

"You made love with her, didn't you?"

It was a blunt question that required a blunt answer. Arthur considered lying, then decided against it. "Once or twice."

"Once or twice?" Chelsea ripped her corset free and flung it to the floor like a vanquished enemy. "You don't remember?"

With growing wariness, Arthur observed the angry little movements of her shoulders as she worked at re-buttoning the front of her blouse. "Twice," he said. "What difference does it make?"

In reply, she twisted around to glare daggers at him. Her hair spilled loose about her shoulders, her elegant mouth was set in a thin, furious line, and her crookedly buttoned blouse did nothing to disguise the turgid peaks of her unbound breasts. Except for the civilizing effect of her eyeglasses, she looked exactly like the lake-swimming brunette in his dreams.

"That was different," Arthur said, determined to fight down a new and nearly debilitating wave of desire for the disheveled bluestocking who knelt so challenging and cold-eyed before him. "Julia was different."

"Yes. Julia and I are quite different."

Arthur had no idea what she meant by that, but he did know one thing. She wasn't getting his point. "Julia and I enjoyed each other's company, that's all."

"Oh."

Arthur set his teeth together. He'd had just about enough of being cast as the heartless despoiler of Julia Tierney's unimpeachable virtue. "Chelsea, I don't know what she told you, but I wasn't her first and probably not even her second."

Surprise flashed in her eyes, but just for an instant, then she swallowed hard and raised her chin. Even though he might have disillusioned her with that little piece of hard-to-digest truth, it was clear that she wasn't going to admit as much, so Arthur drove his point home. "Julia and I were physically attracted to each other. It didn't have anything to do with love or marriage. She knew from the beginning that I had no intention of marrying her. There's a lot I want to do before I settle down."

"Such as?"

"Such as," he said pointedly, "I intend to see the world. That takes time, money, and the freedom to pick up and go whenever the urge hits."

"I see."

"That's not something a man can do if he's saddled with a wife and children."

"Well, neither can a woman," she snapped back.

"A woman? What are you talking about?"

Chelsea pressed her lips together hard, fighting a stab of childish envy. Of course he was aghast. What she'd said was outrageous. Being a man, Arthur could travel alone and do whatever he pleased without raising an eyebrow. To do the same, Chelsea would have to take the same unorthodox route as her Aunt Geraldine. *Get thee to a nunnery, Delafield,* she thought petulantly, and was chagrined to realize that even as this mocking refrain formed in her mind, it was only half in jest.

Deciding to drop the subject since it was bound to get her deeper into trouble, Chelsea struck out on the offensive. "You flatter yourself."

"What?"

"You are so very pretentious."

He looked stunned. "Pretentious?"

"To assume that one tossabout in your bed would cause me to pine after marriage."

"Excuse me?"

Chelsea flipped a strand of hair over her shoulder and injected as much dignity into her demeanor as she could manage in her underclothes. "I propose that while you may possess a certain short-term appeal, you would make a perfectly dreadful husband in the long term. Why, I wouldn't marry you even if you begged me to."

"Begged you to?"

He was finally stirring to anger. Chelsea could tell by the steely look in his eye and the rigid set of his jaw, and she was glad. He had thought so little of insulting her, why not let him have a taste of his own medicine? "Have you considered the possibility that I might be . . . oh, what do you men call it"—she fluttered a hand through the air—"sowing my wild corn?"

"Sowing what?"

"Corn. A woman has the right to be curious, too, you know."

"Curious?" Moving with unexpected speed, Arthur caught her hard by the wrist. "So, that's what all of this is about, Miss Delafield? Curiosity? I'm just one big, rollicky, two-legged science experiment, is that it?"

"Yes!" Chelsea's hand clenched into a menacing little fist. Her violet eyes shot sparks as she tried to yank free of him. Arthur thought he hadn't seen her this steaming hot since the night they'd quarreled on board ship.

He didn't let go of her. Instead, he forced her wriggling body back down onto the bed and leaned in close to her face. "And all that moaning and writhing you were doing earlier, that was just curiosity, too, was it?"

Her eyes were wide but obstinate. "Ye—yes, of course."

She was lying again and very badly, too. Arthur knew he could prove it just by picking up with her where he'd left off, but that would be cruel. A girl like Chelsea didn't fall into bed with a man if her heart wasn't in it. Arthur knew the truth even if she wouldn't admit it.

He bent his head and kissed her hard before releasing her and pushing off from the bed.

"You . . . you reprobate!" she screeched, shooting back up like a jack-in-the-box and scrubbing at her mouth with the back of one hand.

Grabbing an extra blanket that was folded at the foot of the bed, Arthur turned away before she could notice the blatant evidence of her effect on him still straining against the confines of his trousers.

"You cur! You snake!"

Always leave them wanting more, Arthur thought grimly as he snatched a pillow and strode across the room to extinguish the lamp. "Believe me, Miss Delafield, when I say that you are not the corn-sowing type. Neither are you a mere kernel to be sowed. Save yourself for your unlucky husband."

"Knave," she cursed in the dark.

Ah, sweet innocence, Arthur thought, then stumbled over his own discarded shoe. Spouting expletives, he shook out his blanket and spread it on the cold, hardwood floor. He could hear her angry muttering as well as the groan and creak of slats as she moved about on the bed. He presumed she was trying to find her way in between the sheets. Precisely where he wanted to be.

Arthur dropped down onto his blanket and punched a deep dent into his pillow before turning on his side away from her and folding his arms. Innocence was exactly why he'd always kept his distance from No-Girls. Too much damned responsibility. Tonight, in all his hot-blooded haste, he'd conveniently forgotten that time-honored credo, but once burned was plenty enough for him. He'd be damned if he was ever going to let her tempt him again.

**Blake Manor, Leicestershire**

"It is fitting that Caliburn now rests by the seat of the king until he shall rule again," Emory Blake recited cynically.

At the moment, he stood alone in the spacious library of his sprawling country manor, his smoldering gaze fixed upon the bisected remnants of the Glastonbury parchment. It had been delivered by Mr. Beck early that morning.

Lined up next to the parchment was a second sheet of neatly framed and meticulously preserved manuscript. Blake had procured it six years before from a highly bribeable rare book dealer in London. It was part of a missive sent by one of Cromwell's men to his liege, King Henry VIII, reporting on the dismantling of Glastonbury Abbey.

After breaking open King Arthur's tomb, the pillagers had been disappointed to discover that it contained nothing but bones and dust. No sign of what they had been searching for, the enchanted sword. Unfortunately, it had already been too late to further interrogate the abbot, Richard Whiting. By then, his wizened old head had been gracing the abbey gate.

Ah, but that was old news, Blake thought bitterly. After all this time, after the fortune he'd spent tracking down countless false leads, he was now forced to the infuriating realization that all his efforts might have been for nothing. Even with the Glastonbury parchment in hand, he was no closer to piecing together the puzzle of Caliburn's whereabouts than Cromwell's men had been more than three centuries before.

*It is fitting that Caliburn now rests by the seat of the King until he shall rule again.*

"Bah! A meaningless riddle!" Blake slammed a fist down upon the offending words, shattering the glass that protected them. Sweeping the whole wretched conglomeration from his desk, he sent it to crash into the bookshelves and drop to the carpeted floor in ruined pieces. "Superstitious fool!"

It was the long-dead, rotting monk he cursed, certainly not himself. Foolish to believe a man made of mortal flesh could rise from the dead, not so foolish to believe that perhaps a mythical sword could hold the key to earthly power.

Blake noticed a thin trickle of blood oozing from a small cut on his hand just as a timid knock came at the locked library door. Snatching a handkerchief from his coat pocket and dabbing at the self-inflicted wound, he bellowed, "What the devil is it?"

A tremulous voice came from behind the thick mahogany partition. "A . . . a telegram for you, sir."

Thackery.

Scowling, Blake jammed the stained handkerchief back into his coat pocket. "Push it under the door!"

"Yes, sir."

A folded slip of paper shot through the narrow slot and came to rest on the carpet. Crossing the room, Blake retrieved the telegram and scanned the barely legible scrawl of the village telegraph operator. The message was from Geoffrey Dark. *Our friends have left Glastonbury. Bound for Edinburgh. Shall make next contact from there and await your reply.*

Edinburgh? Blake crumpled the telegram. He had sent instructions for either Geoffrey or Mr. Beck to remain in Glastonbury to make sure Pierce's nephew would cause no further trouble. In truth, once robbed of his parchment, Blake had expected the lad to slink back to London, or, preferably, all the way back to America. But Edinburgh? Why Edinburgh? Had Sidney Pierce's nephew stumbled upon a clue that Blake wasn't aware of?

*. . . by the seat of the King . . .*

Suddenly there was something about those words that scratched at the back of his mind, something significant, something obvious that he had missed all along.

But what the bloody hell was it?

Aggravation flared again. Blake covered his face with his hands. Surely, after ten long years of searching for the sword, he was better equipped to decipher the meaning behind the monk's riddle than some callow American youth and his British doxy, yet there they were, heading off in a direction Blake would have never predicted! Why? Why?

*. . . by the seat of the . . . ?*

Blake dropped his hands. He raised his head. A tentative calm settled over him.

Because of business and political interests, he had traveled through much of Scotland. He'd visited Edinburgh twice, but it was only now, for the very first time, that the possible answer began to dawn upon him. Could it be . . . ?

With new excitement Blake crossed the library in broad strides, passing by his favorite Delacroix painting without so much as a fleeting notice. Pushing open a tall casement window, he allowed a moment to calm himself and to bask in the sweet fragrance of blooming maythorn. It was, he thought, the scent of impending victory.

In the courtyard below, his son's nubile nurse perched on a garden bench with one eye on her needlepoint and the other on her energetic charge, who was engaged in his afternoon play.

"My kingdom for a horse! My kingdom for a horse!" Sturdy young legs pumped beneath blue denim Buster Brown knee pants and golden blonde curls flew as Duncan raced along the yard, brandishing a toy sword over his head.

Blake's lips curled into a cunning smile. "It is not on the battlefield that you shall win your kingdom, my dear heart."

It was true that Duncan would never wear the British crown. He had not been born to the purple, but there were other means to worldly power, means that Blake intended to pass on. Land and money were only two of them.

Turning from the window, Emory Blake's gaze sought out the parchment he had destroyed a few moments earlier. *By the seat of the King.* Why, yes, now that it was all spelled out for him, it couldn't be more simple. He threw back his head and began to laugh.

# 20

*In the past, Chelsea's spirits* always soared when she traveled, but today she could draw no solace from the peaceful English countryside that passed by her train window. Even the hustle-bustle of the station in Birmingham failed to stir her enthusiasm.

Their line continued north, running west of the Pennine Mountains to Carlisle and over the border into Scotland. Chelsea kept her attention fixed on the undulating green hills and heathered moors and tried to think about what little she knew of the city of Edinburgh. Instead, her mind wandered back to Arthur, who now dozed across from her in their otherwise empty carriage. How could it have happened that she had fallen in love with him even while she had remained so adamantly opposed to the whole preposterous idea? Wasn't she supposed to have any say in the matter at all?

But that wasn't the worst of it. What was more unbearable was the knowledge that she had grossly overestimated his interest in her. Arthur didn't find her attractive enough to make love to even when she hadn't demanded any sort of commitment from him, and that was a devastating blow to her pride. If it hadn't been for the overriding importance of their quest for Excalibur, Chelsea would have fled back to London, no matter how unpleasant her parental situation there was bound to be.

Luckily for her declining spirits, it wasn't long before their train crossed into the Lothians and steamed into the hilled city of Edinburgh. As the locomotive's whistle shrilled and they slowed to a chuffing crawl to pull into Waverley Station, Chelsea turned to her traveling companion. With the brim of his hat tipped down over his eyes and his arms folded across his chest, he appeared much too peaceful and content.

She jabbed his ankle with her umbrella. "We're here."

"Ouch!"

Arthur awoke with a jerk, his hat tumbling into his lap. It took him a few seconds to regain his bearings and realize where "here" was. Edinburgh. He'd left his dream-lake behind in Avalon.

He replaced his hat and bent to massage his ankle. "Jeez, Chelsea. Easy, would you?"

"So sorry."

She didn't look sorry, Arthur thought as they debarked. This morning, they'd breakfasted in silence in Glastonbury. Their journey to Edinburgh hadn't passed much better. It seemed that Chelsea had retreated into the impenetrable shell Arthur recognized all too well from their days in Philadelphia. He could feel her anger and hurt, but there was little he could do about it. She wasn't the sort of girl one took to bed and then walked away from, and Arthur wasn't ready to sacrifice his dreams of seeing the world by weighing himself down with a wife.

After claiming their luggage and leaving Chelsea to make use of the womens' facilities, Arthur pushed through a swarm of travelers to the ticket counter. He purchased a city map and asked a paunchy clerk about lodgings.

Once made to understand Arthur's dwindling financial state, the clerk tapped an ink-stained forefinger against his whiskered chin and suggested slyly that if he "warn't the nervous type" he might try a place called the MacKenzie on Leith Street. "Jest be sure ye don't wander too far down the Leith wi' your wife in company, sair. T'is a lively neighborhood. Ye ken what I say?"

Despite the man's thick accent, Arthur "kenned." The Leith didn't have a ladylike reputation, or, perhaps it was more accurate to assume that the "ladies" on the Leith weren't "ladylike," but the clerk assured Arthur that the area wasn't dangerous and that the MacKenzie itself, located close to the main thoroughfare of Princes Street, was at least clean.

The walk from the station to the MacKenzie was less than ten minutes. Short enough in real time, but torturously long when one's only company was a mute, hundred-pound iceberg.

Mr. MacKenzie was a cigar-chomping barrel of a man with a thick beard, spiky gray hair, and a metal ear-horn that did little to alleviate his deafness. After Arthur plunked down five shillings for the night, he was left with a paltry six and sixpence. Between now and tomorrow, he would have to figure a way to pad his pockets or he and Chelsea were going to end up conducting their sword hunt from the street.

When they entered their cramped, windowless room, Arthur threw his suitcase onto one of the two cots. "Let's take a walk."

Chelsea's reply was cool. "I believe I would much rather get something to eat."

Arthur's grumbling stomach agreed. Except for a biscuit and tea at the station in Carlisle, they hadn't eaten since breakfast, but with little more than six shillings in hand, whatever they ingested for dinner might have to last them for a while. The later they consumed their evening meal, the better.

"We will," he assured her, "but Calton Hill is close by. According to the clerk at the station, that's where we can get the best view of the city. Maybe we'll get some ideas about where we want to start our search for Excalibur."

"Fine."

Hell had no fury like a woman scorned, Arthur paraphrased in silent aggravation as they left the MacKenzie House and tramped back up the steep curve of the Leith to Princes Street. But, damn it, love had nothing to do with this, and he hadn't scorned Chelsea, he'd merely behaved like a gentleman. Hadn't he?

Using his map, Arthur led them along Waterloo Place to a set of stairs cut into the steep rock of Calton Hill. Once they reached the top, he paused to survey a field populated with neoclassical monuments, prime examples of the extravagant architecture that had earned Edinburgh its nickname of "Athens of the North." Straight ahead, into the distance beyond the city, were the Lomond Hills of Fife. To the east lay the deep blue reaches of the Firth of Forth.

Arthur pointed west with his map hand. "Over there looks like the best place to get a view of the city."

When Chelsea didn't answer, he turned to meet her sullen expression. Her pompadour knot was coming loose. Sable tendrils fluttered in the easterly salt breeze that swept in from the sea. Tired, wrinkled, and frumpy, Arthur thought with a pang of empathy. And grumpy. If it weren't for this last, he might have given in to an irrational urge to take her into his arms and apologize for behaving like such a goddamned gentleman the night before. Instead, he offered his hand. "Coming?"

She hesitated, and Arthur perceived a battle raging behind those distrustful violet eyes. Angry with him she might be, but they still had a sword to find, didn't they? She took his hand grudgingly. "I still fail to see how this is going to help."

A temporary truce, Arthur thought. It was a start. He let his fingers close over hers and began walking through the ruffling grass. "What if our monk climbed this very hill more than three hundred years ago? I wonder what he would have seen."

"He would have seen the Old Town much as it is today."

"Yes," Arthur agreed as they passed a towering monument dedicated to Lord Nelson. "He would have stood over here and looked out over the Old Town of Edinburgh."

He stopped when they reached the edge of the embankment. Below them sprawled a city that had been split in two. North of the Princes Street lay the New Town. Orderly, rectangular blocks, symmetrical gardens, and neat rows of Georgian buildings. To the south, hugging steep, unforgiving inclines, huddled the sooty gray tenements of the Old Town.

Arthur's attention, however, was fixed upon the center point between the two, a majestic stone fortress built centuries before atop the jutting volcanic rock that overlooked the city. Its embattled walls and proud bastions dominated the southwestern skyline. This was the stronghold of past Scottish royalty. Edinburgh Castle.

"What's the most visible landmark?" Arthur asked.

"The castle," Chelsea said, stating the obvious.

"A king's home is his castle." Arthur turned to her. "In other words, his seat."

Chelsea cocked her head to one side. "You think our monk hid the sword close to Edinburgh Castle?"

"I don't know." Arthur watched her face to test her reaction to his latest idea. "What do you think?"

She blinked at him thoughtfully, then looked back to contemplate the ancient citadel. After a moment, she spoke. "Our original assumption was correct. When our monk wrote that Caliburn rested by the seat of the king, he wasn't referring to the Scottish king, he was referring to King Arthur."

"You're certain?"

"Yes."

Despite his disappointment, Arthur wasn't going to waste time questioning her. He knew that she wasn't being contrary to spite him, she was speaking from the wondrous part of her soul that was in touch with the past, the part that had told her exactly where to uncover that broken sword on Cadbury Castle.

Doffing his hat, he turned his back on the city and dragged a restless hand through his hair. "Well, I don't know what to think now. I was hoping—"

"What's that?" she interrupted.

At her sudden urgency, Arthur looked to follow her pointing finger. Behind the tenements of the Old Town, he picked out an elaborate Gothic building set against a backdrop of open greens and a cluster of craggy hills.

He replaced his hat and consulted his map. "Holyrood Palace." His eyes widened. "Hey! There's a ruined abbey right near it. You think that could be what we're looking for?"

"That's not what I mean."

Her words didn't sink in. Arthur was too caught up in a new burst of inspiration. "It makes sense, doesn't it? Who would a monk rather entrust his most valuable relic to than fellow monks? Of course it makes sense! Why, it—"

"No!"

She was already gone, bustling at top speed in a southward direction across the field. He had to trot to catch up with her. "I don't understand. What are you talking about?"

"That!" Again, she jabbed a finger at some point in the distance.

Staying close on her heels, Arthur glanced down at his map, struggling to focus as they moved. "The Queen's Park?"

"No!"

Arthur almost smacked into her when she halted at the edge of the summit. "St. Margaret's Loch?"

"No, no! The hill!"

Arthur squinted at the cluster of hills that loomed behind the Queen's Park, then scanned his map. "You mean, Salisb—" He cut off and his mouth fell open. "Eureka!"

"What is it?"

"We've found it!"

"We've found what?" Chelsea turned to him, her eyes bright and alert behind her spectacles.

Arthur couldn't hold back a jubilant grin. "My dear, intuitive Miss Delafield, you have just located King Arthur's Seat!"

"They've called it Arthur's Seat for as long as anybody can remember. It's an old volcano, and, along with the castle, it was one of the most striking features of Edinburgh's landscape when our monk arrived here in 1539."

Arthur addressed Chelsea from across a small table in a near-empty gaslit restaurant off Princes Street. While she had returned to their room to gather some clothes to be laundered by the proprietor's wife, Arthur had questioned Mr. MacKenzie regarding the history of the area surrounding the eight-hundred-foot hill that spiked along Edinburgh's southeast skyline.

The man was no history scholar, but he had lived in Edinburgh all his life and imparted enough local knowledge to convince Arthur that they had stumbled upon thc answer to their lost parchment's riddle.

"The ruins are all that's left of Holyrood Abbey," he continued, stabbing a piece of steak from his plate. "Much of it was destroyed during what the Scots call the Rough Wooing."

Chelsea cut some baked trout with her fork. "The Rough Wooing? That took place during King Henry VIII's reign."

"Very good, Miss Delafield. It seems Henry became annoyed when the Scots refused to honor a treaty committing their infant Queen Mary to marriage with his son, Edward, and so—reacting as almost any doting father would in his shoes—he sent the Earl of Hertford to burn and sack Edinburgh and anything else Scottish he could touch his torches to."

Reaching for her tea, Chelsea gave him a look of dubious amusement. "Am I to believe that our esteemed, abdomen-scratching lodge-keeper informed you of all this?"

Arthur smiled. "Forgiven your countrymen may be, but

it's rather apparent to me as an outsider that the Scots are not in a big hurry to forget their past grievances against the English."

"Ah, yes." Chelsea sipped some tea. "And quite a lengthy list of grievances it is, too."

"Well, I'll leave that between you and your neighbors. I prefer to stay out of it."

"Perhaps it might do you well as an American to remember where it is you came from. It could have been one of your very own ancestors who took fiendish glee in carrying out the Earl of Hertford's brutish marching orders."

Arthur's fork stopped midway to his mouth. "What?"

"Whether it be through the sins or the virtues of our ancestors, it is our common history that binds us all together."

Arthur had never given this much thought before, but now that she'd brought it up, he was forced to concede. "Touché, Miss Delafield. I shall consider your point in the future."

She didn't reply, but something warmed in her eyes before she returned her attention to her meal. Until now, with the exception of their initial elation over discovering Arthur's Seat, they'd managed to keep their truce crisp and businesslike.

Arthur cleared his throat and endeavored to get them back on track. "Yes, well, the border abbeys sustained the most damage, but even Holyrood Abbey suffered from the Rough Wooing. It did, however, continue to function until the eighteenth century, when the building collapsed."

Chelsea didn't look up as she cut into a boiled potato. "You seem to think that our monk hid the sword near Holyrood Abbey."

"Well, it is right by the foot of Arthur's Seat, and the abbey was still flourishing when our monk arrived here. The Earl's pillagers didn't wreak their destruction until a few years later. Remember, Mary Queen of Scots wasn't born until 1542."

Chelsea shook her head. "For one who claims only a passing interest in the study of world history, your instantaneous recollection of dates is astounding."

Arthur experienced a twinge of annoyance at her words. He knew it was probably because he was tired from their trip, but sometimes, it truly seemed as if he'd spent his whole life either trying to explain, apologize for, or play down his mental capabilities. Shrugging off his irritation, he reached for a bread roll. "If I read it, I remember it."

"A rare ability."

"It's nothing compared to what you've got."

At this, Chelsea's fork stopped moving. She set it down as if she'd just lost her appetite. Arthur realized too late that he'd turned the tables to hit upon her sore spot. When she didn't look up, he decided to press her. "You act as if you're ashamed of it."

She didn't look up. "I doubt most people would understand."

"Who cares what people understand? Did people understand Galileo? Nostradamus? I doubt you should concern yourself with what people are capable of understanding."

Her dark head rose until those lovely, sparkling amethyst eyes met his. "Touché, Mr. Pierce. I shall consider your point in the future."

They gazed at each other much too long.

Arthur was the first to look away. He reached for the butter. When he heard her fork begin to scrape against china again, he spoke. "You know, I've been thinking . . ."

"How frightening," she interjected dryly.

Despite himself, Arthur had to bite his lip to stifle a grin. Oh, she had a sense of humor, all right. Even if she didn't realize it. The problem was, he was getting to know her better than she knew herself; he was getting to like what he saw, too. Ironically enough, if that weren't the case, he probably could have taken her to bed the previous night, and they wouldn't be tiptoeing all around each other now. They would be looking forward to another romp tonight. And tomorrow night and the next. They would indulge themselves for however long they were together, and then, when it was over between them . . . well, it would be over. That was what a satisfying fling was supposed to be. There and gone.

Pushing these disturbing thoughts aside, he began again. "I've been thinking about the money."

"What money?"

"The money from my uncle's will."

"Oh, yes, your inheritance. When was it you said you were going to be able to claim it?"

"I didn't."

"Oh?"

"I can claim it when I find the sword."

She looked up at him. "What?"

"My uncle placed a stipulation in his will. If I deliver Excalibur, I can collect five thousand pounds."

Her eyes rounded behind her spectacles. "Egad. That's quite a tidy sum, isn't it?"

"Even if I fail to deliver the sword, if I make a good effort to find it, then I still collect one thousand pounds."

"Still a tidy sum." Her expression grew more guarded. "But what has this to do with me?"

Arthur pushed his plate aside and clasped his hands on the table. "I think it's only fair that, whatever the take is, we split it fifty-fifty."

She stared at him for a long moment before replying. "That's very generous."

"Not at all. If it weren't for you, I'd still be stumbling around Glastonbury. If we do manage to find Excalibur before whoever else it is we're up against, it'll be because of you and that sword-detecting nose of yours, Miss Delafield. Business is business. The parchment was mine, the nose is yours. A fifty-fifty split seems in order."

But she wasn't listening. Her gaze had turned inward. "Egad, that's twenty-five hundred pounds." Then she muttered something nonsensical that sounded for all the world like, "no nunnery for me."

Arthur noticed that even though she had earlier attempted to straighten her wilting pompadour knot, it was again hanging askew. It lent her a delightfully reckless appearance. Her cheekbones flushed peach in the gaslight, and he thought that he had never seen her look more appealing than at that moment.

It took some effort for him to banish such dangerous thoughts before offering his hand across the table in much the same manner he had over a week before in the Ridgway Library. "Well, are we in business, partner? Do we have another deal, Miss Delafield?"

When she took his hand this time, her smile flashed bright and beautiful and was very nearly enough to undo every gentlemanly inclination he possessed. "Oh, my, yes, Mr. Pierce. We do indeed have a deal."

"How to catch a man?" Chelsea mused to herself as she pressed a cold, wet washcloth to her neck. She appraised her disheveled image in the mirror that hung above a washstand in their room. At the moment, she was quite alone. The blasted man in question was shower-bathing in another room located at the end of their corridor.

By the time she and Arthur had returned to the MacKenzie, Chelsea's spirits had lightened. First, there had been the serendipitous discovery of Arthur's Seat, and now she was in line to collect more than two thousand pounds if their quest proved successful. It was a staggering sum of money. While riches had never held any particular fascination for her before this, she was now in a position to consider that it might be her own freedom she stood to win.

Why, if she were to come into such an amount of money, her teaching career could be postponed. An extended trip to the Continent might not be out of the question. She could hire her own traveling companion, a real traveling companion, not some wrinkled old crone determined to cling to her like a leech.

Not since the day Arthur had placed the Glastonbury parchment in her hands had Chelsea felt such an exhilarating rush of hope. In fact, the only issue that now remained to mar her brightening outlook was Arthur himself. She wasn't so much angry with him anymore as she was plainly frustrated.

Over dinner, she had caught him looking at her with kindling interest, only to have him snatch his gaze away and act as if nothing at all was going on between them. Well, dash it all, something *was* going on between them, and Chelsea had had quite enough of pretending there wasn't.

Taking a clean towel to dry off, she frowned at the mirror. "How to catch a man?"

Her reflection offered no reply.

Chelsea set down the towel and began tugging loose her pompadour. "With a very large net?"

Still no reply. It was clear that the woman in the mirror had no idea how to catch a man. Chelsea was on her own.

Shaking out her hair, she reached for her brush. Perhaps it was time to toss subtlety out the window.

Behind her, a key jiggled in the lock, then the door squeaked open and closed. "Jeez, that water's as cold as a witch's—"

Chelsea turned to look at him.

"Nose," Arthur finished, giving her a mischievous little grin. His hair was wet, his shirt was unbuttoned, revealing just a hint of the strapping male chest she had glimpsed aboard the *Salacia*. A towel was draped casually about his neck. "The bathing room is empty if you want to use it."

"I don't believe so. I'll leave it for tomorrow."

"Oh." He moved to his cot, tossed down the bundle of dirty clothes he'd been carrying, and began rifling through the contents of his open suitcase.

Chelsea set her hairbrush down carefully, drew in a deep breath, then reached to begin unbuttoning the back of her blouse. "All that traveling has me exhausted."

"Well, that's only natural."

Chelsea shrugged the blouse down over her shoulders and shed it, letting it drop to the floor, then she reached back to unhook her skirt. "Perhaps it's all that walking we did this evening."

"Fresh air can do that to you."

She sneaked a glance to see that he was still bent over his suitcase, folding some trousers. She stepped out of her skirt and began to unbutton her petticoats. "All those steep hills."

"Right. Steep."

Down to her corset, her knee-length drawers, and her stockings, Chelsea left her petticoats behind on the floor and crossed to her cot. Perching on the edge of the mattress, she unclipped her garter suspenders, then dropped down onto her back. Lifting one leg, she pointed her toes at the ceiling and began peeling off a stocking. "Tomorrow's another day."

"Yup."

With a flick of her wrist, Chelsea sent the stocking over her head to flutter to the floor somewhere behind her. She lifted her other leg and commenced peeling. "Perhaps we should take a walk round Arthur's Seat first thing in the morning."

"Yeah, I think you're right. We can go out by the abbey ruins and see if—holy jeez! What the hell are you doing?"

Chelsea craned her neck to see past her uplifted leg. All she saw was a white blur that resembled a hurtling towel. The next instant, she was blinded and smothered by something disgustingly wet and smelling of soap.

"You're naked! For God's sake, Chelsea, what's the matter with you?"

Popping up, she clawed at the towel, finally succeeding in yanking it away from her face only to be assailed and knocked back down again by a flying balled-up blanket.

"Cover yourself!"

"I am not naked!" Flinging the towel aside, she grabbed for the woolly bundle. Too late. Arthur snatched it back just before her fingers could claim purchase.

He was shaking it out to full size by the time she sat up

again to glare through crooked spectacles. His eyes were riveted to the floor, his jaw was firmly set, his complexion beneath a day's worth of beard shadow was ruddier than usual.

"I am not naked," she repeated to emphasize her point. "I am merely getting ready to retire for—"

One quick move on his part and the blanket ballooned through the air to settle over her head like a tent. Everything went black.

Chelsea pursed her lips in the dark, straightened her spectacles, then folded her arms stiffly. She tried to remain calm even though her heart pounded at three times its normal rate. She had imagined a slow and romantic seduction. Nothing even vaguely resembling this sort of commotion.

"A lady doesn't go running about scantily clad in the presence of a gentleman," Arthur informed her hotly.

"Hmmm, then all this time I must have been mistaken about what went on at that burlesque house where you used to work."

Silence.

Chelsea waited. The nubby wool scratched her exposed skin, the air was growing uncomfortably close.

"This is different," he said.

"I see."

"Well, it is."

"Hmmmm. Without granting agreement, I'll just move on to say that after last night I assumed we'd gotten past silly exercises in false modesty. We are business partners. Fifty-fifty. That's all there is between us. Anything else would be irresponsible. So, I ask you, what seems to be the problem?"

"You're still a woman, that's the problem."

Chelsea allowed a secret smile to curve her lips. So, he'd noticed. Feeling emboldened, she pulled the blanket down from her face and studied him with speculative interest. "Before this, I never thought of my gender as being problematic. Could it possibly be your gender that is causing difficulties?"

Although she had never before seen the cavalier, smooth-talking Arthur at loose ends, she suspected this was what she was witnessing now. Staring at her with something like bewilderment, he opened his mouth, then closed it, opened it again, then closed it again. Was it possible that he was at a loss for words?

He retreated three steps until his legs met the cot. "I've got to get out of here."

Chelsea's stomach curled into a tight ball. "What did you say?"

"I've got to go out." He glanced about the room, spotted his coat on a peg by the door, and made a dash for it.

Chelsea's newfound feminine confidence had vanished. "B—but I don't understand why—"

"I have something I have to do." He struggled into his coat as if a pack of wild dogs were nipping at his heels. "Stay here. Keep the door locked."

Chelsea couldn't help the trembling squeak in her voice. "But where are you going at this hour?"

"Out."

For a long time after the door slammed, Chelsea didn't move. She had always been given to understand that the great battle lay in the preserving of one's virtue, not in the disposing of it. Dash it all. She couldn't even get that right.

# 21

*With church bells pealing* in the distance, Chelsea and Arthur set out the following morning in a drizzling rain for the ruins of Holyrood Abbey. The dreary weather suited Chelsea's mood perfectly. Arthur had returned to their room in the wee hours of the morning smelling of Scotch whisky, cigars, and cheap perfume.

She was not amused.

With both of them functioning several hours short on sleep, very little conversation passed as they picked about in the mud and soggy remains of an old church tower and nave. Chelsea tried to concentrate as she closed her eyes and pressed her fingers to the cold, mossy stone, but instead of vibrations from the distant past, all she seemed able to pick up were images of Arthur sitting in a smoky pub with a well-endowed strumpet perched on his lap.

"Nothing?"

Chelsea opened her eyes to stare at him. He didn't appear any happier than she was as he transferred their umbrella from one hand to the other.

"It's not here," she said.

"Damn," he muttered, then looked off toward Holyrood Palace where a red-uniformed sentry went through his perpetual back-and-forth march. Behind the palace, Arthur's Seat brooded against the Salisbury Crags and low-hanging clouds of battleship gray.

Chelsea eyed her companion grumpily as she pulled on her gloves. "What we need is access to a library."

Arthur looked back at her with ill-disguised annoyance. "It's Sunday."

"So it is."

"We're not going to find Excalibur in a library."

"But it might help to do some historical research."

"It might," he said testily, "but I was rather hoping that nose of yours would help point us in the right direction."

Chelsea lifted her chin. "My nose is apparently off-duty."

His eyes narrowed on her. "Why do I get the feeling that you're not even trying?"

Chelsea pressed her lips together and glowered. Oh, she was trying, but she couldn't seem to get past the wall of fury that skewed her perceptions. It was all she could do to keep from balling up her fists and pummeling him.

They stared at each other in prickly silence before Arthur broke the impasse. "I suppose we could go back to the room and strike up a game of high-low-jack. Twiddle our thumbs until the libraries open their doors tomorrow morning."

Chelsea wrinkled her nose before turning her back and folding her arms. She hated that he was right. What she needed to do was concentrate on the sword, on the money, on her freedom. That was what was important. That was what she stood to gain out of this whole miserable, rotten mess.

She sucked in a deep breath. "We need to climb the hill."

"Why?" His tone changed to cautious hope. "Do you think it's there?"

"I don't know. All I know is that it's somewhere nearby,

and the only feeling I have about it is coming from the direction of Arthur's Seat."

"All right," he said decisively. "Then that's where we're going."

Taking an eastern approach, their climb to the rocky summit of Arthur's Seat took the better part of an hour. By the time they reached the top, the rain had stopped and the sun was straining to break through a bank of brooding clouds. Even on an overcast morning such as this, the view of Edinburgh and its surrounding countryside was stunning, almost enough to make Chelsea forget her sour mood. Almost. She still wasn't picking up anything useful.

Arthur finally lost what little forbearance he possessed after they walked in circles for more than thirty minutes. "I thought you said all those feelings of yours were coming from here!"

"They were!" Frustrated, Chelsea stopped pacing and glanced about the deserted hilltop in a futile attempt to pin down the source of the emanations that had been tugging at her nerves since they'd come to Edinburgh. The sword was not here, but they were closer to it now than they had been while tramping about the abbey ruins. She sensed that much, but she couldn't extrapolate any further than that. The sword's steady, enigmatic pull seemed to be coming from all directions at once.

Arthur approached from behind. "What do your feelings tell you?"

Chelsea's patience snapped. She whipped about, her hands clenched into fists. "They don't tell me anything! What do you think this is? Some sort of mystical telephone exchange?"

Arthur stepped back, clearly surprised at the vehemence of her reaction. "No, I didn't mean—" He frowned, then began again in a calmer tone. "No, I don't think it's a mystical telephone exchange. Maybe it's just that—" He clipped off whatever he was going to say, slanted her a condescending look, and folded his arms. "Never mind. I think I know what's going on here."

Bristling at the all-knowing, typically male expression on his face, Chelsea raised her chin, daring him to do battle. "What were you going to say?"

He measured her for a moment before deciding to reply. "All right. I was going to say that maybe you're just not in the right mood for this today."

She arched an eyebrow. "Mood?"

"Yes, mood. It's no secret that women have periodic moods. You know what I mean."

"No, I'm afraid I don't. You'll have to explain."

"Explain?"

"Yes."

He appeared taken aback that she'd pushed him this far. "What? You mean, you want me to say it?"

Chelsea waited.

Arthur took a step back and assessed her warily. "Oh, no you don't. I'm not going to say it. In fact, just forget I mentioned it. I don't even want to know if it's time for your . . . mood."

On behalf of all womankind, Chelsea dug deep to deliver him the most withering go-to-the-devil look she could muster before turning her back. "As if I would confide in you."

She was mortified to feel unplanned-for tears creeping up on her. All of her life, she'd always been able to keep a check on her emotions. These days, however, it seemed they soared and dipped and shot about with all the predictability of an agitated hummingbird.

She wasn't sure how long it was before she sensed his approach from behind. Long enough for him to regain some perspective, long enough for a painful lump of emotion-run-amok to form in her throat.

She felt his fingers close about her shoulders and his chin come to rest on the crown of her head. His sigh was one of battle-fatigued surrender. "Chelsea, if it's not that, then what is the matter? Are you angry with me about last night?"

Last night. Chelsea couldn't bring herself to reply. So, it had finally occurred to him that she might not be entirely naive to the ways of the world. Even though she'd led a sheltered middle-class life, she knew of the fancy women, the ones who tucked up their skirts and frequented Leicester Square after the sun went down. And their kind was certainly not confined to London. They were everywhere. In Edinburgh, she assumed they haunted Leith Street. She had suspected as much yesterday when Arthur had insisted they head back up to the high street to find access to Calton Hill rather than following a shorter route that would have entailed going farther down the Leith. She had become sure of it when he'd slipped back into their room last night smelling like a bordello.

"I shouldn't have thrown the towel at you," he said.

Chelsea frowned. Towel?

"Nor the blanket, I suppose, but you caught me off guard."

Blanket? She didn't give a damn about the blanket!

"I know I've been short-tempered today," he continued, oblivious to that fact that he was barking up the entirely wrong tree, "but it's just frustration and lack of sleep and the lousy weather. It has nothing to do with you. I'm sorry."

She felt his hold on her loosen, but then his fingers slid up one shoulder to toy with the hair at the back of her neck. Tingles of treacherous delight shimmered down her spine. Chelsea caught her breath and silently cursed her susceptibility to his touch even when she was so angry, she could throttle him.

"Chelsea?"

She cleared her throat, but her voice still came out an ineffectual rasp. "I'm fine."

He let go of her, and she sensed that he backed a few steps off. His tone became more impersonal. "We can return to the room if you want."

Chelsea filled her lungs with air untainted by the smoke and fumes of the city below them. Her gaze settled on the rolling Midlothian countryside that spread to the southwest of Arthur's Seat. "I think I'd like to try once more."

He didn't sound hopeful. "All right."

Chelsea hunkered down and shut her eyes. The grass reached up well past her knees, but she paid no attention to the clammy wetness that seeped through her skirt and petticoat to chill the skin beneath.

Her monk was here. She had first connected with him in Glastonbury, and now she could sense his benign presence as surely as she could smell this morning's rain in the air, but his guidance seemed maddeningly beyond reach. Perhaps she was still too distracted, or perhaps Arthur was right when he'd accused her of not trying hard enough. Or perhaps she had spent so many years learning to block out her extraordinary senses that she was no longer capable of expanding upon them.

Determined to give one last best effort, Chelsea clenched a gloved fist and raised it to her forehead. She began to whisper to herself. "It is fortuitous that we learned of the approach of Cromwell's men in time to hide the books and relics most valued by the Abbey. . . ."

She repeated the whole text of the parchment. Once through, she began again, whispering the words rapidly. Then again. And again. The words tripped off her tongue like a recited catechism. ". . . of those were hidden with friends in Glastonbury. The rest we brought with us. They will be protected by friends of . . ."

> . . . Benedictines until it is safe for the monasteries to return to England. It is fitting that Caliburn now rests by the seat of the King until he shall rule again.

*With a beleaguered sigh, the young monk set aside his goose quill and reviewed the words he had just written. His Latin was not as precise as that of his learned superiors, his script not as disciplined as his older brother scribes, but there was little he could do about that. Once the ink was dry, he would prefix this page to the others and turn the volumes over to the prior.*

*He rubbed his hands together, blowing on cold-stiffened fingers to lend them heat. With nothing left to do but wait, he rose from behind the sloped writing desk and moved to the window. When he pushed back the shutter, a bracing easterly wind blew back the hood of his cowl. Snowflakes drifted down to melt upon the hard, unforgiving ground. Across the gentle rolls of deadened landscape, a flat-peaked hill rose among many others behind the frozen loch. To his eye, it cut the gray winter sky like a war blade. Fitting, he thought, then frowned.* Opus dei. *His abbot had sent him to do God's work. Had he done well? He only knew that he had done his best.*

Chelsea hit the ground face-first. She smelled mud and clutched handfuls of wet grass to achieve some anchor point. The disorientation that sent her consciousness spinning was more than spatial in nature; it was disorientation of time itself.

She became aware of Arthur's hands on her arms, pulling her up from the ground. "Chelsea! Jeez almighty, are you okay?"

She opened her eyes to an unintelligible blur of browns and greens and gray-blues. The blur closest to her, however, was none of these. It was Arthur, and she grasped at his forearms with unsteady hands as he pulled her to her feet. "Oh, but he was so young!" she cried breathlessly. "Not much more than a boy!"

"Wait. You've lost your eyeglasses." The Arthur blur dropped from sight.

"Fourteen, or maybe fifteen years of age," she continued, unable to contain herself. "He was a porter. He watched the abbey gate, and he also helped in the stables."

The Arthur blur popped back up again. "Here, they don't seem to be broken. I've wiped them off the best I could."

Taking her hand, he placed her spectacles in her palm. "Now, what happened? Are you sure you're all right? What are you talking about?"

"Our monk!" Chelsea settled her eyeglasses on her nose, and the world, except for one annoying streak of mud, slipped back into sharp focus.

Arthur was frowning at her, not understanding and perhaps edging upon worry for her sanity. "Chelsea, what exactly just happened to you?"

"I saw it! I saw Arthur's Seat."

"Chelsea, we're *on* Arthur's Seat."

"No, no, you don't understand!" Chelsea felt as if she might burst with exhilaration from what had just happened to her, but she tried her best to calm down and explain in terms that he could understand. "Arthur, I saw it through his eyes. He was—" Losing patience with the inadequacy of mere words, she glanced about to get her bearings. To the north lay the city of Edinburgh. To the east, the crags and the sea. To the south . . . "There," she said, pointing down. Below them lay a deep blue loch. Just beyond that, a sleepy village nestled in peaceful bucolic surroundings. "It was from somewhere behind the lake, about a mile to the southwest, I think."

Arthur stared at her with an expression of dawning amazement. "You think that's where he hid the sword?"

Chelsea nodded. There was no doubt left in her mind. "I'm certain of it."

"Interesting," Emory Blake commented, squinting into his field glass and focusing upon the two intrepid figures who were making their way around a lake some half a mile distant. "It now seems as if they have a destination. It's almost as if they're following some sort of unmarked trail."

"They showed no such clear purpose as recently as yesterday," Geoffrey Dark remarked tonelessly.

The three of them, Blake, Geoffrey, and Mr. Beck, now stood by the northeastern foot of Arthur's Seat. Blake lowered his field glass and threw a dubious glance at his butler. "They showed no such clear purpose as recently as this morning."

The hint of a scowl chased itself across Geoffrey's implacable features, but he didn't go so far as to disagree. That was because it was true. Blake and the mammoth Mr. Beck had arrived late last night to join Geoffrey here in Edinburgh. This morning, they'd first followed Arthur Pierce and Miss Delafield to the ruins of Holyrood Abbey, then they had kept a discreet distance as the pair had scaled Arthur's Seat.

Blake and his companions had used a field glass to observe the two young people as they had wandered about the summit of the hill seemingly without purpose for almost an hour before descending again and heading off toward the village. It was odd, to say the least.

Blake frowned to himself. "They've found something."

"Possibly," Geoffrey granted reluctantly.

More than possibly, Blake thought. Now more than ever, it appeared that his casual decision to have Geoffrey keep tabs on Sidney Pierce's nephew might have been the wisest move he'd made in almost ten years.

"He's been very lucky so far," Blake mused aloud. "Perhaps we might benefit from that."

"You wish Mr. Beck and I to follow them?"

Blake glanced at Mr. Beck, who remained silent and always ready to serve for the right price. "I think it would be best if you and I take up that task, Geoffrey. I doubt Mr. Pierce has forgotten our friend's face just yet. Mr. Beck may return to our hotel in town and await instructions."

"Very good, sir," Geoffrey said, then inclined his head toward their towering companion, who took his cue and moved off in the direction of the city.

Raising his field glass, Blake focused again on the youthful couple in the distance. Lucky. Pierce was more than just lucky. He was on to something promising, and Blake felt no compunction whatsoever at the thought of taking full advantage of it. In fact, he felt a glimmer of anticipation at the thought of nipping Caliburn right out from under the arrogant lad's nose. The challenge would add a bit of much-needed good sport to the venture.

"Something tells me, Geoffrey, that it shall not be long now." Blake's handsome lips curved into an avaricious grin as he watched the unwitting pair who would lead him to his long-awaited prize. "No, not very long at all."

# 22

*Arthur thought Chelsea made quite* an eccentric picture. A disheveled young miss creeping along on her haunches, unmindful of the wisteria vines that caught in her hair as her fingers worked through freshly tilled garden soil to probe at the stone foundation of the old inn.

The freestanding sign dubbed it THE GRANGE, a charming hostelry with ivy creeping up its thick stone walls, an arbored rose garden, and flashes of colorful blooms lining the flagstone walks. Its outbuildings included a livery and stable.

"Perhaps we should go inside now," Arthur hinted, feeling conspicuous as he stood over his dauntless partner. He was trying to shield her from sight of the country road that wound past the front of the establishment.

Since they'd arrived at the small village, asking questions of various passersby, he'd tried his best to cover for her erratic behavior, but she wasn't making it easy. As soon as Arthur had unlatched the front gate of this peaceful country inn, Chelsea had taken off, bolting around the tree-shaded corner like a hound on the scent.

Arthur had hurried after her, calling that perhaps they should go about their investigation a bit more conventionally, such as, for example, entering by the front door and inquiring for the proprietor, but Chelsea had paid no attention. Now she was crawling about in the dirt.

"Is there something I can help ye with, lass?"

Startled by the deep male voice that accosted them, Arthur swung around to face a robust bull of a man with friendly, though perplexed, gray eyes. Middle-aged and balding, he sported a full gray beard and carried a spade in one hand.

Chelsea took no notice of him as she went about her strange, intuitive business, so the man shifted his questioning gaze to Arthur. "Lost something, has she?"

Arthur knew he had to come up with some sort of an explanation, so he opened his mouth. "My wife entertains an avid interest in late medieval architecture."

The man looked back at Chelsea, who was now craning her neck and shading her eyes to peer up at the second floor above their heads. "Aye, to be sure."

Arthur endeavored to distract the man's curiosity. "A fellow in town mentioned that this inn was once part of an old monastery. Would you be the proprietor?"

"Eh? Oh, er, aye." The man seemed fascinated by Chelsea's strange behavior, but he wrested his gaze away for the sake of politeness. "Balchristie is the name. Ye looking for a room?"

"Maybe. We took a room in the city last night, but, as you can see, my wife has taken a liking to your charming establishment."

Chelsea chose that moment to scramble back to her feet and point to the second-floor window closest to the front of the building. "I should think we would like to take that room. It would afford us an excellent view of Arthur's Seat."

Mr. Balchristie leaned on his spade and squinted upwards. "Well, ye're in luck, madam. It was just vacated this morning. Four shillings will hold it for the night. Another two and six if ye want to take your meals here."

"We'll take it," Arthur said.

Balchristie chuckled and motioned for them to follow around to the front. "Right this way and I'll sign ye in."

Just in case she was tempted by any more urges to plunge back into the vines, Arthur took Chelsea by the elbow and escorted her back along the flagstone walk.

"Ye say ye're fond of medieval architecture, madam?" Mr. Balchristie asked as he pushed open the heavy oak door and held it for them.

"Yes," Chelsea replied, looking about with sharp-eyed interest as they stepped into a cozy parlor room. "Especially religious architecture."

A rustic inglenook fireplace dominated the wall to their right. Ahead, across a room scattered with easy chairs and end tables was an oak counter behind which hung a box full of stuffed pigeonholes, a calendar, a portrait of St. Benedict, and a wooden plaque with hooks and keys. A black cat dozed on a hooked rug by the fireplace.

Balchristie rounded the corner of the front desk and produced a thick register book. "There used to be a little chapel across where the road runs now, but that's been gone for longer than anyone can remember."

"The man we spoke to said the monks who lived here ran a small farming community of lay brothers." Arthur said, drumming his fingers on the counter. He might not have Chelsea's special sensitivity, but he could feel that they were closing in on what they sought, and it was all he could do to keep still.

"Aye. It was a verra small order compared to most and nothing fancy about it. A cloistered priory, they called it. The first floor right over yer head was their original living quarters." Balchristie turned the open register book around and tapped the page. "If ye sign there, sair, I'll see to yer key."

Arthur scribbled *Mr. and Mrs. Arthur Pierce* then dipped a hand into his trouser pocket to extract six shillings and sixpence in coin. Thanks to his successful foray into the Leith the night before, he was now flush enough to get them through another day or two of lodging and meals.

"So, whatever happened to the monks?" Arthur asked, urging the man to elaborate as he pushed the coins across the counter.

Mr. Balchristie scooped up the money before nipping a brass key from one of the hooks behind him. "Well, they took quite a bit o' damage from the English, o' course, but by then their numbers were so few, it dinna much matter. They died out soon after that."

Arthur shook his head, not understanding. "Died out?"

"Aye, some said it was the devil and some said it was an English brother o' their own who brought the plague among them. There was many who would have said there wasna difference between the two. Whatever the case, it was a lucky thing they kept to themselves. The fever dinna pass into the village."

Arthur mulled this over. An English brother? The Glastonbury monk, perhaps? "That's very interesting," he said aloud, "isn't it, my dear?"

No answer.

Arthur turned to see that Chelsea had moved to the fireplace and was now on her hands and knees examining the hearth. He turned back to the innkeeper and offered what he hoped was a reassuring smile. "I think we'll head back to town and see about getting our luggage."

"Is your wife going to be all right, sair?"

"Oh, don't mind her. She's always been wild over fireplaces."

Before the innkeeper could reply, Chelsea piped up from her unorthodox position on the floor. "Would this have been part of the original structure?"

Balchristie cleared his throat. "Oh, aye, madam. Every blessed stone ye see. There's also a supper room, a kitchen round back, and an ale cellar down below. We still use the cellar to store the wines."

"Hmmmmmm."

Chelsea said nothing more, so Mr. Balchristie looked back to Arthur. "I'll be sure to have the room ready for ye when ye return, sair."

"Thank you." Arthur tipped his hat, then hastened over to Chelsea, almost tripping over the dozing cat, who looked up to peer at him with cool insult.

Chelsea was up on her knees now, pressing her palms flat against the wall of the fireplace. "Have you found something?" he asked in a hushed tone.

She didn't look at him. "This is very odd. There's no fire, but it's warm. Feel it."

Arthur put one hand to the stone. "I don't feel anything."

Chelsea shook her head, puzzled. "I can't tell where it's coming from. Even down here . . ." She dropped back onto her hands and knees and felt along the flagstones laid directly before the hearth. "Maybe it's coming from the cellar."

Before she could turn back the edge of the rug, Arthur glanced over his shoulder to see that their innkeeper was observing them with mounting interest. "Chelsea, I think we should get out of here now or Mr. Balchristie might change his mind about renting to us."

With a frustrated sigh, Chelsea stood and brushed off her hands. "So close," she murmured, then raised her head to frown up at a landscape painting that hung over the arch of the fireplace. It was a forest-ringed lake. In the distance, by the shore, a dark-haired woman dressed in a flowing, green tunic stood in profile, looking out over the water.

Arthur took Chelsea by the arm and waved a cheery goodbye to their barrel-chested innkeeper. "Tonight," he said, dropping his voice low and urging her toward the front door. "We'll have a chance to investigate more thoroughly tonight. For now, let's just get out of here."

The inn had a bathing room equipped with a porcelain tub and a tap that ran from two rain barrels below the roof. For two coppers, the stable boy was more than happy to carry up a few buckets of boiling water from the kitchen to create a relaxing bath for any boarder with a whim to indulge in a bit of luxury.

Finished with her washing, Chelsea closed her eyes, immersed herself up to the neck, and rested her head back against the cool curve of porcelain. She was trying to relax tense muscles and clear her cluttered mind. She and Arthur had returned to their room at the MacKenzie House only long enough to retrieve their belongings, pay their laundry bill, and scuttle back to The Grange.

They had found their new lodgings to be quite cozy. Furnished with simple oak furniture, hooked rugs, ruffled curtains, and knitted tidies, it would be a welcome respite for any weary traveler. Why, if it weren't for the monstrous double bed, Chelsea thought it would have been perfect.

In spite of her determination to clear her mind of all troubling thoughts, Chelsea scowled upon picturing that infernally huge piece of furniture. It reminded her of how infuriated she was with Arthur, not to mention herself. She had acted the part of a lovesick fool yet again in trying to seduce him last night. Her only possible consolation was that he might not have realized her licentious intentions. She couldn't help wondering how it might have gone if she'd had any idea about the correct manner in which such delicate affairs were conducted. If that had been the case, he might not have run off to have his desires slaked elsewhere.

Then again, perhaps he would have, the rake.

Chelsea scowled again. Just thinking of him caused her traitorous body to ache for his touch, but her mind's eye rebelled by flooding with vivid images of Arthur and Julia Tierney. She imagined the two of them reclining on said cushy bed, naked as robins and nibbling on grapes.

The image exploded as Chelsea shot upright in the tub. Water sloshed out over the edges to splash onto the floor. Jealousy foamed and spat in her veins. To the devil with Arthur Pierce, his middle-class trollops, his dancing tarts in tights, and his fancy women of the Leith!

Chelsea stepped out from the tub, shivering with rage and swearing as colorfully as any East End ruffian. Snatching a towel from a table, she vowed to banish Arthur from her heart forever. She would concentrate on the sword. The sword and nothing else. The money. She would concentrate on the money and nothing else. Her freedom. Oh, yes. She would concentrate on her freedom. When this was over, she would hop a steamship and cruise around the world. She would bask in the shadows of the pyramids and stroll along the Nile in Cleopatra's footsteps. She would become an . . . an adventuress!

"That's right. That's what I'll do," she muttered, drying her hair vigorously with a towel. "That will show him. Perhaps I shall even take a lover."

Perhaps she would take several lovers.

"Oh, yes, yes, yes," she said, liking that idea even better as she struggled to fasten the front of her corset. She would take innumerable lovers. European nobles, traveling journalists, and daring, dashing, devilishly handsome explorers. She would shock all of society with her wild and wicked behavior.

Feeling refreshed and vindicated, Chelsea finished dressing, grabbed her bundle of soiled clothing, and left the bathing room to pad determinedly up the carpeted hallway in her stockinged feet. When she threw open the door to their room, she found Arthur standing over the washstand with his shirtsleeves rolled up to his elbows. He glanced up, drying his hands with a towel. "That didn't take long. Feel better?"

Chelsea wrinkled her nose. Better. Damned correct, she did. She stamped across the room and bent to pluck up her discarded shoes.

Arthur thought it was an especially well-executed exercise in wordless eloquence. She was angry with him, and she wanted him to know it. What she didn't want him to know, however, was exactly what it was she was angry with him about. All the better to leave him waiting and wondering. Agonizing and sweating.

He mused to himself as he rolled down his sleeves and secured his cuffs. So, if it wasn't her woman-time—and she'd made it clear by the quelling look she'd delivered him earlier today that it wasn't—then what was causing her to behave so irrationally toward him? Hell, he'd apologized for the stupid towel incident. What else was he supposed to do?

Moving to a coat rack to retrieve his waistcoat, Arthur chastised himself for giving in to the temptation to glance at her long enough to notice that she had her skirt hiked up to her knee as she laced a shoe. It served to remind him of how wildly indecent and delectable she had looked the night before with both of those gorgeous legs displayed right in front of his stunned face. It was also a humiliating reminder that he, the suave, experienced Arthur Pierce, had reacted to the whole situation like a complete horse's ass.

He finished buttoning his waistcoat, grabbed his suit coat from its hook and crossed to a rocking chair in one corner to wait for Chelsea to finish getting ready for dinner. He rested his head back and watched through half-closed lids as she stood and moved to the dresser to brush out her hair.

It was still damp from her bath, and he was reminded of how she looked in his dreams when she emerged from that sparkling sunlit lake: water running off skin as soft and perfect as flower petals, palm-sized, rose-tipped breasts, gently flared hips, slim, white thighs.

It didn't matter that she was fully dressed now. Arthur was fully convinced that he already knew what she looked like naked, and he felt a slow, warm pulse of arousal quicken his blood merely upon imagining her.

*"She will lead thee to thy sword."*

The Hamilton voice in his dream had been right. She was leading him to the sword. She was also leading him to something else, something they were both bound to regret if he didn't get a rein on both his appetites and his emotions.

"I'm hungry," he announced, shooting up from the chair. "Let's go."

Chelsea blinked at him in exasperation. Apparently, she wasn't satisfied that he'd sweated long enough. "But my hair isn't dry."

"Nobody will notice." Arthur's hand was already on the doorknob, and it was sweating plenty. "Let's go."

"Egad, wait a moment."

She grumbled under her breath, but she basically cooperated. Arthur drummed his fingers on the door as she pulled her hair back at the sides, tied it with a blue ribbon, then checked her blouse for wrinkles.

"You look fine. Let's go." He opened the door and gestured for her to precede him. Culinary aromas of baked bread and beef stew wafted up from the dining room. Now, he really was getting hungry. For food, that was. It was the dinner hour, and they hadn't eaten since breakfast.

They descended the stairs in silence and passed through the parlor room where two gentlemen boarders were seated in easy chairs, both of their faces hidden behind Edinburgh newspapers.

They found the candlelit supper room quiet and nearly deserted. Only Mr. Balchristie occupied a square corner table. A bowl of beef stew and a sliced loaf of bread sat before him. Raising a hand in greeting, he invited Arthur and Chelsea to join him.

As Arthur pulled out a chair for her across from the innkeeper, Chelsea sat and uttered a tight-lipped "thank you." She thought that it was a blessing that the talkative Mr. Balchristie was present. His steady stream of amiable chitchat served as a much-needed buffer.

Her nerves were on edge. She couldn't tell if this was because of her mixed-up feelings toward Arthur or because of the equally confusing ebb and pull of her sixth sense. Perhaps, if she had, in the past, spent more time learning how to cultivate her extraordinary talents rather than trying to repress and ignore them, she might have been better able to interpret what she felt now. As it was, she couldn't separate her own rioting emotions from all the other disturbing impressions she was experiencing.

"Mrs. McTavish is our new cook," Mr. Balchristie was saying. "She's a recent widow, poor thing. Been with us just a fortnight, but already she's got a reputation for her stew." Raising an arm, the older man signaled toward the kitchen, a separate room that opened off the back. "Here she comes now."

Chelsea was too preoccupied to pay more than polite half-attention to Mr. Balchristie's innocuous conversation. She didn't even look up until she heard the other woman speak.

"Good evening, sir. Madam."

There was something in that soft, purring voice that caused the hairs on the back of Chelsea's neck to prickle. Her extraordinary senses were set to buzzing. When she lifted her head, her gaze clashed with a pair of striking jade green eyes.

# 23

*If Chelsea had expected the inn's* cook to be a plump, elderly, Scottish matron, she was radically mistaken. The woman was tall and appeared to be in her early thirties. She wore an aproned pine green dress over a slim, graceful figure. Her shining, onyx hair was pulled into a severe bun at the nape of her neck, but not even such an unflattering hairstyle could begin to camouflage her exotic beauty.

"Mrs. McTavish, this is Mr. and Mrs. Arthur Pierce. They're visiting from London," Mr. Balchristie said.

"How very nice to meet you." Those ethereal green eyes lingered on Chelsea before shifting to Arthur. "How long will you and your wife be staying with us, Mr. Pierce?"

"Only a couple days." Arthur's manner was openly admiring as he rested an elbow on the back of his chair.

"Well, I hope you enjoy your stay," Mrs. McTavish said. "Tonight's menu is beef stew. May I get you an ale, Mr. Pierce?"

"Now that you mention it, that would really hit the spot. Thanks for suggesting it, Mrs. McTavish."

Chelsea wrinkled her nose. Arthur was grinning like a baboon. Mrs. McTavish, on the other hand, seemed to wear the secret smile of a crafty feline. The hairs on the back of Chelsea's neck were prickling so intensely it was all she could do to resist the itch.

"Mrs. Pierce? Coffee? Tea? Wine?"

"Tea."

As the annoying woman moved away, Arthur had the audacity to crane his neck to follow her progress all the way back to the kitchen door. Fighting an urge to kick him under the table, Chelsea snatched up her folded napkin and shook it out furiously before spreading it on her lap.

"That woman is a godsend," Mr. Balchristie said. "Ye can't know how many cooks I've gone through since my own dear wife passed away just last year."

The innkeeper was still lamenting over how difficult it was to get good help when Mrs. McTavish returned a few minutes later. As she served their beverages and set two steaming bowls of beef stew before them, Chelsea shifted in her seat uncomfortably. The prickles had set in again.

"Why, thank you, Mrs. McTavish," Arthur said. "This looks delicious!"

"T'is my pleasure, Mr. Pierce. Please enjoy your meal."

Chelsea frowned as Mrs. McTavish glided back to the kitchen. She hadn't noticed before that the cook spoke with a subtle accent that bore no resemblance to that of a native-born Scot.

As Arthur drew Mr. Balchristie into a casual conversation concerning the history of the inn, Chelsea tried to place that accent, to no avail. As soon as she tasted her main course, though, she had to admit that, wherever the blasted woman came from, she was a splendid cook.

Mr. Balchristie soon finished his meal and excused himself to see to some outdoor chores before sundown. That left Chelsea and Arthur alone in the supper room except for one newcomer, a well-dressed gentleman at a table behind them. Chelsea assumed he was one of the boarders they'd passed in the front parlor. His face was still hidden behind a newspaper.

Arthur lowered his voice. "So, any new clues?"

Frankly, Chelsea had been so distracted by Mrs. McTavish, she'd almost forgotten the sword, but she wasn't about to tell Arthur that. "No," she replied. "It's all very confusing at the moment."

"Confusing? How?"

"You've got to stop asking those sorts of questions," she complained. "You know I can't explain."

Arthur tore a slice of bread in half and settled back in his chair. "All right. I suppose we'll just have to do some old-fashioned sleuthing until your nose clears up again."

"My nose is perfectly fine."

"No offense intended. It won't do any harm, though, if we—"

He cut off as Mrs. McTavish came through the kitchen archway with her serving tray. She set before them a plate of sticky cakes for dessert, then began clearing their dishes. "Everything to your liking, sir? Madam?"

"*C'est magnifique*," Arthur said, gifting her with one of his dazzling Pierce smiles. "Mrs. McTavish, I can't tell you when it was that we last had a meal as delicious as this."

"You flatter me, Mr. Pierce."

"Oh, but it's true." Arthur nudged Chelsea. "Isn't it true, Mrs. Pierce?"

Chelsea folded her arms and stared straight ahead. "Possibly."

"Why, thank you . . . *Mrs.* Pierce."

Chelsea looked up just in time to catch a glimmer of amusement in the other woman's expression before she turned away to wait upon the newspaper-reading gentleman at the next table.

"She doesn't believe we're married," Chelsea said in a clenched whisper.

Arthur appeared unconcerned as he reached for a sticky cake. "Don't be ridiculous. How can she know that?"

"She just knows." Chelsea watched with narrow-eyed suspicion as Mrs. McTavish moved back to the kitchen. "There's something about that woman."

Arthur gave a rakish little chuckle. "Oh, yes, there's something, all right."

Chelsea glared at him. "She's old enough to be your mother."

Arthur grinned as he pulled off a bite-size piece of cake. "My older sister, maybe, but not my mother. Definitely not my mother."

"She's older than you think."

"Really? How do you know that?"

Chelsea just frowned. She *didn't* know. Not for certain.

After Arthur finished his dessert, he lowered his voice and changed the subject. "As I was saying before we were interrupted, I think we're going to have to get a look at that wine cellar."

"And how do you propose we do that?"

"Wait until everyone's asleep."

"You mean sneak?"

Arthur shrugged as if to say, what else?

Chelsea wasn't sure she liked that idea at all. "I don't know. It seems so . . . so . . ."

"Sneaky?"

"Yes. I rather like Mr. Balchristie."

"So do I," he agreed, "but that's beside the point. What did we travel all this way for?"

Chelsea frowned as she poured more tea and lifted her cup to her lips. Arthur was right, but that didn't make her feel any better about practicing duplicity where their widowed innkeeper was concerned.

Arthur laid a calming hand on her arm. "I swear, you bring out the worst in me. My thieving, scamming ancestors must be turning over in their graves."

Chelsea gave him a questioning look. "What are you talking about?"

Arthur's blue eyes sparked with amusement. "We'll cut him in."

"You mean, Mr. Balchristie?"

"The parchment was mine, the nose is yours, and the inn is

his. I suppose it's only fair that if we find anything, Mr. Balchristie becomes our new business partner. Even though he doesn't know it yet. How's that? Is your conscience soothed?"

In spite of her acute annoyance with him over the past twenty-four hours, Chelsea couldn't resist a grudging smile. "Oh, yes, Mr. Pierce. Much better."

Emory Blake lowered his newspaper and observed as Arthur Pierce and his lady friend left the dimly lit supper room. He felt no pressing need to follow them at the moment. He'd caught only snatches of their hushed conversation, but it had been enough to learn that they were planning to explore the wine cellar later this evening.

"Will you be needing anything else, sir?"

Blake looked up to see the dark-haired, green-eyed beauty appear by his side and set a bowl of savory stew before him. She was no young chit, but Blake found her uncommonly attractive. He detected in those enthralling green eyes a glint of sharp intelligence that might rival his own. Too bad he hadn't the time to indulge in a bit of frolic.

"No, I'm quite fine, thank you," he said, folding his newspaper.

"Do enjoy your meal, sir."

Blake allowed himself the subtle pleasure of observing the enticing sway of her hips as she moved away. Oh, yes, he fully intended to enjoy his meal. And the night ahead.

They had a couple of hours before sundown, so Arthur and Chelsea strolled about the tree-shaded grounds of the inn, soon discovering behind the kitchen a pair of doors that presumably led down into the wine cellar. Noting its location for later, they continued along the country lane back toward the village.

They ended up strolling around the loch, stopping for a while to watch the swans glide through the water. Arthur was glad to see that this seemed to have a calming effect on Chelsea, but his hope that she would reveal what was bothering her was in vain. He was still in hot water, and he had no idea why.

When they returned to their room, the western sky was pinkening toward dusk, but they still had well over two hours until midnight, the hour Arthur had chosen to conduct their clandestine foray into the wine cellar.

Shoving his hands into his pockets, he watched as Chelsea sat on the bed to remove her shoes. Ahead of them stretched two hours of awkward small talk. Arthur didn't think he could stand it anymore.

"All right. Enough of this."

She didn't look up. "Enough of what?"

"Enough of this dancing around whatever it is that's got you so angry with me."

"Angry with you?" she asked sweetly. "Why should I be angry with you?"

"I don't know," Arthur said, deciding that it was up to him to remain calm and rational. He would wear her down with logic. "That's why I'm asking."

She sat up and gave him a look that could have frozen Don Juan's breeches. "Well, if you don't know, I'm certainly not about to tell you."

So much for calm and rational. So much for logic. "Well, that's just plain stupid," he said.

Her cheeks flared a livid bright pink, but she didn't speak. Instead, she rose from the bed with great dignity, took up her carpetbag, and moved to the chest of drawers. Arthur watched in growing frustration as she opened a drawer and began removing the garments that still remained in her bag.

It was then that Fred Sherman's advice sprang to mind. "*The first thing you must do is apologize. In fact, the more obsequious, nose-to-the-ground, dirt-eating you do, the better.*"

But what if he didn't have any idea what he was apologizing for? Arthur considered this for a long moment, knowing what Fred's answer would be. Every ounce of male pride Arthur possessed caused him to chafe at this, yet . . .

"I'm sorry," he said.

Chelsea stopped and looked at him cautiously. "What?"

He chose his next words carefully. "If I'd known at the time that it would upset you, I wouldn't have done it." He waited to see if this would pass.

She studied him with guarded suspicion. "Done what?"

*Damn.* Arthur tossed up both hands in surrender. "Ah, hell! I don't know! You won't tell me!"

Chelsea slammed the top drawer closed and yanked the next one open. It was clear that she was becoming exasperated. So was he. "How am I supposed to apologize if I don't even know what it is I'm apologizing for?" he demanded.

"Apologize?" She whipped around, her cheeks flaming, a pair of lacy underdrawers dangling from clenched fingers. "I think it's a bit late for apologies!"

"Late? Why? What are you talking about?"

"I'm talking about men!"

"Men?"

"You!"

"Me?"

"I'm talking about last night!"

"Last night! Ah ha!" He snapped his fingers and pointed at her. "It's the towel thing! I knew it!"

"No!"

*No?*

Chelsea let out an infuriated squeal and flung her drawers. "I'm talking about you and your tarts!"

"You mean cakes?" Arthur stepped aside in time to avoid getting struck in the face by flying feminine underwear. He wasn't angry anymore. He was back to confused.

"Not cakes! Women, you imbecile!"

Something yellow and frilly came at him. This time, he put up a hand quickly enough to snatch a camisole out of midair. In his mind, he played over her list. At first it seemed an unsolvable muddle, then it all suddenly fell into place. Setting aside her reference to baked goods, it boiled down to two telling clues. Last night and women. No wonder she was so furious. She was jealous.

Of nothing.

She turned her back again. Stockings and garters and corsets blurred together as she yanked the last items from her carpetbag and stuffed them into the drawer. Tossing aside the camisole, Arthur approached her from behind and took her by the shoulders. She made a token effort to pull away, but he wasn't about to let her escape until this was cleared up.

"Where do you think I went last night?" he asked.

"Out. That's what you said. Out."

"You think I went to be with another woman, don't you?"

She didn't reply.

"I went out to hustle some money."

She didn't move.

"I wasn't with a woman," Arthur reiterated so there could be no misunderstanding. "In case you don't know, the only ladies who frequent the streets at that hour tend to charge dearly for their affections, and, believe me when I tell you that I've never paid a woman to come to bed with me."

There was a long moment of should-I-believe-him silence, then the tension drained from her shoulders. "Money?"

Convinced that she wasn't going anywhere, Arthur let go of her and allowed his hands to fall to his sides. "We were busted."

She turned around, her eyes downcast. "I'm sorry. I didn't know what to think. You left in such a rush that . . ."

Arthur cupped her chin so she would look up at him. With her amethyst eyes shining in the waning light of dusk and her ebony hair hanging loose about her shoulders, she appeared to him more lovely and vulnerable than ever before.

"Chelsea, the only woman I wanted to be in bed with last night was you." He knew as soon as the words were out that he shouldn't have said them. Even if they were the truth.

Her woebegone expression began to change. Uncertainty became feminine curiosity. "Arthur, if what you say is true, then why weren't you in bed with me?"

Arthur knew then that he was in trouble. And if he was in trouble, they were both in trouble. It was clear that Chelsea was still unaware of her womanly responsibilities to set sexual boundaries rather than expand them, and, despite his best efforts to remain cool-headed and rational, all he could think of at the moment was what she would look like without clothes. Oh hell, they were in big trouble.

He had to clear his throat to keep from sounding half-strangled. "When I told you the other night that you aren't a mere kernel to be sowed, I wasn't joking. I have no interest in stealing your virtue."

"One cannot steal that which is freely offered," she said, bamboozling him with the kind of logic that he'd set out to entrap her with earlier.

Arthur could hear his own heart beginning to pound in his ears. "This attraction between us is—"

"Unbearable," Chelsea finished, gazing up at him so frankly that he couldn't even begin to deny it.

He tried to drag in a breath but couldn't. His lungs had jammed. The air was suddenly too close, the room too small. "Chelsea, it was never my intention to hurt you, or—"

"You won't." She pressed an open palm to his chest, then moved it in a slow, experimental circle. "I'm not as fragile as you may think."

"Perhaps not, but I can't offer you—"

"I haven't asked for anything." She raised another hand to play along the planes of his chest. Arthur thought she couldn't possibly realize the effect her innocent explorations had on him. Signals of arousal were already racing through his bloodstream.

"You've thought this all out, haven't you?" he asked.

She raised one shoulder in a coy little shrug as she continued to play over him with her fingertips. He realized then that she knew precisely what she was doing, and his body temperature hiked at least another ten degrees.

"I may be a woman," she said, "but I enjoy a bit of adventure just the same as you do. You've caused me to grow curious about certain matters." Her luminous gaze raised to meet his, and there was nothing coy about it. "I think it only fair that you satisfy my curiosity, don't you?"

# 24

*Despite her bold words,* Chelsea's knees were knocking together so hard, she was amazed Arthur didn't hear them. She had never put on such a reckless show of bravado in her life, but it paid off.

In a heartbeat, Arthur had her about the waist and hiked up against him. When his mouth settled possessively over hers, the anxiety in Chelsea's stomach turned into something thrilling and adventurous. Rising up on her toes, she clasped her arms about his neck, relishing his vitality and heated excitement. As his tongue explored her mouth, she let out a shaky moan of helpless delight. He gave a low groan in response as they collapsed together onto the bed.

Clothing. What a blasted nuisance! Hooks, laces, garters, and thousands of buttons. Chelsea's heart tom-tommed as she struggled to shed as much as she could in as timely a manner as possible. It wasn't long before it occurred to her that it was astounding the human race hadn't died out soon after the invention of the corset.

"Ah, damn," Arthur muttered, dragging his mouth from

hers to concentrate more fully upon loosening her newfangled, front-fastening ties.

"Hurry, hurry," Chelsea urged, her fingers trembling with anticipation as she labored to unbutton his shirt.

"Jeez, we shouldn't even be doing this," he mumbled.

"Arthur Pierce, if you run out on me now, I shall never forgive you."

"Believe me, I couldn't run anywhere just now."

She didn't know what he was talking about and didn't care. Just as her corset finally popped open and slid away, Chelsea pulled his shirt off over his head to reveal the enthralling expanse of male chest she'd only glimpsed before now.

"How magnificent," she whispered, forgetting to be self-conscious over her own state of undress as she ran her fingers over lean, muscled flesh brimming with strength and virility.

"I'm an irresponsible cad," Arthur said as he tore down the bedcovers and maneuvered her onto her back. He bent his head to bestow light, tickling kisses across her bared breasts.

"Oh . . . oh, oh, yes," she agreed, threading her fingers through his hair and squeezing her eyes shut. She feared she might swoon as, through the light cotton material of her drawers, she felt his hand skim up, up, up the inside of her thigh. The sensation loosed a shocking and exhilarating rush of warmth between her legs.

"Forgive me, Chelsea," he whispered, grazing his lips over the peak of one breast.

"Ooooh, yes, yes," she murmured. He seemed to be doing something indecent with his tongue.

There was a gentle tug at the drawstring of her drawers, then warm, talented fingers slipped beneath the waistband to caress her navel. And lower. And lower.

"Oh, my God," she gasped when his hand closed upon her, but before she could protest or be embarrassed or even think, his mouth covered hers. He kissed her very hard and very deep, and, by the time he pulled away to nibble a scintillating path down the column of her throat, she couldn't think at all.

She was aware only of the rhythmic press and stroke of his fingers as her whole body tensed, then shivered and slipped off into a stunning oblivion. She sucked in a sharp gasp of air, only to let out a long, breathy *ahhhhhhh* as she was bathed in a pulsating shower of sparkling white light.

*Magic,* she thought when her brain began to form coherent images again. It was the only word she could think of to adequately describe the breathtaking thrill that sizzled in her veins and fueled her thrumming heart. Even though she was coated with a thin sheen of perspiration, she still shivered like a wet pup. "Oh, Arthur," she gasped, "what have you done?"

In response, he gave a self-satisfied chuckle and nipped at her earlobe. "Don't move."

Move? Egad, she was nothing more than a drenched, quivering noodle. How could she possibly *move*? She was disappointed to feel him slip away from her to shed the remainder of his clothing. His comforting warmth was gone, and she still felt a vague ache to be satisfied.

When he came back to her, he picked up her hand and threaded his fingers through hers. Still groggy and tingling, she forced her eyes open. "I had no idea that being ruined could be so stimulating."

He brought her hand up to graze his lips over her knuckles. "I haven't ruined you yet."

Struggling up onto one elbow, Chelsea adjusted her sagging spectacles to peruse his exquisite physique. Her eyes widened upon that part of him which most resembled the thoroughbred stallion she had likened him to in the past. The sight both stunned her and caused a new rush of heat to flood her cheeks. "Oh, dear heavens," she murmured.

Only a hint of daylight still glowed at the window, but it was enough to see that one of them had been seriously misconstructed. Since Arthur had already been with other women, Chelsea was left to conclude that the misconstructed party was herself. She could conceive of no place on her body where he could possibly put such a thing.

"I know what you're thinking," he said.

"You couldn't."

"Yes." He dropped her hand and reached for her waist.

"No."

"Yes," he said again, pressing a reassuring kiss to her lips and urging her back down onto the sheets. "It'll be all right."

"I don't think so."

He kissed her again, then removed her spectacles and tossed them over the side of the bed. "You won't be needing these."

"But I can't see without them."

"I know," he said, thinking that he should have had the good sense to dispose of them earlier. God, she had proven to be even more sensual and enthusiastic than in his wildest dreams, and now he would have to start all over. She was as stiff as a toothpick, about as ready for sex as a new nun, while he was hard enough to drill a hole through the headboard.

Slowly, inch by inch, he urged her drawers down over her hips. "Do you want to stop?"

For a long moment, she blinked up at him in the deepening darkness, quite blind, quite innocent, and utterly irresistible. Part of him hoped she'd say, yes, Arthur, stop, because that would put an end to this harebrained sexual affair before it was too late; the other part of him wanted nothing more than to feel those luscious Delafield legs hugging his waist.

"No," she said. Then she lifted her hips, pushed her drawers down to her knees and kicked them off. She opened her arms to him. "If you say it will be all right, then it will."

Any last vestiges of gallantry dissolved in that moment. Arthur just hadn't the willpower to resist his own impulses any longer. What could one night's pleasurable interlude hurt? She had not asked anything of him. Why had he insisted upon making this so complicated?

He kissed and caressed her and skimmed his mouth over fragrant feminine skin until she began to move and sigh restlessly beneath him. Soon, with his own control wearing thin, he positioned over her, pushing her thighs apart to fit himself against her. They matched perfectly. Almost perfectly, he thought as he began to ease inside of her only to encounter a resistance wholly at odds with her otherwise welcoming flesh.

"Oh, dear," she moaned. "I knew we wouldn't fit."

"We'll fit," he said from between his teeth. "It's just that you have to be . . . broken in."

"Like a shoe?"

"Not quite."

She tightened her arms about his neck. "Other women have got through it. So shall I."

"Yes," Arthur said, but he was breaking out into a sweat that wasn't all due to thinly controlled passion. Other women had gotten through it, but not while he was at the helm.

She closed her eyes and sucked in a breath. "Do it."

Do it? To Arthur, sex had always been uncomplicated. It was nothing more than mutually satisfying adult play, pure, unadulterated pleasure. But this was different. The idea of causing his partner discomfort was not only novel, it was profoundly disturbing. Yes, this was very different. A first. For her and for him.

Arthur dropped his head to touch his mouth to hers, nudging into her a little deeper, pausing when he felt her tense, nudging again when he felt her relax. Which was better? Slow or fast? Had this been a wedding night consummation, he would have found out ahead of time if there was some technique to ease the initiation of a new bride, but this wasn't planned. He was left to depend on his instincts, instincts that were much too far gone to back off now.

He lifted his head, shifted his weight, eased into her still farther. God, he wasn't going to last long. She felt like pure heaven. Her eyes flew open to meet his in the dark.

"Okay?" he asked anxiously, his arms beginning to tremble with the effort it took to both support his weight and be still.

"Yes." She tightened her hold around his neck and urged him gently with her hips. "Now, Arthur," she whispered.

When he hesitated, she arched against him again, urging him onward despite whatever discomfort she was experiencing, and so he braced his knees as well as his nerves, and, with one concentrated thrust, buried himself deep inside her.

Chelsea caught her breath in shock.

Arthur thought he might pass out from delving into such a sinfully lush paradise. Her warm, supple femininity closed around him like a second skin. It took a moment for his drugged brain to catch up with his reeling senses. "Are you okay? Chelsea?"

"Yessss," she gasped on an out-breath. "Ummmmmmm, yes."

She had never felt anything like it. The flash of pain had been brilliant, but it was well worth how it felt to be joined at last. She had to bite down hard on her lower lip to keep from blurting out that she loved him.

He withdrew, then stroked back into her, and she gasped again, but there was no pain in it this time. He repeated the motion, once, twice and a third time, and Chelsea surrendered to his intoxicating rhythm.

Sweat broke out to dapple them both, and when he dropped his head next to hers, his shallow, harsh breathing filled her consciousness. She somehow knew that, after struggling to be gentle with her, he was now losing himself to the same exquisite vortex of pleasure he'd induced her to earlier. Gratified that he seemed to draw such satisfaction from her, Chelsea hugged him tight until the very instant his rhythm faltered.

"Ah, jeez, ah, damn." He groaned, defying instinct and abruptly withdrawing just before his climax washed over him. He shuddered as it wrung the very life essences from his body, overflowing to spill out onto her rather than into her.

Not very romantic, he thought when the blood pounding in his ears began to cool and the pleasure-induced fog in his brain began to clear. But that last-second withdrawal had been necessary. Bad enough that he'd taken her virginity, he couldn't risk getting her pregnant, too.

"I'm sorry," he murmured, lifting his head to press a kiss to her mouth.

Petal-soft lips curved into a teasing smile beneath his. "Arthur, you guilt-ridden fool," she whispered, caressing his cheek, "we fit. How can you be sorry?"

He wanted to laugh, but it might have spoiled the mood, which was very warm and very intimate and more satisfying than he'd ever expected. Instead, he kissed her again. "That's not what I'm sorry about." Then he reluctantly pulled away. "Lie still. I'll be right back."

As he moved off the bed, Chelsea was content to do as he said. The sizzling in her veins had died down to a warm, pulsing glow. It made her want to curl up and sleep.

Letting out a satiated sigh, she hugged herself to compensate for the loss of her lover's warmth. Her lover. She positively adored the sound of it. She positively adored him. She'd suspected it would be like this, had suspected, perhaps, from the very first moment he'd touched her in the garden of her rooming house in Philadelphia. Certainly, she had known the night they'd danced in the grand saloon. Light, spark, magic . . .

"It's not always so, uh, messy," Arthur said.

He felt awkward addressing such an indelicate subject. Negotiating his way across the dark room, he found the washstand, snatched a clean towel, and hurried back to her. "You awake?" he whispered, crawling in between the sheets.

"Mmmmmhmmmm."

Again, he felt silly as he dabbed at her abdomen in the general area where he'd so rudely spilled his seed. "I'm sorry, but, uh, I wasn't prepared, and it was the only way I could think of to keep you from getting, uh . . ." He tried to think of an appropriate euphemism but could only come up with *expectant*. That didn't seem right.

"Mmmmmmm," she sighed, rolling onto her side. She snaked an arm across his midsection and curled up against him like a snoozing kitten.

"Chelsea?"

The only sounds were the soft rustle of night air stirring the curtains and Chelsea's even breathing. She'd fallen asleep.

Moving slowly so as not to disturb her, Arthur balled up the towel and lobbed it to the foot of the bed. He settled back onto his pillow and slipped his arm around her to get comfortable. She sighed in her sleep and moved with him, resting her head in the crook of his shoulder, and it suddenly seemed to Arthur as if this were the most natural thing in the world, to be reclining in bed with Chelsea nestled cozily next to him.

With another hour to pass and his baser drives temporarily quenched, he was left to contemplate what had just happened between them. What could one night's pleasurable interlude hurt? Looking back, he supposed it could hurt plenty when they finally went their separate ways. Would she resent him? Was it selfish of him to want to see the world and experience life on his own terms before settling down to a day-to-day job and a family of his own to support? He had never thought of himself as selfish before.

It was more than forty-five hard-thinking minutes later that Arthur awoke Chelsea with a gentle shake of the shoulder.

Shocked to realize that she'd dozed off, she shot up, trying to remember where she was. The blurred yellow glow of a paraffin lamp greeted her unfocused vision; the cool night air chilled her exposed breasts, reminding her that she was naked. "Oh, dear," she mumbled, hurriedly crossing her arms for both warmth and belated modesty. "What time is it?"

"Nearly midnight."

She squinted, trying to bring the room into focus, but without her spectacles, all efforts were fruitless. She could, however, make out Arthur's fully dressed figure sitting next to her on the edge of the bed.

"Here."

Keeping one arm over her chest, she held out a hand to receive her spectacles. By now, the remembrance of their tryst—every scintillating detail—brought a flood of heat to her cheeks. The tenderness between her thighs confirmed that she had not dreamed it, and now she was left to wonder anxiously if, in her abandon, she might have made a fool of herself.

She settled her spectacles onto her nose only to discover Arthur wearing a grin that made her feel even more exposed and goosebumpy than she already was. "How long have you been sitting there?" she asked.

His grin widened. "A few minutes."

"Do you make a habit of observing unclothed ladies while they sleep?"

"Only this very beautiful unclothed lady." He sounded not the least bit apologetic as he leaned forward to place a light, lingering kiss to her lips.

That kiss, not to mention such blatant flattery, caused Chelsea's stomach to flutter and glow with renewed sensual warmth. Despite the reservations she harbored over her earlier behavior, it seemed that her body was quite blissfully unabashed and game for more festivities.

When he pulled back, though, he cupped her chin, his lake blue gaze sobering to gentle concern. "You okay?"

With his hair mussed and the top of his shirt hanging open, he appeared quite the boyishly handsome swain, and Chelsea's cheeks fired hot once again at the indecent thoughts that chased through her mind. It was undeniable that she couldn't remember having felt more splendidly okay in her life.

"Very," she said in reply to his inquiry, then emboldened herself to toss the question back at him. "And you?"

He smiled, apparently amused at her concern. "Very, too." When he raised his free hand, she noticed for the first time that he offered her hastily discarded underclothes. "But now, Miss Delafield, we have some other exploring to do."

* * *

Holding the table lamp from their room in one hand, Arthur descended the creaking staircase. Chelsea clutched up her skirt and followed close on his heels, thinking that the stairs hadn't seemed to creak nearly so much in the bright light of day. Those incriminating sounds seemed to magnify in her ears to the point where her recently calmed nerves began to bite at her again.

As they passed through the deserted parlor room, the hairs on the back of her neck prickled. Then, there was a sound, a soft *hisssss*, and Chelsea's heart jammed in her throat. They were being watched. She spun around to stare at the darkened fireplace.

Arthur spoke in a harsh whisper. "What's the matter?"

Chelsea didn't reply. Couldn't. Her blood had turned to ice. Menacing furniture shapes and shadows crouched in that part of the parlor, any of which she could have easily imagined into lurking human figures, but what her eyes had trained upon were a pair of glowing yellow orbs hovering near the foot of the fireplace.

"It's the cat."

Arthur had merely whispered in her ear, but he had crept up soundlessly from behind. It was enough to shoot her bristling nerves through the roof. When she jumped, she almost knocked the lamp from his grasp.

"Jeez!" Arthur exclaimed in a hoarse whisper, steadying her with his free hand. "Get a hold of yourself."

She let out a quivering breath and buried her face in his chest. She had forgotten about Mr. Balchristie's cat, the one that had been napping by the hearth this afternoon. Apparently, the animal had returned to its favorite spot to spend the night.

She felt Arthur's arm encircle her shoulders, and it helped calm the hammering beat of her heart. "Sorry," she said, lifting her head. "All this cloak and dagger work seems to be making me a bit jumpy."

"To say the least," he agreed, then laid a finger to his lips and motioned for her to follow.

A moment later, they were outside, creeping around the side of the darkened inn. The night air was crisp and carried the scents of dewy grass and budding roses. A hazy moon cast tree shadows upon the flagstone walk.

When they came to the kitchen door around back, Arthur stopped and held the lamp up. Yellow light splashed out over a pair of battered oak doors that led underground. Earlier, they had been secured on the outside with two dead-bolt latches, one at the top and one at the bottom. Certainly nothing to deter wine thieves or curious midnight explorers. What they saw now, though, proved that Mr. Balchristie was not so trusting after all.

Below the bottom latch, two iron loops had been bolted into the wood. They hadn't taken notice of it earlier because it hadn't been important then. Now it was important. What winked at them in the flickering light was a shiny new padlock.

# 25

*Chelsea's heart sank.* "It's locked."

"Not a problem." Arthur crouched to examine their dilemma more closely.

"You certainly don't intend to break the lock, do you?" She strained to keep her voice low lest the sound carry to open windows overhead.

Arthur set down the lamp. "Do you have a hairpin?"

Chelsea was confused. She'd made a halfhearted effort to coil and pin her hair before they'd vacated their room, but what had that to do with their situation?

"A hairpin," Arthur repeated, holding out a hand. "The next best thing to a key."

Chelsea doubted this, but complied by plucking the requested tool from the bundle at the nape of her neck. "They didn't teach you this at the University of Pennsylvania, did they?"

She caught just a flash of a smile before he turned to concentrate on his task. "No. Some families hand down wealth and some hand down recipes. My family—"

"Never mind. I don't think I want to know."

"Actually," Arthur said as he tinkered with the lock. "I learned this from a guy named Fuzzy Garrison. No blood relation."

"Oh, yes. I recall you mentioning Mr. Fuzzy once before."

"A master safecracker," Arthur said with a trace of admiration. "But he gave it all up for—"

"Love?" Chelsea guessed.

"No, religion. Seems he found Jesus just before he escaped that last time from the Kansas City jail."

As Arthur worked, Chelsea peered around them in the dark. Overhead, a ghostly moon peeked through a tangled web of tree branches. Night sounds nibbled at her skittish nerves. The chirp of crickets, the occasional rustling of a bird in its nest, the squeal of a mouse as it tried to escape a pouncing cat. She had to calm herself. If ever they needed her sixth sense to be sharp, it was now.

"Damn I'm good," Arthur announced as the padlock clicked open. He released the two slide bolts, retrieved the lamp and stood. "So, what's the rule on who goes first when it comes to dark wine cellars after midnight?"

Chelsea was beginning to appreciate Arthur's sense of humor. It helped take the edge off her nervousness. She peered down at the uninviting black pit by their feet. "Gentlemen first."

"That's what I was afraid of." He began his descent. "But stay close, tootsie. We may need that sniffer of yours."

As Chelsea gathered up her skirt and took her first step, she paused to glance over her shoulder. A prickle of awareness skittered down her spine. The feeling that they were not alone. Ridiculous.

The call of a tawny owl echoed in the near distance. It was a night sound just eerie enough to hurry her feet the rest of the way down the steps. She found herself in a vaulted stone cellar that was almost as spacious as the inn itself. Where she had expected to step onto an earthen floor, her heels contacted flagstone.

Arthur was already a half dozen feet ahead, holding up

the lamp to enlarge its arc of golden light. The far walls were still bathed in black shadows, but to her right, Chelsea could make out a row of stocked wine racks, and to her left, a stack of crates and a workbench littered with tools and gardening implements.

"Over here," Arthur said. He was moving toward the north wall below where the parlor fireplace was located.

Just behind her, Chelsea heard scurrying feet—clawed scurrying feet—then the hem of her skirt *whooshed* as something much larger than any rodent she had ever heard of streaked across the floor. With a squeal, she streaked in the opposite direction—toward Arthur, toward the light.

She didn't realize that he had stopped before a wine rack that lined the wall. "Ackk!" she exclaimed smacking nose-first into a shoulder blade.

The lamp wobbled, tossing crazed shadows off the walls, ceiling, and floor, then Arthur snagged her by the elbow, steadying them both. "Jeez, Chelsea. What's the matter?"

"There was a . . . a . . . thing!" she sputtered, nursing her nose with one hand and pointing a trembling finger with the other. "A huge, hairy, monstrous. . ."

"Mouse?"

He was looking at her in much the same way one would perceive a dotty great aunt. She stopped massaging her nose. "Certainly not. It was a . . . a . . ."

"Mouse." His condescending smile informed her that he was needling her on purpose. "Think we can get on with this now?"

So much for appreciating his sense of humor. If she weren't so blasted head over heels in love with him, she would have given him another good kick in the shin.

Lucky for him, he picked that moment to peck a kiss onto her bruised nose. "You're beautiful when you're contemplating homicide, did you know that?"

Despite her resolution to remain unamused, one wondrously light butterfly took flight in her stomach. It made her following scowl less than convincing. "You're maddening."

"Yet inexplicably adorable," he said, then turned back to the wall and changed the subject. "What do you think?"

Chelsea studied the wine rack that lined the stone wall. Rows upon rows of dark, glistening, pigeon-holed wine bottles. Certainly nothing unusual.

"I don't know," she mumbled. And she didn't. That was what disturbed her most. It seemed that her sixth sense had gone awry. Something was very wrong, and she was beginning to suspect it had nothing to do with her fluctuating emotions.

"Up there," Arthur said, pointing to cobwebbed rafters. "That's where the hearth should be. That's where you felt the warmth. You thought it might be coming from down here."

"It seemed so at the time. It's difficult to tell now."

"You don't feel anything?" Arthur asked.

Oh, she felt something. There was more here than met the eye, but as she reached up to touch the bottles and corks, she could get no sense that her Glastonbury monk was with her. Oh, dear. Where was he when she needed him?

"There is something here," she allowed, "but we must find a way to move this rack." She didn't add that she was growing more doubtful about what they might find.

Arthur appeared to have no such worries as he set their lamp down on the floor. "We'll start by lightening the load." Moving briskly, he removed two wine bottles and set them on the floor out of their away.

Working together, it didn't take long to empty the rack. With a lot of grunting and heaving, they managed to slide the rack down along the wall to clear the area they were concerned with. Chelsea stifled a squeal when a huge spider scrambled over the toe of her shoe.

Arthur took up the lamp again to examine the exposed wall that appeared to be constructed of the same rectangular-cut stonework as the rest of the inn. He said nothing until after he sank down on his haunches, then he let out a low whistle. "Well, would you look at this."

Chelsea had no urge to join him down there. Visions of furry arachnids and beady-eyed, sharp-toothed subterranean rodents were still quite fresh in mind. "What is it?"

Arthur ran his fingers along the lines of lime mortar between the stones. "Look at this section compared to the rest."

"I don't see anything," she said.

"The mortar between the stones is a different color, and if you feel along the plane of the wall, there's a definite irregularity. This whole section juts out about a half an inch. Either the workmanship is sloppy or these stones were removed and later replaced." He looked up. "Come down and see."

Beady eyes and sharp teeth glinted in Chelsea's imagination. "Why?"

"What are you afraid of? Little crawly bugaboos?"

"Don't be ridiculous," she mumbled, but something in his tone nettled just enough to incite her courage. Gathering her skirt up to her knees, she cast a quick look around to make sure the area was clear before she sank down and ran her hand along that section of wall. Even if she hadn't felt the physical irregularities Arthur spoke of, she could have told him that something was hidden behind the stones. The problem was, the hidden something she sensed failed to elicit the thrilling shivers of excitement she had anticipated.

She looked up to see Arthur's hopeful expression and tried her best to force a smile. Perhaps she had been expecting too much. That was no reason to dampen Arthur's enthusiasm. "I think this is it," she said.

Blake leaned back against the wall outside the inn, idly cracking his knuckles. Mr. Beck crouched by the gaping mouth of the cellar with his big shoulders hunched and his head cocked, listening for any indication that the two explorers below had stumbled upon something important. So far, the only discernible sound that drifted up resembled the tap-tap-tapping of a sluggish woodpecker. Whatever Mr. Pierce and Miss Delafield were up to, they'd been at it for well over twenty minutes.

Soundless as always and nearly invisible in his charcoal gray suit, Geoffrey appeared by Blake's side, coalescing from out of the dark like a black-derbied ghost. "Perhaps it's time to intervene."

Blake stopped cracking his knuckles only long enough to turn his head. "Not yet. But soon."

The tap-tap-tapping Emory Blake heard was Arthur chipping away at old mortar with Mr. Balchristie's hammer and chisel. The mortar loosened easily; it was clear that whoever had re-sealed the wall hadn't intended for it to stay that way forever. All in all, there were two rows of six stones each.

Once enough mortar was removed, he began to pry the thick stones loose, first with the chisel, then with a crowbar. Chelsea tried to help as much as she could with the few tools available. It wasn't long before the first stone moved.

"We've got it." Arthur threw down the crowbar and grasped an exposed edge of stone to pull it away from the wall. His heart pumped with more than physical exertion when he caught sight of what shouldn't have been behind it—the dull glint of metal.

He lifted his gaze to Chelsea's. In the wavering light, her cheeks appeared flushed. Her eyes were wide with something like awe. "A strongbox?" she asked.

"It could be."

Their initial elation was interrupted by a muffled tap-tapping directly above their heads. They peered up to discern no visible source for the disturbance. There followed a scraping sound that sent an involuntary shudder down Arthur's spine.

"What's that?" Chelsea whispered tensely.

"Mice," he said quickly, although he'd heard plenty of mice scampering behind walls before, and none of them had ever sounded as if they were wielding tiny hand tools. He gave Chelsea a sidewise peek to see if she agreed with him.

"Mice?" She was still staring at the ceiling.

"It must be. What else?"

The sounds stopped. She looked at him, now appearing paler than usual. "Perhaps a restless guest unable to sleep."

Arthur thought about this for a second and nodded. He liked this explanation better. The tap of a walking cane on the floor above might produce such a sound. Perhaps.

They listened for a moment longer, but all remained quiet. Whatever it had been, it was gone now. Arthur looked at Chelsea and shrugged. This time, they tried to make as little noise as possible as they set back to work.

Since the remaining inside stones were already exposed, they pried loose much easier than the first. Moments later, with each taking an end, Arthur and Chelsea pulled out an ironbound leaden chest.

With anticipation churning his stomach, Arthur hunkered down. The chest was in good condition for having been cemented in between face stones for so long. Using the hammer and chisel, Arthur snapped the iron lock and threw back the lid.

The wavering light caught and glinted off silver. Tarnished silver, granted, but there was lots of it. With the possible exception of his Uncle Sidney's mansion in San Francisco, it was more than Arthur had ever seen in one place in all his life.

Silver goblets and engraved dishes and utensils. Crucifixes and medallions. A holy censer and a statuette of the Virgin. A gold-plated chalice with scrolled foliage on the stem and biblical scenes depicted along the sides. And jewelry. Ruby and onyx rings and a gold necklace set with sapphires. A hoard of pearls in a cordovan leather pouch, and enough silver pennies to fill two fists.

But it wasn't until they got to the bottom of the chest that Arthur's blood really began to race. At first it appeared to be nothing more than a bolt of faded red linen, but he knew it was much more than that.

As he lifted it from the storage chest, a faint scent of

mildew rose in the air. Carefully, he set it down on the floor between himself and Chelsea. Whatever was inside was narrow and long and heavy, and when he folded back the fabric, he found himself staring at a sword.

"Jackpot," he whispered.

The hilt, cast in tarnished silver with gold damascening, was shaped into the form of a winged serpent. Its head, with two glinting red rubies for eyes, formed the pommel. At the opposite end, the serpent's wingspread formed the handguard and was inlaid with other gems that winked seductively in the wavering light. Emeralds, Arthur guessed, but it was too dark to be sure, and it didn't really matter anyway.

This quest had long ago ceased being about money.

"Jeez," he said and swallowed hard. "Look at it, Chelsea."

"It's beautiful," she whispered.

*A gift . . .*

In his mind's eye, Arthur saw a splendorous steel blade rising to break the shimmering teal blue surface of a lake. He saw a woman's hand, white and delicate and perfect, offering the jeweled hilt to a young warrior king whose name would live for as long as there were men to tell tales of his exploits. *"It was magic, Arthur. That sword was magic unto itself, a gift offered to him by Merlin the Enchanter and the Lady of the Lake."*

Moving slowly, worshipfully, feeling almost as if he were in a dream himself, Arthur wrapped his fingers around the hilt. In that fleeting instant, all of his boyhood fantasies died.

It was cold.

A taunting voice rose in his mind. *What were you expecting?*

Magic. He'd been expecting magic.

He let out a pent-up breath and tried to dismiss his childish disillusionment. He lifted the sword to examine it with new eyes. The blade was wide at the hilt and gracefully tapered down to a perfect point; it was unscarred and well-balanced, an excellent piece of workmanship . . . but it wasn't magic.

It was just a sword.

He looked at Chelsea. She wasn't paying attention to him. She was staring at the double-edged weapon. And frowning.

"We're rich," he said softly, willing her to look at him.

She did look at him then, but he could ascertain nothing from her expression. Bewilderment? Disappointment? What was going through her mind?

"It would seem so," she said, then shifted her attention back to the sword. She traced her finger down along a groove on the broadside of the blade and frowned again. "Something is wrong."

But before she could elaborate, they heard footsteps on the cellar steps, and by the time they shot to their feet, a tall, dark-cloaked gentleman with an astonishing mane of silver hair stepped into their circle of light. He brushed some dust from the sleeve of a coat that fairly screamed Savile-Row tailoring. "So kind of you to invite us, Mr. Pierce."

"Who are you?" Arthur asked.

"Introductions would be pointless. Suffice it to say that I'm an old acquaintance of your uncle's."

By now, another intruder had joined them. For some reason, Arthur wasn't surprised to see his old friend from the Red Rooster in Glastonbury. "Ah, Mr. Beck," he said ruefully, "I see you've come all this way just to return my satchel."

The big man apparently had no sense of humor, but Silver-Hair condescended to chuckle as he tugged off his gloves. "You so remind me of your uncle, Mr. Pierce. May he rest in eternal discontent, of course."

A third man joined them, this one a good deal smaller and darker complexioned than the previous two. Beneath his black derby, he wore the expression of a bored toad.

"You!" Chelsea exclaimed.

Arthur glanced at her in surprise. "You know him?"

"From Glastonbury," she said, folding her arms and scowling.

"Of course," Arthur said under his breath. "Where else?"

Silver-Hair slapped his gloves against one palm and began to peruse the basement chamber as if inspecting a suite at the Grand Hotel in London. "I'm sorry to say that I came to know your uncle all too well. In fact, it was he who stole the Glastonbury parchment by outbidding me after the deal was supposedly closed. Quite unethical."

"Well, I wouldn't know anything about that," Arthur said warily. "We didn't keep in touch. I inherited the parchment from him after he died."

"Oh, yes, of course. I'm well aware of the terms of his last will and testament." In passing, Silver-Hair stopped to nudge one of the goblets with the toe of a polished boot, then he moved on, not bothering to further investigate the open storage chest. He was apparently unimpressed with run-of-the-mill sorts of treasures. "That's why I harbor no ill will toward you or the charming Miss Delafield, here."

"We're relieved to hear it."

Silver-Hair stopped, turned, and delivered a frosty smile. "I would so like to stay and chat more about your recently departed uncle, but it's getting late, and we really must be off." He extended a hand. "The sword, if you please?"

Although neither of his boon companions had uttered a word or made a move, their mismatched presence spoke volumes. No one was going to get past those two without Silver-Hair's heartfelt blessing.

Arthur decided to try reasoning with him. "Look, uh, Mr. whatever-your-name-is, maybe we can strike a bargain."

"Bargain?"

"Maybe my uncle did steal the parchment from you. Heck, who am I to say different? I know Sidney was no saint. Sainthood doesn't run in our family. But it's no fault of mine, right? You and I have no quarrel, so what do you say we split our profits fifty-fifty? That sounds fair, doesn't it?"

"I think not."

Chelsea grumbled, "Oh, just give him the blasted sword."

"The lady possesses good sense." Silver-Hair flipped a hand in the toad-man's direction. Taking his cue, the man withdrew something from his coat pocket, and, with a neat flick of the wrist, displayed a blade that caught the muted light with a deadly glint.

Arthur took one step back. "Thirty-seventy?"

Chelsea hissed, "Give him the blasted sword."

Both Mr. Beck and the knife-wielding toad were well out of striking distance. A significant fact because it was then that Arthur realized he was armed, too. The weapon he held might not be magic, but it was the most legendary battle sword of all time.

Plucking up his nerve, he tried for his best poker bluffing grin and brandished the weapon. "*En garde.*"

To which Mr. Beck calmly produced a revolver and pointed it at them.

"Damn," Arthur muttered. He'd never liked guns.

"I see you've reconsidered." Silver-Hair flashed that cool smile again and waggled his fingers expectantly.

Arthur gave up the sword. In his mind's eye, he saw five thousand pound notes grow papery wings and fly off into a pink and gray sunset.

"Ahhhh, yes, at long last, Caliburn, Caliburn." As Silver-Hair clasped the hilt, he lost some of that seamless composure. He caressed the smooth blade, his gray eyes glowing with what Arthur thought must be avarice in its purest form.

He felt Chelsea's hand on his arm. "It's all right." There was a calm acceptance in her voice that surprised him. After all they'd been through, didn't she feel even one twinge of regret?

"Yesss, yesss!" With a howl of triumphant laughter, Silver-Hair strode to the cellar steps, his boot heels clicking on stone, his dark cloak billowing behind him.

Arthur decided then that if the twisted adoration he'd seen in those eyes was the closest thing the man knew to love, then he almost didn't begrudge him his ill-gotten prize.

Silver-Hair paused as he put a foot on the first step. "You're very lucky, Mr. Pierce, that I harbor you no ill will. Perhaps our innkeeper will find need to visit his wine cellar in the morning."

"Hey!" Arthur sprang forward, realizing that he meant to leave them stranded. "Wait a minute! You got what you came for. Why leave us down here to—"

But Silver-Hair was already gone, and Mr. Beck made a motion with the revolver that stopped Arthur short.

"Okay, okay." Arthur backed up a couple steps and spread his hands. "But, come on, fellas. Be reasonable."

Toad-man smiled. It was an amphibianlike smile that told Arthur he wasn't paid to be reasonable, the kind of smile that made Arthur especially glad to see the man fold up his sharp little knife and tuck it away before following his chortling master up the steps. Beck was the last to go.

Arthur groaned as heavy cellar doors dropped into place. Chelsea moved to his side as the slide bolts were thrown. They were good and well trapped for the night unless they decided to make a screaming banging nuisance of themselves.

"Oh dear, this is most inconvenient," Chelsea said. "What are we going to do?"

"Wave good-bye to five thousand pounds."

"Oh, I don't know that we ever earned it."

He looked at her, puzzled. "What are you saying?"

She motioned for him to follow her back over to the open chest. "There's something very odd going on."

Arthur was then reminded of her cryptic words just before Silver-Hair and his minions had descended upon them.

Chelsea dropped down to re-examine the treasure spread out at their feet. "All of this is very beautiful and valuable, and there's no doubt that most of it came from a wealthy monastery, but I think it's obvious that none of it came from Glastonbury."

"You're right that none of this was mentioned in the parchment," Arthur agreed, "but we found the sword."

"We found a sword," Chelsea corrected. "It was an impressive specimen, but judging by its construction, my guess is that it was forged sometime in the Middle Ages, not the Dark Ages. I'm not a weapons expert, but it appeared to me as if it might have been used more for show rather than for actual battle."

At her words, Arthur recalled that the blade had indeed been perfect. No dents, no scratches or nicks, no scars of any kind. "A showpiece?"

"No doubt a tithe once offered by a wealthy noble on pilgrimage." Chelsea rose to her feet. "And as for the rest of it, the wealth of most monasteries was kept in silver plate and jewels as well as in coin. This would have been only a small sample of what a large abbey had in its coffers."

"But what's all of this doing here? According to Mr. Balchristie, these fellas weren't interested in all that fancy stuff, they were just farmers."

"And masons, apparently," Chelsea added, inclining her head to the hollowed out section of wall behind them, then she shrugged. "To answer your question, I can only conjecture. It's apparent that most of this was smuggled from a wealthier monastery to be either hidden here for safekeeping or simply hoarded and later pawned for profit. I suppose that depends on the integrity of the monks who lived here."

"And we'll never know that," Arthur said. "They all died before they had a chance to retrieve this stuff."

"It certainly appears that way."

"But I thought our monk really believed he was saving his abbey's holy relics until it would be safe to return them to England."

"Oh, yes." Chelsea nodded emphatically. "I'm convinced our monk believed he was doing a noble thing. He was sent here by his abbot. This might have been a well-known safehouse for keeping holy valuables. After all, who would expect to find riches within the confines of such a humble grange? And if I'm correct, I'd lay wagers that there's more than one treasure hidden within the walls of this old inn. Remember, at the time all of this was going on, even the Scottish border abbeys were being threatened by English pillagers."

Arthur brightened. "That means our sword could still be here."

"Possibly. I've sensed its presence ever since we climbed Arthur's Seat, but what with all these secrets lurking within the walls, it's no wonder I haven't been able to come up with anything specific."

Arthur strode to the cellar steps with renewed purpose. "Well, now we've really got to get out of here." He tried pushing up on the doors over his head, grimacing as he spoke. "I wonder how long it's going to take for our smug friend to figure out he's just run off with some dead duke's sidearm?"

Chelsea followed Arthur, observing dubiously as he tried to budge the unmoving doors. "I suspect he'll come to the truth soon after he examines it under better light." She winced when Arthur finally lost his patience and gave the unrelenting wood door a good pound with his fist.

"Ouch! Damn!"

As soon as he stepped down, Chelsea took his hand to examine his injury. The bruises from his unfortunate encounter in Glastonbury had only begun to fade. Now they would be replaced with fresh ones. "You must be more careful," she admonished. "Crippling yourself certainly won't help matters."

"Oh, really?" He shifted his momentary frustration to her. "And why should it matter? Our situation couldn't get much worse, could it?"

Before Chelsea could reply, their light suddenly dimmed, then flickered. They both turned in time to see the flame in their paraffin lamp gutter and wink out.

Black.

Chelsea immediately began to feel the stirrings of fear that always clawed at her whenever she was left in the dark. "Oh, dear." She moaned softly.

"Shit," Arthur said.

"I . . . I never heard you say that before."

"The circumstances seem to warrant it."

"Oh." Chelsea's feet seemed stuck. She didn't dare move one inch in this dreadful darkness. Already, she was imagining beady-eyed rodents and furry arachnids venturing from their hiding places. "Shit it certainly is," she muttered in agreement.

There was a silence, then, quite unexpectedly, Arthur started to laugh.

Despite her mounting apprehension, she was annoyed. "What's so amusing?"

"Sorry, but it doesn't quite ring true with that accent."

"What accent?"

"Your accent."

"I don't have an accent," she denied, insulted. "You're the one with the accent."

"Don't get huffy. I happen to like your accent."

Chelsea paused, her indignation fading. "You do?"

"Mmmmhmmmm. It stirs my . . . interest."

"It does?"

"Especially when you say my name."

"You mean . . . *Arrrthur*?"

"Mmmm, yeah. Like that. Where are you?"

"Here," she said too quickly, putting out her hands. A split second later, he found them and drew her close.

"When you say my name, it sounds rich, haut monde. Sophisticated. Even royal."

Chelsea let out a tremulous sigh as she slipped her arms about his waist and rested her cheek against where his heart beat strong. "Well, it is royal." She closed her eyes, soaking up the warm security of his embrace. All beady-eyed rodents and furry arachnids could go to the devil. "You were named after a great king."

He squeezed her gently. "You're shivering. Are you cold?"

"No. I . . ." She felt ridiculous.

"What?"

"I don't care for the dark."

"Not many people do."

"It's rather childish."

"Oh, we all have our peccadillos. As for me, I hate to be closed up in small places. It reminds me of the first full day I ever spent in a schoolroom. I thought I'd go crazy from all that sitting."

Chelsea smiled, well aware that he was endeavoring to distract her from her distress. "How old were you?"

"Eleven."

"That was the very first time you ever went to school?"

"Well, my family moved around so much, it wasn't until my sister got married and settled down in Chicago that she put me in a normal school. That was bad enough. After we moved to Philadelphia, it was private school, and that was worse. I spent a lot of time daydreaming about the time I'd be free to travel the world and see all the places I'd read about in books. After prep school came college, and then, well . . . you know."

"You got expelled," Chelsea said. Julia had once told her the details of the incident that had led him from the prestigious University of Pennsylvania to the fledgling Temple College. Something to do with a goat. At the time, Chelsea had been righteously appalled. Now, for some reason, she wasn't appalled at all. That sort of prank was so characteristic of Arthur that now it was all she could do to muffle a giggle by burying her face in his lapel.

"What's so funny about being expelled?" he asked. "It was just a minor misunderstanding."

"Quite right." She lifted her head to look up at him in the impenetrable darkness. She couldn't see him, but she could sense his eyes on her. "The important thing is, you went back to school and received your degree."

He didn't sound so sure. "If it weren't for my sister, I'm not sure I would have bothered. She sacrificed a lot so I could get an education. I owed her that much."

Chelsea frowned, suddenly remembering her angry outburst when they'd quarreled aboard ship. "I'm sorry I told you to go out and make something of yourself. It was none of my concern."

He must have remembered the exchange as vividly as she did because he didn't miss a beat. "Well, you might have had a valid point."

"No. Ten years hence, perhaps, but not now. You're still young. Just by finishing college and earning your degree, you've already accomplished more than most people dream of, and . . ." She paused ruefully upon remembering the rest of her impulsive outburst. "And if you're too smart for your own good, well, that's no one's business but your own, isn't it?"

He laughed. "I suppose so."

"So now you will see the world as you've always dreamed."

"Only if we get out of this cellar." As he spoke, his hands, which had been settled about her waist, began to inch up over her rib cage, exploring. "Miss Delafield, what are you wearing under your blouse?"

Chelsea smiled. She had forgotten all about rodents and swords and disliking the dark. "Why, nothing, Mr. Pierce."

"Nothing?"

Rising up on tiptoes, she touched her lips to his and marveled at the soft warmth of his responding kiss.

"You've become quite a scandal since leaving the States, haven't you?" he whispered against her mouth.

"If I have, it's entirely your fault." They kissed again, their lips parting, tongues seeking, a slow, delicious heat building between them. Earlier, they had made love hurriedly. Now, Chelsea began to get an idea of what it might be like if they had days and days to spend together. Weeks, months, years . . . and the thought wounded her heart. It ruined the moment, and she drew back.

"Chelsea? What's the matter?"

He sounded puzzled, concerned, but she couldn't bring herself to reply. She had not asked anything of him, had not expected anything beyond one or two nights from which she could later draw sweet memories, but she had neglected to take into account the possibility that making love might make it all that much more difficult to part with him. That time had not yet come, but she was already feeling the sting.

"Chelsea?" He cupped her chin, turning her face up to his. For once, she was glad of the dark.

It was then that they were shocked to hear pounding footsteps approaching from outside. At the sound of bolts being thrown back, Arthur moved, shoving her behind him. "Our friends must be back. And I doubt they're too happy."

Chelsea feared he was right. This time, after discovering he had the wrong sword, the silver-haired gentleman was bound to be less well disposed toward their welfare. She gripped Arthur's arm and held her breath. All the better to let loose with an earsplitting scream should it become necessary.

The cellar doors slammed back on their hinges. Moonlight spilled down the gritty stone steps. "All right, ye thievin' devils! Come on outter there or I warrant ye'll regret the day ye was ever born!"

Chelsea let out a cry of relief. "It's Mr. Balchristie!"

"What? Who . . . ?" A pair of thick-soled boots and two hairy shins appeared on the steps. An instant later, their burly innkeeper, clad in a homespun nightshirt, descended the steps. He carried a shotgun in one hand and a kerosene lamp in the other.

"Mr. and Mrs. Pierce?" Cocking his night-capped head, he squinted at his two unorthodox guests in disbelief. "If ye don't mind me askin', wouldna ye be more comfortable in yer own room upstairs?"

# 26

*It was Mrs. McTavish* who had awakened Mr. Balchristie to alert him that there were intruders in his wine cellar; Mrs. McTavish, who just happened to be conspicuously absent when Chelsea and Arthur and their befuddled innkeeper came back inside a short while later. It was Mrs. McTavish who was even more conspicuously absent the following morning when she was supposed to be serving breakfast.

"That woman was about as Scottish as my big toe," Chelsea grumbled as she and Arthur boarded an express train to London at Waverley Station two days later. "I told you there was something odd about her."

"Oh, you were definitely on to her," Arthur admitted. "Right from the start."

Along with the cat, which Mr. Balchristie had taken in as a stray about a month before, Mrs. McTavish had vanished without a trace. Well, almost without a trace. If it weren't for Chelsea, Mr. Balchristie might not have discovered the loosened flagstones beneath the rug in front of his parlor fireplace for another week.

Once the stones were removed, they had discovered not another treasure but a gaping four-foot hole containing a gold and enamel reliquary chest the size of a small jewelbox. Inside, stored in tiny compartments, they'd found a collection of relics. Pieces of bone, splinters of wood, some hair, strips of cloth, and even a tooth. Without any labels to identify them, however, those saintly remains were now left for antiquarians to quibble over.

Whatever else had been hidden along with the reliquary chest was gone, undoubtedly spirited away by the mysterious Mrs. McTavish, but Chelsea had a pretty good idea about what it had been. "So close," she lamented as she found her coach seat.

Arthur settled into his own seat beside her with a philosophical sigh. "It's all water under the bridge."

"I wonder who she really was."

"Just another sword hunter, I suppose."

"One with better instincts than mine."

"No one has better instincts than you, tootsie. Better clues and better luck, maybe, but not better instincts. And you're right, we came damn close to winning this one, which, when you think about it, ain't bad for two amateurs, hmmm?"

"Perhaps not," she conceded, "but it would have been gratifying to have taken part in such a historic find."

"Not to mention to have collected a few thousand pounds for our efforts."

Chelsea forced a weak smile. "Yes." Before that smile could falter, she turned her face away. According to their agreement, she would share half of what Arthur would still receive from his uncle's executor.

Five hundred pounds. She should have been thrilled. It might not be enough to postpone her teaching career forever, but it would be enough to give her time to reconsider her options. She was already toying with the idea of writing to her Aunt Geraldine in Africa. Perhaps she could join her there in missionary work. It might be one way of combining teaching with her desire to experience something more of the world. And maybe it might help her to forget her first, and most likely her last, affair of the heart.

Arthur managed to doze throughout most of their trip to London, and Chelsea, who should have been exhausted enough to do the same, spent her time staring out the window, barely conscious of the landscape that rolled by. When they pulled into King's Cross Station, it was midafternoon. They had no trouble engaging a hansom cab to take them to Bloomsbury.

As they climbed into the conveyance, Arthur was not indifferent to Chelsea's reflective mood. He observed without comment as she settled across from him, folded those graceful, talented hands on her lap, and turned her head to stare out the window. To unschooled eyes, she might have appeared serene and untroubled, but he knew her better than that.

He was sharply reminded of the day they'd traveled to London from Southampton. She'd been disturbed then about returning home, and she was disturbed now. This time, though, he thought she might be worried about facing her parents. At least, he hoped that was all that was on her mind. Unfortunately, that was something he couldn't help her with. She wouldn't be content until she'd set things straight with them herself.

With a frustrated sigh, Arthur rested his head back and thought instead about the events of the past two days. He and Chelsea had agreed that the medieval treasure they'd uncovered in the wine cellar should belong to Mr. Balchristie, but they had accepted a small finders' fee from the grateful innkeeper for turning it up. In addition to free lodging and meals, they'd had enough spending money to purchase a new hat for Chelsea, a pair of shoes for Arthur, and two first-class train tickets back to London. While in Edinburgh yesterday, Chelsea had dispatched a telegram to her parents informing them that she was coming home.

Early this morning, as the first peach rays of dawn had strained over the horizon, they had made love in a sleepy, leisurely, most gratifying fashion. Despite his present concern over Chelsea's recalcitrant mood, Arthur had to smile with self-satisfaction at the remembrance. It was probably a tribute to his youthful vigor that he'd had any stamina left at all, considering how they'd spent most of the previous night.

As he'd suspected, the prim and proper Miss Delafield was an insatiably curious and adventurous young lady in bed. Eager and responsive, she tackled her new sexual awareness with the same kind of single-minded passion that characterized her scholarly pursuits. She had even surprised him after their initial coupling by maneuvering about to straddle his hips, wondering aloud how one went about exchanging positions, but Arthur, being a mere mortal male, had been forced to call for a brief intermission. That was how they'd come to break out a new deck of cards.

Playing high-low-jack in the nude was a new experience even for Arthur, not to mention it wreaked havoc with his ability to concentrate. Chelsea, equally naked except for the spectacles that kept sliding down her nose, had proven to be too much of a delightful distraction. More than one game had ended prematurely in a scatter of cards and kisses.

By the time they had finally drifted off to sleep, they'd consummated their passions twice and Chelsea had learned the rudiments of executing a one-handed shift with the cards. Not bad for one night's work.

Now, however, with each passing moment, Arthur was becoming more frustrated. His disappointment at losing Excalibur had quickly dimmed, but now, aside from his hope that Chelsea's mood was caused by the upcoming confrontation with her parents, he feared that he might be losing something else, something much more elusive and precious.

Ever since breakfast, she had begun to pull away from him. She had barely looked at him and most of her conversation had consisted of ineffectual chitchat. It was hard to believe that after all they'd been through, she might now be intent upon transforming back into the stiff-necked bluestocking he'd known in Philadelphia.

Except this time it wasn't going to work. This time, Arthur knew what lurked beneath all that cool British reserve—a bright-eyed, adventure-loving, lake-swimming brunette—the girl of his dreams. The problem was, he wasn't sure how to get that girl back.

When their cab drew up before the Delafield residence, he followed her out onto the pavement. "Maybe I should go with you. Maybe I can help explain—"

She stopped him with one gloved hand on his arm. "No, it's better if I speak to them alone."

"But what are you going to tell them?"

Her voice was soft, her smile wistful. "That I took an opportunity to be part of the most exciting adventure of my life, and that I shall never regret one moment of it."

Arthur shoved his hands in his pockets, cursing his own uselessness. "I wish I could do something to help. I doubt it'll be easy for them to understand."

"Oh, I don't know. They were young once." Her forehead furrowed as she glanced anxiously toward her home. "Well, I'm fairly sure Mother was, at any rate."

"They both were," Arthur said, "even if they don't like to let on about it. Keep in mind that someday your children may be wondering the same about you."

Instead of cheering her up as he'd hoped, her expression only grew more bleak. "I doubt it." Then she set down her bag, tugged off her left glove, and removed the wedding band he'd given her. She offered it to him wordlessly.

For the second time in as many weeks, Arthur found himself troubled over the return of his cheap pawnshop ring. "I suppose it won't do any good to tell you to keep it again, will it?"

She just looked at him, her answer obvious.

"I didn't think so." He took it and dropped it into his coat pocket with a sigh. "All right. It's settled. While you go face your lions, I'll go see if I can track down Max Hamilton and collect our money."

"Fine. I'll see you afterward."

Before turning back to the cab, he leaned close and looked deep into those enchanting amethyst eyes. "I wish I could kiss you right now."

His reward was a patent Mona Lisa smile. Pretty enough, but not nearly as lovely as her real smile. "I wish you could, too."

Feeling a renewed stab of frustration over the fact that he'd been unable to lighten either her burden or her mood, Arthur turned back to the waiting cab and addressed the driver. "Little James in Bedford Row."

Arthur found Max Hamilton seated cross-legged on the floor of his office. Dressed in waistcoat and shirtsleeves and with Crystal perched alert and watchful by his side, the portly solicitor's eyes were closed, his hands resting on each knee. To Arthur, he appeared to be quite asleep.

"Don't mind 'im." This was Hamilton's secretary. The elderly fellow sported a limp, a cockney accent, and the beleaguered air of a man who'd seen it all. " 'E'll come out of it soon enough. 'Ave a seat while you wait."

After the door closed, leaving him alone with the oddly indisposed Max, Arthur decided to take the secretary's advice. What else was there to do? Choosing an upholstered chair opposite a paper-strewn desk, he passed a few minutes by perusing the decor. Heavy draperies, Louis XV appointments, and a few French impressionist paintings dominated, with, here and there, a dash of the unexpected. An ivory Buddha statuette on the mantle, a Chinese scroll on the wall, an alabaster vase with Egyptian markings, and even a carved ebony face mask that appeared to be of African origin.

"Oooo-mmmmmm."

The sound startled Arthur. A deep bass rumble that seemed to reverberate from the very depths of Hamilton's expansive chest. Just as he turned in his chair to see if the solicitor might be suffering from some sort of physical ailment, the older man's eyes popped open and he looked around. "Mr. Pierce! How delightful to see you again. Would you care for some tea?"

"Uh, no, thank you. Sorry if I'm interrupting."

"Oh, not at all." Max turned his head from side to side, flexing his neck, then stretched his arms and scrambled to his feet with an agility that was surprising for a man of his age and girth. "I was just finishing up. Have you ever tried it?"

"Tried what?"

Max crossed the expansive office, plucked a houndstooth checked suit coat from a hat rack in one corner of the office and slipped it on. "Meditation."

"Not on purpose."

"It's quite refreshing, actually. I picked up the rudiments from a maharishi while passing through the Himalayas some years ago." Settling into a broad leather armchair behind his desk, Max smiled as Crystal hopped up onto his lap. "So, tell me, Mr. Pierce, what brings you to London? I must confess, we weren't expecting to see you again so soon."

It didn't take Arthur long to recount the pertinent details of his two-week adventure. Throughout the recital, Max stroked Crystal's glossy white fur and listened without interruption.

When Arthur was done with his story, he withdrew an envelope from his pocket and pushed it across the desk to the older man. "A letter from a professor at Edinburgh University documenting some of the items we uncovered at the inn."

Max gave him a smile replete with sage wisdom. "Your word on the matter is quite sufficient, Mr. Pierce." But Arthur noted that he took the envelope anyway, tucking it unopened into the top drawer of his desk. "Tell me," he said, his expression growing subtly curious. "This Mrs. McTavish. You really think it was she who retrieved Excalibur?"

"My partner is sure of it, and, as I said, she isn't often wrong about such things."

"Hmmmmm." Hamilton frowned thoughtfully as he scratched behind Crystal's ears. "What sort of woman was she?"

"My partner?"

"Mrs. McTavish."

Arthur grinned. "Beee-yoo-tiful."

"Indeed?"

"And a helluva good cook."

"I see."

At this, Crystal peered up at her white-bearded master and let out a strident meow.

Max frowned down at his vocal pet and muttered, "Yes, Crystal. I was thinking the same thing."

"Sorry I can't tell you more," Arthur said.

"Yes, well, you've told me enough. Be aware that one must be especially vigilant when dealing with such women."

"Oh?" Arthur was suddenly curious himself. "Sounds like you've had firsthand experience."

Max grimaced and moved to set Crystal back on the floor. "That was many years ago, my lad, many, many years ago. I'd rather not think about it, if you don't mind."

The cat padded over to the fireplace and curled up as if to take a nap. Her glowing amber eyes, however, remained open and fixed on Arthur.

"Uh, no, I don't mind at all." Arthur shifted his attention from the watchful feline and decided that it was time to get down to business. "So, Mr. Hamilton, how soon can I expect full payment of my bequest?"

Chelsea stood by the open window of her bedroom, staring down at the street below and wondering how much longer she would be able to maintain the resolve that stiffened her spine. It seemed that Arthur had been gone for hours, long enough for her to unpack her belongings, long enough for her to confront her anxiously awaiting parents, certainly long enough for her to work up a case of spine-depleting melancholy.

Chelsea had attempted to describe her adventure to her parents—purposely deleting any mention of her extraordinary intuition or the fact that she had recklessly indulged in her first *affaire d'amour*. Granted, she had left out an awful lot. It was no wonder that they had still worn such bewildered expressions even after she'd finished her story.

In turn, she had learned that her good reputation was still intact. Instead of telling the truth, that their youngest daughter had lost all good sense and run off in the middle of the night like a madcap adventuress, her parents had imparted to friends and acquaintances that Chelsea had gone to Yorkshire to interview for a teaching position. Quite neat and tidy, and now that she had returned in time to avoid stretching that story beyond credibility, everything could be swept under the rug and thankfully forgotten.

All in all, Chelsea knew that she should have been grateful for how well everything had turned out, but at the moment, all she could feel was utterly dispirited at the prospect of saying her final good-byes to Arthur. Would she ever see him again? She supposed it was possible. His plans included seeing the world. So did hers. Perhaps he would return to London. By then, though, Chelsea might have already gone to Africa to join her aunt.

She perked up upon seeing a hansom cab draw up to the curb. When Arthur emerged, carrying his battered suitcase, she gathered up her skirt and hurriedly fled the house. She met him just as the cab was departing.

"Did you get the money?" she asked breathlessly. It seemed the safest topic to start off with.

"Uh, yeah." He glanced about as if concerned they were being observed. "Where are your parents?"

"Inside." Chelsea had not missed his furtive behavior.

"Miss Delafield, I have a proposition for you." He took her by the arm and led her round back of the house. "I don't think we should discuss it in front of your parents. At least, not yet."

A proposition? Chelsea tried to ignore her pattering heart, the part of her that would have much preferred to hear the word proposal spilling from his lips rather than its less romantic counterpart.

But what sort of proposition could he have in mind unless it had something to do with her share of the money? As they ducked behind her mother's rose arbor to gain some privacy, Chelsea began to suspect that her new financial freedom might be in jeopardy.

She folded her arms stiffly. "Explain."

"Perhaps you should sit first." Taking her by the shoulders, he urged her down onto a wrought iron garden bench. "There." He offered her a solicitous smile. "Isn't that better?"

Chelsea was in love, but she wasn't blind in love. She recognized Arthur's brand of mischief when she saw it. "If you've gambled away my share of the money, I shall—"

"Gambling?" He feigned shock. "Me? Never!"

"What have you done?"

He sank down beside her and took both of her hands in his. "Have you ever heard of the Egyptian Antiquities Organization?"

Chelsea narrowed her eyes, wary at this unexpected turn in the conversation. "Well, of course I've heard of it."

Indeed, what competent history student with an interest in Egyptology hadn't? Based in Cairo, their objective was to locate lost tombs and make certain the contents weren't exploited or illegally exported from Egypt. "But what has that to do with the money?" she asked.

Arthur's handsome mouth curved in a sly smile. "Well, I told Max Hamilton a bit about your special talents, and he was very impressed. He has a friend in the Antiquities Organization who would be interested in obtaining your services. It seems they have in their possession an ancient amulet. They're convinced that if they can decipher the markings, it will lead them to the tomb of some pharaoh . . . oh, what was that fella's name . . . Amen . . . Amen-hammer-toe the second?"

"Amenhotep II!" Chelsea blurted. "Egad! What an exciting find!" She was all but trembling with excitement. The possibility that the Egyptian Antiquities Organization might be interested in obtaining her services set her blood to racing.

How often had she dreamed of what it might be like to take part in the excavation of a pharaoh's tomb? And Amenhotep II, at that! What an adventure!

"I know you were planning on a teaching career here at home," Arthur said, "so I didn't promise Hamilton anything before I could speak with you about it first. What do you think?"

"Think?" Chelsea laughed and threw her arms about his neck, knocking his hat off and nearly sending them both tumbling to the ground. Luckily, Arthur's firm embrace anchored them both. "I would adore it! Oh, Arthur, it's a dream come true!"

"Well, there is one thing."

She stiffened at the tone in his voice. "What one thing?"

"You'll have to travel there on your own, of course, which is where the money comes in."

"The money," she said, her mouth next to his ear. "You have it, of course."

"Well, not exactly."

Chelsea pulled back just enough to assess him. Those lake blue eyes were sparkling full of the devil. "What do you mean, 'not exactly'?"

He gave her a sheepish smile. "I spent it."

Chelsea's hands, which had come to rest on his shoulders, now moved of their own accord to entangle in his collar. When she yanked, they were suddenly eye to eye, nose to nose. "You what?"

"I spent it," he repeated matter-of-factly. "Most of it, anyway."

"Arthur Pierce, I might have been daft enough to fall in love with you, but if this isn't one of your awful jokes, I swear, you shall not live long enough to regret it."

That damnable grin widened. "You've fallen in love me? Really? Was it my dazzling charm or my manly virility do you think?"

Chelsea bit her lip. How often had she nipped off the exclamation during lovemaking only to now have it tumble out in a moment of pure frustration? Blast him. He was altogether too smug. "It was more likely a momentary lapse in good judgment that did me in, Mr. Pierce."

"Ah, yes. Those momentary lapses can be so troublesome. With lifelong consequences, too, if you're not careful, so why not ruin your life completely and marry me?"

Chelsea still had him in a death grip. This was not precisely the sort of position in which she'd ever imagined herself being proposed to. Perhaps she hadn't heard him correctly. "What did you say?"

"Marry me. It seems I've had a momentary lapse of my own, so we might as well wallow in it. Besides, I've got the tickets."

"Tickets?" Now she *knew* she hadn't heard him correctly.

"My dream to see the world suddenly seemed rather pointless without having someone to share it with." He reached into his pocket, produced two steamship tickets, and inched them up between her wrists to display in front of her face. Chelsea's eyes nearly crossed in an effort to focus. The words *Pleasure Excursion* jumped out and bit her on the nose.

"You said once that you wouldn't marry me even if I begged you to, so I'm not begging. I'm bribing. Think about it, tootsie. Paris, Madrid, Rome, Greece, and, of course, Egypt. If we decide to stay in Cairo for a while to dig up moldy pharaohs, maybe you could let me carry your shovel."

"Oh, Arthur," she whispered, her throat tightening. She let go of him and took the tickets in trembling fingers. She stared at the printed itinerary in teary-eyed disbelief. Marseilles, Paris, Milan, Venice, Naples . . .

"Is that an 'oh, Arthur, yes' or an 'oh, Arthur, no'?"

"Oh, Arthur, *yes*."

"Yes? Yes! I'll be damned!" Taking her face in his hands, Arthur pressed a warm, laughing kiss to her lips. The steamship tickets fluttered to the ground, temporarily forgotten.

Much better than the carousel at Smith's Island Resort, Chelsea thought. Pure magic.

Arthur drew back to match his sparkling blue gaze to hers. "Ah, Chelsea, we'll travel the world, just you and me. We'll be a family of two, and then, when the time is right, we can settle down. Maybe we can even have a baby."

"A baby?" she echoed, her eyes rounding.

"Perhaps even two."

"Two?" She tilted her head, contemplating this wonderfully novel idea. Now, that could prove to be a real adventure. "One at a time or two at once, do you think?"

"I'll leave that to you."

"I shall think upon it," she promised.

"Either way," Arthur said, "we must be prepared. Our children are bound to be extremely bright and crafty. A challenge to keep up with."

"Like their father."

"And intuitive and beautiful," he added. "Like their mother."

Chelsea's lips curved into a smile. A smile with teeth. If Arthur found her beautiful, who was she to argue? "And so, Mr. Pierce, how soon do we embark upon our adventurous new life together?"

"Why, Miss Delafield . . ." He kissed her. "We just did."